STILL…, ALL BY MY LONELY
THE ORGANIZATION-PART TWO
BY
BLACK COFFEE

Still..., All By My Lonely-THE ORGANIZATION-part two

Published by True's Relate Publishing
Still..., All By My Lonely-THE ORGANIZATION-part two
Library of Congress Control Number: TXu 1-794-675
**Copyright ©2003, 2009, 2014 True's Relate
publishing/LTBROWN**

**REGISTERED TRADEMARK-MARCA
REGISTRADA
ISBN: 978-0-9892092-0-5**
Printed in the United States of America
Set by: True's Relate
Cover design by: Gregory Spencer of MisVisions Graphics
Logo design by: JayRocOne [age 12]
Photography: www.freddavisphotography.com
**Requests for ordering, scheduling the author for signings and
appearances should be addressed to:**
Black Coffee's websites
http://www.blackdollone.com
www.truesrelatepublishing.com
Amazon.com/Author's page: http://www.amazon.com/-/e/B008S1WOZ2
Support Page on Facebook:
https://www.facebook.com/AuthorBlackCoffeeSupporterPage
THE ORGANIZATION group:
https://www.facebook.com/groups/TheOrganizationByBlackCoffee/
THE TIME WILL REVEAL group:
https://www.facebook.com/groups/BlackCoffeeCrewNation/
Twitter:
http://www.twitter.com/AuthorBlkCoffee
Manuscript Preparation: Black Coffee
blackdollone@att.net
**True's Relate publishing company
P.O. Box 2911
Gulfport, Ms. 39505**

PUBLISHER'S NOTES

This is a work of fiction. Names, Characters, places and incidents either are the product of the author's imagination or are used fictitiously, and any resemblance to actual persons, living or dead, business establishments, events, or locales is entirely coincidental. Any references or similarities to actual events, or to real locales are intended to give the novel a sense of reality.

Still…, All By My Lonely -THE ORGANIZATION-part two

4

CHAPTER NINETEEN
Kid's Wants A Play Of Action

Back at Blake's Estate, their event is in overdrive. Baby Girl, Young D and DeJuan are ruling the basketball courts, as usual. There's been no mention of the Genolli family murders, the 3 of them had committed a couple of hours ago. They're just playing the game, in more ways than one.

The game playing portion is wrapping up now. It's time for *Grand Hustle records* to perform. Baby Girl and her team has just finished yet another day of ruling the courts. The bragging can commence.

"Happy Independence Day!" Baby Girl yells as she rings her last 3 point shot during another undefeated 3-on-3 basketball challenge for her, Young D and DeJuan.

"We make a *hellava* team," DeJuan shouts as Baby Girl and Young D agrees.

"We're gonna be known as *three the hard way*," Young D says as all 3 of them laugh.

The other guest are oblivious to what they're even joking about. For Baby Girl, this is the good and bad times. Her family will return home starting tomorrow, after this 4th of July event. Kid had only returned for the performances. Then he'd left again without saying anything to anyone. He didn't even take his kids with him because that would have involved him going near other folks to retrieve them. What he had done was set up a plan to have Six Nine and Geezy to squeeze his kids in with them, the next day. Then, they would meet him near the interstate. From there, his kids will get into his SUV and they'll head back to New Orleans, from there.

Baby Girl has never felt such a disconnect with a family member, as she does with Kid. She doesn't have a clue of what his connection is with Kierra either. But he seems more loyal to

Kierra, then he is to her. It's something that will have to be discussed, sooner than later.

They go on with the party at Blake's estates.

Meanwhile, Kid is hanging out with Kierra and her 2 friends, Trina and Venetta. Danica has been taken to Kierra's mother's home. That's where the little girl spends the majority of her time, anyway. Kid was seething earlier. He really hates the fact that his plan to have Kierra interfere in his sister's marriage has faced an obstacle.

"You had to have done some real bullshit to fuck it up," Kid says to Kierra.

"I didn't do nothing," Kierra tries.

"It's probably about that fight that you had with his wife," Trina says.

"Yea. I heard it wasn't really no fight," Kid says, "I heard my little sister beat the brakes off of yo ass."

"That's closer to the truth," Venetta says.

"Shut the fuck up," Kid says to Venetta, "Why didn't y'all ho's help her?"

"They had security," Venetta explains.

"*Damn*, Kid," Trina says, "If I didn't know you, any better. I wouldn't even know that Baby Girl was your little sister."

"That shit is beside the point," Kid says, "She needs to be taught a lesson. That nigga ain't no good for her."

The 3 females sit, watch and listen to Kid as he scolds them on what they did wrong. He tells them that the 4 of them are going to have to come up with a sure fire plan. One that will surely get Young D out of Baby Girl's life.

Venetta asks, "I know this might sound kind of crazy but I needs to ask you. Are you in love with your *own* sister?"

6

"Hell no!" Kid yells, "Y'all needs to get off that shit!"

"We already asked him that shit," Kierra says, "At least twenty times."
The ladies laugh but Kid can't find anything funny about anything they've said, thus far.

"Instead of laughing like some defeated hood rats," he says, "Y'all need to use your minds. Let's come up with a real formula for getting rid of that nigga."
Kid knows what Baby Girl's profession is. He's not going to let these females know because that would surely send their scary asses into hiding. What he's going to do, is try and find a way to incorporate Baby Girl's skills into her own husbands demise. At this point, he doesn't even care if she dies too. And that will become more evident to Baby Girl, as time goes on. For instance, what Baby Girl had thought when she went over her agenda, wasn't that far fetched at all. The person who hadn't shown back up at the event and the person who wanted her dead bad enough to hire the 2nd best hitter in the world, Mark Genolli, might just turn out to be the same person.

For the next few days, Young D and DeJuan are impossible to shake or take for Baby Girl. They're on a high that she has never seen before. Young D is, more so than DeJuan. At times, Young D is so animated that it appears DeJuan is too. When DeJuan really isn't acting any different. That part is the most telling to Baby Girl and always has kept her attention. When it comes to DeJuan, that is. She wonders if her husband will ever qualify to be a cleaner. So far, she thinks not. Because he doesn't understand the concept of, less is more. In her experience with rappers who claim to be street killers. They are to braggadocios. To arrogant. More than even Mark Genolli was. Keeping a murder scene a secret, for a

7

chest sticking out, got everything to prove rapper, was unlikely. And to keep 1 quiet with one which was as clinical and technical as the 1 at Mark Genolli's condo, was next to impossible. Reminding Young D of what is expected of him now, is an every day, several times a day, thing for her. Though Young D promises her that he'll never do something as irresponsible as talk about her profession to anyone who are not connected. She still feels uncomfortable, all of sudden and she doesn't like this feeling. A part of her wishes she could start all over again with the Mark Genolli hit. If she could, she wouldn't have shared anything with either Young D nor DeJuan. But she still feels that DeJuan knew more about it, than he let on. And maybe he hadn't even hinted to Young D about his knowledge of the profession. She had been the 1 who had done that. In the heat of the moment and angry over Kierra being at the Galveston show, she had made Young D aware. That was from her need to make him feel jealous and worried that she would cheat. That's how she let him know about that upcoming hit. Something *The Don* would have punished her for, if he were still alive.

She has to get back to basics. She's the best but she can't help but feel that she has been a bit arrogant too. Rather it be because she knows she is the best or not. She can never allow them to ride along again. She will simply explain to Young D that he hasn't handled the after, well enough for her to trust putting him on the front line again. As far as DeJuan goes, that's out of her hands. She can't ask him. Only he can volunteer that information. And so far, he hasn't.

It's 4 days past the 4th of July. All of their guest have gone back to their states and homes. Baby Girl still hasn't heard anything from Kid. Young D has calmed way down and

DeJuan is still, cooler than a fan, as usual.
DeJuan is always so cool, calm and collected. He use to be rowdy too. I remember when it all changed.
Epiphany! May she rest in peace.

Baby Girl thinks back to when she had known DeJuan to be animated and loud. She realizes that it had been in the first 2 years of her and Young D's relationship. From 1996 to 1998. DeJuan use to be just like Young D. Loud and sometimes arrogant and obnoxious. Testosterone driven is a pretty good synopsis of how he, Derrick and all of their cohorts were, back then. They were wild and loose. The movie *Juice,* could have very well been a depiction of their lives. If that were so, then DeJuan would have been the Quincy or Q, of the group. He was the most reserved of the four. He was fucking an older woman, when they met. That earned him the moniker, Q wan rather then DeJuan. But by the time she graduated from George Washington Carver high school, he was dating a different older woman and his persona had changed, quite a bit. He had started to act more like a father figure to Young D and the rest. During the Christmas season of her senior year of high school, DeJuan got a job with Morales Enterprises, as Alfred's assistant. While Derrick and the others were still heavily involved with *The 3rd Ward* label. Still pursuing their music dreams. DeJuan was more dedicated to his job than he was the music, all of sudden. Sure, he was still featured on many songs. But his desire to be a solo artist changed significantly, that season. His job had also helped him to meet the older woman he was seeing and would ultimately fall for. He had met and started dating, Epiphany Douglas.
Epiphany was 18 years old when they met in 1996.

9

DeJuan was barely sixteen. But the 2 of them hit it off, instantly. They were inseparable. Epiphany worked on Addie Mae's kitchen staff. She was Addie Mae's niece, from a sister who had died many years earlier, of cancer. Addie Mae had taken responsibility for Epiphany when she was 6 years old. That was right about the same time Wanda and *Don* got married and Baby Girl moved to the manor. Epiphany was Baby Girl's first friend, who was close to her in age. Though she was 5 years older than Baby Girl. Everyone else around the manor, they considered old. That was before Baby Girl went away to Tristan, for boarding school.

By 1996, Baby Girl had met her brothers and Young D and DeJuan. She brought all of them to meet her parents. That's when DeJuan and Epiphany first met. DeJuan talked himself upon a job and a reason to keep returning, so that he and Epiphany could advance their interest in each other.

By Christmas, they were an official couple. Addie Mae and the other staff knew about the relationship, from the onset. So did Wanda and *The Don*. Everyone knew and no one had a problem with it. DeJuan seemed to be in love and Epiphany was surely in love with him. Young D saw it as a way for him to get to the manor, more easily when he wanted to visit Baby Girl. And for a while, it was. Young D, Baby Girl, Epiphany and DeJuan went on many double dates together. They went to the movies, *Essence Festival, Blues and Heritage festival* and the *Mardi Gras* balls too. DeJuan and Epiphany had plans of getting married, as soon as he turned eighteen. They had talked marriage, long before Baby Girl and Young D would. But what happened in the fall of Baby Girl's sophomore year at LSU, as tragic as it was, forever changed DeJuan's life and his ability to become seriously attached to anther woman.

Epiphany had gone into the city to shop, 1 afternoon

during October of 1998. On her way back from the bus stop, off of Morales highway, she had taken missing. The bus driver confirmed that she had gotten of the bus, at her usual stop. He said she continued up Morales Road, like any other time. But Epiphany never made it back to the home she shared with Addie Mae. Her battered and mutilated body was found a mile off of Morales road. In 1 of the areas of the Morales property, still largely populated with trees and swamp. Alfred's old beagle Joshua and his hound dog Oscar, who have both since died, had found her body. The dogs were dragging her body toward the mansion when Alfred spotted them. He took a golf cart out to where the dogs were struggling and discovered that it was a human body. The sheriff department was called. It was later determined to be Epiphany. She had been missing for a week, by that time. It was later learned that she was abducted at gun point, by some drunken rednecks. Some hateful idiots who were just out looking to fuck with somebody on the racist tip. Epiphany was a beautiful Creole young lady. But the white separatist rednecks saw her as a mixed race baby. She was evidence of the harmony between the races. The thing they hated the most. Epiphany had walked along Morales road, for years, unmolested. But that October afternoon in 1998 would shatter DeJuan's hopes of marrying the love of his young life. Epiphany had been sexually assaulted, numerous times. She was beaten to the point that she was unrecognizable. Too date, no one has been charged with her murder. Though everyone knew who most likely did it. Addie Mae was both angry and distraught. DeJuan went into a funk that lasted for another 2 years. Some say he never came out of it. His maturity level was already higher than Young D and the other guys, in his age group. But loosing Epiphany, took it up another 400 degrees. He has never looked for another serious relationship,

11

since. For years, Young D thought that if he could find his best friend a girl like Baby Girl. Then he would be okay. But DeJuan never took a serious liking to another woman, after loosing Epiphany so suddenly and so gruesomely. What he did do was get closer to Addie Mae and Alfred. He stayed and worked his job, even when Young D moved back to Houston. He visited Houston on some weekends. But he considered the manor his home. Right up until when Wanda died. When Baby Girl moved in with Six Nine, DeJuan finally moved back to Houston. But he was forever a changed man. Young D and their Houston friends didn't comprehend the change. They would tease DeJuan saying, "Somebody done put on a root on you, home boy!"

And they would all giggle and clown him. DeJuan would laugh with them but he never again took part in the infantile type games they would play. He had matured in those years, at the manor. And to Baby Girl, he had picked up something else too. She never could figure it out before. But nowadays, it's obvious. Sure, he was in *The Brotherhood*. But that came as a result of working for the manor. For males, that was automatic. But DeJuan had also managed to impress *The Don* enough that he had allowed Alfred to start him training as a cleaner for *The Organization*.

That has to be the truth.

Most, at the manor, knew that he wanted to hunt down those redneck bastards who had taken his Epiphany from him. They had left their mark by draping her body with a confederate flag. Unbeknownst to Baby Girl, DeJuan had waged a war on anything or anyone confederate. *Racist. Bigoted.* He wanted to learn the craft so he could avenge the death of his love. That was then and still is his motivation. And though, Baby Girl has

12

her beliefs that he is a member of her organization. She still can't mention it to him. He would still have to volunteer that information to her.

I've always been so glad that he is in Derrick's life because he is a great and loyal friend. But I think there is more to him.

2 weeks after Epiphany's murder is when Big Dog died. DeJuan has spent 9 years as a single man since Epiphany was killed. He's had plenty of girls on hand for his sexual pleasure. But neither of them had a real position in his life. He didn't date and he rarely invited any of his girls out to the estate, in Houston. He's come to be known as the loner. He lost a bit of his compassion, along with losing Epiphany. Before she was so brutally snatched away from him, DeJuan would never have been the 1 responsible for breaking in the new groupies. But since he didn't have loyalty to any 1 woman, over the years. The crew bestowed that honor upon him. He would always get the pick of the groupie litter. Young D is the label mate leader but he was usually with Baby Girl. The other guys had significant others or baby mama's, along the way. The others would sometimes be at the hotel with them. So they had to limit their groupie activity. But DeJuan didn't have that problem. He was a single man and living like as such.

New Orleans

In New Orleans, Gus is on a call with Kid. These 2 have been getting tighter, over the years. Something neither of them allow any others to witness. Not thus far. They'd met back when Don Morales use to have everyone from the 3rd Ward Soldiers label out at the manor. He was working on a music deal for them. The deal they eventually signed with Unity

13

records was due largely to the influence of Don Morales and Morales Enterprises. Kid and Gus Davis hit it off from there. That was the time when Gus violated his oath of *The Organization*. He made Kid aware of what he did for the company which is forbidden. From that day on, Kid wanted in and Gus slowly began trying to get him into the loop. Without even realizing or respecting that he was barely in the loop, himself.

Today, Gus and Kid discuss some possible angles they can try. Kid hasn't given up on being a cleaner for *The Organization*. But his reasons are for personal gain, only. That's #1 no-no of the profession. In honesty, Gus had long stopped honoring the Morales creed. His main motivation has always been about greed! That's something he and Kid, definitely have in common. The 2 of them have plans of, not only disrupting order. But also, changing the name on the manor's crest. No one is wise to their scheme. But that's today. Surely, before long, that will change.

The other thing Kid and Gus have in common is they both always underestimated Baby Girl's intelligence. That is sure to be their undoing.

The next few weeks are off time for Young D and his label mates. He and Baby Girl have an anniversary coming up in a week. Young D has something big planned for them.

DeJuan will be in charge of Blake Estate until they return, as he usually is. He'll have to keep his eyes on, not only the label mates. But also on Lil Man, Don P, Annie, Angela and the grandparents. DeJuan is already up for it. He enjoys his responsibility. He's the Godfather of both Lil Man and Don P, already. He has lots of activities planned for the 3 of them to do while their parents are away. He already knows Angela and

Roderick will be a handful. They are now, an *official* couple. It took awhile for Roderick to rub Young D the right way. But he finally has. He and Ricky's mother had come for the 4t of July event and Mike's mother and father came also. The 3 of them were the only ones the boys could afford to sent for, on that first time. But sending their parents on a trip, was a first too. Roderick, Ricky and Mike have made enough money since joining H-Town records to fly their parents to Houston for the Fourth of July. And it was *legal* money. But *The 717 Boys* have a huge, extended family. They couldn't send for all of them this time. David, Baby Girl's brother, had even suggested that he and Kenya host the next 4th of July event at their estate. Then they can meet all of *The 717 Boys* family and friends. Everybody agreed on them doing that but a whole lot sooner than a year from now. Baby Girl had suggested Labor Day. But then she remembered H-Town records would be back on tour, during that time. Her brother Sammy suggested they could work the date out. As long as the desire to host everyone, stays there. Sammy made it clear that that's all they'll need to make it happen. The Philadelphia and Harrisburg folks are anxious to entertain them on their turf.

Angela got a chance to spend some quality time with Roderick's mother, aunt and uncle. Her and Roderick's mother, who's name is Vikki, had hit it off instantly. Vikki and Annie both had a love for *Bid Whiz*, in common. They were partners during this last event and spanked more ass than an over zealous man at a strip club. But there was something about Vikki's visit that stayed on Baby Girl's mind. And its still there today.

Vikki had been very vocal about a domestic violence situation. One that she deals with on a daily basis. She told them that was the *only* bad news about her sons and her nephew being away from home. His name is James Lawson.

James Lawson is a retired NFL football player. He's now her ex-boyfriend because he was very abusive. Vikki didn't want her sons or nephew to end up in jail for killing him. She met James after her husband and the father of her twins, Ricky Sr was killed in an automobile accident. James was good in the beginning, Vikki had told them. He spent time with the twins, who were 14 years old when they met. They stayed together for 5 years. She told them that even though she had broken things off with him, nearly 2 years ago. He still stalks and threatens her. That's something that turned Baby Girl's stomach. A coward ass man who is pussy enough to strike a woman. She extends an open invitation to Vikki to move to Houston or New Orleans. But Vikki said she has to work. Roderick and Ricky are determined to make enough money to take care of her, so she doesn't have to stay Harrisburg and live in fear.

Move a little closer to me. I'll get rid of your headache. Once and for all.

Baby Girl made Vikki, Roderick and Ricky, promise to keep her informed about future actions from James Lawson. Today Ricky calls her phone to tell her about the latest episode.

"Hello," Baby Girl answers.

"Hey misses Blake. This is Ricky," he says, "I need to let you know that my mother stayed at a hotel last night."

"What happened?"

"James called the house, threatening her. He accused her of being with a man, last week. Even though she ain't with him no more. She told him she came to visit us but he didn't believe her. He told her he was going to wait for her to go to sleep, one night. Then he was gonna set the house on fire."

"Oh wow," Baby Girls says, "Where is she now?"

"She went to my aunt's. She's scared to go home."

"Bring her back down here, Ricky," she says, "You and Rod have to convince her to come down here. Just until we can get something done to protect her."

No matter how hard Roderick and Ricky tries. Vikki refuses to leave because of her job. That's when Baby Girl comes up with an idea. She is going to put a job in place for Vikki, with Morales Enterprises. They have locations all throughout the United States. Harrisburg has shipping industry. Morales has a stake there too. Baby Girl is going to see about getting Vikki relocated. Either that or she'll have to kill James Lawson, herself. But both will have to wait awhile. At least until after her anniversary.

17

CHAPTER TWENTY
"IT'S YOUR ANNIVERSARY"

Saturday, the 14th of July. Baby Girl and Young D leave for their anniversary trip. They take a flight to Tampa, Florida. Then they hop aboard the *Carnival Legend Cruise Line*. Young D booked a cruise. They're going to sail the Caribbean for 8 days and 7 nights. They make their way to their ocean view cabin, on the balcony. Neither 1 of them have ever been on a cruise. This is their 6th year of marriage. Young D wanted to do this one, very big. After all, the double life he's leading is about to come to a head. And if he has to come clean. What better place to do it, than far away from home? Then again, this could be more advantageous to Baby Girl if she decides to kill him. He just hopes the Kierra subject doesn't come up this week.

They said their goodbyes to all of their 4th of July guest, last Sunday. After taking them all to their church and feeding them, everyone headed home. Baby Girl had a great time with her brothers from Philly, Atlanta and New Orleans. It's a holiday gathering she won't soon forget. Although Kid did return to the event, for a short time to watch the Grand Hustle family perform, he didn't mingle. Nor did he talk to her. He was visibly irritated and no one really knew why. Baby Girl just figured maybe he had feelings for that Kierra tramp and that he was hot because she wasn't allowed on the premises. Or maybe he was upset because she'd stomped a mud hole in her ass, days prior. Nonetheless, Baby Girl doesn't care. She's planning to confront him, when she returns home, about being around Kierra.

Does he know that bitch wants my husband? I'm sure he doesn't. But he'll know. Just as soon as I talk to him.

Baby Girl had put $10K of the Tito Lopez satchel cash,

on their Rush card. Young D matched it. They'd gone on a huge shopping spree, just for this trip and they plan to spend every penny of the $20K, while on this anniversary vacation cruise. Of course they're bringing back island souvenirs for everyone. Her and Young D are planning to enjoy themselves. While reconfirming their love for 1 another. They also have to be mindful that by now, whomever ordered the first hit on her, knows it wasn't successful. There's always the expectation of another try. So they both came prepared for *anything*. They are both mindful of the dangers. Young D feels very mindful of it. Not being a pro, he still isn't aware of all the areas to watch and be leery of. So he thinks keeping her out of the public eye, may be safer.

"The rest of this day and tomorrow is for me. Me only," he says. "I get you, in the room until we dock in the Cayman Islands. We can only leave out of here to be guest at the captains table. Understand? Our fun day at sea will be spent in this cabin."

She says she understands and she has no problem with being cooped up in a state room with him, for a whole day. And she'll be honored to dine with the captain, as well.

"It's what my dreams are made of, daddy," she says as she smiles.

He smiles too. Then he pulls out a bag of flavor and says, "Look what I snuck on here."

He has the herb and the paraphernalia too. Quickly, he rolls some of it up for them.

After getting blazed, they take to pleasing each other. Baby Girl feels overly aggressive today. She straddles him and rips his shirt open.

"Take it off, daddy," she demands.

He strips completely. She peels out of her clothes as she looks

19

at him, with longing eyes. She grabs his dick and begins to massage it.

"Did my baby miss me?" she asks.

"Well, it *was* a long flight," he says, "He'll settle a sweet kiss, though."

She puts his dick in her mouth. Young D lays his head back and lets out a long sigh. She sucks him in and deep, to the back of her throat. She can hear him gasp for breath and she's imagining the thrills that are going through his body, right now. She wets his dick and sucks it. Baby Girl considers herself a pro, in more than 1 area. At this point, she knows her husband agrees. He's panting as his breathing picks up.

"Oh daddy. He's *so hard* to see me," she giggles.

He can't speak. He's at her mercy at this moment and he isn't trying to escape. She sucks him off in 5 minutes flat. Then he slips his tongue into her pussy. She purrs.

"Oh daddy," she gasps.

"Mmmm baby," he moans as he licks her clitoris while jamming his finger into her tunnel.

She's becoming more moist, in record time.

"She can feel that she missed me," he whispers from his southern position.

"Oh yes, she did," she whispers back, "That flight was *too* long."

They both giggle slightly. He goes to work on her and within minutes, he brings her abundant joy. She comes like this is first touch she's had today. But it isn't. He drove his foot of dick home before they got dressed for the airport. Still he makes every orgasm she has, feel like the first. They spend another 30 minutes fucking each others brains out. Afterwards, they're stilling buzzing.

"That's some *good* ass pussy," he says, gasping for air.

20

"That was some good dick and some good ass weed too," she says, panting as if she's just had a contraction.

"That's that Cush, baby," he says with a grin.

"That one hitter quitter," she adds.

They're both high and marinating in their perspiration. They finally catch up to their breath. She's hungry.

"Oh I know we going out of here for food, right?" she asks.

He laughs and says, "Yes, Lovely. Daddy's gonna feed you."

Satisfied that she will eat soon and satisfied sexually too. They settle in for day 1 and 2, of their cruise.

Day 3, for them, starts with a call to their little men, back in Houston. The family is doing fine. Young D has fun on the shore, planned for them in The Cayman Islands today. It's the first port stop of the cruise. Day 3 is the actual day of their anniversary. Tuesday, the 17th of July.

"Six years since we said, *I do*," she says, "And Derrick, I still do, honey. You're still the man and the only one I wanna hold."

"Eleven years since I first laid eyes on your pretty face," he offers, "And I still haven't seen a more beautiful woman. Misses Wanda gave you the perfect name. *Lovely*."

She blushes. She always loves it when he compliments her. The look in his eyes, shows his sincerity. He's always told her how beautiful she is to him. On the 1st night of their honeymoon, he vowed to tell her everyday, if that's what it took.

He would say, just what he says today.

"Ain't no man ever gonna take you away from me. Just by telling you how beautiful you are or how fine you are. Or how smart you are. Nor how good of a woman you are. Because baby, I'm gonna make sure I tell you that you are amazing to me. Because you are."

He's speaking straight from his heart.

21

"And you do it too, daddy," she tells him, "You always do and I love that, so much. And I love you."

"I love you too, baby girl," he says with a chuckle, as he sees tears form in her eyes.

He knows she's speaking her heart too and that's all he wants is for her to love him back. She giggles as she lays out their clothes which they're going to wear today.

"We're going in a mini submarine, baby," he says, "It's a clear sub. Bubble type of thing. They submerge us. And we travel underwater and see the fish, sharks, octopus. All of that shit."

"Sharks!?!" she gasps, "I don't do sharks."

"Maybe, sharks. But hey. We're protected. We're inside the submarine."

She has a fear of being submerged. She's claustrophobic but she's going to go with her husband. He's the adventurous type. He likes rollercoaster's and fast cars. Motorcycles and even surfing, when he can get to the ocean.

"What should I wear? Are we gonna get wet?" she asks.

"Baby, I'm gonna get you wet, everyday," he says, "Count on that. Okay?"

She blushes and says okay. He's talking about sex again and she could listen to him, all day. But that's all they've done, in two days. She has a killer wardrobe for this trip. Every item she bought during the spree was specifically aimed at turning her man on. But they've got to get to the outside of this boat. At least, 1 day.

"Whatever you wear, is gonna be sexy," he says.

Smiling big and bright, she selects the *Victoria Secrets* 2 piece sliding triangle top with the string bottom bikini. He loves it. She chooses her *Beach Sexy* cover up dress and white sling back sandals. She brings her *Steven by Steve Madden* handbag and *XOXO* sunglasses. She's a vision in all white with gold trim. Just like 6 years ago, today. Young D wears all white too. His *Derrick Blake* beach shorts and wife beater with his all white *Reebok Classics*, match her perfectly. He accents his gear with his *Chanel* sunglasses.

"Tell me, baby. Would I wear *Derrick Blake* and *Chanel*, if I thought I was gonna to get wet?" he asks.

"Yes. Of course, you would," she answers.
They laugh as they head out of their cabin and onto the deck, for brunch.

****

DeJuan is in charge of the Estate and the label mates while Young D is away. He and the guys are having a get together. They're at the 2 houses in the very back where the artist and some guest stay. They've invited strippers. Kierra *isn't* 1 of them. Her and her friends will never be allowed on the property again. The guys on the label have girlfriends and/or baby mama's. They're invited too. DeJuan doesn't have either. He has no kids of his own. Nor is he in a relationship anymore. The guys call him a loner but he stays busy and the guys can't figure out how. He's always got some errand to run or some booklet to study. But he never shares with them what he's learning. "I'm getting a trade," is all he would say.
He always gives the same answer. The only occupation they see him doing is music. He has 1 night stands often. But he's yet to bring a girl to an event and introduce her as his.

"Yeah. That brother will trick with a bitch but he ain't never trying to stick around," Manolo says as he laughs.

"He don't even let them know his phone number," Arafat adds with more laughter, "That brother is cold."

23

"And he makes sure they completely swallow his nut too," Big daddy offers, "So they can't set him up on no *Maury show*, type of shit."
They guys explode with laughter as they carry on.
"He don't love them ho's," DJ Debo gets in it as he mimics *Snoop Doggy Dog*.
Gat Em and High top are rolling on the couch's with laughter, as Manolo, Big Daddy, Debo and Arafat tease DeJuan.
"Haven't found the right one. That's it," DeJuan says.
They finally ease up on him and mingle with the invited guest. DeJuan goes back to greeting the new guest. Bruce and Angela come down for the party. Annie cooked sides for them. They all walk up to the main house and bring it back down.
"Food's here and set!" DJ Debo yells over the mic.
Then he starts the crowd off with their 2 newest CD's. The crowd is receptive to the new music immediately. The party is on and going. Everyone is having a good time and controlling themselves. DeJuan is in charge.

****

"This place is so beautiful, daddy," Baby Girl says.
Her and Young D are on the Grand Cayman Island tour. After the submarine venture, they'd gone parasailing. Young D loved flying above the water. Hanging by a thread is what Baby Girl called it. They had a light lunch on the beach between the submarine excursion and parasailing. Now it's getting towards sunset. The view is spectacular.
"I'm getting hungry, baby," he says.
"So am I," she agrees.
The tour is over. They head back to the ship. They'll sail again soon. But right now, it's time for them to prepare for dinner.

24

They go to their cabin, shower and change into dinner attire. She is very beautiful again tonight. They're going to keep it simple and go casual. A *House of Dereon* dress for her. He wears casual slacks and a *polo* from his own line, *Derrick Blake*.

Last night at the Captain's dinner, they were both sharp as a tack. She was especially elegant in her *Vera Wang* dress and *Jimmy Cho* sling backs that he'd bought her for the captain's dinner. She'd gotten the attire as a *Mother's day* gift. She had gotten him the *Armani* suit and *Kenneth Cole* dress shoes that he wore, as *Father's day* gifts. They were guest at the Captain's table, last night. But tonight, they're having a candlelit anniversary dinner for 2, on the promenade deck. Very sexy and secluded is the area where they'll actually eat.

"You look really beautiful, baby," he says.

"You look handsome, yourself, sexy," she returns the compliment with a sweet smile.

They turn heads as they're being taken to their table. A few passengers recognize Young D and come over for autographs. He's most gracious as he signs each 1. Then he sits and orders dinner for he and his wife.

She asks, "So what do you have planned for tomorrow?"

"We getting wet, all over," he says.

"Oh. Sex in the shower?" she asks as they both laugh. He's always loved her sense of humor and told her she'd make money doing stand-up comedy, if she put a routine together.

"We're going snorkeling and scuba diving in Cozumel," he reveals while still laughing at her wit.

"We're headed to Mexico?" she asks in surprise.

"Yes we are."

She's excited. She's never been to Mexico and she has always wanted to go.

"We've got to shop some too," she says, "I wanna see if I can find something for everybody, in every port."
They'd gotten souvenirs for everyone in the Grand Caymans.

"Okay. We going riding on ATV's too," he says.

"Now that sounds good to me. I'm having a wonderful time, daddy."

"That's all I'm concerned about, Lovely," he assures her, "And my sons at home too, now. I can't leave them out."
They laugh.

"What if Lil Man was on this boat with us?" she asks as she laughs.

"We would be fishing his ass out of the ocean," he says with a chuckle, "Every ten miles."
They laugh hard just as dinner is arriving. Their waiter smiles as he lays the spread out on the table for them. Complete with a smooth *Kendall Jackson Chardonnay*. He sets another bottle of *Dom Perignon* on ice, next to the table. Then he serves their meal.

They dine on succulent Lobster, Steak and Shrimp. For sides, they have over stuffed potatoes and garden salads. A meal fit for a King and Queen. For dessert, he'd ordered *tiramisu* and *Bananas Foster*.

After dinner, their waiter keeps the champagne flowing. Young D takes his wife on the dance floor for an anniversary slow dance. He's in the mood and so is she.
"It's time for our drink orders for the cabin," he whispers in her ear.
He signals their waiter and he comes to their side as they dance. Young D orders *Hypnotiq* for her and *Courvoisier*, for himself. The waiter hurries the order in and requests that it be sent to their cabin. Young D also has their waiter to set up champagne, strawberries and cream plus a late night snack.

"We'll be working on our third child," he tells her with laughter. He adds, "We'll need to replenish."
The waiter hurries off to attend to his duties while Young D and Baby Girl have 1 more dance.

Soon, he escorts her back to the cabin and helps her out of her attire. Then he sheds his and joins her in bed.

"Happy anniversary, Lovely Blake," he whispers.

"Happy anniversary, Derrick Blake senior."

****

"Bitch! You can't come in here!" High Top yells.
He's at the main gate, stressing to Kierra that she is not allowed on the grounds. She's begging him to let her come up and see Young D. From the front gate of their exclusive neighborhood, security had called the main house. They told Annie of a young woman asking for permission to come in to visit her. And said she told him she'd been invited to come out to a party. Apparently, 1 of the invited strippers knows Kierra and had called and told her about the party at Young D's Estate. The stripper wondered why Kierra hadn't been invited. Kierra knows why but she thought maybe since they have strippers, 1 of the guys from the label would sneak her in. She was mistaken.

"D gone bout *his* fucking business, bitch!" Gat Em exclaims. "He's with the woman he loves and he ain't about your yamp ass!"
After hearing this, the security guard orders her to leave. He threatens to call Houston police. Kierra leaves, reluctantly.

In a very foolish move, she calls Young D's phone. Lucky for her, it's not his main phone. It's 1 of the phones they use for the label. Young A or Aristocrat picks up.

"Hello, not this dumb bitch. How are you?" he answers.

"Why are you talking to me, like that? What did I do to you?" Kierra asks.

Young A explains that this is how the number she's calling from, is saved in the phone she dialed.

"It says, '*NOT THIS DUMB BITCH*'. I *swear*. It's in the phone book, like that."

He is cracking his side in laughter. So is Big Daddy, when he hears him explaining why he's referring to her, like that. Big Daddy takes the phone. He already knows who's on the other end because he recognizes the name.

"You know my nigga is not bout *fuckin* wit you," he growls, "Take your ho ass on home or somewhere else."

A few of the others join in and a few of the party guest too. They're having plenty of laughs, at Kierra's expense. She finally takes their advice. She leaves the area. Next, they send the stripper packing, who had called and told her she wouldn't be invited back. Then they get back to their party.

"If D was here," Angela says, "He would've killed her for showing up here, on his anniversary."

"He would kill her for showing up here, *any* day," Big Daddy corrects her.

"If he could beat Baby Girl to her ass," DeJuan offers.

They all agree, without even knowing why he said it like that. DeJuan is aware of what Baby Girl does for a living. He doesn't offer a clue to the clueless.

****

Day 4 is definitely a *get wet* day. The wet starts in bed with a eye opening session of lovemaking, as soon as they wake up. They have breakfast in bed, then a dip in their Jacuzzi tub

28

for another romantic encounter. Young D is getting it all in. They dry each other off and Baby Girl gets their clothes out for their 4th day of adventure. They're in beautiful Cozumel, Mexico.

After they're dressed, they join the other passenger's for beginner's scuba diving. In the group there are some senior citizens, who are *quite* spunky. The 4 senior couples take Young D and Baby Girl under their wings, after they find out they're celebrating 6 years of marriage. The 4 couples have been married a total of 183 years. They have 50 years, 46 years, 43 years and 42 years of marriage. Baby Girl looks at their own, like they have accomplished nothing. They all laugh.

"I thought we'd done something," Baby Girl says as she giggles. "You guys are my heroes."

"Six years is still the honeymoon, sweetheart," 1 of the ladies say.

"Me and Charlie was still going to bed early, way back then," says another lady.

"Does she go to bed early with you?" the 3rd older another lady asks Young D.
Rather excitedly, he says, "Yes! Yes ma'am, she does."
He laughs. Baby Girl ask *that* lady's husband does she still go to bed early with him.

"She don't go to bed at all, hardly," he answers, "And when she does. She just sleeps."
His wife frowns at him and says, "Nothing left to go to bed for, nowadays."
Young D and Baby Girl are tickled with that response. They're really enjoying their time spent with the 4 senior couples.

"If he don't take you to bed early. You need to come live with me," says 1 of the older gentlemen.

"Watch out there now," Young D says, in a *J Anthony*

Brown manor, as he gives him the look to go with it.

They both laugh but Baby Girl is embarrassed, initially. The older women start to flirt with Young D. Baby Girl thinks it's funny. Young D is embarrassed. He just stands still.

"I remember when my John had a stomach like this," 1 of the senior ladies says as she rubs Young D's washboard abs. She snickers.

Her husband John says, "Now if I get to rubbing on this beautiful young lady. You'll get mad with me."

"So will I," Young D says quickly.

They all laugh hard and have a great time. With an abundance of flirting, they learn and eventually, go scuba diving.

The underwater view is beautiful and clear. Baby Girl and Young D hold hands and swim together. They kiss a lot and take many underwater pictures with their waterproof camera. They know Lil Man is going to love these pictures.

After scuba diving, Young D and Baby Girl part from the group for an ATV & Beach Adventure. They ride ATV's to a secluded beach where Young D arranged a private picnic for 2. They spend so much time on the secluded beach, there isn't enough time left to go snorkeling. They shop for an hour. Then it's back to the ship for their next sail. Their going to another adventure port known as Belize. Day 5 is going to be just as fascinating as the first 4. Young D has guaranteed Baby Girl that he will take her snorkeling before the cruise ends. 2 hours before they dock, Young D calls Houston to check on the family and his label mates.

"I want my mommy!" Lil Man yells.

Derrick Jr is being a brat today. It's been 5 days since he's seen his parents, so he's going for broke as he talks to his father on the phone.

30

"What's the problem, man?" Young D asks.

"I wanna go to my mommy house. Tom get me, daddy!" he demands.

He's testy but Young D can handle him. He tells Baby Girl to talk to him, for a bit.

"He's giving mama hell, today," Young D says, as he laughs and gives Baby Girl the phone.

Baby Girl doesn't think it's funny. She gets on the phone with their oldest son. And in only a few minutes, she has his understanding that her and his father are spending a few days by themselves to celebrate the love which brought him and his little brother into the world.

In other words, she says, "Little Derrick. If you don't behave. You won't get a pony. Do you understand me?"

"I want my boney, mommy," he tries.

"Then what are you going to do, right now?" she asks.

He lays the phone down and hugs and kisses his grandmother Annie and says, "I sorry, Nana."

Then he comes back to the phone.

"I be the good boy, mommy," he says while giggling.

"I'm so proud of you, man. I love you," Baby Girl says.

He says he loves her too. She tells him to kiss his little brother, for her and his daddy. He does. Then he remembers her kiss routine. He kisses Annie, Angela, Bruce and Jordan. He kisses every family member she names. By the end of their conversation, he's giggling and having a good time. Baby Girl gives the phone back to Young D and says, "The hard part is done. You can take over. It's play time, now."

He laughs with her as he takes the phone. He talks to his mother. This time without anymore interruptions from his junior. Annie tells him what happened at the main gate, on their anniversary.

31

"She did what?" he asks, disgustedly.

"Young A said she called one of the business cell phones, looking for you," Annie says.

Young D is irritated instantly. He tells him mother that he needs to call DeJuan. Before the ship docks and,

"Before Lovely comes back looking for me."

She had gone back to their cabin to get out there clothing, for today's port side adventure.

In the cabin, Baby Girl picks out her *Marisa Fit cargo utility Capri pants* in camouflage. She selects the *Tattoo Zip Hoodie* with sleeves in gypsy mauve, to go with them. She wears her diamond necklace and earrings, another Mother's day gift from Young D. Her brown suede *Basketweave* t-strap sandals for her feet and *Lucky Brand patchwork Hobo bag*, with her Chanel sunglasses and 2 fuchsia bangles completes her ensemble. For her husband, again staying with his own line. She pulls out a hooded camouflage t-shirt with ¾ length sleeves. The pockets on his jeans are camouflage. She picks his green loafers trimmed in gold, for a perfect match.

"He did say we're going on a jungle adventure, here in Belize. I wanna make sure the mosquito's don't eat us up," she says to herself as she smiles.

There's a knock on the cabin door. Their breakfast is here. After seeing their assigned server through the peep hole, she opens the door for room service.

"Breakfast is here, madam," their waiter says.

She opens the cabin door and allows him in.

He brings in their large breakfast. They have soft scrambled eggs with cheese, T-Bone steaks, buttered grits, toast, bowls of fresh peeled citrus fruits, milk, grape juice and strawberry marmalade. Their waiter sets it up at their table, next to the port hole, where Baby Girl had requested.

She follows the server out of the cabin and heads back to the shore phone to inform Young D that it's time for breakfast.

"Homie. Make sure that bitch get the point, man," Young D says to DeJuan, "I don't ever want her back in Bellaire for any fucking reason. Not even at the main gate."
He's still on his ship-to-shore call with DeJuan.

"D, she got the number from the flyers and posters," DeJuan says, " The ones we pass out and hang, man. She didn't get it out your phone. I made sure of that. She told me how she got it."

"Good looking out, bro. I knew you had it covered."

"No need to worry bout the home front, homeboy. I got it covered, boss," DeJuan says.

"You make the boss's job a lot easier," Young D says.
Baby Girl tips up behind Young D and grabs him around his waist. With a giggle, she says, "I thought I did that?"

"Oh you do, Lovely. But you're the third boss of me."
She laughs as they hug each other. She ask who's on the line now. He tells her, it's DeJuan.

"What's up pro?" she yells into the phone.
All three of them laugh.
"Derrick had me fooled like I was the *H.B.I.C.* Only to find out I've got a couple of toddlers in front of me."
DeJuan says he knows but that's just the way it is. They have a good laugh. Then they say hello and goodbye to all the guys. They hang up.

"Breakfast is in the cabin?" Young D asks.
She says, "Yes and it smells good."
They hurry back to their cabin and have breakfast.

****

33

Kierra has gotten in touch with Kid because she's upset at not being able to contact Young D, all week.

"Where the fuck is he at?" she asks Kid via telephone. Kid thinks, for a minute but he doesn't even need long. He knows what this week is. 1 he has learned to hate with all of his heart. It's the week when, 6 years ago, Derrick Blake had signed on to be the owner of half of his sisters assets.

"This is their anniversary week," he says, "That nigga probably got her off somewhere spending money, like he's happily married."

Even though Kierra wants Young D for herself. She still doesn't understand why Kid hates him, so much. She dislikes the negative tone in his voice when he talks about him. Which is, all the time. Kierra started to worry, around Father's day, when his conversations were dominated with talk of wishing Young D was dead. He wished someone would kill him. Kierra had set out to meet Young D, in order to tell him what Kid said. It was that show where Baby Girl fought her. Kierra had actually gone to Galveston in hopes of telling Young D that Kid had it in for him. Kid had gotten drunk, the night before and let something slip out. Kierra wasn't sure if he realized he'd said it and she didn't want to judge him while he was under the influence. So she never mentioned it to him but she was going to tell Young D. She hoped it would make Young D see that she really wanted to be with him and that she was loyal to him too. She didn't get the opportunity to tell Young D about Kid because Baby Girl beat her ass for being backstage trying to see him. And she reminded her that Young D was her husband. Still, Kierra isn't going to give up. She has to come up with a plan and she feels she needs Kid's help. But what he says next, only keeps her thinking negatively about his intentions for Young D.

"I wish somebody would hurry up and pop that nigga or something," Kid says.

This time he doesn't sound drunk at all. He sounds as sober as a nun. She questions him, for clarity.

"You mean as in, *shoot* him? You're talking this shit again?" she asks.

She giggles as if she's only playing around. Then Kid laughs and pretends he was only kidding too. She *knows* she's kidding but she doesn't believe he is. Fact is, Kid is testing her, to see how far she's willing to go for her greed.

"I got to get a good ass plan for him, though," Kid says, "Get him caught up, real good. I'm telling you. If she ever catches him cheating. I mean like, *in the act*? She'll leave him, for sure."

"So what's the plan? What are we gonna do? And give me a real plan, this time. Stop playing."

He knows she isn't willing to help kill Young D. He could tell by the tone in her voice when he'd mentioned it. So he tells her, he wants to set him up in a hotel room, have him going there to meet a woman. Then send Baby Girl there with lingerie and a note. Like Young D is there to surprise her with a romantic night. This is what he's telling Kierra but that's not the way he's really planning it.

"Meeting a woman?" Kierra asks, in a dislike tone.

"Yeah. Like a call girl or escort," he says.

"If I get to be the escort," Kierra says.

"You wit it? Can you handle it and not give the shit away?" Kid asks with a chuckle.

He knew she would be all for meeting Young D in a room and having Baby Girl catch them, will be sweet revenge for the ass whooping she'd taken in Galveston. Although, Kierra adds in the fact that she'll surely have to take another ass whooping.

She tells Kid, "Hell yeah, I can do that. I've been waiting on that shit, for damn near *eight* years. Her to catch him with me. Fuck yeah. Long as you ain't talking about setting him up to be killed. Like you was talking, before the Galveston show."

Kid chuckles devilishly. He's definitely planning on sending Baby Girl to see Young D in that hotel room with Kierra. Not as Young D, though. But as a *John* that she's suppose to hit. He's hoping she'll show up, see Young D there with Kierra and kill him, out of anger. Kierra is clueless, at the moment.

Will she figure out just what Kid is up to before it's too late?

"What if she has a gun on her or something?" Kierra asks, "He done told me, she packs a gun. What if that bitch shoots me?"

Kid tells her not to call his sister a bitch, "Ever again!"

"Okay. But what if she brings her gun?" she asks.

"To meet her husband? For a romantic night? Get real, Kierra!" Kid says.

He keeps her talking. Finally, they settle on the plan. They're going to go through with it. Kid is going to take care of the details and the pay. Even getting the message to Baby Girl about the date with Young D. He's going to send her the lingerie gift *with* the note. Again, this is what he tells Kierra. But this is not how it's going to go. Not at all.

Kid will pay to send Baby Girl there to hit a mark. He's going to pay Gus Davis. Then put a hit on Young D, after hiring the best cleaner in the world to get him done. *His own wife.*

****

Young D and Baby Girl set off on the Belize city tour. The carnival is taking place when they arrive in town. The tour

36

stops. They get out and enjoy the carnival. The belly dancers are interesting. They aren't all slim and model thin. There are some with *actual* belly's and still, they celebrate in their skimpy tops and *barely there* briefs. Just as the shapelier dancers are. Young D and Baby Girl shop at the expo where she purchases 6 *Medina's* lawn sets.

"They're shipping them home, for us," Young D says, "Those are gonna look good in the yards around the estate."
She says, "The estate is starting to look a lot like the manor."

"Oh hell no!" he says while laughing, "I'm not even close to *The Don's Manor*."
He helps her pick out some handmade pottery, wall art and paintings. They have it all shipped to Houston, then they take in more sights and take pictures with carnival girls and bikini models too. *Saint John's Cathedral* is the oldest Angelic Church in central America. They tour it too.

"We have to get a picture in here," she says as they go inside the church.
They take lots of pictures. There's a breathtaking view inside.

"You know kings have been crowned here," she says.

"A king is here now too, baby," he says.

"My king," she says.
They kiss, then move along with the tour. Their cruise friends, the 4 senior couples are with them again. They get pictures with them, as well. Then the tour guide takes them back to the starting point and they jump on board to the next adventure. It's the *Jungle Buggy & Mayan Cave Exploration*. They ride through the jungle in a monster buggy, 10 feet off of the ground. They check out the *ECO systems* as the guide tells them tales of Ancient Mayans. Then they hop in a Land Rover and trek through the Mayan Caves.

"I feel like I'm in one of those *Indiana Jones movies*,"

Young D says and they all laugh. Even their driver.

"I'm scared," Baby Girl says.

The caves are beautiful but very overwhelming. Young D takes a lot of pictures inside the caves. He's going to make a slide show for all their entire family to see and be amazed by. The family at the manor are included, anytime he says *family*.

"You should come down here and do a video," she says.

"Can I have some of these beautiful women in it?"

"Oh sure. I'll pick them out for you," she says, "We'll get these four that's hanging out with us now too."

He laughs and says, "That's alright. We'll mix them in there too." They all laugh again.

"You are having a good time though. Right?" he asks.

"I am, love. Yes I am," she says.

She smiles warm and lays her head on his shoulders. They've never been closer.

After the Cave expedition, it's time to get back to the ship. They hurry along to their cabin to shower and dress for supper.

****

In New Orleans, Gus Davis gets a text message marked urgent. It's from Kid. Gus calls him, right away.

"This is Gus," he says.

Kid tells him that he wants to meet with him today, to buy another contract. Gus tells him they'll have to meet first thing tomorrow morning. He tells him to be at his office at 9am.

"You know the routine," Gus says, speaking of the deposit.

If it's a hit for Baby Girl, then it's a high profile mark. The fee is $250K minimum. The more the risk, the more additional fees. Kid will have to pay Gus 10% of the minimum, up front.

Gus' fee is $25K on high profile marks. Baby Girl only does high profile marks. Once the mark is set, Kid has to pay the full balance. Any risk turned in by Baby Girl or any additional cost she has, is collected from the agent at her request. She receives 10% when she accepts the package. When the mark is done, she collects the balance. Whatever cost she incurs is paid to her by the agent. Then the agent has to get the additional amount from the buyer. This leaves the agent with the option of buying a hit on the buyer, if he doesn't refund him. Gus, the agent, is paid his full commission, up front. Whether the hit gets picked up or not. The agent gets paid. The agents fee varies with profiles and risk. But the percentage is always ten percent of the base pay. The agent is paid simply for meeting with a buyer and discussing the contract killing of another. This is because of the risk of implication for the agent. In the event the buyer gets hemmed up or turns out not to be bogus. Because Baby Girl doesn't kill for free. If the buyer is trying to pull a sting. Putting money down, loses him the option of being a witness for the prosecution in that sting because that would be entrapment.

Kid is the buyer, in this case. He's setting this contract on Young D. He isn't going to back out nor pull a sting. In this case, Young D is a celebrity. He's high profile and famous. That's more risk. He will have to pay base price of $350K. Gus get's $35K, in the morning. There is never a refund given. If for any reason the mark is not killed, the pro becomes a mark and so does the contract buyer. In other words, if Baby Girl takes this hit, goes through the research and assumes the risk. She gets paid. The only reason she wouldn't terminate a mark would be if she was terminated by the mark. Or if the mark is cancelled by the buyer. So Kid sees this plan as fool proof. Only he may very well be the fool when the proof is unfolded.

In this case, Young D is the husband of the terminator and she won't be willing to terminate Young D, at any cost. So if and when she discovers that the mark is her husband. She will then back track and find the buyer. She'll do this by going to her agent. She'll ask Gus who bought the contract. It's his duty as her agent to reveal this information. But in some cases, marks are set without knowledge of whom the buyer is. Not often but it has been done. There is always a contact person. She has researched a buyer this way, found and terminated him. It was in the case of a rich child molester who was arrested and bonded out. He wanted the victim and her family terminated. Baby Girl's morals and values is always her first law. She did in that bastard ass child rapist. Then gave the victims family his package fee and called it a large donation. There are also times when no physical description of the mark is presented. Just directions, the address or events. Sometimes there's minimal information to work with but Baby Girl has always gotten the job done.

So once she finds out that *her mark* is *her man*, she'll contact Gus. He may say he doesn't have a description of the mark, thus the reason she didn't get 1 either. If she discovers that Gus knew this hit was on Young D, she'll terminate him and the buyer, Kid. Thus eliminating any further attempts to have Young D terminated and definitely as a future assignment on her family. Killing your agent is not the normal thing to do and it rarely happens. But most agents aren't rogues, like Gus. *The Don* knew this but he kept him employed to keep him near. Most assassins are loners. They have no close friends or immediate family. No wives, husbands or kids. No ties. Before becoming a pro, most assassins separate themselves from what ever family or friends they do have.

Baby Girl is a different kind of Pro. She has a husband,

children and a large family. Which became even larger in the past month. So her cover is flawless. She'd be the last 1 the law would suspect. But her strongest point is also her weakest. Anyone trying to get to her can mark her husband and/or her children. Baby Girl is smart though. She knows what her weak points are. But who would've guessed that her brother and agent would conspire against her and why? Best guess. *Greed*!
Gus is disloyal to Don Morales and Baby Girl. He's become, even more rogue. The Don knew he wanted his fortune but Gus wasn't brave nor dumb enough to try, *The Don.. The Organization* is way to deep for rogues to succeed. Gus doesn't even know the depth. Only the pro which he assigns for and that is Baby Girl. There are those at the manor who know who all of the Morales pros are. They don't get any high profile jobs because Baby Girl is first and foremost. But they do have other pro's to take hits for less then $250K. Don was smart not to let Gus go too. But he put him on a short leash. Assisting the Top pro only, which keeps him at the manor and making the most commission. No other family pro can pay him a minimum of $25k. They aren't Baby Girl, the best pro in the business. But Don knew Gus was a rogue. He was dead on point with that analysis and Gus has only gotten worse. He only cares about the money now. As much of it as he can get, at all cost. He's the 1 who had allowed Kid to set a mark on Baby Girl and Young D, 3 weeks ago and he used Mark Genolli'. That was the ultimate betrayal. And even though he'd received the mark, early. He didn't inform Baby Girl until 24 hours before it was to expire. She didn't learn of a hit on her and Young D until they were in play. Gus was suppose to alert her as soon as the mark came across the wire. These actions by Gus are punishable by death. And his death will most likely come at the hands of the pro, he has turned on. *Lovely Walker-Blake.*

41

The next morning, Kid meets with Gus. He doesn't even waste time waiting for the mark info to be set up. He pays $385k, *this* morning.

"Let me get this straight," Gus says, "You're hiring Baby Girl to hit Young D?"
Kid says yes. Gus questions if he really thinks it'll happen. Kid tells him, he's willing to risk it.
"If this ever gets back to her. She's gonna kill you," Gus says, "And me too."
Kid says, "That's a chance I'm willing to take. Apparently you are too. I see you ain't turn down the cash."
Gus smiles with confidence. He's worked with Baby Girl for 8 years. He knows she'll do her research. Once she sees who the hit is, she'll question him as to who set it.

What Gus is going to do is make it impossible for Baby Girl to see the mark's description before she is upon him. If she finds out it's Young D, Gus will simply deny knowing who the mark was, in advance.

"I'm going to make this a hit, by USPS," Gus says, "They're gonna correspond through a PO Box and a dummy text message phone and pager. Right up until hit time and so will you."
Kid tells him his plans about the hotel. Gus incorporates the 2 together. They look over the contract and discuss how it will play out. It is to go as such:

Young D will receive an offer for a lucrative deal which will come from a female. A fake photo of the female will be included with some fake business literature and a pager to communicate with and the name of the hotel, where the meeting will take place. Young D will have to meet her, in her suite to discuss particulars and to close the deal. Gus and Kid feel this will spark Young D's curiosity.

42

Kid says, "He's an unfaithful ass nigga, anyway. He'll be ready to fuck her, if we add in some seductive shit. Now, how do we get Baby Girl there?"

Gus explains. She will receive a date, time, pager number and room number, for the hit. That's it.

He says, "Baby Girl is a pro. She'll do all the research she can. As long as there is no photo. There's a chance she'll hit him. But she's a pro, like I said. She may figure it out before the hit can happen. If she does. We'd better be somewhere else."

****

On day 6, they're in *The Roatan Island*, Honduras. Young D finally gets to take Baby Girl snorkeling. They dive with the Dolphins and go horseback riding too.

The remainder of the day is spent shopping. Then they go back to their cabin to pack all of the new gifts into the new bags she'd bought to bring it all home.

"We got it all packed up," she says, "I'm gonna have the staff to help me pack this for shipping."

He says, "We can ship the Houston stuff home. Then we can fly to New Orleans and check on the Manor. We can give them they're souvenirs and let Addie Mae cook me some Cajun food, before we fly home."

"Extend the vacation, a little more, ha?" she asks.

"We may as well," he says, "We ain't done living yet."

43

CHAPTER   TWENTY ONE
THE MYSTERIOUS JOHN

Baby Girl and Young D bring in the next week in New Orleans, at the manor. They'd bought art and furniture for the manor while in the Caribbean And shipped it to the staff. After spending the majority of the day with the staff, Young D calls up Six Nine to check on that side of Baby Girl's family. Word got to Kid that they were in the city. He alerts Gus and Gus calls Baby Girl with the new assignment. She goes to his office to pick up the package.

"I'm suppose to mark a man without a description?" she asks, "I must be the best. *Damn.*"
She looks over the package or lack thereof. She's got a company cell phone to use, a voice scrambler, a pager number, a hotel name, the mark's name, the date the mark goes into play and instructions as to how she is to communicate with the mark.

"What kind of name is Drexel?" she asks.
"It sounds foreign to me," Gus says.
"I know what it is," she says.
"What is it?"
"Fake. It's a phony name," she says.
She's good and Gus had better make sure his passport is up to date. Take a trip. A long trip and take her brother Kid with him. Because Baby Girl is very smart. She's had the package for only 5 minutes and already she knows the name is made up. "Okay. So I'll make first contact with him. Give him instructions about where to meet me and when. What does he think he's buying?"
Gus says, "You, for the most part. And shares in the new, New Orleans project. He thinks you work for the mayor's office. He thinks he's fucking the Katrina victims out of their land and

possibly, you too. But what he's gonna get is fucked."

"Well, yes. Someone is. That's for sure," she says.

She grabs her package, purse and her keys. She drives back up to the manor. Her and Young D's flight leaves for Houston in 3 hours. She can't wait to get home and see her babies.

****

The month of July is coming to an end. MC Young D is about to get back on the road touring. This will be the western portion of the tour. Arizona, California, Washington state, New Mexico, Nevada, Oregon, Utah and Colorado. Baby Girl is going to travel with him. Her new mark will be in California. The tour will stop in the city where her mark is to be and on the same day, she is to terminate her target. Baby Girl sees this as perfect from all angles. She will be traveling with the label. Her alibi will be solid. The mark's hit date is August 4th in San Francisco. She grabs a copy of Young D's tour schedule. She can't believe her eyes.

"Wow! This is perfect. Derrick's tour stop on the fourth is in, ………..*San Francisco!*"

She pauses for a second and grabs the package. She retrieves the pager number and saves it in the company phone, she has. She burns the page with the pager number on it. Before Young D can return from the mailbox, all of her bases are covered.

Young Dee returns with the mail. He has received an express envelope but he doesn't recognize the name. There's a California return address. He opens it and examines the contents inside.

Who is this?

He thinks to himself, just as Kid and Gus counted on. He's curious. The deal which is being proposed will be ideal for his

45

label and other business ventures. This couldn't have come at a better time. Kid knows what would be the perfect deal for Young D. He's heard him discuss it many times, over the years. So Kid and Gus made it sound perfect. It's an offer he can't refuse. He reads the instructions. He will receive a phone call from the contact. He's to use the voice scrambler when he talks on the phone to her and so will she. He and the female contact are to use text messaging and pagers to communicate, after the initial scrambled call.

"Female? Is this shit legal?" he asks, himself out loud.
He looks in the envelope and pulls out a photo of a gorgeous woman.

"Who is that?" Baby Girl asks.
She walks into the family room where he's going through today's mail. He tells her a company out in California wants to talk with him about investing in his brand.

He says, "This is a picture of the CEO and some info about the deal they're proposing. I've got to examine it carefully but it looks good. *Too* good."

"That's cool, daddy," she says.
She's excited and so is he. She thinks to herself.
He'll have business to attend too. So I should be able to hit my mark without him sweating me, so much.

"It sounds almost too good to be true," he says.
She tells him to have confidence but be smart and think it through, like he usually does. Young D has a brilliant mind for business. She knows he'll make the right decision.
She says, "I've got some calls to make, daddy. I'll be in my office if you need me. Oh! And I want to meet this woman."
She jokes with him as she makes her way to her office. She's about to make the initial contact with her mark.

****

"Did she accept the package?" Kid asks Gus.

Kid is in Houston visiting Kierra. Baby Girl doesn't know he's here. He leaves Kierra in bed and calls New Orleans, first thing this morning, for an update from Gus.

Gus says, "I set it up where I knew she'd take it because she's curious about who the mark is. She gets to be a call girl, so she can change her appearance too. No one will know it's her. Not even the mark. Plus she's wondering why it's so secretive and why they can't have voice contact? I'm sure Young D is wondering, as well. But for him. This is an opportunity to expand his brand and his business. Ultimately, his fortune."

"He can't say no to that," Kids says.

Gus says, "Don't underestimate Baby Girl. Don Morales trained her, personally. From the crib."

"Do you think I am?" Kid asks.

"Yes. Yes I do."

"How am I underestimating her?" he asks.

He doesn't know Kierra has gotten up and is listening, just outside the opening of her living room. She's in the hallway. She can hear every thing he's saying.

"I feel like you don't realize how acute she is," Gus says.

"I know she's sharp. But once she sees him fucking up. Her emotions will take over. She'll kill him and this bitch too."

Kierra has heard all she needs to hear. She goes into the bathroom and closes the door with a slight thump. She wants Kid to know she's up now. From her cell phone, she calls her roommate Trina, who's sleeping in. But she wakes up, still groggy, to answer her phone.

"What up, roomy? It's early!" Trina grunts.

"Get up and meet me in the bathroom. We need to go

47

somewhere and talk," Kierra whispers, "You're not gonna believe what I just heard this nigga saying. Come on. Get up and let's go."

Trina hurries and gets dressed. Her and Kierra grab Danica and leaves. They tell Kid they're going to the *Waffle House* to meet her parents and ask them about keeping Danica while Kierra goes to California with him.

"Okay. Bring me some breakfast back," he says.

Assuring that they will leave and *have* to go to Waffle House to get breakfast. He gives them money enough to pay for all of their food. The girls leave Kid alone to finish his call. He gets back to it as Gus is telling him, Baby Girl is a true professional. He says, "She'll make sure he sees her eyes and she sees his, before she kills him. I told you this, from day one. And that's because the info about the mark thrives on secrecy. Once she sees him. It's not gonna happen."

Kid responds with, "He'll be there with a woman, Gus. *Kierra*. The woman she's made everyone out at their house, bar from their property. She wouldn't even be doing this shit if he didn't think it was fly. Baby Girl is a cultured girl. Don sheltered her. Sent her to private school, overseas and shit. I think she do the hits because D think it's *gangsta*. She was not doing *any* dirt before he came into her life. Now, she's a killer for hire."

"This is part of the family business," Gus says, "Don Morales himself, trained her. And D doesn't even know, she's a trained killer."

Gus doesn't know Young D found out about her profession, 3 years ago. But Kid persists in trying to build up Gus' courage. And his own.

Kid says, "She *will* be catching him in a hotel room with a bitch she's warned him about. She'll wanna know how she got to Cali too. She'll figure he paid for her to meet him there."

Gus tries, "She'll be angry about the woman being there. *Yes.* But she'll be more concerned about why has her husband been marked for termination. She was marked, just a month prior to his termination date. She didn't know Mark was to kill him too. But she'll think about her sons, the family and if her job is the reason why. I'm telling you. She's gonna back track and she will find both of us. Kid, we need a plan B."

But Kid is stubborn. He thinks seeing Kierra in the room with Young D will make his sister angry enough to kill him. This is why Kid isn't ready for the profession. He's emotional. Baby Girl had said this to Gus during the Memorial day event.

"He doesn't understand rage has no part in this killing game," she had said, *"Only the five A's. Accuracy, acuteness, ability and absolute anonymity."*

But Kid is persistent and wants the contract honored. Gus says fine. He won't pull it. At this point, Gus is just trying to save his own life, even if Kid doesn't want to live. They hang up. Kid's satisfied that his plan is in motion. He hit's the shower.

****

"Girl, he's trying to get Young D killed by his wife and he wants me to be a part of it," Kierra says, "And he thinks *I* could die too. Ain't that some shit?"
Her and Trina are at McGregor Park. Danica plays. They talk.
"Oh my God!" Trina says, "How'd you find out?"
Kierra begins telling Trina about the plan *she thought*, her and Kid had going.
"He's flying me to San Francisco," she says, "So I can be in a hotel room that Young D is to come too. But he'd be thinking he's meeting some woman about business."

49

Trina says, "He'll know it's a set up when he sees you. But he'll think you set it up, using business, just to get him to meet up with you."

"But he knows I don't have that kind of loot," Kierra says, "To fly all the way to Cali just to trick him into a hotel room? He'll know I didn't do it alone."

"Then that's when you can tell him about Kid's phone conversation this morning," Trina says, "Then y'all can wait for his wife to come and tell her about her fucked up brother."

"D ain't gonna sit in no hotel with me," Kierra says, "Not *knowing* she's on the way there. No way in *hell*."
She tells Trina that Baby Girl is suppose to show up and find out that her and Young D are together. And then, Kid's fake plan also calls for her to tell Baby Girl about Danica.
"And then, Baby Girl is suppose to get angry and just leave Young D?" she says as she shakes her head in disbelief.

"And you are suppose to have him?" Trina asks, "Is that the shit Kid told you? He thought that shit was gonna go over like that? *Hell*. I know better than that and I don't even know his sister. I don't know *no bitch* who'll leave a fine ass nigga just cause she caught him sitting in a room. I don't give a shit how many kids y'all have. Young D is a rich ass man."

"But she's rich too. Way richer than he is."

"That's why that nigga ain't trying to lose that pussy," Trina says, "but I can't get over Kid. That's his own sister."

"That's the reason D won't tell her about Danica. It's because she'll leave him for making a baby, on her. That's what Kid has been harping on. Now? I don't believe shit that he says. Not after this morning."

"What all did he say?" Trina asks.
She tells her roommate what she overheard.
"I heard him talking on the phone to somebody,"

50

Kierra says, "I heard him ask, *'How am I underestimating her?'* Then, and here is the killer. He said, *'I know she's sharp. But once she sees him fucking up. Her emotions will take over. She'll kill has ass and this bitch too.'* I heard that shit with my own ears. That's when I went in the bathroom and called your room. I had to get us out of there. *Quick.*"

"Sound like he's setting both of y'all up," Trina says.
Kierra agrees, saying, "I heard it from his own mouth."

"What are you gonna do? You can't go to Cali with him by yourself. Not after hearing this," Trina says.
She wants to go too. Just for the free trip. Because she knows Kierra isn't going to do anything that will get Young D hurt. But she knows she isn't going to turn down a free trip either. Kierra tells her she's going to go to California with Kid. She'll pretend she hadn't heard his phone call. She's going to go on the shopping spree that he promised and say nothing about the call. But she isn't going to go in that hotel room. Not at all.

"Hell to the nah!" she says, "He's trying to get me and my man, knocked off."
Her and Trina toast with their water bottles and laugh.

"Two can play this money game," Trina says.
She's all in. Kierra decides to take her along too. She'll tell Kid that she needs Trina there, in case things get too thick or something like that. They'll think of something. It's going to work out because it has too.
Trina says, "Tell him I can't be in Houston, at the apartment. Because you told your parents you needed them to sit for Danica cause I was going out of town."

"I'll say I need my home girl there to keep me focused."

"Just make it work because I wanna be there too," Trina says, "I have to be there. That's Cali. *Shit.*"
They laugh again and let Danica play for a few more minutes.

51

Then they head off to eat. They're going to eat at, *This Is It*. They get some Waffle House for Kid, on the way back.

****

Gus sits at home alone. He's thinking about how he sees this contract unfolding. His gut tells him that Baby Girl will prevail. This hit will not gone down and she'll want blood, once she unfolds this plot. He's planning to save himself. When she comes back to him, he'll say he didn't know the identity of the mark. And that the buyer never disclosed the mark's identity. She'll press him for the buyer, knowing it's against policy for him to give her that information. And he'll refuse to give it to her. Though he knows this buyer has marked her husband. He's relying on the fact that he has watched her grow up and be placed in this field. He's like an uncle to her. He was best friends with Big Dog, a loyal employee of Don Morales and Baby Girl's biological father. But Gus is guilty of the same thing which he's accusing Kid of. Underestimating Baby Girl's intelligence. She is very strong willed. To play her weak, to send or bring harm to her or her loved ones. Or to threaten her position on the family square, are all grounds for termination. Gus had better come up with a *better* plan B.

San Francisco, August 3rd

Kid, Kierra and Trina arrive in San Francisco on August 3rd. They check into the *King George* hotel. Kid knows Baby Girl and H-Town Records will be in the *Prescott*. He got that information from Gus. Baby Girl tells Gus where she's staying when she has a mark to hit, while the record label is on the road. Just in case a hot sheet comes through.

A hot sheet contains a new high profile target, in the same area as another high profile target. This is for Baby Girl's safety, as well as a new opportunity. And Gus can get a new package to her or warn her that another pro is in the same town on a different assignment. Since she doesn't carry her phone on jobs, he can express it to the hotel desk for her. Just in case, she wants to take the new hit too. Or so she'll know that another pro is in the area and to beware. It's for precautions. But this time, Gus is using it to his and Kid's advantage.

Kid knows the contract hotel is *The Drake*. For now, he's taking Kierra and Trina on a huge shopping spree. He is still not aware that these females know of his ultimate plan and they take full advantage of his generosity. They spend $8K, in no time. Plus Kid is feeling extra charitable today. Probably because he thinks his sister will make herself a widow in 24 hours. But why does he really want to get rid of Young D? That story still hasn't been told.

San Francisco, August 4th

H-Town Records are finally at their San Francisco tour stop. They've arrive early. This is going to be a busy day for both Young D and for Baby Girl. She does her regular duties, as road manager and gets the crew settled into their hotel rooms. *The 717 Boys* have gotten better with the road rules and procedures, by now. They fall right in with the rest of their label mates. Baby Girl knows Young D has a banquet room meeting at 4pm, at *The Drake*. That information was in the Express mail with the gorgeous woman's photo. Baby Girl has a noon mark to hit, at *The Drake*, as well. She gets the guys settled into the Prescott. Then she goes over their complete itinerary with the concierge. Everything, as far as the hotel and food, is set. She has Young D to schedule a noon sound check, so he'll be out of her hair while *she* works. He schedules the sound check for 1pm, not noon. He already has a meeting at noon. The one Baby Girl knows nothing about.

When Young D had gotten the initial phone call, the disguised voice told him about a PO Box and where to find the key for it. He was told not to discuss the call or information with anyone or it could blow the deal. That call had come from Baby Girl. From Baby Girl's package, she's under the impression that in the PO Box, her mark will learn of the hotel room where they are to meet and get it on before discussing the business deal. She is to text him, 10 minutes before arriving at the room but she's going to ignore that last part.
I'm not about to tell some anonymous mark that I'm on my way. This could be a set up.

Young D's next information was in the PO Box. This is when the betrayal, gets legs. From this new information, he finds out about the separate meeting. A private meeting, in a suite. He has the name of the hotel where the meeting is to take place, on the same day and at the same hotel as the public meeting. *The Sir Francis Drake Hotel.* The public meeting is at 4pm but he's meeting with the CEO, in her suite, at noon. Room 312. He had shared the public meeting information with Baby Girl. She'd seen the Express mail and the CEO's photo. But the meeting in the suite, the info he got inside the PO Box, he was instructed not to tell anyone about. He feels his wife would be uncomfortable knowing he's meeting this woman in a suite and he doesn't want to screw up the deal. He thinks the woman wants sex with him. If he has to, to close this type of deal, he's willing. He's wondering if he'll be able to meet her, get the deal done, then make sound check at 1pm. Then on to the public meeting at 4pm, where the new deal is probably going to be announced. Which will give him a boost for the show, tonight. Surely, he'll be able to share his news with his fans. He plans to share the news at the *Moscone Center* tonight. Baby Girl plans to attend the banquet room meeting at 4pm too. Her and Young D discuss his schedule while in their room.

"The meeting will last an hour" he says, "Then we can meet the crew for the dinner the promoters set up for us."

"That's here at the Prescott. Right?" she asks.

"Right. At *Postrio* with the famous chef," he says.

"*Wolfgang Puck*," she says, "Cool. All of your meetings are in *Union Square*."

Young D's music show starts at 8pm at the Moscone Center.

"Where is your mark?" he tries.

"Good one, daddy. You already know…"

"…I know. You can't tell me," he says, "Are we back to that? Even after I got to ride on the Genolli hit?"

They laugh. He gets the message. Indeed, they're back to the rules. No discussions about her work until it's carried out.

It's nearly 8am. They get the guys together and they all have breakfast. Then they can all lounge in the rooms until time for sound check. But not Baby Girl nor Young D. Baby Girl has Louis V and *Get to Work,* on the vanity. She prepares her husband's attire for both the 4pm meeting and tonight's show. She wants him to wear the *36mm DateJust yellow Gold Rolex,* which she'd given him for their anniversary. He gave her the *26mm Lady-DateJust.* She's going to wear hers too. He says he'll wear his, all day. But not for the show.

He says, "I don't want to risk someone pulling it off my arm."

She says that's logical and agrees he shouldn't perform in it.

"I don't have to perform for a crowd," she jokes.

He laughs. He's trying to figure out how he's going to get

dressed for his noon meeting, without her knowing. He's relieved when she reveals that she has to leave by 1030am. "To bad your mark ain't in Union Square," he tries.
"We can't have it all, can we," she says.

Since arriving, the previous evening with Trina in tow, Kid and Kierra have been shopping and lounging around in their suite at the *King George Hotel*. There hotel is in Union Square, also. Kierra has her part of the plan down. She is to leave at 10am and go to Room 312 at the Drake, to meet Young D. He's suppose to show up at noon. The room is ready. Kierra has her key. The key for Young D will be waiting for him at the front desk. He has his instructions. Kierra is to go in and wait for him to arrive. Then seduce him in her normal way. But Kierra, after getting wind of Kid's *real* plan, decides she's going to do a plan of her own. 1 her and Trina came up with while talking in McGregor park. Kierra wants Young D for herself. That's true. But she isn't willing to take a chance on getting killed or getting him killed. She would never agree with something like that. She's seen a side of Kid that she wasn't always sure existed. It's evil and cunning. She thinks he wants his sister, for himself. But she's wrong, still. Baby Girl is Six Nine's blood. Still, Kid isn't interested in Kierra romantically. Her eyes are wide open now and it's only a matter of time before she finds out what his real motivations are, for getting Young D out of Baby Girl's life, for good. And it has nothing to do with Kid wanting to assist Kierra in having Young D, for herself.
Kierra leaves the King George hotel and hurries over to The Drake. Trina goes with her. They tell Kid, Trina is going to be a look out in the lobby and she's going to text Kierra, in room 312, when Young D enters the lobby. Kid likes the idea

for Trina to duck out in the lobby when Kierra heads upstairs.

"That's a good *heads up* idea," Kid says with a devilish grin. "That way she'll know exactly when he's in the building." The girls smile and head on off to the Drake.

After they leave, Kid has the concierge at King George, to deliver a package for Baby Girl to the concierge, at the Prescott. He's sending her a key to room 312. Kierra nor Trina knew he was going to do this. What they do know is that it's a set up and Baby Girl is suppose to come. Kid doesn't know that they know that part. That's their advantage, so they're way ahead of Kid. They've already foiled his plan before it even has the opportunity to hatch. Kierra goes up to room 312. Trina goes with her. Kierra goes into the bathroom, turns on the shower then leaves the room. It's 10:15am. Her and Trina go back to the lobby. There, they find a secluded spot, then hide out there to wait and watch for Young D and Baby Girl to arrive.

Kid is in his suite, gloating. He calls Gus, after he sends the package to Baby Girl's hotel. He feels like he's about to pull off a fool proof caper. When in reality, all he has done is embark upon a journey which, if it's successful, will be the ultimate betrayal of a person who loves him and calls him family. He and Gus are the masterminds behind trying to take away the only person in the world whom Baby Girl loves, intimately. All of this is because Don Morales trusted her to own and manage what his family built from scratch.
A multimillion dollar empire. The very thing he saw for her, from the day he learned of her birth.

"I never felt comfortable with her being in charge," Gus admits. "Don's mind must've been ate up with cancer. Or that drug the doctor was giving him for his kidney's, had to have had him delirious. For him to put her in charge of every damn thing, never has made any sense to me. But the rest of these old ass farts around this manor, don't have one problem with it."

"She's very book smart, though," Kid says, sounding as if he's about to defend her. But then, he says, "But she wasn't smart enough to know not to give that nigga D, free run of that damn fortune she inherited."

"The manor *is* running well, you know," Gus tries, "And D has made millions of his own."

"The reason it's running well, *could* be because all of the staff have been there longer than she's been alive," Kid says, "And what D has made, is nothing compared to what he married into. He had to do something or be labeled a gigolo or a gold digger. The staff has been there, long enough to know how things run."

"*Myself*, being one of them," Gus adds, "Don was a smart man. He kept things that he deemed private, away from everyone. She does the same things."

"So she has shit, none of y'all know about?" Kid asks.

"Not only that," Gus says, "But she holds a fortune that none of us know the total value of."

"Is that right?" Kid asks, "If you had to guess what she was worth. What would you say?"

"Oh gosh. Well, gee whiz. It was estimated at over a hundred and seventy million in a Fortune five hundred article, when Don died. That estimated projection was based from the interview they did in the eighties."

"So in two thousand, they guessed it was one seventy," Kid says, "This is seven years later."

"I'd say it increased by another hundred and fifty, at least," Gus says, "Because Don got in on the ground floor of some Microsoft stock. That was when Baby Girl went to high school, in the nineties."

"Oh *shit*. Computer software stock? In the nineties?" Kid asks, "That's some shit I wished I had the money to do, back then. But I didn't know shit about investing either. Nor did I have the real money to put up. I was learning shit from Don. I was hoping he would turn me on to that."

"She was the one who pick the damn stock," Gus says, "She taught Don, me and all of us, how to get around on the computer. The little knowledge we do have. She taught us. She told Don that Microsoft was going to lead computer software. Because all of the students in her school had an easier time with it."

"She gave him the stock tip?" Kid asks, "Why didn't she tell me about it?"

"Maybe she knew you would try to kill her and her husband, one day," Gus jokes.

"She don't have a clue," Kid says, "I'm her big brother. She will never see me as someone who would hurt her and I wouldn't. I just don't want her to lose that Goddamn fortune."

"But you've put a hit on her, already," Gus says as he chuckles. "What do you mean, you wouldn't hurt her?"

"I knew that dude wasn't gonna win," Kid lies, "I just wanted to see how good she really was."

"He was the second best in the world," Gus says, "That means, she's the best in the world."

"Obviously so," Kid says, "Which is why I hired her to kill her cheating bastard of a husband. Before they lose all the shit the Don built up."

"I hear you," Gus says, "But unmolested, she won't."

"But then, that won't cut us in either," Kid chuckles, "We're gonna have to molest her. Just enough to get some of that shit."

"No it won't and we're molesting her, as we speak.

59

But," Gus says, "I still don't think this hit will happen, Kid."

"You hope it does," Kid says, "See, I know how a bitch gets when they catch they're nigga fucking another bitch. They be ready to kill his ass. That's why I wanted it set up, like this. Where she'll already have her pistol."

Gus is feeling cautious, this morning. Kid is feeling his usual cockiness. Neither of them feel any remorse for what they've plotted. God help them, if Baby Girl doesn't fall for this trick.

At the Prescott, Baby Girl has received a package from the concierge. It has Gus' address on it. She takes the package and ducks into the lobby bathroom. The package is very light. Doesn't feel as it there's anything in the envelope. She opens it. There's a typewritten note and card key. The key is for room 312, at the Drake hotel.

"Okay. I'm in," she says as she leaves the bathroom and heads for The Drake. It's 10:25 am.

Young D dresses quickly, for his noon meeting. He knows he has to pick up a key from the front desk of The Drake. He wants to arrive on time, so as not to upset the CEO.

Baby Girl arrives at The Drake at 10:30am. She buys a room on the 3rd floor and pays cash. Then she hurries to the elevator with her Louis V and her *Get To Work* bags.

"There goes his wife," Trina says.

"Yes. I guess that's the lingerie, Kid bought for her, in the bags," Kierra says as They continue to hide out and watch.

Lovely hurries off the elevator and runs to room 300, the room she has just paid for. She needs to change her clothes.

Quickly, she changes into her *French Maid* disguise. The 1 from the Lopez hit. She wants that hooker look and she knows for sure, she has it when she heads down the hall to room 312, at 11am. There are 3 Japanese men in the hall.

They'd just come out of their rooms and are walking together. From their look, she'd guess they are businessmen. Married businessmen, judging my the bright gold bands on their left-hand ring fingers. But they show interest in her, as they stop her for a chat. She doesn't speak Japanese but from their gestures, she knows they want a call girl.

Young D leaves the Prescott for his meeting at The Drake. He arrives at the front desk at 11am. He gets his key and heads for the elevators.

"Oh *God*. Look at my man," Kierra whispers, "Damn. He's looking good in that suit."

Trina agrees with her. 2 fans stop Young D for an autograph. He signs them, takes a picture with each of them, then he hops on the elevator and presses the 3rd floor.

Trina whispers, "It is going down, home girl. They're gonna have a romantic afternoon, after all. Thanks to you."

She smiles at Kierra, who returns the smile. She would rather not see him at all. Then to see him and get killed for it or get him killed.

Baby Girl is still trying to shake the 3 gentlemen in the hallway but they're very persistent. They pull out wads of cash, trying to entice her. She smiles and says,

"Thank you but I have date already."

Trying to speak quickly and break her English, as well. They hand her their business cards and beg her to call them later. They want a date with her.

Young D steps off of the elevator. She sees him and there's no time to move or hide. He's never seen her in her disguise. It's a good 1 and right now, she is hoping he can't tell that it's her. She quickly latches onto 2 of the gentlemen, putting 1 on each side of her. The 3rd one is directly in front of

61

her. She turns her back to the spot where Young D is about to pass them. The 3rd gentleman becomes her shield, in back while she uses the other 2 as side shields. They're much shorter than her, so she slouches down and puts her head on 1 of their shoulders. This prevents her husband from getting a close up look at her. But through her large framed, dark tinted sunglasses, she watches him. He notices the 3 men with their hooker but he's distracted. She can tell. For him, he's more concerned about this mysterious meeting he's heading too. He speaks to the 4 of them without really looking at them, as he continues pass them. He puts on a friendly smile and goes on past.

I can't knock the hustle. He thinks to himself. Not even realizing he has just past his wife of 11 years. She watches him as she wonders.

Obviously the disguise is good. But what the hell is he doing here?

She's thrown off after seeing her husband. But she keeps the 3 men's attention on her. She watches her husband, at the same time. He slides the card key into the door lock of room 312, opens it, goes in and lets the door close.

She's taken back. For the moment, she's forgotten why she's here. She's just watched her husband walk into the very hotel room of her mark. Her mark, who according to her package, always orders a call girl while he's out on business. At least, that's what the package said. She has to get rid of these 3 Japanese men quickly, so she can regroup.

She whispers, "Okay. I call you tonight. We can *licky licky, suckie suckie.*"

Their reaction says they understood the comment. They grin and raise their eyebrows, as they say, "*Ah, Ah*" over and over.

She talks and walks as she hurries them to the elevator and rushes them on it.

"Lobby? Okay. Goodbye. I call you," she whispers as she pushes the button for the lobby and backs off the elevator. The doors close. She has sent them on their way.

Now, she turns her attention back to room 312. As she uses every nook in the hallway to shield herself, just in case he comes back out, she eases towards the door. She stops just outside of it and puts her ear up to the door. She's listening for his voice but can't hear any talking. She can only hear the shower running.

Oh fuck! I know this ain't what I think it is. Is he taking a shower here? Are is he meeting my mark?

She's thinking of using her key, going in and bussing the shit up.

But what if the mark is in here? In the shower. What the fuck is Derrick doing meeting him? And why didn't he tell me?

She decides to go in. But just as she is about to slip the key in the door, she hears the elevator arrive. She ducks into a nook in the hallway. Then she hurries to her room door, slides in her key, opens it and ducks in.

Safe in room 300 now, she looks out of the peep hole. It was just the guest for room 310. They come up the hall, making major noise and go into their room. She heads back to the door of 312. First, she listens again. She can hear Young D calling out, as if he's gotten tired of waiting.

"Hello? Are you in here? Is anyone in here?" he ask.
She hears no other voice. Just the shower.
Who is he looking for?

She can tell the shower door has opened because the water sound is louder now.
He's going into the shower with.., who? What the fuck?

Her mind is moving, a million miles a minute. She feels as though she could pass out.
Please don't tell me Derrick is cheating on me? And he had better not be investing in the new, New Orleans project either! Fucking over his own people is not his style.

She looks at her Rolex. It's 5 minutes before noon. She slips her key in and cracks the door open. She peeps around it. He's not in the room. He's still in the bathroom. She slips inside and eases her way over to the bathroom door. She can hear the shower turn off. Still, no voices but Young D is walking back to the door. She can hear his *Stacy Adams* clicking the ceramic tile on the bathroom floor. Sounds like tap shoes. She ducks into the closet, next to the bathroom. She's got cover now as she peeps out of the key hole. Young D comes out of the bathroom. He has a look of confusion on his face. He checks his Rolex. It's noon and no one is here for his meeting. She's watching him, watching his watch and looking around the room. She's hoping this is not some secret rendezvous, he's having.
But wait. This is where my noon mark is.

She thinks to herself as she continues to watch him and her mind continues to spin. He has checked in the bedroom and found no one. In the kitchen. No one there either. He sits back in the chair and figures that he's there alone.
Sound check, ha?

He looks dejected.

64

Is he mad because some bitch didn't show, who was suppose to be here?

Her imagination is running wild. She can't imagine what her husband is doing here. She decides to send a text message to her mark's pager, from the company phone number she last contacted him with. Just to settle her curiosity. She has it with her. She was instructed to bring it. She sets the phone to meeting so that it won't vibrate. Then she carefully types, *Where are you?*
She turns the phone off, just in case. Seconds later, she hears a message alert tone. Young D grabs for his pants pocket. Then, it hits her.
My husband is in play?

He uses a cell phone and calls the number back. The phone is 1 she's never seen him use before. She's thinking to herself.
When I get back to the Prescott and check this phone. It's gonna be my marks number that called me. I just know it.

She gripes her 9mm. She's waiting for a pro to come bursting into the room trying to terminate her husband. It's 12:25 and no one has shown up. Young D decides to leave a note. Then, he leaves the room. disappointed and disgusted. He's heading down to the front desk to see if there are any messages there for him.

       After he leaves, Baby Girl exit's the closet and quickly reads the note.
To the mysterious CEO. I showed up early, for the private meeting. But you never came. I guess I'll see you at 4pm. I'm very disappointed that this business meeting didn't happen.
MC Young D aka Derrick Blake

"What the fuck?" Baby Girl says.

Quickly, she checks the entire room. It becomes instantly clear to her that no one has ever checked into this room. There is not 1 personal item here.

At the front desk, Young D has checked for messages. There are none. He leaves his info with the clerk, in case someone comes down looking for him. He gets back to the Prescott and sees all of his wife's personals on the vanity.

"I guess her meeting is going well," he says.

He changes his clothes and hurries to sound check. He's very disappointed that his meeting didn't happen. He feels the deal was too good and it wasn't true.

Kierra and Trina were shocked to see him leave so soon. They're curious as to what happened in room 312.

"I got my key. Let's go up and see," Kierra says.

They dash to elevator and hop on when it opens. They head up to the 3rd floor.

Baby Girl has finished reading her husband's note, for the 4th time. Her mind is racing, trying to figure out what just happened here. She can only conclude that he was in play since no female had shown her face. She tucks the letter in her pocket and leaves the room. She goes back up the hall to room 300, to change back into her regular clothes. Before she can close her door, she hears the elevator arrive again. She leans on the peep hole and checks to see who's coming down the hall, this time.

"I hope it's, Miss CEO," she whispers, "I'll just do her ass and call it a day. Trying to fuck my man."

But it's *way* worse. It's Kierra and Trina. She hawks them as they go directly to room 312. Kierra uses a key and goes in. Trina follows.

66

Should I just murk this musty bitch now and be done with it?

Baby Girl is thoroughly pissed off. She goes into survival mode, to calm down quickly.
No emotions, Baby Girl.

She can hear her daddy's voice. She thinks it through. She reads the note again. She finds a clue.
"Mysterious… He didn't know who the person was, he was meeting," she says aloud, "I was there when he got the express mail. I saw the woman's picture. This shit is fake. The name Drexel was fake. And I knew that shit. *Damn.* All of this shit is tied together. And I'll bet you, all the tea in China that the meeting at four pm is fake too. Who the fuck wants my husband dead? First me. Now him. Or maybe it's him, to get to me or vice versa. They can't have either. Who the fuck is it?"
She knows it's not Kierra. She doesn't have the money or savvy to place a hit on anyone. At least, she doesn't think so.
"Could she be in the game and me not know? Or is she a spy? This bitch has been in too many circumstances. It's time to check into her ass, a bit closer."
She can hear the 2 women come out of room 312. She watches them through the peep hole. They come out and survey the hallway. No one is around. She can hear Trina say,
"Wonder why they didn't stay and have a romantic afternoon?"
They hop on the elevator and head back down. Baby Girl changed her clothes quickly while she watched Kierra and Trina go in, then leave room 312. After they get on the elevator, she grabs her things and hits the stairs. She needs to know what these girls wanted with her husband. And did he know they were here, in San Francisco and why? She has a

million questions and no real way to get answers. Not without blowing her own cover. She needs to talk to Gus. But face to face is the only way to handle this one. She'll look into it immediately, though. No doubt.

She makes it to the lobby, just as Kierra and Trina have left out of the hotel. She see them as the hop on the rail car. She can't put together why they're here. She'll deal with that part, later. Right now, she has to get to Young D and keep him alive. Once this west coast leg of the tour is done, she's going to have a face to face with the only person whom she knows, knew that she was to be in room 312.

"Gus!" she says as she leaves the Drake.
She has to get back to the love of her life. He's in sound check. Someone wants him dead. She will not allow it that happen.

****

Kierra and Trina go back to King George hotel. They hook back up with Kid. He inquires about how it all went.

"He didn't even show up," Trina says.

"Your plan wasn't good enough," Kierra says, "Or maybe he wasn't interested."

"He didn't show up?" Kid ask, suspiciously.

"He never came to the room," Kierra says.
She was hoping he would blow his cover and ask did Baby Girl show up. But he doesn't. They can see in his eyes that he's both angry and sad. They can't help but to laugh at him. He's upset and even more determined now, to pull off these hits.

CHAPTER   TWENTY TWO
STRESS FREE WORK PLACE

Daddy Don taught Baby Girl at what point it would be proper to question a package. He gave her the code of conduct on how assignments are to be handled. She was taught the Morales family oath. The Don had said:
"When you receive your information package, this is what you do.
Review, Research, Plan, Execute.
Trust your agent. I will never give you a package that will be detrimental to you or yours. Nor will any agent assigned to you by this family, give you any package which will bring harm to you or yours. We are family and our oath is to protect this family. Anyone going against the family oath is a rogue. If a rogue is discovered to be amongst my family. They are to be terminated immediately. Forever banished from the family and from life."

She replays her daddy's words and the Morales oath, over and over in her mind. Then she retraces her actions from the day she first handled the last package.
When I received the package from Gus, I reviewed it's contents. I researched the info provided to me. I planned my attack. I was there to execute But the target was my husband. My 1 and only. The love of my life and father of my beautiful sons. Loosing him would be very harmful to my existence. This hit assigned to me by my agent was a play on my family. How in the hell can I trust that motherfucker?

She has a conversation aloud, with herself and her deceased father, Don Morales.
"I cannot trust him, daddy. You were right about Gus. He wasn't brave enough to fuck with you. But he thinks he can

do whatever he wants to me. I'm on your honor, daddy. Give me a sign. Please."
She continues to question herself, her upbringing and what she should do next. She didn't ask any questions of Gus, once she reviewed the package. Even though she knew the name was phony. She only pointed out to him that she knew it was phony. That's allowed. She had even looked forward to the challenge of executing a target with whom she had no description of. She trusted that Gus knew what would cause harm to her. Who not to accept contracts from. What lines she would never cross. What lines *he* should never cross. When to reject a contract.
How the fuck could he give me a hit on my own fucking husband?

She's in turmoil with herself and angry, with no real target for it. She's at the Marriot, in Denver. It's been nearly 4 weeks since the botched hit on Young D. H-Town Records are still on the west coast tour and she's still trying to hold on to her sanity. She needs to get back to New Orleans and speak with Gus, face to face. But she isn't going to risk leaving Young D on the road without her. She hasn't told him anything about the hit on his life. How is she going to make him understand that her family is trying to kill him? She hasn't tried to contact Gus since the day before San Francisco. He hasn't called her either. And now, she knows why.
This isn't over. Not by a long shot, motherfucker. You and your buyer are going to have to pay the piper. You went and fucked with the wrong woman's man, Gus. Of all the people in this world you could've fucked with. You chose to fuck with the best.

Colorado is the last stop on the western tour. Baby Girl is anticipating getting off the road. It's the last week of August.

The tour has been in Colorado for 3 days now. On day 1, they visited Teddy Wells in the *Centennial Correctional facility*. It's in Canon City, Colorado. It had been added to H-Town's tour schedule, right after Baby Girl met her Philly family. Young D did a show in Canon City, the same night after their visit with Teddy. JB and Baby Girl are in the process of arranging an H-Town records show, at the facility. They met with the warden the same day of the visit. The warden sees the potential profit's his facility can receive if the show happens. Getting a live performance looks promising for Teddy and the other inmates. Sammy Wells had seen to getting Baby Girl, Young D, Bruce and JB's names added to Teddy's visitors list and Teddy was very glad to finally meet her. Now she has photo's and contact information for all of her siblings and they all have the same for her. Teddy and lots of the other inmates, got photo's with Young D. Even autographs and paraphernalia from the label and a promise that he'll stay in touch with them and give them a shout out at his next televised interview.

Young D has honored that promise at every radio station he's visited since making it. He and Baby Girl are coming back to visit and bringing Tunisia, for their birthdays. Teddy, Baby Girl and Tunisia all have birthdays in the month of October. Young D had also encouraged Baby Girl to set up monthly commissary payments for Teddy. He remembers the plight of a brother, doing time.

Young D and the label mates have gone to sound check. He has long bounced back from the disappointment of not having either meeting in San Francisco, 4 weeks ago. He sums it all up to someone's wet dream. A prank, even. But JB has come though with another offer. He'd met them in Vegas with some of the details. He's pulling a deal together for Young D which will take his clothing line international, like his music is

71

already. That helped him to swallow the San Francisco, non action a bit easier. If only Baby Girl's let down could be stomached with the same ease. But that's impossible. She's going to visit Gus. She can't and will not rest until she does.

After the Denver show, Young D has a surprise for her. They aren't going back to Houston, on the tour bus. They're going to spend another night in the Mile High city. Then fly home later.

"When did you decide that?" she asks.

"Last night," he says.

"It's a great idea," she says, "But what made you decide to stay?"

"So I can help you sleep," he says, "You haven't slept good since San Francisco. I know you're worried about me not getting that deal. But I'm not."

He's right. She is worried about San Francisco but it has nothing to do with the deal or lack there of. She knows the whole thing was a set up. The hit wasn't even professionally handled. The buyer wasn't smart enough to send Express mail to another city, along the tour to keep him anticipating it. In reality, if a sponsor was trying to get an entertainer on their team. There would have been a follow through. No way would he have shown up and no one not be there. Nor leave any messages by note or call. And the buyer hadn't even contacted his management. When Young D called JB that night from San Francisco, after the show to tell him about the blown deal. JB was upset and he voiced it loudly. Because he hadn't heard a word. That's when Young D realized it really wasn't going to happen and that was the first part of the reason JB met them in Las Vegas. Which was the next stop on the tour, after San Francisco. He looked at the package Young D received and

72

called the numbers. All of which had been terminated by the time they arrived in Nevada.

"What kind of international company contacts the artist and not even bother to speak with his management?" JB had questioned, "Before or after the initial contact?"
Young D has the freedom to talk with potential sponsors, on his own. But he prefers that they involve his management and keep things on the table. He had sent that preference to the bogus company. He got a reply back that they had forwarded information on to New York city and to JB. But they hadn't. Baby Girl knew by the time she left the Drake that the whole deal was bogus. But she couldn't tell Young D and she was angrier than JB. If it had been real it would've lacked professionalism and she would've advised her husband not to invest. Her and JB were both mad about the mismanaging of information. Only for JB, it was the legalities. For Baby Girl, it wasn't only that. But the life or death of her man.

JB has returned to New York. Young D and Baby Girl are in their hotel suite. Young D has filled the Jacuzzi tub with a warm bubble bath. He's ordered room service and amenities, for 2. They're in the tub together. Young D is very curious about what has her so preoccupied. She can't tell him about the hit. Not until she has a future victim. But that hasn't stopped him from inquiring. She plays him off by being seductive.

"This was a great idea to stay another night," she says.

"I think so too," he says, "I want to know what's got your attention. You tossed and turned, last night. Like you were having a nightmare. Is this about the hit that didn't show up?"

"Baby I can't talk about it," she says, "but I will tell you that's not it."

"Then what is it?"

She can't tell him the truth. Not until she has a solution and a victim. She's quick on her feet, most of the time. She doesn't practice lying to her husband but today, she has too.

"I dreamed about mama and daddy don after the *Moscone* show," she lies.

"Oh, baby. What's got you bothered?"

"I wonder if daddy is proud of me," she says, "I wonder if mama is worried sick. I want our boys to know them both. It just got me out there, a little bit. You know I get like that around this time of year. This is when I lost them all."

"I know. I'm sorry I didn't say anything about them. But you know I try not too. If you don't mention them."

"You've been here through it all," she says, "I love you so much and I'm so glad we met, at a young age. Otherwise, I would really feel alone in all of it."

"Baby, I'm here for you always," he says, "I have never wanted another girl. It's always been you. And that's because we met at a young age too. By the time I was old enough and had money to really get attention from girls. I already had you and you already had me."

"You're right. You are my best friend, Derrick," she says, "Staying an extra night is perfect. You always know just what to do. And the right time, to do it. I can relax with you and talk about my parents. And cry all night, if I want too."
She smiles. He's giving her a shoulder massage and she's loving it.

"You're so tense," he says, "You can relax now, baby. Daddy got everything under control. It's me and you, tonight. And your nine millimeter."
They both laugh. She thinks about what a good idea it really is. If the buyer is following his tour schedule, they will expect for

him to be on the highway. Somewhere between Colorado and Texas. When in fact, he's laying up in a plush hotel with the best security anyone can have against another attempt on his life. She treated the entire label to a flight back to Houston. Then gave the driver time off, earlier then had been planned. With pay.

They've left the tub and made their way to the large king sized bed.

"You set everybody up good, after you found out I wanted to stay longer," he says, "They love you for that."

"Good. Now. I need for you to set me up too," she says, "Set my dick on out, daddy."

"Yes ma'am."

He rolls her over on top of him. With both of his hands grasping her face, he sticks his tongue into her mouth. She takes it. They kiss with fervor. With passion, like they haven't seen each other in years. He pulls her ass towards his chin. She knows he wants to taste her. She wants to taste him too. Before sitting on his face, she whispers,

"Can a lady get a little bit of that sixty nine action, up in here tonight?"

"You can have anything you want, baby," he replies, spinning her around and pulling her pussy to his mouth. Before she can get a good grip on his dick, he has already plunged his tongue into her soft tunnel. The sensation makes her purr. She grabs his 12 inches as if it's a lifeline to safety from a 40 foot drop over a cliff, into hundreds of jagged rocks below. She puts his dick in her mouth and submerges half of it quickly. Sucking in hard. Nearly pulling his load out prematurely. He gasp.

"Ah shit. That's good, Lovely," he whispers.

She moans. He's lapping her clitoris with the speed of *Usain*

Bolt. Then he holds it between his lips, slightly pinching it as he sucks it hard.

"Oh, daddy!"

He's relentless. Both of their faces are so intense as they trade pleasures.

She cums hard. He holds his in. Straining every muscle he has, not to succumb to her strong suction which is demanding his orgasm be released into her throat, at once. Feeling his about to blow and not wanting it too, just yet. He pulls her away from his dick, so he can maintain. Still he sops up her nectar like it's the sweetest thing he's tasted. He moans while he eats her pussy. She's going wild. Gyrating her body, all over the bed. Raising her hips wildly to meet his mouth. And he's right there, lapping and loving every twist. Before she can calm down, he flips her over onto her stomach and lays on top of her. Then pulls her ass to him and enters her pussy from the back. Instantly, he pounds her flesh.

"Oh, Derrick," she yells, "Oh it's so deep, daddy."

As if that's permission to fuck her crazy, he gets up on his knees, pulls her up onto her knees as her upper body rest on her elbows. They're doing it doggy style. He's hitting her hard as she screams in both passion and pleasure. But she's also feeling the pain. Before long, she can feel his drops of sweat, dripping on her ass cheeks. He's getting a work out. She tries to look over her shoulder. Tries to get a glance of him as his hard thrust push her forward. Forcing her head to drop and dangle, as well. She does manage to get a glimpse of her man. He's a workhorse when it comes to sex. His face fashions indiscriminate grimaces as he pounds against her ass. Pulling her at the hips to meet his bull. She can see his face and his eyes. He glances at her and flashes a slight smile. He whispers, "Who's pussy is this?"

76

"It's yours, Derrick," she whispers back while trying to handle his rhythms, at the same time.

This makes her voice wiggle. He looks back to his work. Fucking her hard while he reads his name, tattooed on the small of her back. He knows this pussy is his. His signature is right there, above her ass. There's 1 on each of her inner thighs too. He has plans of looking at those again, before he slumbers. He watches his name as it jumps, jiggles and bounces. He's focused on it. As if there are instructions there, on how to properly please the woman who adorns it.

"You liking this, baby?" he ask as he pulls her up to his chest.

"Yes."

He turns her over for some missionary and reenters quickly. She pulls his shoulders to her as she captures his lips and with her tongue, demands that he give her his tongue again. He accommodates her. Both of their bodies are stretched flat out, hard working as a heart racing pace is being kept. Their goal is to give the other the ultimate pleasure. He whispers to her. Telling her how good her pussy is to him. How much he loves to please her. How much he loves to feel her and fuck her.

She cums on demand. That's what he wanted to hear. She yells *Oh's*, *Ooo's* and *Ah's*, as she screams his name and tells him how much she loves, "The way you fuck me, daddy!" And him assuring her, "I love fucking you, Lovely. I have since day one."

He gets his nut within the next 5 minutes. It's aggressive. Same as his fucking her was. His nut feels like he's losing all of the stress he had built up as he anticipated San Francisco. He's over it now as he spirals to new heights in the mile high city.

They're laying in a bundle of warm, sweaty flesh with sounds of whispering talk and pauses to catch a breath. They are both winded and satisfied, as they hold each other tight and drift into a deep sleep.

****

Last night, Baby Girl dreamed of her father, *Don Morales*. It was so vivid and real. But when she woke up, she burst into tears because she realized that he was indeed, still dead. But he was here. In her home office, in Houston. This home wasn't even built when he died. The only thing she could take from her dream was, he'd honored her wishes. He'd brought her that sign she'd asked for. In her dream, The Don said,

"Daddy's little girl was not raised to second guess herself. For I, The Don, put faith, belief and trust in you to carry my name. Carry it, Baby Girl. When you were still a little princess. I saw your strength and ability to maintain, in any surroundings. You pressed on even when we you left alone, in a foreign country and you made friends and followers for life. You found a man, much like both of your fathers. My princess is a queen now. With a new castle to grace and protect. Guard it with every ounce of passion and the know how that I bestowed on you. Just as you do with the manor that I left to you. It's your call. You are the boss. I am so proud of you. Wanda and Big Dog are too. We love you."

She has her sign and without another thought, she plans her attack. The 1st thing she does after she finishes crying, is make contact Alfred at Morales manor with her plan. Alfred tells her to give him a little time to organize and when he calls her back, it will be time for her to come home.

It's 2 weeks after Labor day. Baby Girl is in her

CLK63, *her work car*, on I-10. She's between Lafayette and Baton Rouge now, in route to New Orleans. She's just gotten back on the road after a stop for lunch, in Lafayette. She'd called Chadrella from Houston and invited her to meet for lunch. She did and they talked like they were still in college at LSU. Chadrella talked about her father's drug overdose and how the case was going.

"They're calling it a death by overdose," Chadrella had said. "But we refuse to accept that, as a fact. They're making my father out to be a dope addict."
Baby Girl listened as Chadrella talked but she didn't offer any advice or suggestions.
Hell. He was a dope addict and he'd been a dope addict.

Baby Girl thought that to herself while Chadrella rambled on. She finished her lunch as quickly as possible, paid with cash, said goodbye to Chadrella and hit the road again.
She reaches Baton Rouge a half an hour after. It's 2 hours later and she has reached the city limits of New Orleans. Since *hurricane Katrina*, each and every time she comes home, she surveys the land on her ride in. Much of the damage is still present with exception of the flood waters and black families sitting on their roofs. And a bloated floating dead body, here and there. Everything else still looks like the city exploded. She's looking at the blighted conditions and having the same thoughts she'd had after the Gulfport hit.
They ain't doing shit to bring all of the citizens back home. Hell, they got new plans circulating the city. For a whole new look. I hope the bitches responsible for the catastrophe, after Katrina, become a mark. I would love to get some justice for my comrades and people who are still suffering. Still evacuated. Still homeless. I would do them shits for free.

79

"And I still feel the same damn way," she says aloud. She crosses *General Degaille* and presses toward Morales highway. Soon she's entering the wrought iron gates of her property. Finally at the end of her 7 hour trip, she's parking her Benz in her private garage at *The Manor*. She's come to give Gus his walking papers. Or something of that sort.

She kills her engine as she thinks over her plan of attack.

Daddy told me <u>emphatically</u> to never allow Gus into the office. <u>My office</u>. And to never let him have access to the computer. <u>My computer</u>. Nor any pass codes or bank accounts. Daddy Don told me that Gus Davis' only job was to arrange packages.

"But that motherfucker can't even do *that* shit right," she says aloud.

He's a rogue. He's broken the trust and violated the Morales' family oath. He's going to be terminated before I leave this manor.

"God willing!"

She grabs her *Louis V* and her *Get To Work* bags, first. Alfred meets her inside the garage and takes her suitcases up to the master suite. She'd already given orders that her visit be keep secret. On the low. No announcements. No staff at the foyer. She wants to get in here without the fanfare. She's here to get her work done and get back to the home where her husband and children still slept when she parted.

"I'm home to do daddy's work," she tells Alfred.

Alfred knows what this means. Baby Girl has a job to do and it involves some house cleaning. The senior house staff are the only people who knows she's here. Alfred, Cherry, Charles and Addie Mae are all in the know. They've worked for the Morales' since Duke Morales, *The Don's father*, was the head

80

of the family. They helped raise The Don and Baby Girl. They know the order of the family's business. They were all left in The Don and Wanda's will, as Baby Girl's guardians. Her happiness, well being and safety is and has always been, their *top* priority. This was an order from *The Don*. They never took it lightly and they won't, this time either. Neither of them have alerted anyone else of Baby Girl's arrival. Gus has no idea she's at the manor. That's exactly the way she wants it. He lives on the property. He's lived in 1 of the staff homes for over 30 years. But for Baby Girl, that still doesn't make him family.

"Your dinner is served, baby," Addie Mae says.
She's made Baby Girl's favorite dinner. Three fried chicken drumsticks, white rice, brown gravy, macaroni and cheese, cabbage, sweet corn bread and sweet potato yams. She serves her in the mini kitchen of the master suite. Seeing that meal cooked would've been enough for Cherry, Alfred and Charles to know that Baby Girl was home or coming home. Subtle signs like this, use to be ways of communication at the manor. In time, it shall be again.

Alfred and Charles go about their day as if nothing has changed at the main house. They announce her bogus future arrival to the rest of the staff, as they always do. With the importance of a royal heir and the preciseness of a well oiled staff of house and grounds management. Everyone knows what they're duties are. The formal announcement went, as such.
"Misses Baby Girl and her family will be at the manor, one week from today. Everyone prepare the grounds and her property, for their arrival."

The phony announcement serves it's purpose. Gus hears the announcement and breathes a sigh of relief. He feels he has a week to prepare his getaway. Once again, he has underestimated Baby Girl's intelligence. He gathers info for other jobs. His plans are to keep her busy. Away from New Orleans, away from the manor and away from him. He had searched out these hits. He didn't wait for a buyer to bring it in. That's another no-no. This type of action is known to bring unwanted attention and heat, to *any* organization. Still, he's done it anyway. He gathers 4 packages for her and calls her phone. He tells her, he'll mail the information to Houston.

Calmly, she says, I thought we couldn't do that. Can we do this, Gus? Isn't that against the code?"

He fumbles for an excuse as he speaks in an almost whisper. He says, "In certain circumstances, we can forward work to you. Without you having to come, in person. This is one of those times. I know you can't arrive for another week-"

"You usually bring it to me, when I can't come," she digs, "Can you now?"

"I have other obligations, Baby Girl," he tries.

"Other than *me*?"

"No marks but other family business," he lies.

She knows he handles no other business for her family but she pretends to accept his lie. She tells him to mail the packages. He knows he has violated. As far as she's concerned, he could've saved the breath he used to come up with that lame excuse. He's going to die, in less than 24 hours. She's going to kill him. She hangs up with him.

He may not know he's dying, in less than a day. But surely, he knows he deserves too. That's evident to her by the simple fact, he's telling her he's going against the families oath.

There are no other obligations before family business. Who the fuck do you think you are? You're dissin' everything my daddy built here. And why? Because I'm a female? I'm the fuckin' boss. Not you. You think you can bullshit with me and I'm just gonna continue to trust you? Hell no, motherfucker. You're going to meet your maker.

She thinks about how far she has come in the profession. She also wonders has Gus ever sent her out to hit someone, for his own personal reasons. He may as well be guilty of it. Because he's going to die. He has to go. It's the only answer she comes too. She plans her attack and prepares her weapons.

****

After Baby Girl had gotten back to Houston, from the west coast tour. She had done something she'd never done before. Prepared a target package. She set the hit, while calling on the senior staff, for more research. She planned it and she's going to carry it out. Gus is the mark. She's reviewed him and researched him. Everything about her skills and loyalty says it's his time. And before this time tomorrow, she will execute him. Gus has been marked for death.
It's time for me to accept my responsibility and run my daddy's businesses. He came to me in my sleep and reinforced his wishes. I'll run it. The way he wants it run. I am gonna be the agent for my family, from here on out. This way I'll know this phase is being run correctly too.

She grabs her *Get To Work* bag and goes into her bathroom. Not to leave her personals. Not at all. Because she's keeping them on her. This mark will expire right here in the main house and on the property. In *The Don's* office, which is now her office. Gus will get to come into the office but he'll never tell anything about what he sees in it.
First, she's going to take a long relaxing bath. Then

83

she's going to do another thing, she usually hadn't done before a hit. Decide who's going to replace her as the pro for the Morales Organization. She slips into the Jacuzzi and her bubble bath.

Once Gus is dead, I become the agent in charge of assignments. I have two pro's trained and ready to be sent out for marks. I'm going to train more. I'm getting this family back to full staff. The Morales Family will rule forever.

After she finishes her relaxing bath, she goes into the Don's office. Even though she's the boss, the office will always be her daddy's. She has brought along her 9mm with the silencer and a machete. She lays them on the desk. Then she checks the closet to see if the senior staff has everything prepared. She opens the door to the closet. They have fulfilled her request. She reaches into the closet and pulls out the rolls of plastic used to cover furniture and carpet, when painting. Like clock work, Cherry and Alfred come to assist her. They cover the carpet and anything else that may get blood stained. They leave the desk, as it is. Cherry brings out the empty wooden box which had come from the cellar. These boxes have symbolism. They have been used throughout the years by the family, to stash severed parts. Severed parts of rogue members. Whatever body part the member uses to violate the family, usually a hand or tongue, is removed when they're terminated. For Gus, it will be his left hand. He writes with his left hand.

"That's the hand he used to sign Young D's package into play," Baby Girl says, "That's the hand I want."

Then she tells Alfred, she's ready for him to make the call to Gus. Cherry goes and gets in position. She has to open the door and send Gus into the office to meet with Alfred.

Cherry goes to the front door and alerts Charles that

they're ready for him to pick up Gus. Then she waits in the foyer for them to return. Addie Mae has coffee brewed with the fresh baked teacakes, in the servers quarters. These are Gus's favorite. He asks for them, every time he stops in at the main house. Alfred sits at the Don's desk. Something he's only done, once before. It was when he'd help The Don clean house of a rogue hit man, nearly 30 years ago. 4 years before Baby Girl was even born. Now she's the head of the family and he's going to help her to get things back on track. This is what separates the senior staff from the others.

Alfred picks up the phone and calls Gus. He answers the call to his home phone. Alfred tells him they have a matter up at the main house that needs his urgent attention. Some papers have come, by way of the city constable. They imply that someone is about to take ownership of the manor. The city needs over $40 dollars in back taxes or they will Foreclose.

"I do believe Baby Girl and Young D have fallen behind on the taxes," Alfred says, "Or perhaps it was an oversight. Seeing that they have to travel, so much."
He tells Gus he needs him to come up and tell them what they should do next. Gus says he's on the way. Alfred tells him Charles is already coming down to get him. Because it's just that urgent.
"We're sorry," he says to Gus. "But I'm afraid we panicked and didn't want to wait for you to walk up or drive. The papers say the Foreclosure is in progress and it will be affective before close of business, *tomorrow*. We'll need somebody to go with me to access the family's funds and then get the money to the tax assessors office, first thing in the morning."
Then Alfred strokes his ego, saying "You're better at this kind of business, than any of us."
"I can do the money business," Gus says and smiles.

When Baby Girl set up this package, she decided to play on Gus's greed. For a long time, she has speculated how much he yearns to be the head of this family. She figures he has always wanted to know how much the estate is worth. So he could come up with a way to dupe the staff into putting him in charge of it. Thus he could take as he pleased.

Baby Girl watches the camera's. She sees the limousine pull back in front of the main house. Charles hops out and lets Gus out. He walks him to the door and Cherry opens it. She's leading him to the office. Baby Girl goes into the closet, taking the 9mm and machete with her. They're only a 2nd option.

Gus comes into the office where Alfred greets him in the normal manner. Gus looks around. Then he asks,
"Is the office being renovated?"
Alfred answers Gus, saying,
"Misses Baby Girl wants it painted, to her liking."
In his usual voice of talking down on Baby Girl, Gus says,
"But Donnie liked it, *this* color. I think she should be taking care of these taxes. Instead of redecorating. Don't you think?"
Alfred shakes his head, affirmative.

That's when Addie Mae comes in bringing coffee and teacakes. Gus is overjoyed as he digs in. Addie Mae sits the coffee service tray on the hutch, then leaves. Gus makes him a steamy cup of coffee with 2 sugars and 1 teaspoon of creamer. The way he always has it. Alfred passes on the teacakes but he does take a cup of coffee. He drinks his black. Gus looks over the papers on the desk. His eyes go straight to the account information on the bank forms. He gawks at the large amount showing on the total assets sheet. The billion dollars in cash, land and assets is something he has wanted to possess for a lot of years. Alfred asks him can he help. Gus gives him an arrogant look, before he answers.

"Well, of course I can, old man," Gus gloats, "Ain't that what you called me up here for?"

Alfred replies, "Well. Not exactly."

Baby Girl emerges from the closet. She walks around in front of the desk. Gus sees her and flinches. She has her 9mm in her hand. It's pointed at him and cocked. Gus knows not to move a muscle. Instantly, he tries to reason.

"Lovely Girl. What's the gun for?" Gus asks.

"It's not a gun. It's a weapon," she corrects him.

"Why do you have your weapon drawn on me?"

"Why would you give me, my husband, as a target?"

"What? Your husband? When did I do this?" Gus asks, as he pretends to be ignorant about the anonymous mark.

He tries to appear calm. He lays back as if he hasn't a worry in the world.

"That's what I just asked you," she states.

"I had no idea who the mark was, Lovely girl-"

"Do not say my name again. Just answer the questions I asked you. Why would you allow Derrick to be a target?"

"I didn't. I had no idea who the target was. You know it was non-descriptive. Very secretive. *Anonymous*."

"I know that's how you set it up. So you didn't know who the mark was?" she asks.

He says no. He didn't have any idea of who the mark was. He says the buyer came in, paid in full, gave him the information and left.

Upon saying this, Gus leans back in the Don's chair, even further, while rocking from side to side. He really feels like he's in charge or at least, that's how he wants it to appear.

"Who is the buyer?" she asks.

"You know I can't divulge that information," he tries.

"In this case you can. The buyer set a detrimental mark.

87

He marked a family member. You, as my agent, are to guarantee that no family is ever harmed by family and you failed. Who is the buyer?" she asked, "And this is the last time you get the opportunity to answer me."
He gobbles down a whole teacake and half his cup of coffee. He begins to rock arrogantly in the chair, again.

"I can't tell you that," he says.

"You can but are you're refusing too?" she asks.
He nods yes. He is about to speak again but suddenly he can't.

Gus is stricken with a sudden case of paralysis. Just as Mark Genolli had been. He can't talk nor can he move a muscle. His eyes are fixed on Baby Girl. She stands in front of the desk and talks to him.

"First, you refused to talk," she says, "Now you can't talk. Cat got your tongue, Gus?" she's being coy now.

"These papers are phony, Gus. Just like the name you gave my husband. This estate is in great shape. I know this is bad news to you but the taxes are fine. Oh and I did a great job with this package. Don't you think?" she asks.
Gus sits and slobbers. Addie Mae comes in to take the remainder of teacakes and creamer, so she can dispose it all. Before exiting, she looks at Gus.
She says, "Shame on you for going against mister Duke. Against mister Donnie. *Die*! You damn fool."
She takes the tainted items and leaves. Cherry goes with her. They go and dispose of the Pancuronium filled teacakes. Pancuronium had also been added to the creamer.

Back in the office, Baby Girl has her peace. She reminds Gus of all the times he's sent her on marks and how she'd trusted him. How that trust started to dwindle, after he had shown her that he didn't have faith in her. That same night he'd come to her home to notify her that there was a hit on her. When he acted as if she wasn't superior to Mark Genolli. She pulls a chair up in front of the desk. She's feeling herself now and she wants to imitate *Tony Montana* in *Scarface*. She sits down in the chair as *Tony Montana* had done when he went to Lopez motors to kill Frank Lopez. She points her weapon at him. Then she speaks.

"Let me remember exactly what you said," she starts, *'Miss Lovely. I don't want you to get too damn cocky. Be careful.'* That's what you said to me, Gus."

Gus slumps over in the chair. Alfred slaps his forehead and makes him rock back. Forcing his body to straighten up.

Then Alfred joins Baby Girl in the broad mentality manor of speaking. First, he slaps Gus' forehead again. Then he says, "Who was you calling an old man. You maggot."

Baby Girl quotes Tony Montana, saying, "He's a *cockkaroach*, Mr. Alfred. Or a *hassah!*"

They both chuckle for a split second. Charles comes into the office and says, "His car is ready."

Baby Girl stays in her Scarface character, a little bit longer.

"Do you think I'm gonna kill you?" she asks, as she looks into Gus' eyes.

She tells Charles she has a few more things to get off of her chest. Gus' eyes run water. It's involuntary but if he could, he would cry right now. She can see it in his eyes. He knows he's going to die.

"When I did the Chadwick hit. You called my cell phone. I wondered how did you know I'd have it but I said nothing. You've been watching me and my husband. That's the only thing I can conclude. He brought my personals with him. He also brought our children. You son of a bitch," she struggles not to be emotional, as Charles reminds her to carry out the plan as she'd planned it.

89

Charles says, "No emotion, Baby Girl. You're a master."
She tells Gus that she knows he has a problem with her being in charge. She says, "When I said to you, *'From this day forward, no work goes out that I'm not aware of'*, it made you angry. I saw it in your eyes, on Memorial day, when you tried to give my work to Kid. What's going on with you and Kid? Is that where I should look?" she poses a question or 2.
She has thought about Kid, as a spoiler, a few times. She hasn't quite figured out just how involved he is. Nor why he would be. But she will. Soon. It's time to execute. She says her last peace.
"You think I'm going to kill you? I ain't gonna kill you," she says in her Scarface tone. Then she looks at Charles and Alfred and says, "Charles, Alfred. Drown this piece of shit!"
On cue, they pour a liter of Seagram's Gin, his favorite drink, down his throat. He gags but it goes down. Then quickly, they roll Gus to the front door and down the handicap ramp, in Don's chair. Charles had brought Gus's car up from his home. He and Alfred put Gus into his driver's seat and adjust the seat for him, as he would when he drives home drunk. He would always sit close to the wheel. Cherry rolls the chair back to the office, where she will clean and sanitize it.
Charles opens the passenger door for Baby Girl. She keeps her gloves on but gives Charles her 9mm. She won't be needing it. She gets in and starts up the car from the passenger side with Gus behind the wheel. She puts his window down half way. He tries to grunt. She slaps him. Then puts his hands on the wheel. She says, "Shut the fuck up."
She puts the car in gear and it begins to roll. She steers it towards the large bayou on the property. She reaches her foot over and slightly presses the accelerator, gets the car up to a speed of 30 miles per hour. It's rolling good. She opens her passenger door and flings herself out onto the ground.

Gus' Cadillac Seville rolls on toward the water, then plunges into the bayou doing 40mph. It slowly sinks to the bottom. Baby Girl runs back to the main house. Cherry has her bags already in her CLK63, in the garage. She hugs them all, hops in and heads back to Houston. The senior staff will take it from here. They go back into the Don's office to get things back to normal. They'll wait for someone to discover the car floating. Once they do, the senior staff will go into action again.

Blake's Estate. Houston

Almost 7 hours later. In Houston, Young D is starting to worry about his wife. He hasn't heard from her since she kissed him and pulled out at 8am, the previous morning. He assumes she's working. It's nearly 4am. He's just finishing a studio session. It's time for bed.
To DeJuan, Young D says, "I wonder if she got her phone with her."
"Yeah. I bet she do. But don't call her," he says, "She'll think you don't trust her."
Young D walks down to the kitchen. He feels his best friend doesn't understand how Baby Girl prepares for a hit and doesn't want him to act as if he can't trust her.
She always leaves her valuables and personal items. She didn't this time.

He thinks to himself. Even though he wants to call her. He opts not too. Not this very minute.
Just inside of Houston, Baby Girl is making her way home. She has had questions going over and over in her mind. On the drive back, she's thought about how she'd felt about Gus, the night he met Kid in her home. When he had tried to

91

give Kid, 1 of her packages. Then how she felt the night after the Lafayette hit. She thinks again about the questions she had asked herself, that night while Young D was pumping gas.

Does he know Derrick has come to meet me? That's not against the rules. Nor is my having my phone, after a job is done. What the fuck is going on and why is Gus really calling me?

Lastly, she had thoughts about the hit on her life, 4th of July week and how Gus delivered the announcement. How arrogant his tone was. How *impatient* he seemed with her. The lack of confidence he showed in her ability. Why was he so impatient with her, all of a sudden?

The Don use to say Gus was a sucker for a good line. And if someone offered him a chance to be a boss. He would step on infants and children to get there. Even Big Dog never liked him either. But The Don gave her the information on him which ultimately led to his execution.

"He's a follower, sweetheart. He worships man. The want for money and power, rules him. He can never hold the power position in my organization. He would lose it all, for sure," The Don had said.

The Don was a wise man. His words resonate through her mind, on a weekly basis. She still hasn't put it all together yet. Or maybe she isn't ready to accept what she's thinking. But she knows there's an explanation. There's a way to find out who the buyer is. She'll have to go back to the manor to research the buyer for the San Fran hit and it's properties. She'll have to go back soon, anyway. Once Gus' body is found, she can go back announced. Then she can go through everything with care. Take her time and look at every entry, every deposit and every transaction. Baby Girl is the best at finding the impossible. Being ahead of her time. She's been early on everything in her life. From birth to school and college graduations, to finding true love. She will put it all together. It's only a matter of time.

Soon, she's pulling into her garage at her Houston home. It's 4:45am. Young D comes out to meet her. He has waited up. He hugs then kisses her. Then he picks her up and carries her inside. Kissing her, all the while. He takes her straight into their bedroom and lays her on their bed. He lays down next her and holds her. He had been afraid for her. He's just relieved that she's made it back home safely, once again.

DeJuan grabs her things from the car and puts them in the master bedroom, for her. Then he leaves their room.

"Lock that door for me, partner," Young D says to him. DeJuan does, just that. Then he goes back up to the studio. His best friend and wife can enjoy each others company and then sleep. He's going to watch the property until everyone stirs again.

CHAPTER   TWENTY THREE
HOLLA BACK!

Young D and Baby Girl are at Annie's house with their sons. It's Friday, late afternoon. They're prepping items for the tour bus. Young D's Midwest tour will kick off the following Monday.

Once the clothing and linens are done being folded and are packed away on the bus, Young D is taking the family and the labelmates to his restaurant *H-Town Cuisine*, for dinner. The label is 2 years old, this month. They're going to celebrate this milestone, as well as their new compilation CD, *"H-Town's Finest!"* It will be released in 2 weeks.

Baby Girl is relatively quiet today. Young D can tell she's distracted and he wants to know why. He had inquired about her most recent job when they finished making love, earlier this morning. Still she hasn't been forthcoming with any details. She said she was extremely tired and she would tell him about it later. He isn't sure if she's being totally honest with him or if she's hiding something. Based on her actions since coming back home, he believes the latter. Young D isn't at all, patient about her keeping secrets. Though he has 1 of his own. Maybe knowing the magnitude of his secret is the reason he's so paranoid about her having one. Either way, he's going to keep pressing her until she comes clean.

She's never stalled about telling me details of her kills, after the fact. Not even before I went with her to do in Mark and his driver. But there's something new. What's the deal? Was it a industry person, this time? Had to be somebody within a days drive, if it was. Who could it be and why is she so secretive, all of a sudden?

He looks at her as she packs the final towels into the last bin and fastens the lid on top. The guys grab it and load it on the bus.

Finally the tour bus is ready for another month long tour. Young D's labelmates head back to their houses. They have to wash up and get dressed for dinner and a night of celebrating their success.

Young D sits down at his mother's island counter, next to his wife. He looks at her. She looks at him briefly. Then she looks back to their youngest son, Don Prince.

It's just me against the world...oooo, oooo.......it's just me against the world baby...ohh ooohhh....I got nothing to loose.......it's just me against the world.......stuck in the game.......me against the world, baby.

Baby Girl's cell phone rings. It's the New Orleans manor, ring tone. Baby Girl lets Young D answer her cell phone while she continues to feed Don Prince.

"Hello," he says as he answers her phone.

Then he listens to the person on the other end of the line. It's 1 of the staff from Morales Manor. Young D's face displays a look of shock. Suddenly he turns and looks at Baby Girl. He's about to announce that Gus Davis is dead. But the look on Baby Girl's face assures him that she knows it already. He can see it in her expression. He can also sense that she wants him to play it off. So he does.

"Baby. I got some bad news," he says, "They just found Gus' car in the bayou. And he was still in it."

"Oh my God!" Annie says, "What happened?"

Young D shares with his mother Annie and his sister Angela, what the staff are telling him on the phone.

He says, "They pulled his Seville from the bayou on the

95

property. They're saying he was intoxicated and he must've fell asleep at the wheel. And he didn't come around in time."

"Oh no," Baby Girl plays along, "I need to talk to the staff and calm them down. We need to go down there too, daddy. We'll need to make arrangements for him and have his things moved to daddy Don's office. He handled some *real* delicate stuff. I don't want it in the wrong hands," she finishes before reaching for her phone.

Young D hands her the cell phone and takes Don Prince so he can finish feeding him. Baby Girl talks to Cherry. Her and Young D both play the scene off. Baby Girl tells Cherry that her, Young D and the family will be there, as soon as possible.

"We'll be flying," Baby Girl informs Cherry, "I'll call you back with our itinerary. Okay?"

"Yes, dear," Cherry says and they hang up soon after.

Baby Girl goes back to feeding their baby boy, Don Prince. At this point, Young D is overwhelmed with curiosity. He can barely contain himself.

First, he helps Lil Man aka Derrick Jr down from his high chair and washes him up. Don Prince is done eating too. Baby Girl cleans him up. Young D feels an urge to get some privacy for him and Baby Girl. He comes up with a quick solution.

"Mama, can you get them dressed for us?" Young D asks, "I need to take care of Lovely."

Annie says, "Of course. I've got some more of that new gear that you bought for the boys. And its still here at my house."

Angela chimes in and adds, "Me and mama got my nephews. Go take care of my sis-in-law."

Annie and Angela will get them dressed for dinner, so Young D can take his wife home and console her on the lose of her family.

96

"Go comfort, Baby Girl. Bless her heart," Annie says sadly, "Another death in her immediate family."
Baby Girl has already handed Don Prince to Annie. Angela hugs her. Baby Girl walks out of the house without another word. Annie and Angela figure she's really grief stricken. They can understand, full well, why she would be. She'd already lost her real father named Big Dog. The Don too and he was the father that raised her too. Plus she lost her mother Wanda, just after she'd turned old enough to vote. Annie and Angela always saw Gus as a father figure to Baby Girl. They figure she has to be hurting, really bad. Young D knows she's not. He just doesn't know the particulars but he plans on finding out, in a matter of minutes.

As they're leaving Annie's house, DeJuan is coming up from the guest houses. He's approaching them.

"I'm going to the main gate," DeJuan says, "Some unwanted guest. Again."
Baby Girl inquires about who it is. She asks, "Somebody looking for a date?"

"Some niggaz who've been trying to get us to listen to their demo," DeJuan lies. "They done tried this shit, a few times. I keep telling them we'll set up a meeting at the office downtown."

"I guess y'all not moving fast enough, then," she says.
Young D gives him a blank stare because he knows who it is, without a doubt. He knows it's Kierra. Danica's birthday is next week and she's looking for him to give her money for the birthday party. She's started to communicate with Corleone, down at *H-Town's Finest clothing store* since she's restrained from coming near Young D's home property. Young D has told his half brother that he was giving her the money for the party. But Young D didn't say how or when. So Kierra decides to

force the issue. She figures if she shows up at the gate and has the guard to call down there. Then someone will bring the money on up to her. Anything, just to get rid of her. DeJuan is going to take care of it, right now. Young D and Baby Girl walk on to their home. DeJuan hops in his Denali and drives to the main gate.

He spots Kierra before he gets there. As soon as he pulls up to the gate, he jumps out and heads straight for her.

"How many times do I have to tell you to stop coming around this community?" DeJuan ask Kierra as he steps outside of the gate.

She says she wouldn't have come but she needs to get the deposit paid to *Chuck E. Cheese* by tomorrow.

"And I know y'all gonna be leaving again, to go out on the road," she says, "I had to catch him now. Is he at the house?"

DeJuan tells her that's none of her business, as he's handing her a cashiers check. She laughs, takes the $500 check and leaves. DeJuan has given her $100 for every year of the little girl's life. Danica is turning 5 years old, next Thursday. Young D has gone up by $100 each year, when he gives Kierra money for her daughters birthday.

At their house, Young D has asked Baby Girl what happened with Gus Davis? And did she kill him? Baby Girl tells him that Gus drowned.

She tries, "You heard it yourself. You answered the phone, daddy."

He says, "And that's *another* thing. You never just *let* me answer your phone either, baby."

She counters with, "I do when my hands are busy. I was feeding, Don P."

"You wasn't even surprised when you heard it, Lovely,"

he says, "I could tell by your expression, baby. You wasn't surprised by the news. Just admit it to me. Why are you keeping secrets from *me* now?"

She tells him it's complicated. She says, "But as soon as I *can* tell you. I will. It's better that you don't know about this, right now. When it's cool to tell you. You know I will, Derrick."

He doesn't like that answer. But what choice does he have?

"When will you be able to tell me?" he asks.

"I don't know," she says, "But it will not be before he's buried. Just know that. Nor will it be before I have some of the answers as to *what's* going on and why he had to die."

She has just thrown Young D a cross. He's confused, for sure. But he recovers quickly. He asks, "Did you do him? That's all I'm wanna know."

"Not alone. He was a rogue," she tells him.

That only makes Young D even more curious, as he wonders. *Who helped her? How did she find out Gus was untrustworthy? What did he do?*

She tells him she's going into her office to make flight reservations for tomorrow afternoon. Then she's going to lay out their clothes for dinner tonight. And afterwards, they can take their bath together and get ready.

He sits on the chaise in their bedroom, dumbfounded. He wants to know why Gus was killed. He wonders if it has anything to do with the hit on her from the Genolli family. The 1 he'd participated in, with her. He isn't going to accept *not* knowing what's happening in his wife's life. His feelings stand as they are now. She's going to tell him something and soon.

She'll have too. I should've been the one who killed that Mark Genolli, motherfuckah. And that Gus Davis asshole too. I know he's the one who tried to kill my wife. The mother of my boys. My

99

only love. Why won't she tell me? I don't even know why she's protecting his bitch ass. She killed him for trying to set her up. So what? What's the big secret about? Was someone else helping him? Fuck! I have to know what went down and why!

Celebration Dinner, Downtown Houston, Texas

Miss Deloris Flowers, from Harrisburg Pennsylvania, calls while they're all at dinner. She's upset because she has her 3rd flat tire, in 3 days. She's convinced that James Lawson is defying her restraining order which she has against him, once again. She's also convinced that he's sneaking onto her property to slash her tires. But facts wise, she can't prove it. She hasn't witnessed him around her car or her home.

After receiving her call, the twin brothers from *The 717 Boys*, Roderick and Ricky leave the dinner table. They head out to the patio of the restaurant so they can hear their mother clearly.

"I'm so sick and tired of this, sons," Deloris says, "I keep waking up to flat tires. Yesterday my neighbors and I swept the driveways, just to be sure there wasn't any nails or glass or nothing. That was after I woke up to the second flat."

"I just wanna know one thing," Roderick says, "Is it that fool *James*, mama? Let me know. I wanna know."

"I can't say, for sure, Rod," she says, "But I have a flat tire, again today."

"And there was no glass or nothing around. Nor on the driveway?" Ricky asks.

"No," she says, "There is *no* glass. And I actually parked on the grass, last night. So even if it *was* glass on the driveway. I didn't park there. I pulled on the grass, for that very reason."

100

"Then you know it's somebody who's doing it," Roderick says, "Mama. I want you to move down here. Move down here with us."

"Rod's right, mama," Ricky adds, "He might get inside the house, the next time."

"I have to work," she says, "I have a job to go too."
They continue trying to convince her to move. But she gives them more reasons why she's obligated to stay in Harrisburg. Soon Baby Girl joins them on the patio. She's concerned about their mother too.

"How is she?" Baby Girl asks, "Anything new?"
They tell her what their mother has just told them. Baby Girl asks them to put Deloris' call on speaker phone and they do.

"Hello, Miss Deloris," Baby Girl says.

"Hi, Baby Girl," Deloris says, *"How are you, dear?"*

"I'm good," Baby Girl says, "But the question is. How are you? I hear you're having a problem keeping air in your tires?"

"Yes I am," Deloris answers, *"This is the third day in a row. But I have no proof-"*

"That's all the proof *I* need," Baby Girl says, "Do you have some vacation time coming up?"

"I do," she says.

"Then I want to come out and visit," Baby Girl says, "And I'm bringing your sons with me. They need you and they need for you to be okay too. I've noticed how distracted they've been lately. They can't get any recordings done because all three of them are worried about you."

"Oh dear," Deloris says, *"I had no idea. I don't want them to be worried,"* she adds.

"They're worried about their mama and aunt," Baby Girl says, "I lost my mom. So it rips my heart out to see

101

somebody worried about losing theirs. That's gonna stay on my mind until there is some settlement."

"*I had no idea this was bothering them, so much,*" Deloris says, "*Not all the way down there. To be honest. I was happy for them to get signed. Because I didn't want them to go to jail, for killing him. Or worse.*"

"Then come visit for a week or two," Baby Girl says, "The label is going to send for you. Be ready in three days. No questions asked. Either that or we will all be up there to kill his butt. Do you want that?"

"*Him dead?*" Deloris asks. Then she answers, "*Yes. But I don't want you guys to do it. I don't want that kind of trouble for anyone who matters to me. James Lawson is not worth it.*" While Deloris is answering her, Baby Girl is thinking.
I'm going to kill him anyway. I just need you alive, long enough for me to get there and get things in order. Then it's goodbye to his bullshit. Forever.

Baby Girl says, "I'm gonna come get you and I'm bringing your sons and your nephew with me. We'll be there as soon as I return from New Orleans. And before they go back out on the road," Baby Girls adds, "Deal?"
Deloris tries, "*I'll have to see if I can-*" before her son cuts in.

"Deal? Come on, mama," Ricky interrupts, "We want you to leave there. At least, for this time when we can't be there to protect you."

"Are you ready?" Roderick asks, "If not. Get ready."
They all make pleas into Roderick's phone. Deloris is hesitant to answer.

"What did you mean by, *or worse*?" Baby Girl asks.

"*I meant. I didn't want him to end up hurting them,*" Deloris says.

"I wish he *would* think about hurting me," Ricky says, "I'm not six years old, no more."

"Mama excuse my language," Roderick says, "But we'll bust his ass if he ever tries to come near you or us. And we won't leave no one around to witness it. All I want you to do is pack an overnight bag. We'll get what you need when you get down here."

"We're not waiting longer than three days," Baby Girl says to her and her sons, at the same time.
"We'll be there to bring you on vacation, in three days."
With that, Baby Girl goes back into the restaurant and leaves them outside to come up with the particulars. She'll arrange their flight before leaving for New Orleans, tomorrow. She tells the rest of the family what's going on and what she's planning to do for their new labelmates mother. Her husband agrees.

"I'm going too," Young D says.

"I'll go too, if you want," DeJuan offers, "Just say the word."

"I'll need somebody to protect the property," Baby Girl says, "DeJuan will you watch out for everybody here in Houston. Until we get back?"

"Of course, I will," DeJuan says, "All y'all have to do is let me know what you need and it's done."

"We all will," High Top offers and all of the other guys cosign him.

"Good. I need my family to be okay," Baby Girl says, "That's why we're going to get Miss Deloris. She's our family now and we have to protect her too."

"It's done," Big Daddy says.
Roderick and Ricky rejoins them after hanging up with their mother. They come back inside, just as the entrees are being placed on the table.

"She's coming," Ricky says, "She'll be ready when we get there."

"She's coming if I have to drag her," Roderick adds.

"When are we leaving?" Mike asks.

"In three days," Baby Girl says.

"I hope y'all find that bastard and beat his ass," Annie says, " I can't stand a man who hits on a woman."

"My daddy wasn't violent," Young D offers, "He was just a deadbeat."

"No. He wasn't violent," Annie agrees. While chuckling, she adds, "And yes. He was a deadbeat."

"*My* daddy was the one who was violent," Angela adds, "But he's dead now."

"You didn't kill him, did you?" Roderick asks as he chuckles.

"No. He died in a car accident," Angela says, "It was five years ago."

"The way you drive," Ricky jokes, "You probably ran him off the road."

"No she didn't," Annie says, still laughing, "But somebody did. They just never found out anything about the other car. All it left was skid marks and nothing else. I just didn't wanna take no more ass beatings from him. At one point, I thought my son had done it. He was always threatening to kill him if he'd ever caught up with him."

****

Early afternoon of the next day, Baby Girl, Young D and their sons arrive at *Louis Armstrong International airport* in New Orleans, Louisiana. Charles is there to pick them up. He gets a skycap to retrieve their bags and loads them into the limousine. Young D signs several autographs and takes pictures with fans on their camera phones, before they can get to the limousine and away from the airport.

Once they get in the car, they head straight to Morales manor.

"The first time I ever came to New Orleans," Baby Girl recalls, "I was riding on a greyhound bus with my mama. I use to love it so much back when daddy Don would tell that story." Charles smiles and says, "I came and got y'all too, Misses Baby Girl. You was a beautiful baby girl. The Don was in love with the idea of being a father to you. Before you had ever even *graced* his mansion. I knew he was in love with Miss Wanda too. You two were the only people who could put a smile on his face, with just the mention of your names. He talked about y'all, all of the time. We knew everything it was to know about both of you. Long before we ever laid eyes on you. And now, you're here with your own family. A strong husband and two handsome young men."

Her and Young D smile and thank him for his compliments.

"I notice you have two brand new car seats, back here," Young D says as he laughs and adds, "with my sons names." Charles says, "It's how the Morales family *welcomes* it's heirs. We did the same thing for your wife, when she came in on that greyhound bus with Misses Wanda. She's the boss, *solely* now. And your sons are her heirs. They get the royal treatment. Just like she does." Young D likes that a lot.

Charles drives them on to their estate. The staff are waiting on the landing, for them. They get out and greet everyone.

Lil Man takes off running through the Mansion while Cherry gives chase. Lil Man loves this huge mansion. Cherry's assistant Maggie, takes Don Prince from his car seat and places him in the antique baby carriage. It's the same antique baby carriage Baby Girl was strolled in, as an infant.

"Misses Lovely. Mister Derrick," Cherry says, "I'm sure you want to get comfortable, after your flight."
She has caught up to Lil Man and brought him back to the parlor. She's going to get him dressed for horseback riding.
Alfred is in the parlor with Baby Girl and Young D.
He says, "I'd like to take the two of you out to view Gus' accident scene."

"Yes. We wanna see it." Young D says before Alfred can finish offering.
And though Alfred is aware that Young D knows about Baby Girl's profession. He also knows Young D doesn't know about the senior staff and their *overseeing* duties when it comes to her profession. If Baby Girl decides she wants to make it known to Young D. She can. But Alfred or no one else is going to volunteer any information about what actually happened to Gus. Not to Young D. Not to the junior staff. Not to anyone. Baby Girl is the boss now. They all move under her tutelage.

Alfred, Baby Girl and Young D head out to the scene of the crime. Gus's body was long moved to the Coroner's office. Charles had gone to meet with the coroner and taken the wooden box with him. The *Jefferson parish* coroner's office has been on the Morales payroll for decades. Charles had left the box with the coroner. The coroner and the morticians will mummify the left hand, then secure it in the box, for the Morales Estate. Charles will witness the left hand of Gus being put into the box. Then the box will be sealed and given back to him. The box will then be placed in the Morales family burial vault. However, the remainder of Gus's body won't be. He'll receive a regular burial through the parish. Unless some of his family shows up and claims him. The Morales family certainly will not.

Alfred, Young D and Baby Girl have made it to the

scene of where Gus' death occurred. Alfred is giving Young D the update on what's been reported on Gus' death.

"So he had too much to drink, fell asleep and drove off in here?" Young D asks with a doubtful tone in his voice. He's asking Alfred but he's looking at Baby Girl.

"Yes sir. That's how it was explained to us," Alfred says.

"Where is the yellow police tape?" Young D asks.

"They've removed it already," Alfred says, "The coroner gave his cause of death as accidental. There was no crime. There was no need to leave the property taped off. Shall we head back to the main house?"

Young D, Baby Girl and Alfred walk back to the manor.

Addie Mae has lunch ready for them. She sends her assistant to summon Cherry and Lil Man.

Addie Mae says, "Bring me that handsome fellow. I made his favorite brownies."

Addie Mae is Lil Man's godmother. Cherry will be Christening Don Prince in December. The Sunday before Christmas.

Alfred turns to Baby Girl and says, "I took the liberty of having Gus' records and property moved into the Don's office, ma'am. I left it all, as is. I know you want to be the one who sifts through it. Correct?"

She tells him he's correct. She doesn't want anyone to see those registers. No one. But her.

****

Back in Houston, DeJuan is holding down the Fort. This weekend at *Houston's Finest Clothing*, they're launching the new *Derrick Blake* line for toddler and infant boys. The first 200 customers receive an advance copy of the labels 1st

107

single from their new CD. Young D and Baby Girl are still in New Orleans. They'll be back tomorrow so Young D can make the autograph session. Young D calls DeJuan and Corleone to check on the progress of the new launching.

"What's going on, brother," Young D asks Corleone, "How's business?"

"We've had over five thousand paying customers come through here already," Corleone tells him, "And it's just two thirty."

"You opened at nine. Right?" Young D asks.

"Yes," Corleone answers, before adding, "And I won't close until nine, tonight."
He tells Young D that the autograph session is scheduled from 4 to 6pm, tomorrow. And he expects him to be there. Young D lets him know he'll be there. Then he asks to speak with DeJuan.

After taking the store phone, DeJuan updates him on things at the estate and in the studio.

"We're working hard in the studio, bro," DeJuan says, "And we've had no drama from Kierra or anyone else."
That's good news to Young D. They hang up.

But later, during the same evening, Ricky and Roderick gets a call from their mother Deloris. She has gotten her vacation days approved but she has some more bad news. She had her 4th flat tire and this time, she saw the culprit.

"It was James, wasn't it?" Roderick asks.

"Yes it was," Deloris says, "I saw him. As plain as day. He stuck it four or five times with an ice pick."

"Mama hang in there," Ricky says, "Uncle Mike is on his way to get you. You're staying with them until we get there. I don't wanna hear nothing about, *no*."

"I'm not going to say no," Deloris says, "He's already

108

pulling up. He told me he was on the way and to call you all."
Uncle Mike is the father of their cousin Mike. The 3rd guy of
The 717 Boys.

"Good. Stay there until we arrive," Roderick says,
"You're off tomorrow?"

"Yes," Deloris says, "So I can get packed for the trip. I
asked for three weeks off and I told them I had to go on tour
with my sons." They all laugh.

Then Ricky adds, "Just stay with Uncle Mike. He'll bust
James' ass if he shows up, over there. And since you don't have
to work. You don't have to go out nowhere, mama. We're
getting everything you need when you get down here. Okay?
Please?"

"Okay, twins," Deloris says, "I promise. I want go out
anywhere before y'all come. Except to get into the car with my
brother."

Both Roderick and Ricky feel comfortable with that answer.
And even more, knowing their mother will be safe at their
uncles house, for a day and a half. Until they get there to bring
her to Houston.

****

Business for the Morales family isn't only about hitting
marks. They have tax paying legitimate businesses, dating back
100 years. *Morales Printing Company* publishes everything
from Novels to the parish newspaper. While *Morales Shipping,
Trucking and Freight* logs millions of miles per decade.
Distributing goods all over the world by roadway, water and
rail. *H-Town Records* label uses both of these businesses for it's
printing and shipping needs. Then there are the 7 restaurants
throughout Louisiana. The oldest 1 which opened in 1927 is in

109

Lafourche Parish. It's still in business today. Another business is *Morales Sporting and Wildlife*. These are the fishing and hunting camps throughout bayou country. Plus the Southern, Midwestern and Northwestern states too. These camps are frequented by sportsman from all over the world. Morales Manor also owns a string of Dry Cleaners, Laundromats and Blue's bars in the southern region. The Don had bought Baby Girl a 12% share in *Clear Channel Broadcasting* which oversees 3 FM stations in the New Orleans area. Hundreds, maybe even thousands of stations, worldwide. That's another plus for her husband Young D and her brothers' music labels.

But the Morales name will always be synonymous with politics. There has been a Morales in Louisiana politics since the early 1920's. Baby Girl has 3 step uncles and 4 step siblings in office, too date. But the Professional cleaning business is the most lucrative for Baby Girl, personally. She'd earned a BS degree in Business Management with a minor in Elementary education and Sports Medicine, while at LSU. She hasn't put her degree to use since leaving the 3rd Ward Soldiers office. The income she pulls in from hitting targets, dwarfs any monies she would have made while working at any of the other family businesses. On a *pay-per-job* ratio, that is. She inherited an Empire which employs over 3500 people. The Manor sits on 210 acres. Or 5% of Jefferson parish. It employs 102 staff members. Gus was employee number 103. Baby Girl's Empire is huge and she accepts her position.

It's after 5pm now and Baby Girl finally gets a chance to get into Don's office. She's going to look over the records which had been moved in from Gus Davis' quarters. There is crate after crate. Bin after bin of logged information. Letters, tapes, CD's and DVD's full of all the information Gus had used to put together packages. Packages which covers the past 20 or more years. Gus' computers and disks are here too. Gus kept excellent records. However, when they moved them up the main house, they didn't keep the cases in chronological order.

"I should be able find who I'm looking for," Baby Girl says, "I have to get it organized first."
What she needs to have to help her unmask the mysterious buyer of her husbands death, is here. *Somewhere*. But it's going to take some time to find it.

She takes a seat in her father's chair and pulls the 1st bin forward. She pulls out the 1st folder. It's 1 from her father Big Dog's files. She files it away and pulls another. It's Teddy Jones. He was Big Dog's partner. She files it, as well. She labels this crate 1980's and pushes it away. She pulls another 1 forward. The 1st folder she pulls from this bin has 2007 on it. This is *her* case file. She's the only working pro for the family and has been for several years. She starts out filing and organizing all the information. She's looking for all the assignments which was handled by her. She finds the bin which contains the info from her 3 hits at the end of May 2007. She pulls the package on Dennis Montgomery and looks it over thoroughly.

"Nothing out of order here," she says.
Next, she pulls the Chadwick Donaldson file from May 30. She looks it over. There is a CD disc with it. She pops it in the laptop computer on the desk and opens it. She runs the disc to see it's contents. The properties on the CD shows there are sound recordings on the disc, as well. She opens 1 of the SR's which is titled, *"Conversation with Brad."* She plays the audio. It's a phone conversation between Gus and Kid.
What the fuck? He was discussing my job with Kid? Since he couldn't give him the package. He gave me up.

111

She listens intensely. She hears Kid telling Gus,
"That nigga Young D went to Lafayette today. Kierra told me she went out to their property and fucked with his crew. But he wasn't there. They said he was out of town with his wife."

Baby Girl is incensed. Immediately, she thinks about the white t-shirt but she maintains her composure. There's more to hear. Kid tells Gus to call her phone. This is when he hangs up with Kid. The next sound recording is Gus talking to her.

112

CHAPTER TWENTY FOUR
THE UN-COVERING

So that's why he called me. But why is Kid checking up on me? And why the fuck is Kierra in my husband's business? That stinking bitch!

She taps her fingers on the desk as she thinks, long and hard. A part of her wants to ask her husband why would Kierra be at their property and relaying information to Kid. But she knows better than that. It would be a rookie move to become emotional about *any* phase of her work. Still, the woman in her wants to know more. *Immediately.*
What's going on? How is Kierra involved in this? She was at The Drake in San Francisco. But how? Is she Kid's woman? Was he there?
Okay. I'm going to have to ask Derrick. But let me figure out the best way to do that.

She *has* to talk to Young because she needs to know what connection he has with Kierra.
How well does Derrick know her and why would she be in his business? I have to find a way to get that info. Without letting too much go, too soon. Why would Kierra be telling Kid anything about Derrick and me? As if we're not suppose to be with each other. Still, why was Gus discussing my assignments with Kid. Or with anyone?

There are lots of questions to be answered and she's going to get to the bottom of this conspiracy. *Sooner than later.* Someone wants her and husband dead. She can't figure out if they want them both dead, *equally.* Or is 1 of them is marked because of their association with the other. She figures it has to be a mark on Young D. Because a mark on her, would be professional enough not to include her family members. She would be the *primary* mark. In the professional cleaning business, family members and friends aren't normally marked. If they are killed it would usually be because they were present when the primary mark was hit. The same way Billy the driver got hit when he was with Mark Genolli.

So this is someone who wants to kill Derrick. But why? How does Kierra fit into this picture? And why is my brother telling her our damn business?

She takes the files she's viewed, thus far and locks them in the safe. Then she locks the office up and leaves it. She's going to talk to Young D, this instant.

Young D is on the lanai of the staff's dining room with their sons. They're enjoying a cool drink of homemade lemonade and toasted sandwiches. Cherry and Maggie are with them. These ladies are dedicated to Baby Girl and Young D's children. They hardly loose sight of the boys whenever they visit Morales Manor. Lil Man loves the horses. He's coaxing Cherry for another ride, at the time Baby Girl joins them.

"Would you like a cool drink and a sandwich, Misses Baby Girl?" Addie Mae calls to her from the main kitchen.

"Yes," Baby Girl says, "I'm starving."

Addie Mae brings her a toasted Club and a tall glass of lemonade.

Addie Mae says, "Supper will be ready at eight, prompt."

Baby Girl says, "Okay." Then she looks at Young D. She tells him, "Baby you've been asking me about work. I'm ready to talk. We can talk about things, tonight. I'd say we do it after supper. In private."

"Do you wanna do it now?" Young D asks.

114

"No," she answers, "Not until we're alone. I have some things to go over with you."

"Cool," he says.

She enjoys her sandwich while they watch their sons go for a horse and buggy ride. Lil Man wants to ride a horse but Cherry convinces him to get into the buggy.

"If you ride in the buggy. Your little brother can ride too," Cherry says.

Lil Man is okay with making that sacrifice.

"Tom on Prince. Lets ride the horses," he says, giggling as he climbs into the buggy with Cherry, Maggie and Don Prince.

They take off for a ride around a large portion of the 210 acre Estate. Young D figures this is a good break for a private talk.

He suggests, "Let's talk now. Come on."

She agrees with him and starts to pick up her food. He helps her to carry her food and they go up to their master suite.

Charles has returned with the wooden box from the mortician. Alfred assigned 3 staff members to the funeral home. They're in charge of the obituary and arrangements for Gus's funeral. The service can be held on Thursday. *Maybe*. Something else Baby Girl will find out about Thursday, is that it's Danica's birthday. But for now, Alfred has the staff to put the box in his private safe. He'll present it to Baby Girl to seal it in the vault. But right now, she's in a private meeting with her husband in their master suite. The staff are use to this. Only this time, the meeting isn't about romance. It's about what she knows is trickery. Baby Girl wants to get to the truth without giving away details of what was actually going to happen in that *"The Drake"* hotel room, in San Francisco. Not until she can figure out who wants her husband dead. At the present time, she's more interested in knowing what did he

115

think he was going to that hotel room for.

They sit in the lounge of the master suite, as she finishes off her sandwich. After she's has the last bite, the conversation begins.

"What's on your mind?" Young D asks.

"You," she says bluntly, "I know about the meeting."

"What meeting?" he asks.

"The meeting you had at the *Drake*," she says, "What was happening?"

"You know what happened," he says, "Nobody showed up. We was both there."

"Yes. We both were. Weren't we?" she says, realizing he's not going to be forthcoming about the earlier meeting.
She continues, "I'm not speaking on the ballroom meeting. I'm asking about the one at noon, in the Drake hotel room."

"I don't know what meeting you-,"

"Don't lie, Derrick. You were there," she says, "I know you was meeting a woman there too."
Young D decides to deny any knowledge of a noon meeting. He knows he wasn't cheating. He still thinks it was a legitimate company, who didn't bother to show up or cancel the meeting. Only because his label is very sought after globally, these days. He's honoring the secrecy because he thinks they'll call him again later to apologize and reschedule. Baby Girl is disgusted with him, at this point. She hates to be lied too and she always has. But since he has decided to be deceitful with her about having a meeting in a hotel room or even being there. She doesn't bother to tell him about the hit on him.
"So you deny having a meeting or being in a hotel room at the Drake?" she asks for clarity.

"Baby, I told you about the meeting at the Drake," he says, "No other meeting happened. That's all I know on it."

"Kierra was there," she says suddenly, as she waits for his reaction to the mentioning of her name.

He looks at her. His eyes are narrow and angry.

"*Kierra*? In San Francisco?" he asks, "I don't know nothing about Kierra being in San Francisco. Or her being in no hotel room."

"Why is she in your business?" she asks, "What do you know about her?"

"From what I know, she's a stripper," he says, "You need to ask your brother Kid about her. He seems to be closer to her than anybody I know."

"Oh I plan too," she says, "You can believe that. I just hope he'll be honest about the bitch. I'm not gonna be fighting your whore's, Derrick-"

"She's not my ho or nothing else, Lovely," he says quickly, "You're my wife and my only woman."

"Then tell me the truth," she demands.

"I have and I'm done with that," he says as he's set on not telling her the particulars of his noon meeting.

He doesn't have any idea of why Kierra's name is even being mentioned. He thinks his wife is trying to trick him into admitting something else and she using Kierra, only because she's been a thorn in her side lately. From the t-shirt to the fight backstage in Galveston.

"Okay. Fine," she says, "We're flying home at one thirty, tomorrow afternoon. Get packed and be ready to go."

"What time are we flying to Harrisburg to get Miss Deloris?" he asks as he tries to keep the communication going.

Baby Girl walks out of the suite, leaving him in there alone with his guilt.

She never answers his question. Her mind is on bigger issues than his whore's, anyway. Besides, she'll get to the truth.

117

But in her *own* way. She's going to speak with Kid.

Young D is clueless as to how she even knows about the noon meeting. It never dawns on him that she knows because she was paid to know. If he would allow his imagination to flow past, *"My wife thinks I'm cheating."* Or *"I can't let her find out about my guilt with Kierra,"* then he would probably be closer to knowing why she's questioning him about the noon meeting. But his mind never unwinds that far, on it. He decides to call DeJuan back and see if he knows how Baby Girl found out about his secret meeting that never took place.

Meanwhile, Baby Girl tells Charles she needs to use one of the cars from the fleet to run an errand. He inquires about the errand. She tells him where she's going.

Charles says, "Okay. But I'm going to drive you."

She doesn't argue with him. He's watched her grow up. He knows her mannerisms. She's agitated and he can tell. He wouldn't be keeping his word to Donnie Morales if he allowed her to leave the manor alone, in a emotional state. She gives him a slight smile. She knows he's right. She chooses a 2008 Land Rover LR2 limited edition, from the garage. Morales Incorporated with it's elite status, is privy to automobiles before they're released to the public.

Charles starts it up and pulls it out of the garage. He buffs it up to bring out the full shine. Then he'll pull it in front of the mansion.

Baby Girl goes and grabs her *Hug-a-thug* bag, for convenience. At this point, she trust no one outside of her children, herself and her staff. And still, her husband and his family and labelmates. She knows he wasn't cheating in San Francisco. But she's knows he's lying. What has her upset with him is, he doesn't even know that she knows for certain that he wasn't cheating. And still he decides not to come clean about

118

the noon meeting. He wants to be cavalier about it.

As she waits in the parlor for Charles, she starts to wonder.

If he was cheating, he would lie about it. He could care less if I think he's having an affair. That's how I feel about it.

She's thinking to herself as Young D comes down from the suite. He finds her in the parlor, waiting for Charles to bring the SUV around.

"Are you going out somewhere?" he asks.

She doesn't answer or even acknowledge his presence. He comes closer and asks again. She doesn't blink. He bends down and gives her a kiss her on her cheek.

He says, "I called DeJuan. He said he didn't know Kierra was there either. And whenever you get back, we can talk about the private meeting, baby. I'm not doing anything dishonest and certainly, not with Kierra. I can't stand that tramp."

He exit's the parlor and goes back out on the lanai where the staff are having a much needed break before supper. They're pleased to see him arrive back.

"Is Misses Baby Girl joining us?" Sara asks.

She's one of the maids on Cherry's staff too.

"She going on an errand," Young D says, "She'll be back by supper time. Or I'll be going to get her. Wherever that is."

As Baby Girl heads out the main door to join Charles in the LR2, she smiles to herself.

He'd better be ready to talk to me. He knows me. I don't fall for the lies.

She's happy he corrected his earlier actions. But right now, her focus is on hearing what Kid has to say, without telling him too much.

Charles drives her straight over to Kid's home. Charles gets out and accompanies her to the door. He knows this is an unannounced visit, so he rings the doorbell. The housekeeper answers the door and leads them to Kid's guest area.

"Mister Walker will be right down. Would you like a drink, Miss Lovely?"

"That's *Misses* Baby Girl," Baby Girl corrects her, "And no thank you. I just wanna talk to Kid, for a few."

The housekeeper excuses herself as Kid enters the room. Charles waits just outside of the guest room door but still within earshot. He has taken on the role as Baby Girl's protector. It's always been a natural thing for him, as it is with all of the senior staff. They don't get to do this much since she met Young D. He's all of the protection she needs, in normal circumstances. Kid makes his way over to her.

"What's up, little sis?" Kid asks.

He's all smiles. In her opinion, he looks like the cat that swallowed the canary. In other words. He looks guilty.

"I'm sure you know about Gus' accident?" she asks.

"Yeah. I caught it on the news," he says, "That was some terrible shit. Terrible the way he went out."

She agrees with him. Then she gets to the point of her visit.

"I found out some disturbing information in his files," she says, "It made me wonder if you and him were in cahoots or something. Were you?"

"He was trying to get me some professional work," he says, "But ah, we both know how that turned out. You shut that down, pretty damn quick."

"Is that it?" she asks. "Was that all it was?"

"We was casual friends, Baby Girl," he says, "I still spoke to the man, even though he couldn't employ me."

"I know y'all were still speaking. That's why I'm here."

120

He looks at her as if he's about to go on the defensive. She can tell he's agitated and a bit nervous. Everything in her says he and Gus were up to no good. She presses him for more.
"When y'all did speak. What was it about?" she asks.
She wants to see if he'll admit to the phone call during Memorial week. The 1 she listened to a few hours ago. But Kid stalls, for a few seconds.
Six Nine shows up, comes into the room and saves Kid. At least, for now. He's just stopping by to see if Kid wants to accompany him to the manor to check on Baby Girl. So he's happy to see that she's here.
"Hey, Baby Girl!" Six Nine says, very excited to see her. "I was headed your way to check on you. I heard about Gus."
They hug and she thanks him for his concern.
"Why don't both of you come for supper?" she asks.
Six Nine says, he will. Kid says, he has other plans.
"Oh, okay. Well as you already know. Jordan is living with us," she says to Six Nine. "I would've brought him but he's in school. He loves the gifts y'all sent him for his birthday too. I just want you two to know. I expect for you to visit, a lot more often. To see Jordan and my sons too."
Jordan had just turned 13 years old in August and started 8th grade. Six Nine is glad he's enjoying the money he'd sent to him and the brand new *ATV*, he'd just bought him for his 13th birthday.
"I'm gonna head on out to the manor and see how everybody's doing," Six Nine says. "I'll be there. So I'll see you when you get back home, Baby Girl."
He says goodbye to Kid and Charles. Then leaves, heading to Morales manor.
That's when Baby Girl gets back to her conversation with Kid.

121

"Were you in San Francisco on August fourth?" Baby Girl asks Kid suddenly.

Kid says, "No. Why?"

"Ugh. I guessed you were," she says.

"No. I wasn't, Baby Girl," he says, "How do you figure I was in San Francisco?"

"Cause your girl was there," she says.

"My wife was here. At home with me," he says.

"I meant your girl, Kierra," she says, "I saw her."

Kid tells Baby Girl that she's wrong. Kierra is not *his* girl.

"If she was in San Francisco. She didn't come with me or for me," he says, "Maybe you should ask your husband about her."

Baby Girl tells him, she knows he's never liked the idea of her and Young D being together.

"From day one, you treated him wrong," she says, "You never welcomed him into the family. It doesn't matter *to you* that I love him and he loves me. Why don't you like Derrick?"

"He loves *him*, Baby Girl," Kid says, "He fucks around on you. Right under your nose."

"That's *your* bitch, Kid," she says, "When she's around our label. She fucks with the labelmates. *Not* Derrick."

"Maybe not anymore. But she was," he offers.

"Whatever, Kid. I saw where you and Gus was trying to take part in the New Orleans project. What's that about?"

He seems stunned that she knows of their involvement in her business. Though he tries to act unaffected. Then he tells her it's a new business venture for the city.

"It's a way of fucking Katrina victims out of their land and homes, is what it is," she says.

Kid becomes angry instantly. His voice starts to rise. His face is bent all out of shape too. He looks more caught up than ever.

Just like he looked her had, when he first walked in to this room. Only he has a frown on his face now and not that shit eating grin he was wearing, previously.

"I'm a Katrina victim, just like them and you," he tries, "I can't fuck over myself."

She presses him. He's a big piece to this puzzle. She wants to put it together, as soon as possible. She tells him she knows the new project for New Orleans involves landscaping, parks and other venues. Which will be located where, what's left of the 9th Ward is. Among other things. The citizens of New Orleans are being booted out of their homes for corporations.

"So you're accusing me of being a crook now? Because I know your husband is a liar and a dog?"

Baby Girl shows no emotion.

"No. I'm telling you what the project is," she says calmly. "Now, if you're a part of it. Then take your lumps. But the project is on some bureaucratic bullshit that's fucking my people out of their homes."

"Like Young D ain't fucking you out of yours," he says, more angry than before.

"Where the fuck did that come from?" she asks.

"Baby Girl you come from a cultured home," he says, "I know Don had outside shit going on. But you? When you first came around us, you was a debutante. You still had the English accent from going to school abroad. Now you kill people for a living. You fight every other month. Some ho Young D been fucking with or that you think he's fucking."

"That's not the truth but what is your point? I'm gonna hold up for me and mines," she says, "Derrick has nothing to do with me fighting, Kid. I fought more girls out there in the third ward, for y'all. Than I ever will, with Derrick. You act like he has me doing what I do. My profession was taught to

123

me by my father. Not Derrick. My job doesn't always call for me to kill someone. Sometimes it's just to whoop their ass, real good. But that's neither here nor there. Just tell me this. Why is your bitch in my husbands business?"

"Oh he ain't told you?" Kids says, "They have daughter together. She'll be five, next week."
Baby Girl looks at him with rage in her eyes. She keeps her voice calm. Even though, on the inside she's at boil. She looks him square in the eyes. She has to say her peace.

"I know you blame Derrick for you and I not being close. But that's no reason to bring shame to him as a man or as my husband," she says, "You and your friends are the only ones who say and feel, like that. Like your friend, Gus. I didn't need people coming at me with that, *'He's the reason that you don't have a conscience' bullshit. If you feel I don't have a conscience, then that means one of two things. Either your name is already on my list. Or it's most likely going to be on my list. My suggestion to you would be this. Spend your time and energy trying to change your fate. So I don't have too. GOD is the lead I follow. Nobody's gonna run me. Any Dirt I do or have done. I did it, All By My Lonely!"*
Hearing this, Charles steps inside of the door. He senses Baby Girl is about to make an emotional kill. He cannot allow her to do that. Kid sees him and says nothing more.
Charles says, "Misses Baby Girl. I'm ready to take you home."
She clutches her *Hug-a-Thug* bag to her side, with her hand still in it. Her finger, still on the trigger. She stands facing Kid. Quiet as ever. Charles clears his throat, then he walks in and stand next to her. She stares at Kid with a lost expression. Charles knows Baby Girl has no feelings for her step brother, whatsoever. She has her killer eye on him. And again, Charles can't allow her to slip up like this.

124

Charles says, "Misses Baby Girl. We'll be leaving now."
With that, she turns and follows him to the SUV.

Everything in her wants to turn around, go back into the house and blow Kid's fucking brains out. But she knows *that* would not be professional. She hops back into the SUV limousine, in the front passenger seat, as usual.

"His time is coming. I can feel it," she says as she sits shotgun in the passenger seat of the LR2.

"Sooner than later," Charles replies, as he starts up the Land Rover.
He drives her back to the mansion. It's 7:15pm. They have to prepare for supper.

CHAPTER TWENTY FIVE
MEANT TO BE

Young D and his family arrive back in Houston, in the nick of time. DeJuan is at the airport waiting for them. Young D has just enough time to get to his store for the autograph session at 4pm. Baby Girl still hasn't spoken a word to Young D. Though, before she left for Kid's house, he said he wanted to talk about his secret meeting. But while he's with his fans, she goes about her duties, tending to Don Prince in the back office. Lil Man sits at the table with Young D as he signs autographs and takes pictures with fans. Baby Girl decides to wait in the back until the session is done. She doesn't feel like faking it and acting like they're a happy couple. She's not happy, at the moment.

Young D wraps up the session shortly after 6pm. DeJuan drives them home. During the drive, DeJuan senses the tension between his best friend and his wife. Young D tries to play it off but Baby Girl doesn't. They arrive at their Houston estate.

Lovely goes directly into their home office. Young D stops in the kitchen briefly. He retrieves the mail from their Island counter. Then he joins his wife in their office.

"Baby, do you wanna finish the talk about the Drake or not?" he asks.

She says nothing. She brought some more of the interesting looking files home with her. She wants to look them over, this evening. Before their flight to Harrisburg, tomorrow.

"Can we talk now?" Young D tries again.

"Not now. I'm busy working," she says.

Her eyes doesn't leave the file in her hand. Not as long as Young D is looking at her. He sits down in a chair directly in front of her desk. He has the mail from yesterday. He sifts through it. She peers at him from over the edge of her file.

Oh God. Please don't let him have a child out there, on me. I'm already crushed by the news. He has never said a word about him and Kierra. Let alone a daughter.

She looks back at her file, when he stops reading the letter in his hand to look back up at her.

"You have a letter too," he says.

He places an envelope on the desk in front of her. She reads the name in the return address section.

"Teddy Wells. Number three, zero, one, one, seven," she says, "It's from *Teddy!*"

She's excited to hear from her brother. She lays her file down and tears the letter open. Teddy has written to tell her how he's doing, how much he enjoyed meeting her and how he's looking forward too seeing his daughter, her and Young D, again.

"He's looking forward to us coming back, next month," Young D says.

He'd gotten a letter too. He's still reading his.

"So. Are we still going?" she asks.

"I don't see why not," he answers.

"I need to call Tunisia's mother to see if she'll allow her to go," she says, "After all. School is in session."

"I wanna talk to you, baby," Young D says.

"Oh. Now you wanna talk? It's about what you want now?" she asks and her patience is very short. "Is that it? You were *'done with that'* when I *wanted* to talk about it. So why now, Derrick? Ha? Is it because you didn't get any sex last night? I'm sure you got a whore to fulfill that need too."

She overflows. Showing her hurt and vulnerability. She didn't mean to expose herself, like this. She quickly composes herself and looks back at her file. He looks at her but says nothing. And as suddenly as he'd come into the office. He gets up to leave the office. He gets to the door, then turns back to look back at her.

"For the last time. I don't have a whore, Lovely," he says, "I have a wife, for whatever needs a female meets for me. Oh yeah. Go on and act like you're not paying me any attention. Okay. And by the way. Your file is upside down."

He leaves the office. Leaving her alone to sulk. She slams the file down on the desk and covers her face. She feels the urge to cry but she doesn't. She's learned to hide her emotions, well. Thing is, Young D can get a rise out of her. He always could. But like daddy Don had told her. *That's how it should be.* But this child by another woman, shit that Kid spoke on. Baby Girl simply does not believe. She sees how her husband is with their sons. She knows there's no way he could have a child out there and not have her be a part of his daily life.
Can he?

For now, she has to remove those thoughts from her mind and focus on the files. She has to know who's purchasing these contracts on Young D. If she can find the buyer. She can find out more about the Kierra and Young D situation.
If there really is one.

She figures if he won't come clean about a hotel meeting. He won't admit to having a child with another woman. As she's reading the 1st file, she notices some notations in it from *The Don*. The file she's holding is 1 of her 1st hits. She notices where her father inked out her salary amounts and initialed them. Then he left a note explaining where to find this information.
It's on his computer.

128

The Don had done everything he could to protect her from his disgruntle employees. Gus, being 1 of the main ones. She compares the packages then, with the one's since Don passed. She notices the changes. Gus was doing things his own way. Leaving things sort of open where it could be easily seen and decoded. She logs into her father's files from her desktop computer. She checks and rechecks the official books. Making sure Gus hadn't left the empire vulnerable to the feds either. She's please to see that this mishap was only in his files. Don's files are as she'd expected them to be. Properly camouflaged and impeccably organized. Looking over Gus files, she's without a doubt, positive as to why Don left her in charge if anything ever had happened to him.

Because Gus was trying to set him up. Take him down. That sorry sour ass mother fucker! He wished he could be my daddy. Maggot food!

Don has every job set up by Gus, linked back to Gus and only Gus. It was done through his computer. And no doubt, the senior staff has been keeping it current since his passing. Baby Girl feels even more secure than she had before getting her hands on these files.

"Daddy Don was brilliant. He never left himself compromised. I have to be the same way," she says aloud.

She takes a break. She has to call Southwest airlines to book their flight for Harrisburg. She has to call Philadelphia also.

She gets the reservations for her, Young D, Ricky, Mike, Roderick and Big Daddy. After that's done, she calls Tunisia's mother and ask if she can fly down to Houston, to go with her and Young D to visit Teddy.

"You know she's in school, right?" Tameka asks.

"Yes, I know. But it's for our birthdays," she says, "I

129

promise you, if she brings her school work. I'll make sure she do it and I'll help her with it too," Baby Girl tries.

Tameka ask when is the trip. Baby Girl tells her, they're going for the weekend of October 20th. Teddy's birthday is on the twentieth. Tunisia's is on the twelfth. Of course, Baby Girl's is on the 4th. Tameka finally says she'll allow her daughter to go visit her father. He hasn't seen her since she was 3 years old. Baby Girl thanks her. Then she tells her, she'll call her back with ticket confirmation.

"I'm about to schedule the flights now, okay?" she says.

"Okay. Take care and thank you," Tameka says and they hang up.

Baby Girl makes the arrangements for Tunisia to fly down to Houston, round trip. She also makes reservations for them to fly out to Colorado, round trip. She updates her season pass. These are open end tickets which she can use at anytime to go anywhere in the continental United States. She may be hurt by the info she'd heard about Young D. But there's still someone trying to kill him and she's going to follow him. She going to follow him around. Even on tour, without his knowledge. She won't be seen by him or his labelmates. Not unless she wants to be. If he's having an affair. Then she should see some evidence of it, at that same time. But she's not going to believe what Kid said. No way will she ever do that.

She calls Tameka back with the ticket information. After they hang up, she gets back to her files. She's going to find something which will help ease her mind tonight. But first, she has to tell *The 717 Boys* to get packed. Plus she has to pack her and Young D's things for Harrisburg. Then she'll get back to her files.

****

In the mean time, Kid is on a phone call with Kierra today. Kid says, "I told Baby Girl about Danica."

"What do you mean, you told her?" Kierra asks.

He's called her in Houston to let her know that he has let the cat out of the bag. He has told Baby Girl about Danica being fathered by Young D. He shares some of he and Baby Girl's conversation with her too.

Kierra is pissed. She knows her days of black mailing Young D, are over. She knows Baby Girl is going to demand a paternity test before she agrees to let Young D spend another dime. She also knows this is going to be disastrous. Not to mention, Young D is never going to set eyes on her again. Kierra is sure Baby Girl has shared this information with Young D and he's done with her and her daughter, for good. She isn't happy with Kid for opening his mouth and giving up her money train.

Kierra asks, "Why would you tell her? What did she say?"

"She didn't believe me," Kid says, "She just thought I said it because I hate his ass."

Kid is chuckling but Kierra is panicking. She has to run interference. She needs to know what has happened since Kid told Baby Girl about Danica. She hurries, so she can get Kid off the phone. She has to know if Baby Girl and Young D have discussed her and Danica. She hangs up with Kid. She calls Corleone, at the store, to see if he's heard any news.

Corleone tells her, he hasn't heard any news about it and he doesn't want to hear anything about it. He hangs up without giving her a chance to say anymore. Kierra yells out loud, after Corleone hangs up on her.

"Fuck! I wonder if she's mad at him. Is she leaving him or what?"

Kierra isn't giving up yet. She's going to try to contact DeJuan and find out more information. She has to check his schedule before calling him. He hates to be interrupted when he's in the studio.

What she doesn't know is he hates to hear from her, worse than Young D does. DeJuan wants Baby Girl and Young D's relationship to stay solid. He's wanted Kierra out of the picture for years and he is about to get his wish. Further, his schedule is showing he's in the studio and Kierra isn't able to call him.

****

The following morning Young D, Baby Girl, Big Daddy and The 717 Boys board a flight for Harrisburg. In 7 hours, they're seated in the living of Deloris' house. She's already packed and ready for their return flight. It's in 2 days. Baby Girl didn't even bother to bring extra security for Young D because she's almost certain of who the buyer is. Though she doesn't want to believe it. Her main objective in the next 2 days is to get a lead on James Lawson while securing Deloris. She has Ricky to drive her and Young D to downtown Harrisburg.

She visits Morales Enterprises office. She's there looking into finding job placement for Deloris Flowers. The CEO of that office is very open to hiring Deloris, on Baby Girl's recommendation. But Baby Girl tells him, she'll be in touch. After getting to the office, Baby Girl thought better of placing Deloris in *that* office. Simply because that office is still in Harrisburg. She needs to convince Deloris to move south. That way, she's nearer to her sons and the entire family. Then Baby Girl can guarantee her safety. She has the CEO in Harrisburg to draft a letter for her and send it by CC mail to the CEO's of Morales in New Orleans and Houston. The letter recommends Deloris Flowers for hire, at either office. With a

132

letter of recommendation from the Empire's owner, Deloris Flowers is sure to receive a letter inviting her in for an initial interview. With that done, Baby Girl turns her attention to baiting a trap for James Lawson.

First, she treats Deloris, The 717 Boys, Deloris' brother Mike Flowers, Sr and his wife Edna Flowers, to a free night at *The Courtyard by Marriot*. All expenses paid. When Deloris learns of the full day of spa treatments her and her sister-in-law will receive tomorrow. She can't resist.

"I'm there, honey," Deloris says, "Thank you, Baby Girl and H-Town records."

"You're welcome," Baby Girl says, "Now let's head on over there."

Just like that, Baby Girl and Young D drop all 6 of them at the hotel. They leave Big Daddy there with them for extra look out. Then Baby Girl and Young D head back to Deloris' home.

With Deloris out of the house, Baby Girl is free to bait James Lawson at her will. She drives Deloris car, using a GPS system to get around. Her and Young D have dinner. Then they return to Deloris' house for the night.

As Baby Girl is pulling into the driveway, she spots a pickup truck, just down the street which is occupied. She can see 1 head, of what looks like a male occupant.

I just hope that's you James. Come on down.

She pulls Deloris' car into the garage and closes the door. James Lawson will think it's Deloris because he won't see who gets out of the car and goes inside. Her and Young D lock the car and go on inside the house.

"Don't turn the lights on, daddy," she says, "Not until I can make sure all the curtains are closed. I think that was Lawson sitting in the Ford, in front of her neighbors house."

"He's a bold ass bitch, to be sitting out there in plain view," Young D says.

"That's true," she says, "Especially with as many times as Deloris has called the cops on him. You would think a police car would be sitting out there. Or at least, riding down the block, every five minutes."

"Now baby. You know them folks don't come unless they can get a drug bust," he says, "Or claim it's gang related."

"Unfortunately that's the truth, ninety percent of the time," she says, "So many women die every month, at the hands of their domestic abusive mate. The police don't seem to be as eager to patrol these type of houses. But if they could prove Roderick or Ricky was profiting from drugs. They'd be here every hour."

"Now, you got it," Young D says as he chuckles.

The secure all doors and windows before turning on the light in the living room. Baby Girl goes and turns on the light in Deloris' bedroom and in her bathroom. This way, if James is out there and comes on up to the house. He'll think it's Deloris, as usual. Baby Girl and Young D turn on the living room TV and sit down on the couch. Young D is impatient.

"Can we have our talk now?" he asks.

"No Derrick," she says, "That matter is closed for now. I don't have the energy to discuss it, right now. Let's get her back to Houston, safely. Then we'll get back to *our* issue."

"I don't like that answer," he says, "But if that's how you want it."

"That's how I want it," she says.

"Fine," he says and the subject is closed.

****

In New Orleans, the senior staff have set the Gus Davis funeral date. After some thought, Baby girl had given them the okay to take care of his burial. She told them she wasn't going to pay for anything elaborate. If his family hasn't come forward by now. It's probably because he had done nothing significant for them, in all of these years. She had remarked to Alfred, Addie and Cherry that she couldn't remember ever meeting anyone who claimed Gus as a relative. Not since before she was a teenager. The senior staff told her he'd been estranged from his entire family and they'd written him off because he never supported any of them. Truth be told. He had left his wife for the fortune he thought he could get from Donnie Morales. His wife's family was partial to the Morales rival political family and her father threatened to disavow her, if she followed Gus to Morales manor. She couldn't turn on her father and Gus wasn't willing to stay with her. Not and lose the benefit of being connected to the most powerful man in the southern region, Donnie Morales. The regional power expanded to national, just before Wanda and Baby Girl came into the picture. The Morales' are a very powerful family. There endeavors of the business and political kind are well known throughout the world, these days. Alfred tells Cherry to just send the order for the obituaries to their printer and she does. He contacts Baby Girl and makes her aware of the date.

They're still relaxing in Deloris' home when Baby Girl's cell phone rings. It's the manor's ring tone.

"Do you want me to get that too?" Young D asks.

"No. I got it," Baby Girl says and opens her phone. She heads toward the kitchen for some privacy. She has her *Hug-a-Thug* bag on her shoulder, out of habit. She leans against the kitchen counter as she listens to Alfred give her the particulars on the funeral service. Suddenly, she hears a bump.

135

Sounds like it's coming from the garage. With the kitchen light still off, she cracks the door open quietly, then flicks on the garage light. And there he is. *James Lawson*. He has broken into Deloris' garage.

He's startled by Baby Girl's presence. She makes eye contact with him. She still has her phone to her ear. Alfred is still talking. James is frozen in her stare, for what seems like an entire minute. Then, when he can speaks, he asks,
"Who the fuck are you."

"The person who has permission to be here," Baby Girl says, "Why the fuck are you here?"
Alfred stops talking. He knows something is in play. He listens.
Baby Girl says to James, "Now. Miss Deloris Flowers gave me her keys and her permission to sleep in her home. She never told me anyone else would be coming here. So again. Who the fuck are you and why are you here?"
Alfred asks her, has she dialed 911.
He says, "You'll need that for your alibi, Misses Baby Girl."

"Yes I have," she tells Alfred while never taking her eyes off of James Lawson.
She has her cell phone propped and held in place by her shoulder. With her left hand which James can't see, she'd dialed 911 on Deloris' house phone which hangs on the wall, just inside the kitchen door. Harrisburg Police and Alfred are listening to her exchange with James Lawson.

In the living room, Young D can hear her talking to someone. He comes into the kitchen to see who she's talking too. She signals him with her right hand to come and take the house phone. He does. She continues watching James Lawson. Her right shoulder holds her cell phone in place. Her right hand is on her 9mm. She wants to end Deloris and *The 717 Boys* agony, so badly. But she's smart enough to know she'll need a paper trail first. 1 of her own. James isn't threatening her but he is trespassing. He's also in violation of a court order. Tonight, she's just going to hold him until police arrive. Young D has relayed all the information to the 911 operator, who have already sent 2 police units to the address.

Within minutes, the police are there and James Lawson is arrested. But something much more significant happened during this entire incident. Baby Girl has a visual of him now. He's as good as dead. She want stop until he is.

As the police lead him to the car, she hangs up with Alfred and calls Deloris at the hotel.

"He was here," she says.

"Oh my God," Deloris says, "Are you guys okay?"

"Of course we are," Baby Girl says, "James is a coward. He didn't even try to get close, after he saw me. He just asked who the fuck I was? I asked him why the fuck was he here?"
They laugh.
"Miss Deloris. We leave a eight am, day after tomorrow," she adds, "Enjoy your spa day tomorrow. Your house is safe and sound."

"I see that," Deloris says, "Thank you again, Baby Girl. For everything you've done."

"Oh I'm just getting started," she says with a giggle, "You have a relaxing day before we fly out. We're going to be *just* fine."
They hang up.

CHAPTER TWENTY SIX
SEEING WITHOUT BEING SEEN

Today is the day. The tour bus will be leaving for the Midwest tour, in a matter of minutes. Deloris is going on tour with the guys and so is Angela. Only Young D doesn't want to leave without being on speaking terms with Baby Girl. He makes the first move, by going to her.

He says, "I know you don't wanna speak to me but I can't leave home with us, *not* talking. I know you're angry and I'm sorry for whatever has made you upset. I love you, baby. Nothing or no one will ever change that. Do you believe me?"

She says, "Yes. I believe you."

She leaves it at that. She's not going to come around as easy as she did when they were teenagers.

She continues, "A lot of things have changed since you first left New Orleans in two thousand and came back here. There are something's that *can't* be reversed, Derrick. I've never loved *anyone else,* in my *whole* life and I'm not ready to start now. Now. Do you believe *me*?"

"Yes I do," he says.

He feels good hearing this from her. She is a soldier with special training on how *not* to show emotion. Still, with Young D, she can't help but show it. That's because her love for him is true. He knows that. He also knows that she's been hardened since loosing all of her parents at such a young age, as she was and so suddenly too.

He continues, "I promised your parents I would take care of you. I'm gonna do that, baby. I'm not gonna let you stop me from keeping my word to mama Wanda and The Don. You know that too. Right?"

She walks over, *really* close to him. She stands face to face and looks into his eyes. She gives him a very passionate kiss.

Come on, be real. She misses him too, by now. Don't get things twisted. She's a woman who's hurt. Scorned, even. By more than just him. But at this moment, none of that other shit really matters. It's about her and the man she loves.

She has some work to do before she can have that all included talk with her husband. But she *is* going to get him vindicated. She's going to cease these hits on his life too.

After the passionate kiss, he asks, "Will you meet me on the road?"

"I'll try," she answers.

But in reality, she's going to be at every stop he makes. Rather he knows she's there or not. She's not going to miss a turn. Someone wants him dead and she can't afford *not* to watch his every move. She's just praying that he isn't up to no good and that he isn't having an affair. Because she doesn't want to catch him being unfaithful. That would truly tear her heart apart and she'd have to face some fears, she's not familiar with at all.

****

Kierra calls Annie to ask if Young D can see Danica today. This is Kierra's last ditched effort to try to find out who knows what about the daughter she has. Young D had already told mama Annie about Baby Girl mentioning Kierra while they were in New Orleans. Annie advised him to call it all off and come clean.

Annie said to Young D,

"Don't say shit else to Kierra until Baby Girl knows the whole story, son. I'll handle Kierra's stupid ass if she calls here again."

Today, Annie relays what she'd said to Young D, to Kierra. She also tells Kierra that Young D and Baby Girl have already

139

discussed Danica. Even though they haven't yet. Annie tells Kierra that Baby Girl knows the whole story, even though she doesn't. That 1 untrue statement from Annie leaves Kierra dumbfounded. She doesn't know which way to turn now. Annie finishes off the conversation quickly. Annie says,

"Don't call or contact my son in the future. Let them contact you. Him and his wife will schedule Danica's visits out here, from now on. Young D will not be coming to your place at all. *Anymore*. Do we understand each other?"

Kierra says she understands. She's crushed too. Annie hangs up the phone without saying goodbye.

Annie had already wished her son and the labelmates well, when they departed for the tour. She views that last call with Kierra as just a little more insurance that Young D will have a wonderful time. Baby Girl had to go to New Orleans to help the staff prepare the grounds for Gus's funeral. Or at least, that's what everyone except the senior staff is led to believe.

****

Young D's 1st tour stop is an Air Force Base outside Chattanooga, Tennessee. Baby Girl is already here. She had flown in, copped a rental car and checked into the same hotel she'd booked for Young D and the labelmates. She had left Houston with Annie and security, thinking she was heading to New Orleans. Only the senior staff at the Manor knows she's in another town. Annie was more than willing to keep Lil Man and Don Prince.

Baby Boy's label are on tour with Young D and the labelmates. Soldier's label will be meeting them in Kentucky. Before Young D can even get settled into his hotel room and then, get off to sound check, Baby Girl has already peeped out

140

out the hit man who's there, to off him. She's got the jump on this hit man. She knows that already too.

"He's a rookie, definitely," she says aloud, "Nothing but a rookie. And there is no professional family backing his ass either. He don't even have sense enough to act like a fan or an artist trying to get signed." She shakes her head and smiles. "Sometimes these asses make my job, *too* easy."

H-Town Records and Baby Boy's label are all in the hotel bar. The hit man is too. And so is Baby Girl but she's in camouflage. She's at the first booth in the far corner. The bar has hanging ferns and potted trees, for her to hide behind. She has a good visual on her husband, all the guys who are with him and the hit man too. The concierge has just told Young D and the guys that their cars are ready to transport them to sound check. They prepare to leave.

After they leave out, get in the hotel cars and head to sound check. Baby Girl moves closer, so she can get a fix on the hit man who's now, her newest mark. She doesn't think he knows her but she's going to test that, right now.

She gets up and walks passed him at the bar. Just past him, she stops. She turns to the bartender and orders an apple martini. The new mark starts to flirt with her.

"Classy drink for a classy lady?" the hit man says.

"Who me?" she asks, looking around and smiling shyly.

"Of course, *you*. You're gorgeous," he says.

"Well thank you," she says, "What's you're name?"

"Damien."

"You mean like Satan? Six, six, *six*?" she asks as she giggles flirtatiously and he laughs too.

Then he says, "I do believe the name is synonymous with the book and the movie. But I'm more like Jesus."

"Oh okay," she says, "I don't know if I'm gonna tell

141

you my name yet. I'll have to see if we have anything in common, first."

They talk for a few minutes. It doesn't take long for Baby Girl to figure out, they have nothing in common. Damien is retired military. A *Corporal* in the *Marines*.

"So where are you from?" she asks.

"Different places," he says, "But I'm here now."

He's definitely a hit man but he's not a pro.

Next, she decides she's going to ask him another question.

"Before I tell you my name. I want you to tell me. Why are you here tonight and do you have plans?" she asks.

"I'm gonna catch a rap show," he says, "It's over at the *Air Force Base*."

"*Arnold* air force base? You mean that MC Young D show?" she asks in excitement.

"Yes. That's the one."

"You don't seem like the type who would be a fan of MC Young D," she says, "What songs by him, do you like?"

"All of them."

"I'm not familiar with his titles," she says, "What's his biggest hit?"

She asked the last question just to see if Damien was even familiar with Young D's music.

"How about you just go with me to the show and you can hear all of his hits," Damien tries.

He doesn't know any of Young D's songs.

Baby Girl figures he's going to try to knock him off at the show. She concludes that Damien is definitely a rookie. She further sums him up as a *shell shocked rookie*. Especially, if he thinks he can do a public hit on MC Young D. She sets her mind on his demise as she finishes the last sip of her drink. Then she says, "I think I'll take you up on that date, Damien.

My name is Cherry. Cherry Jones. It's very nice to meet you. So are you staying here?"

"Yes I am," he says, "I'm in room seven seventeen. And I'm here alone too."

Wow! His room number is the same as our newest group, 7-1-7 boys. I guess that's another sign. Okay, daddy Don. I'll do him there.

She laughs to herself.

"I'm so sorry to hear that," she says while laughing. Then she adds, "That you're here alone, that is. How about I meet you in your room for drinks, before we go to the show?"

He's all smiles. He thinks she's interested in him.

Actually, she is. But not in the way *he's* thinking. She's only interested in getting him alone so she can take his last breath.

"We have to appear as if we are not together though," she says. She wants him to believe she's a prostitute. After all, she is dressed like one.

She tells him, "You can leave first and go on up. I'll go freshen up. Then I'll meet you in your room in one hour."

Damien says, "Sounds like a plan," and leaves immediately.

Baby Girl knows in order for Damien to hit Young D at his show, he'll have to do it from a balcony position. Which means he has to have some type of high powered weapon. She's going to bring her detection equipment with her, to his room. Her detection equipment will alert her, if there are other weapons in the room.

****

Meanwhile in Houston, Kierra has called Kid once again. She tells him how disappointed she is that he had told their secret. His demeanor proves that he doesn't give a damn

143

how she feels. She senses that he is only out for himself.

How could I have been so stupid enough to think that this foul nigga actually cared about me?

She's thinking as she seethes. She certainly likes Young D, much more than she likes Kid. And she has decided she's going to let Young D's family know what Kid has been up too.

She remembers she's prohibited from visiting their estate and his mother doesn't ever want her to call them anymore. But she's going to get the word to them, by any means necessary.

"Why are you so quiet?" Kid asks as he notices she's just holding the phone.

Realizing that she has been thinking and plotting and not even talking to him, she says,

"I was just wondering why you haven't come to visit me, in awhile. Danica's birthday is Thursday, you know? And you said you had my back, through this whole deal. It doesn't feel like that too me."

She tries that to keep him thinking that she believes in him.

"I have to go to Gus's funeral," he says, "I'll get out there after that, though. Is that okay?"

"I guess it's gonna have to be. Bring me some cash and make it rain like you use too," she says, as she giggles.

"You know me," he says and laughs too.

She says she'll see him when he gets to Houston. They hang up.

Now she has to figure out how she's going to get the word to Young D about Kid wanting to kill him.

****

Lovely knocks on the door of Damien's room. He opens it up and lets her in. She activates the weapons sweeper.

"I need to use your bathroom," she says suddenly, "My

144

dang eyelash is falling into my eye," she lies.

Damien shows her to the bathroom. She goes in and locks the door, then quickly checks her sweeper.

It's a hit! There are other weapons in this area.

She needs to know if Damien is just an avid gun collector because the alert has picked up 4 weapons.

She returns to the front room with him and starts a conversation about war and weapons. He likes this subject. She can tell by how his eyes lights up when she says,

"Weapons of war."

"Are you the type who carries weapons everywhere?" she asks, "Cause some marines seem to be a little bit programmed, in my opinion. Do you have weapons in here?"

"Nah. Of course not, Cherry. Well okay, yes. Just this one," he says as he grabs himself and laughs hard.

He has the audacity to grab his genitals and laugh.

She pulls her 9mm from her hug a thug and shoots him in the head. He falls from the couch, onto the floor.

"Mine packs more punch. I know you agree," she says with a slight smile.

She searches his room and finds a return ticket to Houston.

"Oh. A homeboy, ha?" she says aloud.

In his pocket, is a book of matches from *The Anatomy*. This is the same strip club in Houston, where Kierra works.

That bitch is becoming more relevant, at every damn turn. I will definitely be going to see her ass.

Aloud, she says, "He's a rookie for sure. I'm definitely getting closer to this buyer. I smell a rat and it smells like that stank bitch."

She leaves the room. Then she checks out of her hotel, returns her rental car and leaves. Cherry Jones aka Baby Girl has left the Air Force Base.

She's going back to Houston to check for the next hit. She can make arrangements from her office and fly out to the new destination. There's no reason why she wouldn't be traveling to those destinations. After all, she has always accompanied her husband when he's on tour. She has every reason to be there.

Angela flies back to Houston to help Annie out with the boys while Baby Girl is out of town. She'll rejoin the tour at a later date. Deloris is still out with the guys and she's having a great time. She has missed being able to watch her sons perform and the energy of the shows are electric. The fans are going crazy and this makes her proud. She feels she owes all of this enjoyment to Young D and Baby Girl. For giving her sons a chance to shine and also, for giving her the opportunity to breathe freely without looking over her shoulders for James Lawson. In Baby Girl and Young D's opinion, she's given them all the payment they want by helping their newest artist remain calm. She's doing that by being out of Harrisburg and out of the reach of James Lawson.

Speaking of *James Lawson*, Baby Girl has kept up with his movements. He wasn't allowed to have a bond until after his initial court appearance on the trespassing and breaking and entering charge. Afterwards he was allowed to bail out with the orders, never to return to Deloris Flowers property. He's still not allowed within 100yards of her. That order of protection had been extended for another 12 months. This only made Lawson angrier. He's even more determined to not only find Deloris. But this time, he plans to kill her. That's the words she's heard from her friends and coworkers. On the

146

same day he'd gotten out, he went right back by her job site. This is exactly what Baby Girl had hoped for and she was happy when she heard it from Deloris. James Lawson is on the offensive which will make him easier to be terminated. The police departments tend not to look as hard, for those who murder someone who is a constant nuisance to the community. Baby Girl's putting together a package for James Lawson day. She calls Deloris, who is on the tour bus heading to the next stop. She discusses more of Lawson's habits with her.

"I just want to know if he's dumb enough to bother your brother and his wife?" Baby Girl asks Deloris, "trying to make them tell him where you are? Is he that relentless?"

"He won't asks my brother because he knows he'll beat his ass on site," Deloris says as she chuckles. "But he's always going to try to track me down. Going by my friends houses and my job. Like he's doing everyday. That's why I'm glad I'm on the move for three weeks. Because he'll find out where my sons have moved too, if he hasn't already. And he will come south if he can find a clue as to where to find them and me."

"Oh. So he's a persistent coward too, ha?" Baby Girl asks as she chuckles slightly. Then she says, "Well our security are more than trained to keep him off of our property and away from you. So don't you worry about that part."

"I really appreciate that," she says, "I wish I could have that when I get back home."
Lovely figures this is a good time to introduce to Deloris, a hint about moving south permanently.

"You got a letter here from one of the biggest companies in the country," she says as she smiles, "I have a clue about what's in it."

"A letter?" Deloris asks, "What do you think it is?"

"It's from one of my families largest industries," she

147

says, "It's a job offer. I recommended you. I had to do it for Roderick, Ricky *and* Mike. They want you out of Harrisburg, Deloris. You may not be worried about James but they are. It's all they've talked about since signing and having to leave you there."

Deloris says, "I don't want them to worry about me. But a new job? Where will I stay? How will I handle two mortgages? I haven't gotten my house in shape to sell it."

"Let me worry about all of that," Baby Girl says, "You just enjoy the tour. And when you get back to Houston, we'll come up with some answers. Alright?"

"Alright," Deloris says, "Thank you again. I feel like I'm always saying that."

"That's what family is for," she says, "And you're family now. If you could, you'd do it the same for me."

Deloris says, "You're absolutely right. I would, in a heartbeat."

"Enjoy this peace of heaven," she says, "We'll talk when you get back."

They hang up. Baby Girl adds to the James Lawson package.
I really want you to come and visit me.

****

The tour moves on from Arnold AFB to Chattanooga, then on to Nashville by Wednesday night. After Nashville, he's going into the state of Kentucky. He'll hit Bowling Green on Thursday and Lexington on Friday. He'll play Louisville on Saturday after he attends Gus' funeral in New Orleans, with Baby Girl. It's Wednesday night. Baby Girl is in Houston and planning to visit *The Anatomy strip club*, to see what leads she can come up with. She has asked Angela to go with her to the club.

148

Angela laughs and says, "I *am* twenty one, sister. I can get up in there now. *Legally!*"

"Yes you are legal," Baby Girl answers. "But you can't drink when you're with me. We have to be undercover. I'm checking out something. I really need you to keep this a secret. Can you do that for me? I promise I'm not applying for a job." They both laugh hysterically. Then Angela says she won't tell. She knows about the Young D and Kierra situation. She's known about Danica since day 1. Her, just like their mother Annie, has been on Young D's case about telling Baby Girl the truth for years. Angela is more than willing to go to the club with her sister-in-law. She's curious to see what information Baby Girl is going there to check out. And she hopes it's about Danica. Even though Baby Girl won't say what it is she's checking into. It doesn't matter to Angela. She's going with her to the strip club. She has her back 100% on whatever it is she wants to do while at the club. Angela's hoping she'll beat Kierra's ass again too. But she'll have to see what happens when they get there.

Baby Girl and Angela leave for club, within the hour. Angela is excited and a little nervous too. Nervous only because she doesn't know the reason they're going. Baby Girl's phone rings.

I've been really trying….baby! Trying to hold back this feeling, for so long. And if you feel,…. like I feel baby. Come on! Oh, come on! Oooooo! Let's get it on!

That's Young D's ring tone and she's been expecting him to call her. He has another show tonight.

"Hello," she says.
Young D is calling her from Nashville, Tennessee.

"What's up beautiful girl?" he asks.

She smiles and drives on.

"Hey daddy. How are you? Are you at the venue yet?"

"I'm in my dressing room, smoking my show blunt and sipping on some Cognac," he says.

"Sounds like you got it all together," she says with a smile. "I guess you don't need me on the road, anymore."

"I needs my pre-show, baby," he says intentionally trying to sound sad. "These shows have been whack."

She laughs and says, "That's not what the reports and polls say. Fans are overwhelmingly pleased with the performances."

He says, "It's a set up. They don't want you to come out here to save me. They want me, all to themselves."

"Oh! Is that right?" she asks, still smiling.

"Hell yeah, it's right," he says as he smiles too.

"Well they won't get that," she says as she giggles.

He's in a great mood and so is she. Her and Angela are driving to *The Anatomy*. She exits onto *Old Spanish Trail* and pulls into an empty parking lot. It's just down the street from the club. She doesn't want to pull in Anatomy's lot, for fear of excessive noise and men howling at her and Angela, through the windows. For then, Young D will hear it and ask where she is.

"Nah they can't have my baby girl's dick," he says. "He misses you, Baby Girl."

Young D is feeling very fresh tonight. They haven't been intimate since Saturday morning before flying to New Orleans. It's been 5 days which is a record for them. Since they've been married, they have never gone more than 2 days without indulging. Unless she was on her period, after the birth of their children or his was locked up. Other than those cases, never have they let 48 hours pass without sexing each other.

She giggles and says, "I miss him too. Perhaps I need to come out there and visit him, for a private and stand up meeting."

"You took the words right out of my mouth."

"I'll take something else right out of your mouth too," she says, showing him that she's horny too.

"You can put a few things in my mouth too, baby," he says, "Like those nipples and that pearl tongue. I'll take some of that regular tongue too."

She's engaged in the conversation, so deeply that she nearly forgets Angela is in the passenger seat. Angela shakes her head and rolls her eyes. Then she smiles and looks out her window. She's use to how Young D and Baby Girl talk to each other. They've been together for 11 years.

Baby Girl tells him, "I'm coming out tomorrow. I can meet you in Bowling Green." Then she looks at Angela, "And bring Angela back with me."

Angela smiles and shakes her head, *yes*. She wants to get back to Roderick. Young D agrees and it's settled. Even though his only sister is coming back to meet her boyfriend. He doesn't care. Him and Baby Girl may have a communication problem concerning Kierra and Kid. But their sex life takes a back seat to no one or nothing. She's going to Kentucky tomorrow and she's going to fuck her husband. *Very well!*

Satisfied that she's coming to be seen by him, Young D says goodnight. But before hanging up, he says, "Now I'll call mama's house and talk to my sons before I go to work."

"Okay. They were asking for you, earlier. So do that," Baby Girl tells him, "And tell mama I'll be up there to get them if she needs me too."

He says okay. They exchange I love you, then hang up.

Baby Girl has got to get inside this strip club and see how it goes down. Her and Angela are both nervous. Neither of them have ever been to a strip club. They don't have a clue of what to expect. They arrive just before 10pm. It's still, very early. They're able to pick the table of their choosing.

"We wanna be low key," she says to the bouncer.

He sits them at a corner booth on the left hand side but right next to the stage.

"*Man*. This is low key?" Angela asks with a smile.

The bouncer smiles and says, "You two are some of the prettiest guest we have in here. We want y'all to be seen, just a little bit."

He smiles and tells them he'll be sure and keep the vultures off of them. With that, they say they'll stay. Then they thank him.

Before they can warm their seats, the waitress stops at the their table. She tells them that 2 gentlemen would like to buy them a drink. They decline but Baby Girl asks her to point out the gentlemen and she does.

After she leaves, Baby Girl checks out the 2 gentlemen without them being aware that she's looking. They appear to be regular customers but after the waitress tells the gentlemen they've declined the drinks. The 2 men come over. Baby Girl tells Angela to be cool and follow her lead. It turns out, the 2 guys are part owners of the club. They welcome them to *The Anatomy*.

"We always like to personally thank *every* new patron of our establishment," 1 of them says.

"Do you ladies dance? Or are you just here to be entertained?" the other 1 asks.

"We don't strip," Angela says, "But we dance."

Baby Girl cosigns her. Then she looks at 1 of the guys lapels. He has a picture pin of *Damien*. She looks at the other guy and he has 1, as well. There's a waitress and a bouncer who are wearing 1. In perfect fashion and right on time for Baby Girl, Angela chimes in and asks, "Who is that on those pins?"

Baby Girl says, "I was just about to ask the same thing."

"His name was Jeff. Jeffrey Daniels. He was one of our bouncers," guy 1 says.

Again, perfectly timed, Angela asks, "What happened to him?"

"He was killed two days ago. In a hotel, up in Tennessee," Guy 2 offers.

Baby Girl breaks in and changes the subject before Angela can volunteer any information about her brother just being there, 2 days ago, doing a show.

Baby Girl asks, "How do y'all hire people to work here?"

Guy 1 says "Through auditions, for the dancers. Applications, experience and word of mouth, for the other employees. Our silent partner is from New Orleans. He's heavy in the music business but he put up the money, eight years ago to get us going. He hires the dancers."

Again Baby Girl has to stop Angela from volunteering that New Orleans is 1 of her homes.

"Where is the bathroom?" Baby Girl asks, moving to get up from her booth, "Angela come on and go with me."

Angela follows her to the bathroom. Baby Girl has to get her sister-in-law away from the table. She has to give her the #1 rule about privacy. And at the same time, she has to make it seem as though it's to protect them.

"Don't tell them who your brother is or where we're from. I hear that these types of people be checking your wealth," Baby Girl says, "They'll make us buy up a minimum, if they find out we're loaded." They laugh.

Angela says she understands and she won't volunteer any information to anyone.

Good. Don't get me caught up, up in here. I love you but you've got to learn not to be so friendly. Let others do the talking and you learn from them.

153

As they head back to the booth, they see Kierra. She's going into the back room where the other dancers had gone. They duck into their booth to keep her from seeing them.

Baby Girl says, "We're leaving pretty soon, girl. Before your brother finds out we've been in here. He's gonna kick both of our butts. You know he got folks, all over Houston."

They laugh. Baby Girl is satisfied to know that the dead hit man worked here. She's sure he was sent from here too.

He was hired by the silent partner? A buyer would know Derrick's family. Those guys didn't seem to know me or Angela. The silent partner is the key. Who is he? I wonder was it Gus? Who sent the hit, God Damn it! Surely, the two owners would have recognized me, if they had sent the hit.

She gets a few phone numbers from bouncers and waitresses, for future references. Her and Angela leave before midnight. Kierra had danced once, before they left. Angela acted as if she didn't know her. Baby Girl had watched how Angela watched Kierra. She knows Angela knows this girl's face because she had been at their events. So why didn't Angela make reference to it or her? Why didn't she speak to Kierra?

Maybe they know the same shit that Kid told me. I'll find out, that's for damn sure.

Angela still wonders what it is that Baby Girl went to check out. She doesn't know her and her reaction toward Kierra, was 1 of the things, Baby Girl was checking for. Baby Girl got just want she needed at *The Anatomy*. They head home.

****

On Thursday, Baby Girl and Angela met the bus in

Bowling Green. Young D and Baby Girl end their loveless streak with a romantic lunch in his suite. She continues on to Lexington with them, on the tour bus. Deloris seems like a totally different person, away from Harrisburg. Baby Girl brought the letter and gave it to her. Deloris reads it and realizes she's being offered a job at Morales enterprises, in Houston and New Orleans. She can pick which 1 she wants. Baby Girl tells her, she can live in 1 of the homes on their property, in either city and all she'd have to pay is her monthly expenses. Or she could help her find a home, now or whenever she decides she wants to look for one. Deloris is excited about being near her twin sons and her nephew. She's excited about the high 5 figure salary she's being offered, as well. Baby Girl seems sure she'll take 1 of the positions.

****

Today Baby Girl and Young D fly to New Orleans. It's early Saturday morning, the day of Gus' funeral. They attend the funeral but have to get right back on a flight. They have to meet the tour bus in Louisville before 8pm.

Before leaving, Baby Girl grabs 12 more files to review while she's out with Young D and the labelmates. Kid was at the funeral. He and Six Nine come to the manor before Baby Girl's flight. Her and Kid meet in Don's office.

"So Kid. You've been wanting to do some work. Are you still up for it or not?" she asks him.

She is determined to make him believe she's comfortable being around him. She wants to appear unshaved by what he'd said to her and Danica. So far, it's working. He expected her not to speak to him, at all.

"Yeah. What you got?" Kid asks.

155

She passes him 1 of the 4 hits Gus had shopped out for and she isn't going to touch either 1 of them. She has removed any and all resemblance of a Morales hit, from the packages. She feels like these were done as set ups anyway. Now, she's going to see if they really are. Based on whether or not and *how*, Kid acts on the 1 she has handed him. She tells him, she has a flight in 2 hours and they have to get going. Kid takes the package. She shows him out, then locks the office. Her and Young D say goodbye to her brothers. Charles drives them back to *Louis Armstrong international* and they fly out to Louisville.

CHAPTER   TWENTY SEVEN
DIRTY RAT

From the tour, Deloris calls her brother and tells him to hire the movers. She's going to take the job in Houston so she can be closer to her twins and her nephew. Her brother likes the idea and even ask, if he and his wife can find employment too. Deloris mentions it to Baby Girl. She tells Deloris to let her brother know, she'll put in a recommendation. She also says, whichever moving company he hires, needs to be able to do the moving in 1 day. The same day the huge truck comes, it needs to take all of Deloris belongings at that time. She says this because she knows James Lawson will still be stalking the house. When they fly in with Deloris, it's only going to be for 1 day and if they left orders with the movers, James would surely show up to terrorize them. Baby Girl has suggested they have the police there on moving day, as well. But she isn't insisting on the police.

"Just for protection," Baby Girl says, "Because they'll keep a car or two, around the house until we leave. But not for more than a day."
Deloris' relays the info. Her brother says he'll take care of everything and the movers will be there when they come in. Satisfied that his sister will have a new start, he thanks Baby Girl for all that she's done.
As he laughs, he says, "But I still want that recommendation."
Baby Girl tells him, she'll do it as soon as she gets Deloris settled. They hang up.

Then Deloris calls her job and puts in her resignation. She tells them, she's forwarding a letter by *Express Mail* and it should arrive in 2 days. By the last day of the tour, she has found a seller for her house. There will be a potential buyer coming by, on moving day.

"Everything is falling into place," Deloris say as they head off to the venue for the last show of this tour.

****

This leg of the Midwest tour ends. Baby Girl, Young D, DeJuan and *The 717 Boys* fly back to Harrisburg with Deloris, to meet the movers. The buyers come by in the late afternoon to look at the house. They love it and want to buy. Most of the furniture is packed and they're cleaning the rooms as the furniture is taken out. There are 2 police cruisers assigned to the house while the movers are here. This is the safest Deloris has felt in years. While she guides the movers and throws out what she doesn't want to take, Baby Girl is building more to her package for James Lawson. She has his address from court records and she's going to smoke him out as soon as Deloris is settled. Deloris had told her that James would stalk her, all the way down south if he had a clue of where she was. So Baby Girl is going to see to it that he gets a clue and a free plane ticket too. So she can light his ass up like a 4th of July sparkler. She'll set it up and make it look as if he's won the ticket. But the clues on Deloris' whereabouts are going to come from a fake enemy who just "Wants to see her get what she deserves, for leaving him."
He won't have 1 iota of an idea that the demise my clue will be seeking, will be his.
They get the house completely emptied and cleaned. Baby Girl tells Deloris to leave her car there, overnight. Her and Young D are going to stay at the house and put her in a hotel until tomorrow morning's flight. Deloris agrees.
Baby Girl and Young D drop her and the boys off at the hotel. Then they drive back to the house, as they had done the

last time they were here in Harrisburg, Pennsylvania. Baby Girl is hoping to see *Deloris' pain in the ass*, on this trip too.

"I'm so glad Deloris decided to move," Young D says, "And I'm glad we have a house ready for her too."
Baby Girl says, "So am I. She's got five bedrooms. Plenty of room for her brother and sister-in-law too. That's if they want to come down early."

"Rod, Rick and Mike are gonna stay with her," he says, "So that really works out."
They're cuddled in front of the fireplace on a pallet in the now, empty house. They enjoy a nice little candlelight dinner of Chinese food with some stimulating conversation. They'll get to the heavy discussion when they're back in Houston. Baby Girl's mind is on extra work. She's expecting James to show up, again tonight. She knows how persistent he is and she's hoping for a close encounter of the *last* kind. She doesn't *quite* get her wish.

Her and Young D enjoy each others bodies. Then later, as they cuddle and keep each other warm, James Lawson shows up. Neither of them see him. They know he's been there because he leaves a message that no one in the neighborhood could miss. He sets Deloris' house on fire while Baby Girl and Young D are still inside.

They're able to get out and move Deloris' car, just before the flames take over. It's a good thing they wasn't asleep yet. But they were still undressed. They had just enough time to get dressed, grab their things and hop into the car. Then pull it out of the garage and into the street. The fire department was there as they were pulling the car out. They was able to put out the blaze. The good news is the house didn't burn to the ground but it may as well had. More than 50% of it is burned beyond repair.

Deloris and the boys show up just as the flames are contained and the house is still smoldering. Deloris cries while her sons console her. She cries for more than an hour. She had lost her husband while living in this house and she raised her twin boys from birth here, also. She has a lot of memories in this house.

As she cries, she says, "Thank God I got all of my stuff out today."

"That's why I suggested you get the movers to get everything, in one day," Baby Girl says, "I had a feeling he'd come back and try to end your happiness. He'll get his."

"He damn sure will," Young D says, "If he brings his ass out in the opening and stop hiding, to do his dirt."

Roderick adds, "Like the bitch that he is. That motherfucker is a punk ass bitch."

"He tried to burn us up while we slept," Ricky says, "He thought my mother was in there. I'll kill that dude. I swear to God, I will."

As she looks at Young D, Baby Girl says, "I would too."

Young D can see the disappointment in her face. He realizes she was hoping to kill him tonight.

"I'll get my chance," she whispers to him as they all head to back to hotel.

They have to get packed for their early morning flight. Deloris' brother will sell her car, from his yard. Roderick and Ricky have already bought her a brand new *Mercedes*. It's waiting for her in the garage of the 5 bedroom home on Young D and Baby Girl's property. She will be thoroughly surprised.

They arrive at the airport and go through security quickly. Lovely had their driver make airport security aware of how delicate Deloris is and what she's been through in the last 24 hours. Security gets them through to the secure area in a hurry, as they watch for anyone fitting James Lawson's description. Baby Girl wasn't asking them for all of that. But her trusty 9mm is tuck away in her checked luggage. Young D had told her that if James Lawson had shown up. Him, DeJuan and the 717 boys would've beat his ass to death. They all enjoy a laugh until their flight is ready to board. Deloris breathes a sigh of relief when she heads to the tarmac.

"I think things are going to work out just fine," Deloris says as they board the flight.

"I'm counting on it," Baby Girl says as she winks her eye at Young D and they smile.

They board, take off and arrive back in Houston, on time.

The next week is spent getting Deloris moved into the biggest guest house. The 1 with a living and a spacious family room. Her furniture arrives. They get all of it placed for her, as well. DeJuan and DJ Debo move into Young D and Baby Girl's house. Them, along with the 717 Boys had been staying in the house which Deloris is getting now. Deloris will start her new job, 1 week from Monday.

****

For Baby Girl's birthday, Young D throws her a huge party. She turns 25 years old. Derrick gives her a diamond necklace with a 15 carat diamond and pearl pendant. She scolds him for spending so much money on a gift for her.

"You're my wife, Lovely," he says, "You know I always have spoiled you."

After saying goodnight to their party guest, they have a grand night at *The Crowne Plaza hotel* in downtown Houston. DeJuan is left in charge of their estate, once again.

Kid didn't call Baby Girl for her birthday. Nor did he send her a gift. Six Nine attended her party, along with the rest of her brothers. In fact, Gee Dog and Geezy are still here. Baby Girl hasn't heard from Kid since she handed him the package prepared by Gus, days ago. She still hasn't told Young D that she suspects Kid of being the buyer of the contracts on him either. They've been going through the motions and waiting for the best time to have their revealing talk. Also he still doesn't know that she knows about Danica. He still doesn't know that she knows about the meeting in the hotel room at the Drake. But he knows she knows something. Because she has asked him, repeatedly, "Are you sure there isn't something that you want to tell me about San Francisco? Or something about anything?"

His answers have always been the same,

"Yes I'm sure," and "No, I don't."

They'll continue going through the motions until time permits them to have a real conversation. 1 where she can take time and explain the formula's on her work computer, to him. She wants to show him the ins and outs of how marks are set. How she is able to trace them and how she goes about setting 1 in motion. Then she can better explain to him, how hits had been set on him. Especially the 1 *she'd* received. The 1 totally shopped, purchased and arranged by her own family. In the name of *The Organization*.

Baby Girl and Young D return from the Crowne Plaza hotel the next day, looking fully flushed. It's figured they were up all night talking and fucking. Only the latter guess is true. They didn't talk about anything important because the computer wasn't there.

They arrive home to find out that James Lawson had

162

contacted Deloris' brother. Deloris tells them when she called her brother to give him her updated information. He told her he'd seen James, today. He said as he was leaving his place of employment, James approached him and asked him where was Deloris and where did she move too. He said he grabbed James and started whooping on his head but their security broke it up. He also said James left a chilling message with him. He said he knew she had moved away to be with her twins. And he knew her twins was traveling with that rapper, "MC Young D." He also said he would find her, no matter where she went. And if he can't have her, she won't be with anyone else.

That's exactly what I was hoping for. I think it's time to give him a little hint.

****

2 weeks later, Tunisia arrives from Philly. She's excited about seeing her father. Sammy and Kenya came with her. They want to visit Teddy, as well. The 2 of them, Tunisia, Young D and Baby Girl visit Teddy on the 20th as planned. Baby Girl and Young D bring Lil Man and Don P along so they can meet their other uncle. Teddy has made Tunisia a gift for her 9th birthday. Teddy's birthday is today. He turns 33. Him, Lovely and Sammy discuss their memories of their paternal father Big Dog Roger Walker. They have a great visit and takes lots of pictures. While there, Baby Girl confirms the show date at the facility. It will be the week between Christmas and New Year's. December 28th is the date. There are still a few kinks to iron out but the show at *Centennial Correctional facility* in Canon City Colorado, is a done deal. The benefits are better for Young D then the prison facility. He gets a huge tax write off for the year 2007. Baby Girl loves that part.

163

They return to Houston and prepare for Halloween. Annie has gotten costumes for Lil Man, Don P, little Corleone and Jordan. Young D and the crew will have to go back out for the 2nd leg of the Midwest tour, in a few days. They'd done Missouri, Nebraska, Arkansas, Kansas and Oklahoma, after leaving Kentucky. They still have to hit Ohio, Michigan, Indiana, Illinois, Wisconsin and Iowa. Then they'll hit the southern states between Thanksgiving and Christmas.

But this week, Baby Girl and Young D are planning to have a real talk about the communication problems, they'd experienced down in New Orleans, a month back. It's past time they iron out these confusing nicks which are causing a hiccup in their day-to-day lives. Halloween night presents the perfect time for that much needed talk.

Annie and Angela take the kids trick-or-treating. Young D and Baby Girl are home alone. Feeling he hasn't another minute to spare, Young D goes into his safe and grabs the express package envelope he'd gotten from that PO Box. He hands it to Baby Girl.

"That's what I got in the mail, right there," he says, with a desperate look on his face.

He shows her the part where he was instructed *not* to mention *anything* about the noon meeting.

Secrecy is the key.

"Now baby I'm not gonna lie. I was wondering if the chick in that picture was the one holding the meeting," he says, "I wanted to know why it had to be a secret. And why I had never seen or heard of her. I wanted to know who she was."

"I've seen her," she says, "at The Anatomy. She's a waitress there."

"What are you doing at The Anatomy?" he asks.

"Working. Doing research for my work," she says, "I'm

164

glad to know you don't go there. Thanks for not knowing this girl."

"You're welcome," he says, "But what kind of work were you doing at the strip club?"

He inquires about it strongly. He wants to know what the strip club has to do with her profession.

She says, "The last hit on your life. It was from a bouncer, *Damien*, who was employed there. I found the information on daddy Don's computer when we were in New Orleans. Before the Arnold Air force base show. So I flew into Chattanooga, checked into Courtyard, same one with the crew and you. I saw you guys in the hotel bar before sound check. The hit man was there too. Watching you."

"*Damn*," is all he can say.

"I got acquainted with him. He was ex military, so his base credentials allowed him to go all over the base," she says, "He was set up nice. Had lots of weapons and I took them all. Then I popped him in his dome, checked out and flew home. That's when I got Angela to go with me to the strip club."

"*Damn*. I had a feeling when they said they found a man dead. They was sweating the *hell* out of us and you didn't tell me shit."

"Not on the phone, I couldn't. I knew not too," she says, "And I couldn't stay there. Not and risk being found there with gun powder burns on my hands. So I flew home. But his name was going by the name, Damien. He was sent from that strip club. He had matches in his pocket from that club. So Angela and I went to Anatomy. We went the night that you were in Nashville. I was talking to you on the phone and we decided I would meet you in Bowling Green."

"Oh that night?" he says, "I was missing you, so much. I was just glad to hear your voice. I wasn't checking to see if

165

you sounded distracted. I was just glad to be talking to you and getting answers that were in complete sentences."

They laugh.

Then she tells him all of the employees at Anatomy were wearing a pin with Damien's picture on it.

She says, "But they was calling him, Jeffrey Daniels."

She tells him she doesn't think the employees knew at all of what he was up too. Nor what he was really killed for. But she thinks the silent partner knows everything and the silent partner is the 1 behind the hits on him. She stops just short of telling him who she really thinks the silent partner is.

"And the silent partner is from New Orleans. I thought it could've been Gus. That's all I have, so far. That's all I can really share. But more is coming, sweetheart. I promise."

"Hits? On me? Since when?"

"San Francisco. That's what that noon meeting was suppose to be. Me killing you," she reveals to him.

He's shocked. He's totally confused now. She breaks it down for him and tells him about the whole episode. From the voice scrambled first call. To the 2nd canceled meeting at The Drake.

"It was all a set up," she says, "There never really was a deal honey. It was an assassins game."

"How did you get a hit on me, Lovely?" he asks.

She tells him Gus gave it to her when they returned from their honeymoon cruise.

She says, "It had no description of the mark. Just the date of termination, company cell phone, a voice scrambler, hotel room number and a fake name. Room three twelve. Right?"

"Yeah. That was it," he says, "That was the room I went to and waited and waited. But no one ever showed. So I left a note."

"My key to the room was delivered to the front desk at

166

the Prescott," she says, "I was there, in the hallway. Then later, in the room."

"*What*?" he asks, "*Where*?"

She tells him, she was there and how he passed her in the hallway with 3 Japanese men. She tells him, she was the hooker. The long legged hooker in the hallway being swooned over, by 3 men half her size. They giggle shortly.

He says, "Damn. I knew those legs looked familiar. But baby, I wasn't trying to stare at no hooker….., that woman…., well, at you. *Wow*. How did I pass by my own wife and not know her? You said you was in the room too? How? Where?"

"I came in, right after you went in there," she says.

She tells him she came in the room after he turned off the shower and she took the note he'd left for the unseen CEO. Young D is still in disbelief. She shows him the note.

"Isn't this the note you left?" she ask as she unfolds the piece of paper from the hotel Drake stationary note pad.

He takes the paper from her hand and reads it.

To the mysterious CEO. I showed up early for the private meeting but you never came. I guess I'll see you at 4pm. Very disappointed, MC Young D aka Derrick Blake! ☹

He can't believe she has the actual note that he wrote. Even more, now he believes she's correct about a hit on him.

"Where was you hiding at?" he asks.

"That closet outside of the bathroom with the golden goose floor lamp, next to it. I even sent you a text message from the closet," she says.

He's convinced she was there but he's still amazed at how easily he'd fallen victim to a hit on his life. He always prided himself on being the protector. The 1 who looks out for them and their sons. Their family and friends. She has always told him the killer-for-hire industry preys on that *very* thing. So

167

they'll create packages that go at your very strengths, your core beliefs or your chauvinisms. She also tells him most marks are personal. When it comes down to it, they are. Even if it's 1 about saving New Orleans from land developers or what have you. The bottom line is always about money for someone and that's personal. Now, he wants to know who marked him.

She says, "I still haven't found out yet. But that person who set this one up with Gus is moving on his or her own now. Because this hit with this guy from Anatomy was entered after Gus was dead. He was planning to hit you at the show."

Young D listens intensely now. He wants to understand her methods. He's starting to see how much she does love him and wants what's best for him, as her husband. Then she tells him that Kierra and her friend came up to the room, as well.

"They had a key to that room too. After you left, they came up and went in. They came right back out and was like, *'Why didn't they have a romantic afternoon together?'* I don't know what they were talking on but it was clear to me, they didn't know about the hit. Or it didn't seem like they did. And both of them work at this strip club. I still think it's the silent owner from New Orleans. I'm working on finding out who he is while protecting your life, *my son's father's life*, at the same time. I don't think these two strippers was in on this hit. Not to harm you. But who knows? I'll tell you one thing. I will. *Soon.*"

"Who was with her? Trina? The one who came to the events?" he asks.

"Yes. That's the girl but how did they get to San Francisco?" she asks.

He says, "Hell if I know. But I do know their broke asses can't afford to travel, like that. Neither one. It was probably some John they've been fucking around with. How about you ask your brother Kid. He's all in with them and the club too. When

168

I first said that to you before. It was for a very good reason, Lovely."

She says, "I know it was. I really do believe that it was. And if I find out who paid for them to travel and who paid for that room. I'll have the buyer. I'm sure of it," she says with a confident smile.

He catches himself, after putting her onto Kid. He doesn't plan to say another word. Not after he realizes by mentioning Kid, he has put her on to his own little secret. If she goes to question Kid, in his defense. Then Kid, being an avid hater of his, will surely tell her about the child he has with Kierra. Young D doesn't know Kid has already told her that part. He's hoping Kid won't tell her. He's thinking that surely Kid wouldn't break his little sisters heart like that. Even if he does hate him, for whatever reasons. He may not like him but he loves Baby Girl. Or so he thinks. But he does know with her finding out her only love has fathered a child with another woman, will break Baby Girl's heart. But Baby Girl already knows about the child with Kierra. She doesn't have the heart to tell her husband, she knows. Not until she has exhausted every other possible avenue to clear him. She already knows that look he has on his face, right now. He's nervous about the fact that he has told her to challenge Kid. He knows Kid doesn't like him. But he doesn't have a clue of just how much he hates him. Nor does he have any knowledge of any involvement Kid may have with *The Anatomy*. Baby Girl doesn't know that yet either. But she's watching her husband as he fidgets. She knows he only does this when he's nervous. And she has a good clue of what it is, that he's nervous about.

I don't have the heart to tell him about the little girl. He looks so nervous, right now. Let me let him off the hook, for now. I'll know all I need to know before we discuss an outside kid.

169

"Let's go into my office, daddy," she says, "I need you to see how your termination packages roll up on the network. You may have some clues that'll help me break this thing wide open. You asked to be involved. You are *now* involved."

He does just that. He follows her into the office. She turns the computer on and pulls up the locator. They spend the better part of the evening going over the network. They spot 2 upcoming dates for new hits on him. She looks at him.

She says, "I'll get the jump on these hits. It may be the Pantango's. They might be trying to end the Morales reign. They probably think I'm training you."

"You're going too," he says, " I need to be ready for all this type of shit."

She smiles and says, "I may do that, one day soon because I am allowing you to see my computer. But for now. Trust me, Derrick. You're safe. Even if I'm not there or you don't see me there. Trust me and don't ask me anymore. But you are safe. I'll always be there. Even if you don't know I'm there."

"Like Arnold Air Force base?" he ask as he kisses her on the cheek.

"For sure. I'll never let anybody take Man and Prince's daddy from us," she says, "They'll have to take me first."

"Damn. I'm a made man," he says as he peers over her shoulder at her computer desktop.

He stands behind her as she sits in her office chair. He plants kisses on the back of her neck. She shivers and smiles. They get back to the network, for now.

"The buyer has figured out that the Anatomy dude, Damien Glover is dead," she says, "See these packages here with your name on *this* line? They're new. One is set for Indiana. The other one for Iowa. They're trying to make it look like a hate crime. Same way they did with Epiphany

170

Douglas, *DeJuan's only girlfriend*, some years back. There's another thing, daddy."

"*What*?" he asks.

"Whomever is setting these marks up don't know about the network. Because they would know I have a visual of it. Now that Gus is terminated," she says, "A pro would never do that. So it's not the Pantango's. This buyer is not a pro. It's not a key family's network doing the packaging either. There is no crest. This is someone who was allowed access. Just as I'm allowing you access. Which is why it's forbidden. I have faith that you wouldn't violate this trust, Derrick. Or I could be termed as a rogue. Another thing that could get me terminated. So this person is emotional. They may or may not be doing this to set me up. That part I don't know yet. I don't know if the buyer is that smart but Gus wasn't. Or he would still be here. My guess is, the buyer isn't either. It's my job to put a stop to this. And him or her."

She catches herself. She doesn't want to give him the impression that she has a person in mind. He looks at her. He fights off the urge to ask about Gus' demise. He's certain she was involved. But the need to know the details are killing him softly. He decides not to ask. He knows she will tell him when the time is right. Who is trying to kill him every single day, takes precedence over how Gus had died anyway. How he's going to stay alive, is what he's concerned with.

"Derrick you are my first, my last, my everything," she says, quoting the now deceased *Barry White* as she mimics *Chris Tucker* in *Money Talks*.

They smile as she continues, "You are my first and only love, Derrick. That's the best insurance policy a person can have."

"I wouldn't have it any other way, Lovely Blake," he says.

171

They kiss for the next minute. He takes his tongue in and out of her mouth, down to her neck and breast. He's heading south when the house intercom comes on.

"The boys are back with their candy! Come let them know what they can have to eat, tonight!"

It's Annie shouting from house intercom, just outside of the door. She wants them to come to her house to see and separate, their 2 sons treats.

"We'll finish later," Baby Girl whispers to Young D.

"Can I bring some treats to bed too? he asks, being silly. They're giggling as they meet Annie at their front door. The 2 of them ride back up the driveway to her house.

DeJuan and the labelmates had gone out with them to get trick-or-treat candy too. He has been on guard tonight, as usual. While Baby Girl and Young D are gone to Annie's house to sort candy. He has to get the guys in line and ready to hit the studio.

"We head out tomorrow, brothers," he says, "Let's get to the studio and get busy."

The guys go to the house studio at Young D and Baby Girl's home while their bosses are gone.

Derrick and Lovely help Annie and Angela pick through the huge bags of candy the 4 boys have collected. Man is demanding he get to eat all of his *NowandLaters* and *Snickers* bars. While he makes his case, the adults chuckle.

Lil Man says, "I need to eat these ones and these ones, right there."

After noticing he's getting a laugh, he becomes more animated. Just another evening with the junior version of Derrick "MC Young D" Blake Sr. Suddenly, Baby Girl's cell phone rings.

"It's just me against the world…oooo, oooo…….it's me against the world baby…ohh ooohhh….I got nothing to loose…….it's just me against the world…….stuck in the game…….me against the world baby….."

Her cell phone rings and cuts off the laughter. It's someone calling from Morales Manor again.

"Oh boy. What now?" Young D asks as he looks at his wife. He asks, "Should I answer?"

"No. I got it," she says, expecting this call to be good news. She answers, "Hello?"

It's Alfred calling to tell her that Kid has been called in for questioning.

He says, "Kid has been implicated in someone's murder in the seventh ward. He hasn't been charged yet. They're just asking him questions."

"Do I need to come?" she asks.

He tells her no and says, "If Kid needs anything. We'll be here to handle it. If we need you to come. We'll call you back."

She says okay and they hang up.

Then she shares the news with those in Annie's kitchen.

"Kid has gotten caught up in someone's murder, out in the seventh ward," she says, her face non expressive.

"Every time that phone rings from the Manor, it's bad news," Annie says.

"Not necessarily," Baby Girl says as she smiles.

Young D winks his eye at her and smiles too. At this moment, he knows without a doubt that his wife is on his side, when it comes to Kid. This means the world to him. He appreciates her for loving him, unconditionally too. To prove his worth, he has now decided he's going to tell her all about Danica, at their next sit down. He can't hold it in any longer, anyway. She loves him and he loves her. The Don and Wanda had told them they

173

were meant to be. Their love had been blessed by both sets of their parents and her real father, as well. Love is strong enough to survive any adversity is what Young D had been told. He just hopes it's true!

Baby Girl's mind is on something totally different. Something Young D wouldn't know unless he was in the know, on the pro circuit. Or unless she tells him. The hit that got Kid called in for questioning was apart of the trap Gus had for her. The 4 packages he'd thrown together to side track her from getting to him and the buyer, who was and still is, trying to kill her man. It was also one of the packages that the buyer of the hits on Derrick would've known about. If Gus had been forthcoming with the buyer. That's why she didn't give Kid that little bit of information. She didn't tell him Gus had generated that hit for her. The fact that he took it, gave her a little confidence that maybe the buyer isn't him. But she's still not sure. Because Gus could've been double crossing him too, by not even telling him what and who the hits where on that he was setting her up with. The point is. Gus is dead and has no way of telling Kid anything else now. His only choice, if he wants work in the pro assassins business, is to work through *The Organization*. No other family will give him work, due to the fact that he's associated with the Morales family. Don Morales was part owner of The 3rd Ward Soldiers label. The share that passed on to her and another reason why she could see Kid being angry and wanting her out of the way. But why would he want Young D killed? She doesn't have that reason. She's certain Gus, being the power hungry rogue that he was, never told Kid the particulars of the hits he was doing, as a double cross. But she's sure Kid knew he was planning to set her up. And for his part in it, she has no sympathy for him, whatsoever.

174

November comes in with the labelmates, back on the Midwest Tour. The 1ˢᵗ week of November they hit Ohio. The Cincinnati show rocked but not without some controversy. They did have a little civil disobedience where fans started to a riot with police. But this was caused mostly because of the overzealous Police department. *Katt Williams* will be even more embarrassed when he hears about this 1 and how they treated some of the concert goers. As if the murder of *Tip's* manager and friend, *Philant Johnson*, wasn't appalling enough for the city of Cincinnati. Or cause for Katt to speak out again. The police looked even worse than the criminals they arrested when they get caught trying to entrap fans who were going to the concert. The report on that night, said that a record number of fans were arrested during the concert for having drugs and/or paraphernalia. But a follow up story which came out after they had moved on to the next city, flipped the script drastically in favor of the fans. It wasn't until it went nationwide on *Countdown with Keith Olbermann*, that the nation and world got an inside view of how some police departments operate at urban events. Also in the urban communities. The national story was, plain clothes and undercover officers were selling drugs to ticket holders. Then the uniformed cops, who were patrolling the inside of the venue, were arresting the ticket holders for having the drugs. The story was more of a feather in the cap of MC Young D. Than the scar that the police were trying to put on his show. It gave rise to his song, *The Inside Look*. This song was about how the governments, from local to national, are the real drug dealers. And how they participate in the drug game and profit from it. Which is another reason why his good friend and colleague *Tip better known as T.I.,* along with many others, call it the trap. This story would aid in the firing of 10% of the Cincinnati police force. That was justice enough for Young D, Baby Girl and their entire label.

After Cincinnati, they did Cleveland, Toledo and then Columbus, before moving on to Michigan.

Baby Girl is excited about the Detroit stop. Her and Young D have a faithful friend who is also the chairperson of MC Young D's fan site; *Christina "Shady Lady" Hailey*, who lives there. The label had given out free tickets on the website, for his truest fans. Young D is anxious about meeting and hanging out with these particular fans because they've gone the extra mile. They had written poems and battle rhymes from an online competition, which *Shady Lady* had on the site. The top 4 winners will get to spit their winning verses, on stage with Young D and the labelmates. Another 200 fans from the site with free tickets will fill up the pit. This is a heavily anticipated show which makes Baby Girl wonder why a hit was scheduled for Detroit.

Because the buyer isn't a fan. He isn't a network person either. I was right. I was dead on. This is personal and emotional.

"That's gonna be crazy love in the State Theatre, bro" High Top says.

The entire label are hyped for the show, already. But Detroit isn't until Thursday night. They have to hit Grand Rapids, Lansing and Bay City, before Detroit.

When they pulled into Detroit, they checked into the Marriott and then got off to sound check. Sound check was so hyped because about 75 fans were apart of the set up crew. They were in the venue as the H-Town records label rehearsed for that show. That gave Young D and guys, *killer energy*. They were all looking forward to the show and when they did it. They rocked it. The fans participation was awesome. They

176

brought *Shady Lady* on stage and introduced her and the fan site, to the crowd. Before they could get to Battle Creek, which was in 2 days, Shady Lady had already emailed Baby Girl telling her that the fan site size had tripled from 600 to over 1800 people, in 2 days. That made the entire label excited. They advertised the site on every show, after Detroit. They'll rap up Michigan in Flint and Battle Creek. Before moving on to South Bend, Indiana next Sunday. There are hits on Young D's life, starting again in Gary, Indiana.

Baby Girl has her laptop on the road with them. She knows the hit on Young D is coming up in Gary. They're doing South Bend tonight. Tomorrow is the Gary show. She watches the network closely for any changes. She's watching the people around them, even closer. Just in case, there's a quick change in plans. She's prepared for anything. She tells DeJuan to stay extra close to Young D, out here on this tour.

"Anybody not traveling with us or not on our team, from here on," she says, "is suspect."
DeJuan is more than ready. He takes his job as a rapper, seriously. But his job as best friend and security detail to Young D, overshadows anything else he has going on. Even his own rap career.

"I'm on it," he says to Baby Girl.

****

Back in Houston, Kierra is preparing to go to work when Kid drops by unannounced. She isn't really thrilled to see him but she plays it off. At the same time, she's more nervous than anything. Especially after she knows he wanted her to help him to get Young D killed when he flew her to San Francisco. She will never trust him again. But she doesn't want

177

him to know that she doesn't. He might just set her up too.

"Hey stranger. I thought you forgot all about me out here in Houston," she says as he strolls into her apartment.
Kid had used his own key. Another thing she'd forgotten is that he has a key to her place.

"Not at all," Kid says, "I've just been busy, baby. How's business at the club been for you?"

"It's been okay but not as good as it use to be," she says, "Nobody's dropping them stacks on us, these days. *Shit.* I'm doing good to clear two stacks *[two hundred dollars]* a night."

"We're gonna change all of that, as soon as we expand." Kierra looks at him, in surprise. She hasn't heard about any expansion. She tells him so. He says it's something he's been thinking about.

"So are you gonna invest in Anatomy now?" she asks. She's surprised to hear him talking about her job.

"I been did that," he reveals, "Years ago. But I'm a silent partner. So keep that to yourself. I don't want the gold diggers coming out," he lies.
What he really doesn't want is for Baby Girl to get wind of any affiliation he has with The Anatomy. What has really brought him to Houston is damage control. After he was questioned on the hit he delivered, which was given to him by Baby Girl. He started to think, just maybe she doesn't know how to package. Or maybe she set him up, intentionally. Because she doesn't want him to do hits. She wants them all for herself, was his line of thinking. He's also thinking she has been on the prowl for the buyer of that hit that she was suppose to do on her own husband. She had to be on the right track because she had snuffed out and killed the hit he'd sent from The Anatomy. He has found out she was in his club and was told that there is a silent partner. He doesn't want her to know he's the partner.

Because if she does find out. He knows she's smart enough to figure out that he's behind the Kierra hustle and the hits against Young D.

If Baby Girl knew about his partnership. Then she would figure out that he'd made certain Young D met Kierra. When he'd sent him back to Houston with no music deal to speak of. He figures she'd conclude that this was *all* his doing. It was his plan, all along, to ultimately get him out of his baby sister's life. If she knew this, she would be only half right. But Kid can't afford for her find out about his affiliation to the strip club. That's the glue to keeping him on speaking terms with her. So he's adamant that Kierra doesn't let his secret partnership slip out when talking with anyone else. Not even Trina or Venetta. He hasn't tried to set a hit on Baby Girl since Mark Genolli. Baby Girl's just too damn good for that. He would have to do her, himself. *Probably*. After Young D is dead, he'll comfort her and get her to trust him, 100%. Then he'll get rid of her and take her fortune. That's when Kierra, whom he has always wanted for himself, will finally be able to live the lavish life she's craved for, for all of these years. He can make her, his stick up girl. A prostitute and armed robber, all-in-one. He has hopes of doing that without her wanting to be Young D, as she's hoping. He had promised her, years ago but he already knows that will never happen. He knows Young D is a typical guy. He might cheat, from time to time. But even Kid knows Young D isn't about to leave Baby Girl. Not for any other woman in this world. This is why he wants to kill him. That will be the only way to get him out of her and Kierra's life. Kierra is the woman whom Kid *really* wants and he always has. Framing Young D as the father of her daughter, has been his biggest attempt at trying to separate him from Baby Girl. But he doesn't want Young D to want Kierra. That part has worked out to his favor because Young D doesn't want Kierra and he never has. She's been forcing him to see her, for all of these years, by threatening to reveal their secret.

Well, it's not longer a secret. Still, Baby Girl is with Derrick and still, as he sees even tonight, Kierra wants Derrick for herself. Kid feels she will sell him out before she'll turn on Young D. So Kid has decided he'll kill Kierra too, if he has too, to keep her quiet. But he'd rather not. He's going on emotion with this plan to break up Baby Girl and Young D. But he consistently underestimates Baby Girl's intelligence, maturity and strength. He also underestimates her love for her husband. And vice versa. Kid thinks she'll take his word over her own heart, just because she'd looked up to him when she was 11 years old. He was her protector in the 3rd ward, back then. But she has grown up, big time. Does he think this is enough to constitute Baby Girl choosing his word over Young D's? If so, he really is delusional.

Kid sits on the couch at Kierra's apartment while she gets dressed for work. She's moving through the apartment and talking to him. Anything to avoid sitting down and having face to face contact with him.

"So you're my boss?" Kierra says to him as she laughs. "Well, I need a raise, then."

"Don't start that money hungry shit with me, Kierra," he says, "Your ass is taken care of."

"By D, though," she says, "Not by you."

"Give it time, baby," he says with a devilish grin, "Just give it time."

She's aware he wants to kill Young D. That part, she's not okay with. Kid doesn't know she's figured that out. He thinks she's dumb. She isn't going to risk him finding out that she knows, though. He would kill her, for sure, to protect his secret. She figures it's about money and status because that's all Kid has ever wanted. To be the biggest and richest man amongst all his brothers, peers and in the music business. He had stepped on a lot of toes to get his small fortune. And he would step on his own mother to make that small fortune bigger. His family members weren't exempt, back then. So she figures they aren't now either. She's not willing to help him hurt Young D and that's final. Even if Young D doesn't want her. There is no way she'll ever help anyone to hurt him. She's heard enough of his conversation and she's not interested in the situation he had dealt with in New Orleans and the 7th ward murder. She knows it's something his greed got him into. She isn't even enjoying his company today. She's ready to get him out of her apartment. She tells Kid she's ready for work.

He was going to go to the club, after leaving her place, so he drives her there. While in route, he receives a telling phone call. She can only hear his end of the conversation but she knows it has something to do with Young D plus Gary, Indiana and carrying out a very important mission.

D's on tour out there, right now. He'll be in Gary, tomorrow. I think Kid is trying to kill him out there. Just like I think he was trying to do in San Francisco. Of course, he is. But he knows he can't use me for a second time. Because then, I'll know he's trying to kill him. I'm not okay with that part. I may not ever have him, away from his wife. He might not ever leave her, for me. But still, I don't wish for him to be dead. I have to let him know what Kid's ass is trying to do. I have to find a way to get the word to him that Kid is trying to have him killed.

"*Damn*, you're quiet," Kid says and breaks her thought. He's finished his phone call. They're minutes away from the Anatomy club.

"I was just wondering why you won't just take care of me," she says, "Instead of helping me to get D to do it. I use to think you liked me but now I don't. I think you like D's wife."

"That's ridiculous, Kierra," he says, "I do like you. I like you, so much, that I wanna see you get money from all sources. And we can save mine."

She doesn't believe him anymore. She's seen through his lies. She's heard him on malicious calls. *Twice.* She just wonders now, if he has a plan somewhere that includes her death, as well. She doesn't answer his reply. She only looks at him a smiles.

They arrive at The Anatomy and park. Kierra jumps out and runs in, acting as if she's stressed about having only a few minutes to change.

"I think I was suppose to kick things off, tonight!" she yells back to Kid as she bolts from his S-U-V. "I've gotta hurry up and get my ass in there and get dressed!"

She goes straight back to the dressing room. That's where she hops on her cell phone and calls Corleone.

She tells him about the conversation she'd just overheard from Kid. But she tells him it was someone in the club that she'd overheard from Kid's end and he was talking about a killing D while he is in Gary, Indiana.

"And they said it's gonna happen in Gary Indiana," she says, out of breath. "Please, Corleone. Just get the word to him. You don't have to say it's from me. I honestly don't want him to get hurt and definitely not killed. Okay?"

Corleone says, "Okay."

They hang up and Corleone calls his half brother instantly. He tells Young D what Kierra has just said.

"Okay," Young D says, "Who did she say she heard it from?"

"She didn't say," Corleone says, " As a matter of fact, she didn't even want me to say that she had told me. But I figure if it turns out to be some truth to it. Then she deserves that little shout out."

"Okay," Young D says, "If it turns out to be credible. I'll let you give her a shout out. I still don't want to have shit to do with her. Credible or not."
They laugh and hang up.

Young D relays the news to Baby Girl, who knows this already. But after hearing that *this* news came from Kierra, even without hearing whom she'd gotten it from, Baby Girl thinks of Kid. In her mind, all roads lead to Kid. And in her opinion too. She's going to speak with Kierra, personally. *Face to face.* She knows Kierra is sincerely concerned for Young D's safety now. Especially, after this last tip and she's knows exactly why too. So yes, she's going to confront her but she's going to talk to Young D first. They need to get to this matter of this daughter, he supposedly has with Kierra. They're going to handle it while they're out on this tour. It's time to get this shit and everything else, out in the open. She wants to know why her brother hates him, so much as to tell such a damaging lie on him. She feels like if Kid's hate for Young D, allows him to tell her something, so hurtful and to try and pay for a hit on him. Then his hate could also allow him to want her dead, as well. His hate could also be powerful enough to cause him to fabricate the whole thing.
But apparently Kierra believes it. Or does she?
That's the part Baby Girl hasn't figured out.
Is Kierra on Kid's side with claiming Derrick as the father of her daughter? If so, how can she claim to love Derrick? Or is she being used and fooled, right along with Derrick? She's not on Kid's side. And that probably changed after the San Francisco

183

hit attempt. After I whooped her ass, in Galveston. Maybe I beat some sense into her. She called Corleone with the news of tomorrow's hit. That says she doesn't want it to happen. She wouldn't furl Kid's plan if it was her plan too. So while I've got her on my side. I need to get everything out in the open and dispel this bullshit, once and for all. While getting the truth out, all at the same time.

But at the moment, her husband's life is still on the line. All of these other issues will have to be handled after she dumps this next hit attempt. She'll get with Young D, Kid and Kierra about their triangle, in due time. But first, she has to furl this next attempt on her man, by any means necessary.

CHAPTER   TWENTY EIGHT
A FAMILY AFFAIR

On November 12th, they arrive in Gary in the early Monday morning hours. H-town Records has 6 shows left on the Midwest tour. They will going home for only 2 days and that's for Thanksgiving. After Thanksgiving, H-Town Records will tour the southern states.

In Gary, Baby Girl and DeJuan have their security guys extra thick, around Young D and the labelmates. With all that she has on her mind, Baby Girl still can't sulk and be upset, like the typical wife who's found out a secret her husband has. Her training as an assassin is the reason she's not emotional about it. Her training taught her to always be loyal to your primary and your family. No matter what other entities come into her life. She has to remain vigilant and focused on protecting her primaries. *Her priorities*. At this point, her primary Derrick *"MC Young D"* Blake has a price on his head and a baby on the side. She's only focusing on the price on his head. The latter, isn't life threatening. Her priorities are straight. She must spot the hit man and identify him. Her, Young D and DeJuan are in her and Young D's hotel suite at the Marriott, in Gary Indiana. *Home to the Jackson 5.* She powers up her laptop and pulls up the network. She goes over the package carefully.

The hit man's information should be added by today. It hasn't been yet but it's not even 5am. If it was her job, she would've demanded she be listed at the same time she'd gotten the package. This way, all others takers would know that she's the leader and if they wanted to play on her. She could take care of them early. That would leave her maximum time to prepare and focus on her mark. But whomever this hit man is. He isn't *that* confident. Which tells her, he's nothing like her.

He's a rookie. Probably a gang banger or an ex-con. Someone who has killed before but wasn't trained by the network.

She's thinking, if the buyer were smart, he or she would've tried this hit in Detroit. When the fans had been allowed in the pit, on stage and backstage too.

"The buyer is a rookie too," she says, "As far as setting up the hits. He isn't using an agent. It's someone who was use to working *through* an agent, though. Most likely Gus. Because now, the packages are very underdeveloped. They aren't thought out nor organized."

"They're personal ha?" DeJuan asks.

"For sure and emotional too," she says as she looks her husband. "This is someone who is angry at you, Derrick. For some reason. It's like a vendetta. Like you have something they want or they're afraid that you'll get something they want."

"That's why I think it's one of these niggaz in the business who can't sell shit," Young D offers, "And they mad at me because I'm getting my bread."

Baby Girl agrees with him, to a certain extent. There have been many artists writing beef raps aimed at him. But she's glad he has chosen the high road when it comes to beefing with other artist. He's a mature young black man. He loves his people and he's not going to spend studio hours and money, to trash talk anyone. Still she agrees it could be an industry person but she doesn't believe it in it's entirety.

Kid is an industry person. And if he's the 1 trying to have him killed. Then it doesn't have shit to do with record sells. Kid's label matches Young D's label sells, almost dollar for dollar.

H-Town records has the edge now. But 3rd Ward Soldiers have been in the game longer. Lovely *"Baby Girl"* Walker Blake sees

186

revenue from both labels. Her cuts are the same for each label, as well. Her monthly check from H-Town is only slightly higher than her monthly income from 3rd Ward Soldiers.

"It's about more than that though, Derrick," she says, "You haven't received any death threats. Remember? That's how it was when it's was just about the music business. This is more personal."

DeJuan asks, ""So who has personal beef with you, man?"

Young D can't think of a single person who hates him enough to want him dead.

He says, "I don't have a clue, DeJuan. Lovely says it's someone who wants something I have. I know it better not be her. One of the benefits I have of having a wife who's only been with me? Is I don't have to worry about no jealous ex-boyfriend being mad cause I have her."

They laugh at his comment. And an ex-boyfriend *could* never be it but he's not too far off.

"It could be someone who wants her now, since she's become an heiress," DeJuan says as Lovely looks at him. "Money is the number one motivator, for some people. Those who have never tasted loyalty."

That's it! I'll bet Kid's ultimate motivation is the same as Gus' was. Greed!

****

In Houston, Annie and Angela have heard about the hit out on Young D, from Corleone. Annie is worried, so much. She has to call her son. She catches him in his room while Baby Girl and DeJuan are still there. Annie's worried about the assassination attempt, so much, she wants them to come home, immediately.

187

"I don't think you should do the show," Annie says, "Honey, someone is trying to kill you."

"Mama I have to earn a living for all of us," Young D says, "I've got the best security, it is. It'll be alright. I don't want you worrying."
She says she'll worry anyway and her, Angela and Corleone are coming to join them and bringing the kids too.

"If an asshole is going to fuck with my child," Annie says, "He's gonna have to take us all."
With that, Young D knows no matter what else he says or tries, she's coming anyway. Baby Girl overhears the conversation about plane tickets. She tells Young D, the family account is set up for them for any and all travel. She knows Deloris is not coming back out. She's training in her new job. But Annie is a mother who's concerned about her son and her grandkids father. She's coming. Regardless of what else is going on.

"Lovely said to use the family account for the airline tickets," he says, "Have a safe trip out, Mama. I love you."

"I will and I love you too, son," she says, "I love all of you. That's why I'm coming."
They hang up and he tells Baby Girl who will be coming with Annie. Then Baby Girl calls Danny in Atlanta, right away. She tells him to fly to Houston on the family account and stay with Bruce and Jordan, so they don't have to miss school.

Danny will fly out by 8am. Annie and the rest, their flight doesn't leave until noon which gives Danny time to get to Houston before they leave. Cherry is going to be there too. She has agreed to stay at the Estate with Danny and run things until some of them return. Her 1 hour flight leaves New Orleans at 830am.

"Danny and Cherry are flying to Houston to be there with Jay and Bruce," she says, "I have to get more rooms, so mama Annie, Angela and Corleone will have somewhere to sleep."

"We've got a three bedroom suite." he says, "My sons have rooms."

She rolls her eyes at him as she smiles and says, "Okay. Now we'll need two more rooms for the three of them."

Young D says, "Baby, they wanna stay in our suite. Angela is probably gonna spend her time in Roderick's room, anyway. But with this hit shit going on. Mama has already said, *'I don't want to be intruding but I am going to be wherever you are.'* She's planning to stay in our suite."

Him and Lovely smile. She knows exactly how Annie feels. This is a mother and son bond, so much like the 1 she has with her sons. She agrees they can all stay in the suite with them, "And Angela can come and go as she pleases."

"I don't know about all that," Young D says, still trying to be the overprotective big brother.

All 3 of them smile. Then Young D gets to what's on his mind, more than anything else.

"But we still need to talk about some things," he says, "So we'll need some privacy, at some point."

"I think we do too," she says.

They kiss.

****

The crew have sound check, after breakfast. Baby Girl goes with them and brings her laptop along, so she can keep *up-to-the-minute* information on the hit, at her fingertips. At sound check, she finally receives some information.

"Another one from Houston, ha?" she says, "The buyer must be from Houston. Hmm. I wonder if he is. Or just wants

189

it to appear that way. Who are you *muthafucka*?"
She looks into her database for his identification photo. It pops up, in a instant.

"He is an ex con. Well at least he don't have to worry about going back to jail," she says aloud, "He's going to hell, this time."
She downloads his arrival information.
I've got him!

She tells DeJuan his flight information and they put together a plan and a package for *Hiram Jones*. That's the name of the newest hit man from Houston.

"We need to be there when he gets off the plane," DeJuan says, "We can go to the airport and have a sign with his name on it."
Baby Girl agrees with his idea. But this guy will already recognize her and Young D.

"I feel like this hit is personal," she says, "Whomever the buyer is, is hip to all of Young D's family and labelmates. He may have passed this information on to the hitter, this time. We'll have to catch him slipping. But we're going to the airport. That's for sure. DeJuan try to disguise yourself up, a little bit. You're going to make the initial contact. I just hope he doesn't know you by face."

****

Annie and the family arrive in Indiana, shortly after 5pm. The concierge at the Marriot has ground transportation there and waiting for them. DeJuan is at the airport too. But he's there to meet Hiram, the hit man. He brings along a sign with his name: "Hiram Jones" printed on it. DeJuan is

190

disguised as a chauffeur. He has the Lincoln town car, Baby Girl rented per their package plan, as transportation for Hiram Jones. This will be his final ride, if their plan works out. DeJuan is going to drive Hiram to meet Baby Girl and Young D at the waterfront. Hiram doesn't have a reservation, at any hotel. Baby Girl assumes his plans are to hit Young D outside, somewhere. He's probably planning to hit him after the show, as Young D is leaving. So Lovely plans to give Hiram an up close and personal view of her man before she kills him. She also wants to know who the fuck hired him. She's going to try to get that information out of him before she kills him. DeJuan and Young D are going along on this one.

Meanwhile, Annie and the gang arrive at the suite and get comfortable. She ask where Young D and Baby Girl are, first thing. She's told they're at a meeting with the promoters and will be back soon. She's satisfied with that answer.

DeJuan dials Young D's phone, just as Hiram Jones is walking toward where he's standing. He's holding the sign with Hiram's name on it. Baby Girl told him to do that. With DeJuan's Bluetooth on, they can hear everything that's said without Hiram knowing he's even on the phone. Hiram was expecting a car to be waiting for him. He feels like DeJuan is legitimate. He prepares to follow him to the car. DeJuan reaches for his bag.
"I got it player," Hiram says quickly.
He doesn't want DeJuan to touch, let alone carry his duffle bag. That's a sure sign to DeJuan and Baby Girl, who's listening, this is the right guy. Hiram grabs the bag, himself. DeJuan pops the trunk. Hiram is hesitant about placing the bag inside. He acts like he wants to keep it at arms length.

"I'd rather keep this by my side," Hiram says.

"No passenger is allowed to bring any over sized bags into the car," DeJuan says, "It's just like an airline. If it doesn't fit on your lap or the floor. Stow it away."

DeJuan tells him how it's going to be.

"That's the rules, sir. Take it or leave it."

Hiram doesn't want to be stranded without a ride from the airport. So he reluctantly puts his bag in the trunk and hops into the back seat. DeJuan jumps into the drivers seat and pulls away from the terminal. DeJuan is listening to Baby Girl and Young D tell him exactly where they are. Then Baby Girl, through his Bluetooth device, confirms that Hiram is in the car by telling DeJuan to make small talk with him. Like asking him where he's from and what's the purpose of the trip. The questions chauffeurs usually ask.

"Are you from here?" DeJuan asks.

"No."

"Is this your first time visiting Gary?" DeJuan asks.

"Yes."

"Here on business---"

"Just drive the car," Hiram spits, "Damn the chatter. I just need you to drive me, man. I don't wanna chat."

He passes DeJuan a note with *Allen Whitehill Clowes Amphitheatre* on it. This is the same venue where Young D and H-Town records are performing, in a matter of hours. This is also, all the validation DeJuan needs to know Hiram is the assassin. He drives under an overpass and quickly exits to the docks. Before Hiram notices they've taken a wrong exit, DeJuan stops abruptly. He pops the locks and Baby Girl pulls the door open. She already has her 9mm cocked and pointed at Hiram before he can adjust.

"Get your ass out, Hiram," she says, "Now!"

192

He moves slowly. Sliding towards the open door, as he looks at her. He knows she's got the jump and she can tell he knows who she is and what she does. Without a doubt, she'll have to kill him and the buyer that hired him too. Because that buyer is giving out her valuable trade information. She backs up a foot and gives him room to stand to his feet.

"Move away from the car," DeJuan orders, not wanting to cause any damage to the rental.

Nothing that could throw suspicion their way. Hiram moves from the car. DeJuan searches him.

"He's clean," he says after a minute.

That's when they allow Young D to step out from behind a huge pillar which helps to hold up the overpass above them.

"Pop the trunk, Juan," Young D says immediately.

DeJuan does so and Young D grabs the duffle bag. Then he turns to Hiram Jones.

"When I look through this bag. Am I gonna find information in it which is going to tell me, you came here to kill me?"

Hiram doesn't answer. Baby Girl can see his expression. He knows his game is up.

"I already know you're going to find that info, Derrick," she says, "Because I'm the best at what I do. Finding and execution marks. Check the bag out, so you can make my fuckin day."

She's looking directly into Hiram's eyes. He looks puzzled and caught. She's smiling devilishly. She wants to do this piece of shit, so bad. She can taste it. But she wants his employer's name, first. Young D looks inside the bag.

"Bingo. He's the hit man," he says, "Who hired you?"

Hiram won't snitch. He climbs up. Young D asks him again. DeJuan moves toward him. Hiram still won't give up his source.

"Derrick we need to go," Baby Girl says, "We have a schedule to keep."

"Do his ass, then," Young D says.

She does him with 2 rounds. 1 to his head. 1 to his heart.

They pull all identification from his body and leave him there. Then they drive back to the Marriot.

Baby Girl puts all of Hiram's belongings in her Hug-a-Thug, along with her 9mm. They search the duffle bag completely, before they leave the hotel garage. As they had expected, there is another lead to *The Anatomy*. Kierra's lead was credible but Lovely knew that already. Still, she needs to know just how Kierra is getting her information.

DeJuan says, "Bro, this is someone from home, man."

"Or someone who wants it to look that way," Baby Girl says.

Hiram has stationary from the club. He has several notes written from a tablet with Anatomy stationary.

"He has the venue address on this pad. A photo of the tour bus and one of Derrick. Plus a list of the buildings surrounding the Amphitheatre. He was the one, alright. Let's go."

They bring his duffle bag with them. DeJuan is taking it to his room. They'll pack it for shipping and have it mailed to the manor. They go to DeJuan's hotel room. Baby Girl disassembles the H&K G36 rifle which was in the bag. She's the only 1 who knew how too.

"This is antique military issue. They don't sell these in the hood. I've shot one of these before. Possibly this same one. It does major damage and it feels familiar. I own a few of these through The Enterprise. I inherited them. Hiram's buyer has got some cash and a weapons connect too. Because these kinds of weapons are easily tracked. Only a few people own them, outside of the military. But it's an old weapon, I do believe.

194

Pack this shit up in the box. I have to make a phone call."

She goes to her and Young D's suite. Her sons are there and are happy to see her. She stops, kisses them and plays with them for a few minutes. Until the newness of seeing her wears off for them.

She tells Annie, "I need to make some calls before show time. Then they'll have me all evening, after that."

Annie tells her to handle her business, as she says, "I got my babies. Where is my son?"

"He's right behind me," she says as she dips into the bedroom to call Alfred.

She tells him to check with their arsenal guardians and suppliers.

"I need the run down on a M I [military issue] G36," she says.

She gives him the serial number, for good measure. But a weapon of this caliber isn't going to be hard to track down, as she had told Young D and DeJuan. These aren't usually sold individually. They were made for combat organizations like the U.S. Military. Alfred takes the information and tells her he'll get back to her, ASAP.

"That's a bet. Call me when you can," she says.

They hang up.

Young D and DeJuan arrive at the suite with the package ready for shipping. Lil Man thinks it's a gift for him, as they hand it to Baby Girl.

"Can you get this mailed for us?" Young D says, to throw his mother off the fact that Baby Girl already expected the box. "And man, I'm taking you to that mall, next door and let you pick out what you want. Okay?"

"Okay!" Lil Man cheers.

"Lovely can you get that out, tonight?" Young D asks.

"Of course I can," she answers.

195

She takes the package and calls the concierge. While Young D plays with his sons, DeJuan contacts the security detail and brings them up on how they are to line up for tonight's show. Even with the hit man taken down, they aren't going to relax. They will never relax on Young D's security. Not with Baby Girl around because she won't allow it. Young D is a precious commodity. He is *her* air and he's, "Oh *so* necessary, baby."

Once the package is in the mail, Baby Girl and Young D go into their bedroom for pre-show. They have 3 hours before show time but he wants to talk and so does she.

"I want to get something off my chest, baby," Young D says. "Please hear me out, first. It's not something I believe. But it's what's been told to me and I feel like I should tell you about it. So it won't be any secrets between us."

"You've been told you have a daughter with Kierra?" she asks, shocking him into an abrupt silence. She adds, "Is that what you wanna tell me?"

He's stunned. He had no idea she even knew about this. Yet she has known for a long while. Young D is shocked speechless. Seeing that he's unable to speak, she assumes she's guessed correctly. That's what he was about to say to her. She asks him if he was. He nods yes and looks sad.

"How long have you known this?" he ask her softly.

"Kid took the liberty of telling me, the day after Gus died. At the time, I felt like he only said it to make you look bad because I was grilling him about faulty shit that he's into," she says, "But it does make you look bad. I didn't believe it then. Should I now?"

"No," he says.

"Why shouldn't I?"

He says, "Because I don't believe it. Mama don't either. No one else does. She doesn't look like me or any of us."

"Wait. Your mama or no one else does?" she asks, "Who all knows about this?"

He hesitates, then looks up at her and says, "Everybody."

"No the hell everybody doesn't," she says, growing angry for the first time. She says, "I didn't know. And Kid said this daughter is five years old. Is that true?"

"Yeah."

"Oh Derrick. *Damn*! How the hell could you keep this shit from me?" she asks.

"I wanted to tell you, baby," he says.

"You should have. If you wanted to. You would have." She's calming her emotions, so she can speak clearly.

"I've tried so many times," he tries, "The night at mama's when you was bathing the boys. I was gonna tell you."

"When? Which night?" she asks.

"After Memorial Day? Well. After we came back from Lafayette. And before we went to NYC."

"When I found that funky ass t-shirt?" she asks, "Was that, that bitch's smell on your clothes?"

She already knows it was. She smelled that funky perfume when she whooped her ass, a week later.

"Yeah," he says.

"Don't come with the one word answers, Derrick," she says, "It's time to spit it on out!"

She's heated and though she has control of her emotions. It's noticeable. Still he feels like a weight has been lifted off of him. Now that she knows the only secret he has ever kept. He feels relieved. That may very well change, before this day ends.

"She was blackmailing me," he says suddenly, "Every damn time you left home. She wanted me to see her. I hate that bitch. I made a mistake, baby and I didn't want this shit in the media either."

197

"When did you first meet her?" she asks.

"It was back when I left New Orleans and came back home with no record deal. You was in college. You was always gone or not answering your phone. Having different numbers and all of that. I would try to come visit you. But you would tell me not to come because you had plans for the time I would've been arriving. I thought you had moved on and was seeing another man. Plus your own brother was telling me, you had a man at LSU."

"I didn't have no other man, Derrick. You were my man, *then*. Just like now," she says.
But she's thinking of every word he's said. Something sticks out in her mind as suspicious. She has to say something. "Someone on the inside is feeding her information. Every time I left home? How did she know about every time I left home?"

"No one was feeding her anything. Not from *my* camp," he says, "No one in my camp would ever tell her shit."

"Someone did. What's this other man stuff about?"
He says, "Because you never had time for me and I wasn't use to that. You always wanted to see me before that."

"Before what? *College*?" she asks.

"Yeah. You would tell me if you had plans, ahead of time," he says, "That changed when you was at LSU. Anyway, Kid introduced me and her, one night. He said he wanted me and DeJuan to meet him, about possibly coming back to his label. Or at least that's what he said to me. We met at the Anatomy. He introduced me to her and kicked it with us, that whole week. Even on *that* night, he kept telling me you had moved on. That you found a college boy, who was feeling you. And he was taking you out of town, all the time. He said that was why you never had time for me. When I would ask you why you didn't want to see me. You would say something very

198

important came up and that you had to go out of town. So I thought he was telling the truth. I called the manor. The Don would tell me, you had business to take care of. And that you had more important business which had to be your first priority."

"The other man was and still is, *my profession*."

"I know that now. But back then. I didn't," he says, "I didn't find out what your other priority was, until two thousand and four. Before then. All I had to go on was what your father told me or what Kid was *steady* telling me."

"I've never cheated on you. *Ever*! And if I ever thought you were. I would bring it up to you."

"You didn't about *this*," he says.

She doesn't say anything.

"A lot of the times when I went to her. It was because it got to a point at LSU, where you didn't have time for me at all," he says. "I didn't know what you was doing. Nor what secrets you had. So I was hurt. I thought you was seeing another man and didn't wanna tell me. During that time, Kierra was there. It's like she knew I was down without me even telling her. Just like she knew when you was out of town, without me telling her."

"The child is five years old. We've been married for five years. There is something *so wrong* with this picture."

Although in her mind, she knows that Kid is the link. That's the part that hurts the most.

He says, "I found out about her pregnancy after you and me got back tight again. I had always said if you came back to me. I wanted to marry you. That didn't change because of her."

"It should've made you be honest with me, Derrick. This whole marriage is a lie. My children or not your only children. Do you know how much that hurts me? I've been faithful to you. I've been honest with you. I even broke code

199

and brought you in on the profession, so you wouldn't feel like I was keeping secrets from you. But now. I find out I am a fucking stepmother!? My son's have an older sibling? Oh hell no! Hell no! You are just like my biological father, aren't you?!"

Outside, Annie and the others can hear their argument. Annie puts a video on for the boys to watch, so that they won't hear their parents arguing.

Inside the bedroom, the argument continues.

"Baby. I'm sorry to even be..-"

"She wanted you *every* time I left. Did she have you *every* time I left?" she asks.

He hesitates. She looks at him. For the first time, he can see hurt on her face. He hadn't seen this look since 1996. Since college, she'd become non-emotional. Nothing seemed to phase her. Now, he knows that was her craft. Tonight she isn't an assassin or an heiress or security tech. She's a young lady, a young wife, who's been hurt by her husband and only love, *affairs*. She ask him again,

"Did she have you every time I left?"

"No way. *And* I shut it down," he admits, "I didn't wanna see her at all."

"When did you shut it down, Derrick? When was the last time you was with her?"

"May. When you found the shirt," he says, "That was the last time I fucked with her, Lovely."

"And you lied about the fuckin shirt. You, Annie, DeJuan. All of you are playing me for a fuckin fool!"

"No, baby. We're not-"

"Don't come with that baby, shit. Don't even patronize me. Fuck no! Hell fuck no!" she screams.

"Lovely. Please!" he tries.

She storms out of the room and out of the suite. Saying nothing to anyone in the family area, she gives both of her sons a kiss. Then she leaves the suite and the hotel.

She didn't even pack her bags first. She left with her work tools only. Young D knows this is bad. His mother tries to suggest some things he can do. But he follows Baby Girl.

DeJuan had gone to drop off the rental car. He's returning in a cab, just as Baby Girl is rushing out of the hotel. DeJuan gets out of the cab and she jumps in. Before leaving, she has a message for him.

"I'll call you once I get settled," she says, "Keep your eyes on Derrick, please. I have to be alone for awhile."
The cab pulls away. DeJuan is confused. He looks up and sees his best friend Young D coming out of the hotel.

"She left me. I told her about Danica and she left me," he says, "I told you she would."
DeJuan can see tears welling up in his eyes. He brings him up to his room to calm him down and talk about what he wants to do next.

201

CHAPTER TWENTY NINE
FAMILY FUED!

Baby Girl flies into Houston's *Hobby Airport,* grabs a rental car and drives home. Cherry is still there and so is Danny. She packs a bag of her necessities to take with her to New Orleans. She's going to stay at the manor until she knows without a doubt, who's trying to kill her and her husband. She's still mentally torn about Young D's latest revelation but she's still his wife. His safety will always be atop the list of her concerns. 1 reason she wants to be at the manor is to view The Don's computer. The other reason is to get to Gus' computer. Plus to be close enough to spring a visit on Kid, at a whim.

Her and Cherry get everything in order at the Houston homes. Deloris helps them. It's her day off from work. Baby Girl wants to know how she's adjusting to living in the south.

"It's a lot warmer here," Deloris says, "But my job is great. I have my *own* office and *not* having to look over my shoulders every minute, is something I'll have to get use too."

"You're safe now," Baby Girl assures her. "Even though your boys got you a new car. You still don't have to drive it. You have a driver who's also trained as security too. So you can feel safe *anytime* you're outside of these gates too." Deloris smiles and says, "Security follows me everywhere. Like at my job, if I have to go to the bathroom, he'll go in there first and make sure its safe. I feel like a superstar."

"You are," Cherry says, "You have sons and a nephew who think you are."

"And they want you to be protected like one," Baby Girl says, "That's exactly what we're going to do."

"They're doing *so* well," Deloris says, "I asked them to stay out of jail and do good in their lives."

"And they truly did," Baby Girl says, "That's why I

wanted you to give them something to be proud of and something to settle their minds, at the same time. With you here *and* safe. They can focus on their careers without wondering if your life is at risk."

Deloris smiles and thanks Baby Girl for what has to be the 100th time. She tells them the insurance company has offered her a nice settlement for her home and property. She's going to sell the property and keep the money for her new start in Houston.

She adds, "And if my brother gets a job down here. I'll have some money to help them get here and get settled."

"I think that's a wonderful plan," Baby Girl says with a smile. "I'm looking for placement for them too. But it may have to be at one of the New Orleans companies. We're huge in the New Orleans area."

Before Baby Girl and Cherry's flight to New Orleans departs, Alfred is on the phone calling her with his findings on the H&K G36 rifle.

"It belongs to the manor," he says.

"The gun I took from Hiram was my *own* property?" she asks in disbelief.

"This is true. It's the property of the manor," Alfred reiterates. "I've already received it, unpacked it and double checked the numbers, along with Charles. It was Don Patrick Morales' marine issued rifle."

Alfred has just told her the rifle she confiscated from Hiram Jones, actually belonged to The Don's grandfather.

She says, "So Gus was letting go of any and all of my daddy's property and business."

"He was a rogue who deserved to die," Alfred says, "I am increasingly happier each day, that you are in charge and on the job too. Because you don't believe in second chances when someone has wronged the family. Donnie has to be so very proud of you."

"Well he should also know already, that I'm not nearly finished," she says, "And Alfred?"

"Yes dear?"

"I'm gonna have to contact Emilio," she says, "I have a feeling I've been used as a mercenary, in some cases. The only way I'll know, for sure. Is by viewing files from another family agent's computer. Emilio Pantango will do that for me."

Alfred says, "But if you make contact, he'll feel cornered."

"I'll do it by phone," she says, "And I'll let him know, *immediately*, that this is for the good of The Organization. And Alfred, the Morales name will not suffer. I put that on his life."

He says, "Okay. Baby Girl, you're sounding like Donnie now."

They laugh. He adds, "Oh yes and I have to give you a bit of advice. Only because I've known you, your whole life."

"Okay. You've earned the right too," she says, "You don't even have to qualify yourself to me, Sir Alfred."

"I just want you to check on Young D, daily," he says, "He's worried sick, about you."

"I will. I promise you that," she says, "We'll talk more, when I get there. I'll be back in there, long before the work day ends. I have to see a man about a dog."

She gives him their flight information. He tells her, Charles will be at *Louis Armstrong* to pick them up, on time. She knows that means Charles will be ready to take her to, *just off of St. Claude avenue*, to handle the next *hit man*. They hang up. Baby Girl and Cherry board their flight, on time.

****

In Harrisburg, James Lawson has received a free

204

airline ticket. The ticket *has* to be used between certain dates. But the destination is open ended. It's a free round trip to anywhere in the Continental United States. He thinks he's won it from a mail-in contest, he always enters. But in fact, the ticket was paid for in cash, by Mrs. Lovely *"Baby Girl"* Blake. She knows he'll use the ticket to stalk Deloris. If he knows how to find her. Baby Girl is going to help him with that too. Sort of.

The free ticket isn't the only perk James will receive. At this time, he already has a new pen pal. The new pal says he has known him for a long while. Since the days of his relationship with *that woman who has the twin boys*. The woman who's husband died in a terrible accident, a few years before he met her. The pal also tells him, he knows the woman has left him and forbids him to be in her and the twin boys lives. After he'd helped her raise them. On the last letter from this pen pal, the 1 that came the day before the free ticket. James was told that this pal would have Deloris' new whereabouts. The pal promises to tell him where she has moved too. But the pal isn't able to help him get there. The pal did tell him that Deloris has moved down south. Somewhere in Louisiana or Texas. James is extra excited today because he now has *free travel*.

"Now. All I have to do, is wait for my pen pal to give me the info I need, on exactly where to find her," he says with an evil grin on his face.

He's thinking of how convenient this ticket has made his revenge quest. Baby Girl's hoping he's seeing the ticket as a means to an end. Because once he receives his next letter from her, *disguised as his pen pal*, he'll know a destination to use his free ticket for. It'll be to a place where he'll meet his end. *By necessary means.*

Baby Girl calls to check on her sons, as soon as her and Cherry land in New Orleans. She knows they're up and running around by now. It's near lunch time and it's the next day, after she'd stormed off. Everybody on the tour has been asking about her.

"I'm doing fine, sweetheart," she tells Annie, "I just needed to clear my head, after the talk Derrick and I had. That's a lot to swallow."

"I've been after him to tell you, from day one," Annie says, "I am the one who told him and I didn't find it out until we were about to go to New Orleans for you and him to be married."

"Yes. I know the little girl is five," she says, "The same number of years we've been married."

"That's not my grandchild, though," Annie says, "A mother knows her babies. That little girl does not have my sons blood in her. We had a test done and it said yes. That's the only reason I make him take care of her. But he wants nothing to do with either of them."

"He told me," she says.

"He's being set up. My gut tells me that," Annie says, "Only I don't have the resources to check into it. Do you, Baby Girl?"

She says, "I'll be looking into it, mama Annie. That's my husband and he *is* the father of my children, *only*. I'm gonna prove that. But I don't want him to know I'm doing *anything* to help this go away. I want him to remember this feeling, for a long time. So he'll know not to fuck over me. Ever again. I've been faithful to him, *entirely*."

"I know you have. He does too."

"And I always will be," she says.

Annie says, "You're not leaving him then. Are you? Because

206

I don't want you too. He needs you."

Baby Girl can she's relieved and near relief tears too.

"He's all I know and all I wanna know," Baby Girl says, "There's no way in hell I'm gonna leave and let some trick have the rewards of my years of hard work. But he's gonna have to understand that honesty has to be the key to our relationship. Or I *will* leave. I don't know where I'd go, from him. But I won't be disrespected. Not when I'm being loyal. I don't wanna ever leave, so he has no other choice but to get right." They laugh.

"I hear you, girlfriend and I agree with you," Annie says, "I've always been on your side and I am now too."

Baby Girl says, "I'm still here, mama Annie. Just keep his head on straight, *out there*. And keep my babies smiling. I'll see you sooner than later. Okay?"

"Okay, Baby Girl," she says.

They hang up. Baby Girl and Cherry hop into their limousine and Charles drives them directly to the *MEPS center*.

The newest hit man's name is Kevin Moore. He's a staff sergeant at the *in-processing station* for the U.S. military. He trains other military personnel on how to process in new recruits and get them shipped off to their boot camps and home bases. But Kevin Moore has a side job, as well. That's the 1 which brought his name across Baby Girl's wire. He's a metro police officer, by night. His night job is where he acquired the handle of *hit man*. Sgt Moore is what American media refers to as a *corrupt cop*. Another name for a rogue. Sgt Moore has been keeping the streets free of competitive drug dealers, while getting paid handsomely, at the same time. His handsome pay comes from the dealers who have him on their payroll, *specifically* to thwart out others dealers. In other words, Sgt Moore is a legal street sweeper, doing illegal things for illegal people. For Baby Girl, he's nothing. She has the police chief on her payroll. She had considered turning him in and making a mockery out of both of his careers. But he has to die. She's not the least bit surprise that he would be in the company of her brother Kid. The more she learns about Kid's acquaintances. The more she wants him banished from her existence. Once again, he has underestimated her intelligence. And shown total disregard for her power and authority, when he hired this sub par, beat walking, part time, fancy security guard to go up against her. It's almost unfair to Sgt Moore, to have to give his life for taking side jobs. Only because he hadn't felt that his pay as a protector of America was enough. She can sympathize with his position of needing to supplement his income. But he can't have her husband and the father of her son's, jacket payment as a subsidy. It's sad to have to take out 1 of America's brave ones. But she can't risk leaving him alive. She only hopes he isn't wearing his soldiers uniform when she does him in. That's a uniform she respects, to the utmost. But he isn't doing the honorable thing by that very uniform. Not when he's aiding drug dealers in infesting the streets of New Orleans with drugs. *No way*! Sgt Moore is about to be discharge from the military today. He can thank her for the, otherwise dishonorable discharge he would've received had she turned him in. This way, he gets to keep his honors, pins and medals. Everything except his life. He's going to die today.

Charles pulls the car down Poland avenue and parks. Baby Girl gets out but leaves her hug-a-thug. She'll have to go through several security clearances before gaining access. She's dressed casual and wears a pair of her *Pastry* sneakers. She doesn't want to attract to much attention. She has to get around to Dauphine street to get inside, where she can get access to the parking area. She's prepared to go through in-processing procedures, if necessary. It's noon and she has 6 hours before Sgt Moore expires. She arrives inside and her credentials provided by Alfred, gets her in. She's placed in a group of cadets and future soldiers. They've just announced that lunch will be served at 2pm. Her lead also told her, she had missed her morning sessions and would have to make them up. She says okay. Knowing that her, *as Sharon Nix*, wouldn't be around to complete the process. She feels blessed that the buyer who has also set *him/her* self up as an agent now, doesn't have access to the network. For if that were so, she would only be able to nab potential hit men as they came after her husband. Because the network would allow for other pro's to see the mark's information. She's thankful that this buyer of death marks on her husband, isn't backed by any family. Whomever he or she is, they're still going to die, as well.

****

The tour is in Anderson, Indiana today. Young D had barely gotten through last nights show in Gary, after Baby Girl left, so abruptly. He's been down every since she stormed off.
"*Derrick. Son.* You're gonna have to eat lunch," Annie says as she shakes him to wake him up.
He didn't attend the after party in Gary which was given in his and H-Town records honor. Instead he had told the others to attend, if they wanted. But the bus was leaving for Fort Wayne at 1a.m. That was only 1 hour after the show ended. *The PA, The 717 Boys* and everyone from *The Kilo Clique* except Young D, attended the party for about 30 minutes as the bus waited outside. Young D signed autographs on his tour bus until the others returned. They arrived in Fort Wayne at 4am. Annie

209

and Angela handled the check-ins. The guys had partied, all the way in. While Young D spend his time in the bus studio, going over new tracks. As soon as he got to his suite in Fort Wayne, he got his sons and went straight to sleep.

"I'm not hungry, mama," he says as he rolls back over. He had ordered both of his sons, back to bed for a nap, around noon. He hasn't been up. He had skipped breakfast and sound check. It's 2pm eastern time now and time for lunch. Annie has to make sure the kids eat. She wants her son to eat, as well.

"I'm gonna get Man and Prince up, so they can have lunch," Annie says, "Son, I want you to try to eat something too. I'm bringing a plate back in here, for you."

"Alright, mama," he says as he pulls the pillow over his head.

She grabs her grandsons and leaves the bedroom.

Angela takes Prince and heads to the bathroom to get him dressed for lunch.

"Corleone will you get Derrick's plate and take it in there, for him," Annie says, "And tell him, *I said*, he has to eat half of it. Because he didn't eat anything for breakfast."

"Yes ma'am," Corleone says, "He hasn't been in a good mood since Baby Girl left."

"I know. But he's gonna have to shake it off, so his son's won't feel this split," she says, "They're gonna be ready to wrestle with him, after they get full."

"Like usual," Corleone adds and laughs.

Annie takes Lil Man into the bathroom to get him dressed while Corleone takes his half brother his lunch plate.

****

Baby Girl makes her way to the door that allows access

to the parking lot. She spots Sgt. Moore's vehicle. It's in a secured parking lot. She has an ID to get her out there. She takes her time and swipes the badge provided to her by Charles. Alfred had sent all the tools she'd need to complete this package. She accesses the parking lot and attaches a tracking device to Sgt Moore's Ford Taurus. Then she makes her way out of the center and heads back up Dauphine to Poland and hops back in the limousine. Cherry is there with the monitor.

"It's on and already transmitting," Cherry says.

"He gets out of there at five o'clock," Baby Girl says, "He expires at six."

"That gives us just under five hours to work with," Charles says.

"Let's see if he leaves for lunch," Lovely says, "His car hood was ice cold. Which tells me, he hasn't driven anywhere since coming to work. But they do offer lunch and dinner, on site. I need to pick up some things for me to have at the manor. Let's just watch the monitor for the next hour and see if he leaves for lunch. If he doesn't. We'll run out to *Read Blvd*. I can get what I need from the *Eastside mall*. We got him tracked so we can catch up to him, even if he does leave."

Charles asks, "Do you wanna get him for lunch or after work."

"Whenever it's convenient," she says, "Whichever unfolds first. All I need is one minute with him. I wanna know if he'll give up the buyer."

"Then we'll wait here through lunch," Charles says and they do just that.

****

Young D picks over his lunch, managing to eat barely
211

half. But it's enough to satisfy his mother. DeJuan tells him he's secured a 2nd slot for sound check and he has to make this one. Whether he wants to or not. Young D says okay. He lays back on his bed and stares at the ceiling.

"She's not gonna stay gone, partner," DeJuan says.

"What makes you so sure?" Young D asks.

"Because she loves you. Nobody in the world has more love for you, than Baby Girl does. You may think she's not around. But something tells me that she is. She's gonna need time to digest what you've told her, man. But she will not let your life be at risk. Not even if she's mad at you."
Young D says, "I miss her, already. I don't feel motivated to do shit."

"That's what I'm here for. She told me to take care of you until she gets back," DeJuan says, "So that tells me she's coming back. Now let's go!"
DeJuan laughs as he pulls Young D off the bed and onto the floor. Young D decides to get on up and get dressed because DeJuan isn't taking no for an answer.

He goes to sound check with his label mates. They have a pretty solid run through. He also eats pretty good before going to the venue. Annie and DeJuan are both glad to see that he's come around, just a little. Baby Girl still hasn't called him since leaving. Hearing from his wife, would give him the boost he needs. Especially if he could have her for pre-show. But that's not going to happen, *this* evening. She's busy saving his life.

****

Sgt Moore doesn't leave the processing station until 5pm. He darts out of the parking lot and makes his way to the nearest *Popeye's Chicken & Biscuits restaurant*. Charles follows as Cherry watches the monitor. Baby Girl prepares her weapon. Sgt Moore goes through the drive through, gets his order then speeds through the city to the crescent city connector and onto his New Orleans east apartment complex. Charles lays back and watch to see which apartment he enters. Baby Girl says, "Jay seventeen. Twelve minutes. In and out."

She hops out of the limo and sends Charles for a quick ride while she heads up the stairs and to the door of Moore's apartment. She listens through the door. He has his stereo on, playing *WQUE 93.3 fm radio. DJ Wild Wayne* is on with evening drive show. She listens closer as she hears the shower come on.
It's time to go in.

Using her tools, she compromises the lock and pushes the door open. She peeps around it and sees no one. She's inside, in seconds as she cases the apartment. She eyes his cell phone and chicken order, sitting on the counter. He's in the bathroom. No one else is there.
Perfect!

She ducks behind a blind wall, next to the kitchen and grabs his cell phone in one of her gloved hands. She searches his phonebook and finds Kid's name and number.
Figures!

She dials Kid and lets the phone ring a few times, then she hangs up. She does this, 3 more times. Then she places the cell phone back on the counter and eases into the bathroom.

Before Sgt. Moore knows it, she has the 9mm pointed at his head. He's in the shower, naked. She tells him to step out

213

and sit on the toilet. He does. He's already begging for his life. She's numb to it. She needs some information.

"Do you really wanna live?" she asks.

"Yes. Please. My wallet is in my pants. In the bedroom," he tries.

"I'm not here to rob you. I need some information. Are you ready to talk to me?"

"Yes."

"You were hired to kill someone in Iowa, correct?"
He stalls. She's fresh out of patience, as she says, "Okay. Since you have amnesia. I may as well go on and protect my client."

"No. Wait please. I was hired to kill a rapper guy," he says, "I'm suppose to fly to Des Moines, in a few days. Kill him and fly back."

"Who is the rapper?" she asks, "Tell me his name."

"MC Young D," he says.

"What do you know about him?" she asks.

"He dropped an album in March. It went platinum, last month. He's from Houston,-"

"Do you know about his family life?" she asks.

"He's a father and a husband. He's married to a wealthy woman from here, in New Orleans. I was hired to kill him because he's trying to take her for her money."

"Is that what you were told?" she asks.

"Yes."

"By whom? Who hired you?" she asks.

"I'm not at liberty to say-"

"So you don't wanna live, then?"

"His name is Kid. That's the only name I know. He sent another guy to do the bidding," he says, "But he owns a record label here in town. That's all I know. I *swear*."
She knows she's being lied to, about that part. Kid's number is

in his cell phone. There had been 4 calls and 12 text messages between them, within the last weeks. Sgt. Moore hadn't erased his previous calls and texts.

Sloppy motherfucker he is. And a dumb ass for trying to lie about it too.

She reels him in, slowly.

"Kid. From *Third Ward Soldiers* label?" she asks, "Cause I'm sure they told you that much."

"He is. That's the one," he says, "He was on the phone and he said he owned a label and a few clubs. This guy was messing over his sister and trying to take her inheritance money. He couldn't let that happen."

"Sergeant Moore are you a gullible person?" she asks.

"I don't know what you mean," he says.

"I'm MC Young D's wife. I'm Kid's brother, *Six Nine's*, half sister. The only person trying to rob me is Kid. Okay?"

He says okay. But he's beginning to shiver from sitting there on the toilet, still wet from the shower. He ask if he can put on some clothes.

"No. You're not gonna feel the cold, much longer."

She pulls the freezer bag from her pocket and pulls it over the 9mm. Using her wristband as a seal, at her arm level. Then she fires 1 round into his forehead and 1 into his chest. She leaves him slouching off of the toilet, shower still running. She has her spent casing in the freezer bag. She plugs the tub and leaves the shower at full force. On the way out, she grabs his wallet and all the jewelry she can see. She leaves the cell phone in plain view and takes his chicken dinner.

"No use letting this go to waste," she says as she pulls her hoodie back over her head.

It makes her look like a boy and in this case, that's okay with

215

her. She runs down the street and meets Charles. He pulls up. She gets in. They drive away clean.

"I got the tracking device from his car while you were inside," Cherry says.

"Good job," Baby Girl says, "I guess you and Maggie get to go on that shopping spree, after all."
They all laugh as they head back to the manor.

Baby Girl flies back to Houston, later that night, to get a few more of her things. Anything else she needs, she'll shop for it in New Orleans or have Cherry and Maggie pick it up for her when they go on their shopping spree. She still hasn't talked to her husband but she has talked to her sons. Annie and DeJuan are in charge of keeping her aware of how Young D is getting along. She wasn't happy to hear that he wasn't eating well. She's going to get on to him about that. While at the house is Houston, she grabs the mail and opens the things that look the most urgent. She finds a deed to a *McDonalds restaurant*.

"He got our sons their own McDonalds," she smiles, "He's a *good* daddy."

By the time the tour leaves Wisconsin, Baby Girl has moved some of her things to the Manor, in New Orleans. Young D has called her for the last 3 nights, begging her to come back out on the road with him. She has refused. Young D sees it as her leaving him. She sees it as, time to heal her mind and track the buyer, at the same time.
What Young D doesn't know, is she's been in every city his tour has stopped in. With the exception of Fort Wayne, Indiana. Annie and the children are still on the road with him and holding up just fine. She has to see her children, even if it's just sneaking a peek at them from city to city. Young D doesn't

know that she has tracked and terminated the hit man. Des Moines is where the hit was to take place. It's the next stop on the tour. Baby Girl is 3 steps ahead, on this one. She has already knocked him off. She doesn't tell DeJuan because she wants him to stay on his toes.

"I'm starting to feel that all of this stuff goes together," she says to Addie Mae and Cherry.
They're sitting on the lanai, sipping cappuccino's and snacking on tea cakes.
"Kierra and her daughter plus Kid, was involved from day one. I have to find out what his real motivation is. If it's greed. Then he's the one who tried to have me killed too. If his motivation is the entire fortune that I have. Then why would he kill Derrick? Unless he sees my husband's death, as some kind of collateral to him. Oh I'm shooting him down! The father of my sons is never some damn collateral! He's top of the line! He should know that, just based off the number of his hit men, whom I keep sending back to him in a box!"
Cherry asks, "You're still going out to Iowa, aren't you?"

"Of course I am. He's still my husband and I still love him. I'm not gonna let anyone harm him. Not if I can help it."

"You've already gotten to the shooter, correct?" Addie Mae asks.

"Yes ma'am. After his day job," she says, "And nothing else is showing on the network. But you can never be, too sure. I'm going back out there. So I'll have a visual too."

"That man has called you at every waking minute, sweetheart," Addie Mae says to her. "He's sorry. I know he loves you. This business makes it very hard to have a personal life. Because your significant other, when they don't know what you're doing, can feel left out. Or cheated on or not needed. You see we're single, don't you? Give him another

217

chance. I'm not saying today. But *soon*. Okay? Because I don't *bit more* believe that is his baby, honey. No more then the man in the moon."

"He said he doesn't either," Baby Girl says, "I didn't believe it when Kid first said it to me."

"And I say you shouldn't now. Trust your instincts and use your resources," Alfred finally chimes in.

The senior staff has her back. They want what's best for her. And they feel that Young D is. Alfred had told her this same thing, the same night she left the tour. When he'd called her back with the information on the weapon she'd gotten from Hiram Jones. He told her not to leave her husband.

Alfred says, "Like I told you that night. Just like that gun belongs to the Morales family? So does Young D. He belongs in it. The Don *loved* him *with* you. He knew he would take care of you and do right by you. It all smells like a set up to me. That young man took being blackmailed because he didn't want this shit out in the open, for you to be hurt by. I don't think it's his. Look into your sources, for the information. Investigate who told you about it. I'll bet you'll find out there's a conspirer somewhere in this mess. Close enough to harm you. And that's who I wanna grease."

"We figured Gus let the weapon loose from this property," Charles chimes in, "Now how hard is it for you to put that shit together? Not hard at all, Baby Girl. Because you already know."

"It's Kid, isn't it? He's the buyer. But I want to know why he wants Derrick dead," she says.

"Then you shall find out," Cherry says, "And then, Kid dies Baby Girl."

218

She lands in Des Moines, 6 hours to show time. She calls DeJuan and makes him aware that she'd already taken out the mark, 2 days prior. She sends him newspaper clippings, so he knows whom it was.

He looks at them then destroys them, immediately after showing them to Young D. DeJuan now knows that Baby Girl has been out to every tour stop. He informs Young D, who shrugs his shoulders. She won't come to see him nor will she call him. He hates this but what can he do? She wants her space.

Later, she watches as he goes into the venue at the Des Moines show.
He cut his hair off!

She's surprised to see that he's shredded his braids. He's rocking a fade. Not even a fro, which he'd done before. He looks very handsome and mature with a clean cut. She misses him. She wonders how their sons like the new look. She misses her little family, a lot too. But she has to clear her mind before she can go home. She has to clear her man too.
I'm gonna contact Emilio.

Emilio Pantango, now the number 2 guy. A distant 2, at that. She calls him from her rental car. Outside of the venue, in Des Moines, Iowa.
"Hello," Emilio says.
She introduces herself and quickly lets him know who she is. He knows her immediately. And immediately, he thinks she's coming for him. She calms his nerves on that notion, quickly.
"It's not about you, at all. It's about the past. Can you get to the network?"

He tells her yes. She tells him to pull it up. He does. She needs to know what leads where associated with some previous marks. She has to know how many of her past marks where, indeed legit. And how many were personal. Emilio, through the network connection, sends her the regular marks. The ones that were network. She reads the information as it downloads to her IPhone.

Dennis Montgomery, Chadwick Donaldson and Tito Lopez.

"That's it?" she asks Emilio.

"Well, yes. For *this* year," he says thinking she feels he's being deceptive. "Nothing else was on the wire except the ones you're reading. I didn't attempt to go at them, if that's what you're thinking. I knew I wouldn't get them before you. I didn't even do a plan."

She feels honored that he knows to stay in his place. And that she is the best.

"But what about the mark in Mississippi," she asks.

She sends him the place and date of the mark. She never had his name.

"No. Nothing on the wire for that one," Emilio says, "But my father told me that one was personal. That was set up for B&G Landscaping."

What!?! Is that Brad and Gus Landscaping?

"Let me send you something on the New, New Orleans project. That should help you understand it better," he says.

He sends the information down the wire.

Brad also known as Kid was in business with Gus, alright. There was something major, they were planning. They were using her and her abilities, to take out the competition. Anyone who was vying for the New Orleans recovery project, they used her to take them out.

"The guy who had the lead on the project, his name was

220

Gilbert Haussmann," Emilio tells her, "He also owned a restaurant in Mississippi-"

"Percale's restaurant?" she asks.

"Yes. That's it," he says, "I wasn't sure of how to pronounce it."

"Oh *GOD*! What the hell did those assholes have me mixed up in?"

She asks aloud. Before ending her call with Emilio, she tells him, "Look. I know you're in the network and you're behind a crest, just like I am. But sometimes we're gonna have to communicate to keep rogues and regular street people from taken the dignity out of our profession. You can call on me, anytime there is a network problem. Make your reasons clear and I'll be there for you. Just as you have been here for me, tonight. I'll do the same."

He agrees with her and tells her to call on him anytime, as well. Especially if she knows of work that she's not going to go after. He says he would love to have it. She tells him okay and they hang up.

She sits outside of the venue in her rental car. She's thinking of how her and Emilio can change the profession to a more trustworthy 1, while keeping the dignity of each family in tact. Before long, she can see patrons leaving the venue. The show is done.

After an hour, the crew load onto the tour buses and pull away. She follows the buses until they exit onto interstate 35 south. It's 3 days until Thanksgiving. They're heading home. Young D calls her phone, just as he has done each night since she left. She considers not answering it. But she misses his conversation, amongst other things. She answers. She needs to hear his sweet voice.

"Hello," she says.

"Hey baby. How are you? I miss you," he says, trying to get every thought out in 1 line.

"Hey, sweetheart. I'm doing okay. I'm still working. I miss you too. And ah, I like the haircut," she says.

He smiles. He knows she's near.

"You was there, at the venue," he says, "I knew it, this time. I could feel your presence. You've been close to me, all day. Until just recently. That's why I called. I felt a disconnect. I just wanted to hear your voice and know you're okay."

"I'm okay. I'll see you soon," she says.

"I hope so," he says.

"I will, Derrick," she says.

They hang up. She drives on to the airport as she goes over her mental notes.

She has so much more information on the buyer now. More than she'd had the night she killed Hiram Jones. Sgt Moore was such a gracious mark to have given Kid up on the Des Moines hit. He had also given her some bonus information, as he was trying to stay alive. He had spilled his guts, so she didn't have too.

"Kid Walker had also set the hit up on you and your husband. The one by Mark Genolli and associates. For the fourth of July." She did thank him for the information but she killed him anyway. She also took his valuables and his dinner. As if she was going to leave a witness. No way!

Tonight she returns the rental car and hops her flight to New Orleans. She's got some family business to tend too.

Or not so family business. How dare you smile in my fucking face. Come to my home and hug my babies. But you want me and their father dead. Why Kid? What the fuck did we ever do to you?

She's in flight, thinking to herself and trying to figure out why

222

someone whom she's loved like a blood relative. Now wants her and her only love, dead. There has to be a reason and she's going to know what it is. She has too. But whatever the reason or explanation Kid has to give her. Will not be enough to save his life. She can hear Cherry's words in head.
"And then Kid he dies, Baby Girl."
She is absolutely right! This is war muthafucka!

"The Pantango's and the Genolli's will never be our friends, Baby Girl," Don had said to her, *"Never accept an offer from either family."*

Emilio hadn't made her an offer. What he had done, was sent her a link to information which proved her family had been up to no good. She's sure he took pleasure in sending that little bit of information down the wire, for her eyes only. He wasn't daring enough to open the file to the network public. No, he wouldn't dare do that. For he would be at risk of facing the wrath of *Baby Girl*.

Even though Emilio had been kind enough to tell her about it. That still isn't enough. She has to pull it up for herself, without using the link to verify it's legitimacy and see the network hits, with her own eyes. She has made it back to the manor. She's in the office with Gus' computer in front of her. She pulls up the network. Emilio had been honest with the information he gave her.
The information is legitimate.

She knows without a doubt that she had been used. She's looking at Gus' computer and there isn't anything on it about the Haussmann hit, in Mississippi. She sees several of the arrangements for hits on her and Young D, though.

"Manfred Hurst, Mark Genolli and Billy Campanili were hits on me. All done by Gus. Using my father's links and hardware," she says, "So the man I killed at *Swegmann's*. Was sent to kill me, by my own damn agent. Gus tried to make it look like he was from the Genolli family. That low down sucker. With a name like Manfred, he deserved to die. Hurst was a fitting last name too."

She smiles to herself briefly. Then she says, "Gus was a piece of shit and I'm glad he's sleeping with the fishes."

She's thoroughly disgusted with Gus and the way he'd continued to stab her dead father in the back. This leaves her with 1 question.

"Why would he make Morales family information accessible to the Pantango's? Unless he was really trying to destroy everything my daddy Don had built."

She reads on. She knows it's very likely the Pantango's can use this against her family later. That is, if a meeting of the bosses were to ever be called. It's her job to get her family business in order and eliminate any risk of shade being cast upon the Morales name.

"It would be my pleasure," she says as she jots down a few notes on her stationary. "Daddy Don. This is on my word to you. No shame will ever come to your name. I'll lay down my own life before I allow any shame to come to my family's name."

She's in the Don's office. She had arrived from Des Moines in the very wee hours of the morning. It's late evening now. She's been cooped up in this office viewing files, since her return. Only breaking for a meal, here and there, at Addie Mae's insistence.

She had a visit from the Orleans Parish police commissioner, earlier today. Concerning her brother Kid. The commissioner told her about the murder in the 7th ward and how Kid was suspected to be involved. It was the murder of a drug dealer. She knows his involvement, already. Sgt. Moore was probably the primary on it but couldn't get it done. She had given the package to Kid, herself. He most likely did the hit. Only because he thought it was professionally set up. But it was actually 1 of the ones that Gus had mastered. Kid didn't know any better. Like the right hand not knowing what the left hand is doing. Kid and Gus were partners in the business of ripping fellow New Orleanians off. The commissioner was here to talk to her as an alibi for Kid, for the night of the murder. But he didn't get what he came for. Baby Girl looked for ways to spin that incident and that visit, to her advantage. It proved easier done, than said.

"He had you listed as a reference, is why I'm here," the commissioner had said, "If I hadn't saw your name. He would be on a slow bus to Angola."
Baby Girl couldn't help but feel the irony of that visit. He listed *her* as his reference.
If he knew what I know now. He wouldn't tell anyone else that.

She did a lot of thinking during that meeting. She didn't trust Kid anymore and was already baking a cake for his ass.
Is he dry snitching? Or is he sincerely thinking I'm gonna do the family thing? Like use my prominent contacts to help him beat this rap? I am not!

What had in fact happened was, Kid had done the wrong thing with the package. He had given it to some other guy. Some street thug. He had given it to a rookie in his organization, to carry out. The rookie was apprehended shortly after the murder. And told the police that Kid had sent him to kill this

225

rival drug dealer. With the promise of a hefty payout after the hit was complete. The commissioner had paid her a special visit based on the respect he has for the Morales name. He'd giving Kid the benefit of the doubt, after he knew Kid was connected to the Morales name. Baby Girl did her damn best to change that.

"Sir. The Morales family doesn't deal with drugs," she had said.

"I am sure of that point, Miss…."

"Misses Blake," she had said.

"…Misses Blake. I've known this family, all of my life. I would never let Duke Morales suffer any backlash from some common street punk. Nor some street thug, turned music mogul. The Morales built this parish, to what it is now. They helped my family to get set up here and they helped me to become commissioner too. Loyalty goes a long way," he had said.

Is he prompting me for a campaign contribution? Bastard!

"The Morales family always takes care of it's friends, commissioner. Just the fact that you know my family, so well. Assures me that I have nothing to worry about when it comes to my stepbrothers' troubles," she had said, "And we look forward to sponsoring your next association ball. Just let us know when."

With that, the commissioner was okay to leave. He had solidified his stance with the Morales family and let her know she had nothing to worry about. Her family's name would not be associated nor tarnished, with the murder in the 7th ward. He left and she went back to her more pressing business of researching the files.

"What an ass. Kid would fuck up a wet dream!" she

says aloud, after thinking back over this mornings meeting with the commissioner.

"No way will you use me or my family to clean up your shit. Not when you've been trying to destroy us, all along. This is war. Your ass is going to burn, just like the roof. Burn muthafucka burn!"

She amuses herself as she works. She researches the other information given to her by Sgt. Moore. Low and behold, she finds the Mark Genolli hit on Gus' computer.

"Son of a bitch! He made the package! Kid paid for it!"

She thinks back to the days, just before the 4th of July event. Gus showing up in Houston, late. With the announcement about the hit on her life. The same night she'd caught Kierra backstage, at the Galveston show. She now wonders why did Gus even bother to warn her about the Genolli hit on her.

"If he wanted me dead. Then why tell me? I wasn't even accessing the network then. I was still trusting him," she says to herself. "I guess he was trying to cover his own ass. Which is the same ole shit."

Then she rethinks what happened prior to and after the Galveston show. When she had found Kierra backstage and whooped her ass. She wonders had she ever been apart of bringing harm to Young D. Or was she always, only there to fuck him.

"Did they send her to harm Derrick, that night? Or was she there to warn him? I don't think she was ever trying to do physical harm to Derrick. I was right to whoop her ass though. She was trying to *fuck* my husband."

She remembers 4th of July and how Mark Genolli and Campanili had come into the picture. She sees where he was there on a job. To take out, not only her. But Young D also.

"Gus didn't mention anything about a hit on Derrick, that

227

night either. He only told me about me. And it was late, at that. Maybe he was hoping Mark would get one of us. He was an arrogant bastard. But he died arrogantly too."

She smiles. Then she recalls when Kid showed up at the event but not wanting to stay, after learning that Kierra and her friends weren't permitted on the property anymore.

"He left with her and stayed gone, all day. He didn't return until it was time for *Grand Hustle* to perform. He was irritated as fuck, when he did come back. Perhaps he'd seen the news and knew his pro's had become marks, themselves."

For the first time, she's beginning to see the full picture. Kid is the living mole. Gus is the dead one.

"Kid never gave a fuck about me, as far as I'm concerned," she says.

She has spent nearly an entire 24 hours, locked in her daddy's office. But the things she has discovered while in this office. Have given her new light and a whole new direction. She's hell bent of doing Kid in. She's going to call her family before she shuts her eyes tonight. She knows what she needs to do about Kid. But what she doesn't know, is that she has a huge surprise coming her way. A surprise that's very needed. Rather she realizes it or not. It's coming and it just might do her heart and soul some good.

CHAPTER THIRTY
THE HEALING PROCESS [LOOSE ENDS]

"Do you guys have bags, sir?" Charles asks Young D, as they meet up at the gate where his flight has just arrived at *Louis Armstrong airport.*

"Yes we do," he answers with a smile.

He had hopped a flight from Oklahoma City and brought their sons with him. He couldn't even wait for his tour bus to make it to his next destination. He has to get to his wife, right away. He has to see where her head is, as far as their marriage is concerned.

"We're going to see mommy for Thanksgiving," he'd said to their sons, as they left Annie and the rest to ride the tour bus on into New Orleans.

Charles gets a sky cap. The sky cap gets their bags to the limousine while Young D secures Lil Man and Done Prince in their car seats. Young D lets Lil Man tip the sky cap, handsomely. Within minutes, they're in route to the manor.

At the manor, Baby Girl is still working. She's been cooped up in The Don's office since she arrived back at the manor. She has vowed not to stop until she finds what it is she's looking for. Suddenly, the *net-to-phone* line rings. She knows it's business or a person who's in the business. That's the only way to have the network's number. She answers.

"Hello."

"I'm trying to get in touch with Lovely Walker Blake, please," a male voice on the other end says.

The voice sounds friendly. It also sounds like, whomever he is, he knows her well enough to be chuckling as he talks. She wants to know who it is, this instant.

"Speaking," she says.

"This is Teddy Jones, junior. My father is…."

"…..Big Teddy Jones, who worked with my father….."

"…..Big Dog Walker. And he worked for your father, The Don. Yes. You're right. So is this Lovely?" he asks.

"Yes it is. Is this little Teddy?" she ask as she giggles.

"Big Teddy," Teddy Jr says as he laughs, "I'm twenty three years old now."

"Oh so *old*?" she asks as she laughs too. She adds, "I'm twenty five. Just made it, last month. You'll be twenty four on the fourth of December. I remember."

They catch up on past memories, for a bit. They use to be pretty good friends when they were kids. That was before she left for *Tristan Academy*. Her real father Big Dog and his daddy Big Teddy, whom they called TJ, were partners and worked for The Don. They were 2 of the best pro's in the game, ever. Until Baby Girl.

"Daddy had me to call you," Teddy Jr says, "We're coming down for Thanksgiving. He's been channeling the network. He wants to talk some things over with you. He feels he can shed some light on your present situation."

"My present situation?" she asks, "Oh. Yes. Y'all have been watching the network, ha?"

"Yes indeed," he says, "Daddy watches that thing like it's the NFL network. He doesn't like what he's been seeing. Especially in the last two years."

They both laugh at his NFL comment.

"Daddy Don use to stay in this office, a lot," she says, "I didn't know he was watching the network, back then. But I know now. It can keep you glued to it, for days. If no one made you get up and move."

"We're gonna do our part for the crest, of course," he says, "Daddy says he is and always has been, committed to The

230

Don, *The Organization, The Brotherhood* and *Morales Enterprises*. And ain't *shit* changed."

She feels honored as she graciously accepts. She's happy to know Teddy Sr, who's now in his retirement, is still accessing the network. He has seen the unfavorable hits, logged and attributed to the Morales family and he knows something in the milk ain't clean.

"I look forward to seeing you again, little Teddy," she says, "I have a brother named Teddy too. You remember we talked on that? Big Dog's sons, in Philly?"

"Yes I do. I remember Big Dog had children spread out across the nation," Teddy Jr says as he chuckles, "He got around like *Tupac*." They laugh.

"Well that's true," she says, "But one of the sons from there. He has his mother's last name. I met them all. Teddy, who's doing time, told me that Big Dog had his mother to name him after your dad. He just turned thirty three. He's doing a bid out in Colorado."

Teddy inquires about what Teddy Wells had done to get locked up. She tells him. Then he tells her, they'll be driving down from Shreveport. They're leaving in the morning.

"Well come on down. I know big Teddy remembers the way. I'll let Cherry know y'all are coming so she can get a suite ready. I'm so happy you guys are going to be here."

They talk a few minutes longer. Then hang up.

She is about to get back to her files, when she hears some very familiar pattering of little feet, out in foyer and hallway. She can hear her husbands voice too. She gets up from the desk and goes out into the foyer. She is greeted by Young D, Lil Man and Don Prince.

"Hey mommy!" Lil Man screams, "Glad to come to my other big house. I tell my daddy I wanna see my mommy."

Her oldest son screams as he jumps up into her arms and hugs her as tight as he can. He's very excited to see his mother.

"Hi baby! Oh you feel so good and you're dressed so cute, in your daddy's clothes," she says, near tears when she hugs and kisses her oldest son.

"This not my daddy clothes, mommy," he says quickly. "This got my name on it. My name just like my daddy name."

"Okay. You're right, man," she says, "Mommy is so tired, she forgot. I'm glad my son is so smart. So you can tell me better." She giggles with him.

Then she has to do the same for Don Prince, as he mutters "Hey mommy. Hey mommy."

"Are you saying mommy?!" she says, as she can't stop a tear or two, from rolling down her cheek. "Don Prince can say mommy!" she yells, very excited and emotional as she hugs and kisses him too.

Though he can't speak clearly. Don Prince giggles uncontrollably which lets her know he's missed her, a lot too. She's just heard her 8 month old saying mommy, as best he can. It warms her heart. She's knows her sons have missed having her around. She'd vowed to do better on her attendance to them. But those plans were forced to be changed when she realized there was plot in the works to relieve them of their parents. That took priority in her day to day dealings because she knows she'll have to be alive to be there for them. And so will Young D. He may be thinking the same thing as he stands there, looking at her. She can see the pain in his eyes. His longing to be near her. She can't resist hugging him too. He can't resist kissing her. She lets him. She missed him, so much. It's been a week and a day since she felt his touch. The way he's holding her now, assures her that he's thinking the same. It's been awhile since he felt her touch or any type of intimacy.

232

"Thanks so much for coming," she says, "And bringing my babies."

Young D says, "I had too. Today is *The Don's* birthday."

They laugh. Don Prince makes 8 months old today.

She asks, "What are Annie and all the labelmates doing for Thanksgiving?"

"Driving the tour bus here." He tells her, "They should arrive before morning. Deloris is flying in from Houston."

She tells him that Danny, Bruce and Jordan are already here.

"They flew in yesterday," she says.

"That's what gave me the idea," he says, "That and my junior's *insistence*."

"I can tell he was a bit much to deal with," she says as she smiles, "He's wired up. How did he do on the flight?"

"It bugged him out, like always," he says, "He went in the cockpit before we took off and didn't wanna come out."

"He always does that," she says, still smiling. She adds, "We need to think about flight school." They laugh.

Young D is relieved to see her smiling and laughing. He was hoping his arrival would find her in the mood to see him. So far, it seems so.

"Looks like this will be a Happy Thanksgiving, New Orleans style again," he says as they hug again.

Cherry and Maggie swarm in on the boys. They take them and their bags to their section of the mansion.

"We'll have a full house for the holiday, I hear," Addie Mae says as she comes in to greet Young D.

He tells her, his family and his entire label will be here for Thanksgiving dinner. Then Baby Girl informs her that Teddy Jones Sr and his family of 6 are coming too.

Addie Mae says, "I am so excited to cook for a house full again. It's been lonely around here, with just the staff to feed. We can

233

finally use the formal dining room again." She's tickled pink.
She tells them they will have enough people to have dinner in
the grand dining room. It seats up to 200 people.

Soldier, his wife Debra, their family and label are
coming. Baby Boy's family and label are coming. Young G's
family and crew, Geezy's family and crew and Markie D's
family and crew are all coming to the manor for Thanksgiving
dinner. Plus Six Nine, his wife Sandra and Roger Walker III.
Him and Kid's mother Joyce Wesley, her daughters and their
families will be here too. Along with Baby Girl's brothers and
their families from Philly, as well as Deloris' brother and his
wife. They are all coming with their families. They'll have over
half the capacity for Thanksgiving. Full capacity with all of the
staff friends and families included. Kid is the only 1 who hasn't
answered his invitation. But Baby Girl feels certain he won't
be here.

****

Young D's tour bus arrives just before 3am., the
morning before Thanksgiving. They're greeted by the staff and
shown to their quarters. Young D and Baby Girl will see them
later. They're in the master suite.

"Baby, this is our anniversary too," he says.
She giggles and adds, "I know it is."
The day before Thanksgiving is a very special day in their
relationship. Baby Girl lost her virginity to Young D, 11 years
ago today.

"I feel like I need to start all over," he says, "I don't
want you to think I don't value our love and our relationship.
Because that would be so far from the truth. I treasure you,
Lovely. I always have."

234

"You don't have to start over," she says, "Let's just make another vow to be completely honest with each other, from now on," she says, "And respect the others decisions too. I think we can move on from here."

Then she lets him know that she isn't just staying here because she wants her space.

"It's so much more than that," she says, "I'm here because it's also the best way to run down that buyer. Gus's computer has more of his personal notes on it. Plus the employees are here to add their two cents. I got a call from Big Teddy's son. They're coming for Thanksgiving. He has some input on the way Gus left things. That's gonna blow this thing wide open, Derrick. And that's exactly where I need it to be. I want light to shine on every wrong that Gus did."

"Okay. The O G's are coming out for this one ha?"

They laugh. She tells him about the commissioner coming by.

"He's got my back too," she says, "And I have yours, still. Nothing will ever change that or stop us."

"I'm just happy to hear you say that," he says, "This whole month has been miserable for me. I thought I'd lost the most important person in my life. After my sons, of course."

"No matter what or who it is. I'm gonna find the buyer and kill him or her," she says, "Nothing or no one can ever stop me from loving you. Except you. So rest your head on that one, Derrick. You're my husband for life. Just know that my main job has to be, to make sure that your life is long and prosperous."

She doesn't tell him about Kid, right now. She's holding that card until she finds his link to Kierra. She has got to get that one figured out. Her main goal is to clear her families name, as well as her husband's and hers too. This is the only way she can insure that their sons will have mommy and daddy around, with no false information out there which will draw heat from other pros. TJ is going to help her get that part of it worked out. And this time, when TJ comes back into the loop. He'll be there to straightened things out and make sure they flow smooth and honestly. Just as the network intended for them to flow, before a rogue like Gus got into the mix and managed to bring sludge to *The Organization*. She feels an extra boost of confidence, knowing that her father's former partner and her daddy's loyal employee has her back. She tells her husband how good that makes her feel.

"I have your back too, baby," he says, "I'm gonna be touring the south, starting Friday. Right here in New Orleans. I hope the tour will give you enough time to get some satisfaction. Because I want you back in my life, on a daily basis by the time it ends. And as my wife, *completely*. It doesn't matter to me if we're here or Houston or wherever. As long as you're with me. Long as we're together. Because I need you."

"I need you too, Derrick. I'll have this wrapped up before Christmas," she says, "Give me until then to get this buyer tagged and cancelled. That's the only way I'll be able to rest."

"Then it'll be a good Christmas, for damn sho," he says, "I've missed you, like crazy. You know I love you, like a fat kid loves cake, don't you?"
They laugh again. Then indulge in each other.

Tonight's lovemaking feels magical to her. His reactions lets her know he's feeling it too. Tonight, he's more emotional then she's ever seen him, since meeting him 11 and a half years ago. His sex is on point and his pillow talk is so soothing. She's missed her husband and she doesn't try to conceal that fact. She wants him to know that she will love him for life, as long he respects her for as long as he lives. She's going to do her damn best to make certain they have a long life together.

That starts with exposing Kid. She wants to expose him without putting light on herself. Because she's the 1 who's going to kill him. If everything she's learned, proves to be deliberate. And shows that he had a hand in it. Then that will be another hand which will become the property of Morales Manor and *The Organization*. It's as simple as that.

****

Teddy Jones or TJ and his family arrives in the late morning. He, Alfred, Charles, Teddy Jr and Baby Girl go into the office to talk, first thing. Once they're inside the office, she learns that Teddy Jr is a pro also. And he wants to work for The Organization and *her* family.

"It's the only place for you to be," she says, "We can definitely work that out. We'll both be following in our father's footsteps. That's what you use to say, before we were even aware of what it was that they did." They all laugh.

Then Big Teddy tells her a bit about Gus' history. He gives her the background on how Gus had become an agent, in the first place.

TJ says, "It was only suppose to be temporary. A trial period, so to speak. Just to see if he would work out. Don wasn't leaving him there, permanently."

Alfred adds, "But The Don got weak. Then he passed away before the changes could be made. Gus was never suppose to be in charge, once TJ retired from the field. So after we got rid of Gus. We contacted Teddy about taking the job, The Don wanted him to have."

They show Baby Girl notes The Don had given to all 3 of them, stating that he wanted TJ to be agent for The Organization.

237

They were signed and dated, a year before The Don passed away. He had initially wanted Big Dog to be the agent. A month after Big Dog's death, is when these letters were written and sent out.

Charles says, "Gus got the letter. So did TJ. We ask him to get in touch with you, so that you, the head of the family, could make this right for The Don. It's now time to make this right."

He shows her where, in The Don's letter, this stipulation was set up.

"So you were suppose to be my agent, all along. Not Gus," she says, "Why weren't you given the position by my father?"

"Because I had to accept it, first," TJ says, "He offered it to me, right after Big Dog passed on. But I said no. I was going through a depression, for awhile, Baby Girl."

"A depression? For what?" she asks.

"Well the first time I was asked. I had just lost my best friend, Big Dog. Shortly after that, I lost my wife," TJ says, "That's when Don asked me and I told him to give me more time. He said okay. After that, all the rest of my friends died. All within a three year time span. Big Dog, Audrey. That was my wife. Then the Don and lastly, Wanda. It took me another three years to get my edge back. By then, Gus had dug in and made it impossible for me to get the leverage I needed. He had your trust and you had a clause in place that allowed no contact from outside pro's or their agents. Unless you permitted them by name."

"But I thought that was a rule that was in place before me," she says.

"No Baby Girl. It wasn't," Charles says, "And we wasn't allowed to instruct you on how to run *The Organization*. We thought you implemented that rule. But later, we learned it was all Gus. So that's when we started doing things to expose him to you."

"And allowing you to see the difference between Gus' computer and the networks," Alfred says, "We knew you would figure it out. The Don did too, obviously. Because he put you in charge of all of us. When Gus got to comfortable with his greed. You caught onto him."

"We would never have let it go as far as ruining this conglomerate, Baby Girl," Charles says, "But we had to give you time to discover it and you did."

TJ says, "Yes. And I called Gus numerous times, over the years to stake my claim. But he, being a rogue already. Never took my calls. Alfred and Charles just told me to hang in there. You'd find him out. Then I could surface. That's what I did."

"We made sure he surfaced too," she says, "He was helping a buyer to mark me and my husband."

"Just a buyer? You know how to find out who that is and how many he's done, right?" TJ asks.

"Not exactly. I've been in here nearly nonstop since I got here," she says, "Going over his files, computers and ledgers. I've only found the buyer for two jobs, so far. But it's been a lot more jobs than that."

"Well Baby Girl. That's what I'm here for. To help you find it," TJ says, "You're not looking in the right place. Focus on the invoices from his wall safe. That's where the meat is."

Alfred says, "But not today though, Baby Girl. Addie Mae will have a hissy fit if we stir up old spirits, on the day before she has a house full. You know where it is. After Thanksgiving is done and some of the guest clear out. We'll get right down to it."

It is something about the way Alfred said: *Addie Mae and Old spirits* that catches her attention. There is potential to find something huge in Gus' files and she can sense it. She senses she'll find, not only the buyer of her and her husbands death certificates. But something that will give closure to Addie Mae, as well.

Oh my God. Addie Mae? Old spirits? I wonder if he had anything to do with Epiphany's death? I can't wait until I can get into that safe.

Alfred shows her the key to Gus' quarters. She's satisfied knowing she has the inside information she needs to get to what she wants to find. This key is an insurance policy which assures her of a path into the details of the conspiracy by Gus and Kid.

As a final gesture of solidarity. She calls the commissioners office. She invites him to Thanksgiving Dinner. She tells him she has invited all of her family. But she would rather Kid not show up at all. The commissioner chuckles for more than a minute before he speaks.

He says, "Me and my family will be there, for sure. As I told you when I visited. And I can help Kid find some where else to spend Thanksgiving."

They hang up.

Then she says, "Kid won't be here tomorrow. And after dinner, we need to grab a *sock-it-to-me cake* and a *sweet potato pie* and head to Gus' quarters."

"Sounds like an all day event for which we'll need lots of energy," Teddy Jr adds.

They all laugh. Sock-it-to-me cake and sweet potato pie has always been TJ's favorite. It was Big Dog's too. Every time Addie Mae cooked the 2 desserts. Everyone at the manor knew Big Dog and TJ was coming home.

Thanksgiving dinner is elaborate. All of Baby Girl's family are here. All of their friends and colleagues are here. All of her brothers are here with their families. Kid's wife and children are here. But Kid had been taken into custody, late last night, on a murder conspiracy charge. The commissioner called them, right after his confirmed arrest, to let them know he wouldn't, *"be able to make it to dinner."*

Baby Girl has told Young D the news about Kid and he's there to witness the call from the commissioner. He smiles. Young D loves the weight his wife has to throw around. Him and his labelmates have been talking around it all, during this spectacular day.

"You're a boss, baby!" he says, "I'm married to a boss." She smiles. He gives her a kiss, while they're seated at their large dinner table. Lil Man is clowning in the children's section of the dining room. Young D is clowning in the grownup section of the dining room. The announcement was just made that Kid may be released tomorrow or Monday. Baby Girl wouldn't care if they kept him longer than a day or two. She's going to find what she needs, once all of the guest are gone and out of here. Then she can get down to the work of finding and trapping, yet another mark. It's just another day in the life of Lovely "Baby Girl" Walker Blake.

****

The following night, the *House of Blues* is packed for the H-Town Records performance. Baby Boy, Soldier, Young G, Markie D and Geezy all join the show. Baby Girl leaves the concert with no voice left. Her vocals had been pushed to the limit. Young D's next tour stop is in Mobile, Alabama tomorrow. So she has a long talk with DeJuan. He's put in charge of Young D's security because she has to stay in New Orleans. She tells him not to worry. If a hit attempt shows up on the network. She'll get out there to them, *pronto*. DeJuan says ok. As long as Kid is incarcerated. There isn't much he can do, as far as setting up hits. He's in a solitary holding cell. He isn't allowed any contact with the other inmates. Baby Girl feels secure with him behind bars. She has to take care of getting her husband and his team on the road. She makes sure the staff has loaded the tour bus for the following morning. Addie Mae has stocked lots of treats for them. Charles and his team get all of the traveling guest to the airport. All of their guest return to their respective hometowns. Man and Don Prince are staying in New Orleans with Baby Girl. Bruce and Jordan are staying until Sunday. They'll go back and return to school on Monday. Annie, Angela and Corleone fly back to Houston with Little Corleone and Young D's grandparents. Danny flies back to Atlanta.

After the tour bus pulls away from the manor, Saturday afternoon, Baby Girl is ready to get back to her research. She summons Alfred, Charles, Teddy Jr and TJ to Don's office.
"It's time. I need to get in that wall safe, today," she says.
The 5 of them take the *Sock-it-to-me cake* and a *sweet potato pie* that Addie Mae set out for them. They get into the limousine and drive down to Gus' quarters.
Alfred opens the front door. They go in and go directly to the wall safe. Teddy Jr cracks it easily. Baby Girl is impressed.
"It's my specialty," Teddy Jr says.
Once the safe is open, Baby Girl sees Gus' money invoices from all the hits he's done since Don passed away. She pulls the 4

242

large stacks of organized receipts out, first. The money in the safe is most likely hers too. She takes it out and places it in her Gucci backpack.

"Put the money on the couch nigga!" she say as she quotes *Juvenile*, a popular artist for New Orleans 3rd ward.

Then she pulls out the lone file from the safe and puts it in her briefcase. She sits down to go over the invoices. She's only interested in the ones from 2007. She takes that stack. The 4 gentlemen sift through the others. They're already finding discrepancies. Baby Girl surveys every hit, for this year. She can't believe her own eyes. Everything she needs is right here. It was here, all along!

"Every damn hit on my husband was funded by Kid!" she says as she sucks in her jaws and puckers her lips.

She's heated already, as she holds up a stack of receipts, an inch thick.

"The hit on me with Mark Genolli of all people, was funded by Kid too. That was suppose to be me and Derrick. And oh yes, the five hundred grand is *indeed* mine."

She smiles as she pats her backpack. The 4 gentleman chuckle. Teddy Jr likes her style.

"She took out the Genolli's best two men, who were number one and two in the world. At the *same* time," TJ tells his son and Teddy Jr is impressed by that too.

"Wow! You took out the only two, *by network*, who could've had any chance of getting you," Teddy Jr says, "I am *very* impressed."

"That's my specialty," she tells him as she puts on a smile.

But she isn't really in the mood for smiling. She's only smiling at Teddy Jr to keep from going berserk. From the time she'd reopened the manor. Kid has been trying to take her out. Then she sees the invoice for the man at the supermarket. *Manfred Hurst.*

"*Damn*! My first time back at the manor, after the repairs. And he was trying to off me," she says, "A rookie showed up at the supermarket after the last *House of Blues* show. Kid hired him and Gus set up the hit."

Charles says, "She did him clean too. In the bathroom of the supermarket. They didn't even find him for 6 hours. She avoided camera's and all of that shit too."

Teddy Jr looks at her with glossed eyes. He is thoroughly impressed. Plus he's feeling her, on a personal level too. After all, they do have history. Not famous history. But history, nonetheless.

TJ says, "That mark at Percale's in Mississippi. That was personal. The dude's name was Gilbert Haussmann. He was a big time land developer. He's worked with Don Morales before. He was about to help the Katrina victims to get their land cleared. And he was gonna help them get their homes rebuilt, at no cost to them."

"So why would they want me to kill him?" she asks, "Because that one was personal too. Emilio Pantango let me in on that bit of info. I was away from my desk."

"I'd say they have plans for the property. Wouldn't you?" TJ asks.

"That new, *New Orleans project*! Dang!" she says.

She needs a minute as she gets up and walks outside to get some air. She's highly upset now, because she realizes they made her a direct part of something she absolutely disagrees with. She would never *willingly* deprive any Katrina victims of assistance. She's a Katrina victim, herself. She had 2 properties damaged during that Hurricane. The people who were displaced and who were the most adversely affected, from

Katrina. Are *her* people. She loves her people, just as her parents did. Everyone of her summer breaks was spent volunteering for something, *community* related. The Morales are known for giving back. Not taking away. *Not ever*! How dare them put her in a position which supports greed and annihilation of her *own* race. She walks back into Gus' quarters with a new attitude.

"Alfred, I need you to set up some meetings. I want a meeting with the ward committee's. One with the mayor's office and community councils," she says, "I want to know how far this new, New Orleans project has gone. If it's possible to make it one meeting. Then that's fine too. I want to reverse what they have signed my family up for."

"I agree with you, whole heartedly," Alfred says as he tells her, he's proud her for what she's about to do.

Then he tells her, he'll get on the phone setting the meetings, first thing in the morning. The 4 gentlemen then suggest that she bring all of the contents from the safe, back up to the mansion. Then she can read them, at her leisure. She agrees to do that, with their help. Together, they pack it all and place it in the limousine. Then they drive back up to the mansion. She hops out with her work and goes straight into the office. She locks the door and digs in.

CHAPTER THIRTY ONE
FOR BETTER OR WORSE OR WORK

There is 1 result Young D would love to see come out of all of Baby Girl's digging and researching. That would be, the utter and complete revocation of Kierra's claim on him as the man who supplied the other half on her daughter. It's true to say Baby Girl would love to see that, as well. But today that often used term, *if it were a snake it would bite you*, most definitely applies. Everything needed to give some everlasting relief to their hopes of having a *true* marriage. Void of anyone's claim on 1 of them, is in the same room with Baby Girl. It's merely staring at her. Begging for her attention. But she's to busy looking for the big answer, to find it.

Out on the road, less than an hour and Young D is already missing his family. The last 2 nights in New Orleans had solidified his position in, not only Baby Girl's life. But in the Morales family. His return to the manor was something the staff wanted to see. For they want him and Baby Girl to remain as solid as a rock. And to have a long fruitful and productive life, together. So at every turn, while he was at the manor, the staff gave him the royal treatment. They made sure he knew, they were on the side of them and their marriage. But the thing that hovers in his mind today, is how sweet the lovemaking was on his first night back. Since pulling away from the mansion, his mind has only been on holding his wife next to him again. The feeling has him so engulfed that he can't even focus on the show he has to deliver tonight. A prophet would say his inability to think of anything other than his wife, right now. Could be because he knows he left another young man in her midst, who from all others observation, was quite taken by Baby Girl and her genius. Whatever the reason for

Young D not being able to shake her loose from his conscience. He gives in to it and just calls it the force that draws him to her, like bees to honey. Or flies to shit, for that matter. He can't shake the feeling that tells him, he needs to be nearer to his wife. It has taken him over, to the point where he has the bus driver to take an unexpected detour. They stop at the house in Mississippi, for some privacy. He calls Baby Girl, who appears to be suffering from the same inability to focus that he is. When she sees his number on her Iphone caller ID, her face lights up as she answers. "Hey Derrick. What it do, baby?"
He can tell she's grinning.
He says, "What's good, baby? I'm in the sip. The house is looking good. They got it back to livable again. It really looks good."
His mood is jovial. She likes it. It means he's relaxed on the issue of her leaving him and is now determined that he will have constant contact with her. He wants her to know his moves, so she knows what he's up to, at every waking moment. She likes the sound in his voice as he says,
"It really looks good."
Her response is, "So does business. It's a family affair or a feud. Depends on which side of it, you're on. But it's nothing that can't be cleaned up. So just go on and mark that off the list."
He laughs. He knows by the tone of her voice. She's referring to Kid and that she's found more dirt on him. That makes his day even brighter.
"You clear anything out yet?" he asks with a chuckle.
Meaning, has she killed anyone since he left.
She says, "Not yet. There's nothing dirty enough, *this* weekend. But surely by the beginning of the week. You know Monday's are catch up days, for your girl." She giggles.

"You need to catch up with me, in Birmingham. So you can get me dirty. Then clean me up."

She tells him, she might be able to come to Birmingham. Because that show is on Monday. She asks him if he wants her to bring the boys out too. He says yes. He wants his whole family out on the road with him. Any time it's possible.

"So we can shop for Christmas," he says, "And we can see what they're flocking too, while we're in the stores."

"I will do my best to make the show, Derrick," she says, "And I hope I'll be bringing some good news with me too."

"It'll be good, period," he says, "As long as you're coming. It can't be anything but good for me."

He laughs. She catches his drift and laughs too.

"Get on to Mobile. Before I have you turning around and heading west," she says as they both laugh.

They hang up before allowing their horny tones to get the best of either of them. Young D gets his bus back on the road and Baby Girl gets back to her work.

There's some new news that she hasn't shared with him yet. It's about her latest hire, Teddy Jr. She's going to tell Young D about the new pro. But not until they're face to face. She has never had a male within her age range, working this closely with her. *Ever*. She does wonder how this will affect her husband. She reminisces on what he'd said when they were in Gary.

"One of the benefits of having a wife who's only been with me." he said, *"I don't have to worry about no jealous ex-boyfriend, being mad because I got her."*

If Baby Girl had ever come close to having a boyfriend, prior to Young D. Teddy Jr would be him. It was the summer of 1991. She was 8 years old. She had come home from Tristan Academy for her summer break, to volunteer in the city parishes, as she usually did with Wanda. Big Dog and his partner TJ was having a barbeque at 1 of the houses on the property, which they shared whenever they were in town. They had invited more than 200 women and only about 50 males was there. Those were the types of parties those 2 were always having. During this time, Baby Girl didn't have any idea Big Dog was her real father. She admired him because he was always extra nice to her. Thinking on it now. She wonders if all the half naked women hanging around him, had ever bothered her mother.

I doubt it. Mama loved daddy Don. They was always passionate with their PDA's. Just like Derrick and I. She only had eyes for daddy Don. He wouldn't have allowed Big Dog to be around, if mama still liked him. Of course, she didn't care who he had around his place. She was the lady of the mansion and married to The Don. His boss!

Lovely concludes that her mother had been over Big Dog, years before her and Don Morales were married. This is what both of them raised her to believe. Besides, Big Dog never acted as if he was bothered by his boss having the woman that he'd taken for granted. Baby Girl knew Big Dog and TJ were 2 of the main employees of The Don. They rarely hung around the manor. Now she knows why. They were always delivering packages. But during 1 of the rare times when they were at the manor and had a barbeque. Baby Girl was home from school. 1 of the women at the barbeque had a little boy with her. He was 7. Him and Lovely met that day and became fast friends. He was the only person in her age group who had ever come to any of their parties. He stayed on the property for a week, with his mother. They stayed in the house with TJ and Big Dog. Baby Girl and the little boy had started to like each other, by weeks' end. And by the time him and his mother went back home, she had experienced her first kiss. It was nothing that made the earth move, by any means. Nothing like what she had gotten when her and Young D first kissed. Her first kiss was closed mouth, lips tight and teeth clinched. They were next to the main pool house, right here on the property. That boy's name was Teddy Jr. He was cute then. He's flat out gorgeous now.

I wonder if he remembers that? Of course he does. He'd better. I cried when he left and I know he did too. Because I saw him crying as they were driving away.

She smiles as she reflects back on the days of her puppy love. It was something innocent and sweet.

"*Whoa.* Derrick came into my life and took me from puppy love and playing with baby doll's. To straight up, real love. With the moaning, rubbing, touching, passion marks and swapping items with each other. Anything else that people do when they're going steady. We did not pass go. Did not collect two hundred dollars," she says aloud as she giggles to herself. "He was the sugar for my sweet tea. The mint to my dewlaps. And he still is, today."

She laughs as she thinks about how much her life has changed since that innocent kiss between her and Teddy Jr. It was innocent and harmless. Still, it wasn't with Young D. So far, he thinks he's the only person who has ever been personal with her. So she has no idea if he'll brush it off. Or if he'll accuse her of keeping a secret. But she'll have to tell him. Because she doesn't keep secrets from her husband. She never lies to him either. She's trying to remember if she had ever mentioned Teddy Jr. She can't recall ever saying anything about him.

Maybe in 1996 when we first got together?

He surely wouldn't remember it now. Or knowing Young D, he would. He didn't say anything about it over the holiday, so she figures she never told him. But with Teddy being back in her life. She has to tell her husband about the kiss. If she gets to go to Birmingham in a couple days. She'll tell him then. Face to face and let it all shake out.

"And then I'll have to tell Teddy Jr that he's going to be working for *both* of us. Oh this should be *real* good. "

He's gonna feel cornered. Especially with his secret, just becoming exposed.

With all of the tension which surrounds her knowing about Danica and Kierra, Young D will probably be as paranoid as hell with another man around. Especially 1 who has the honor of being Baby Girl's *"1st kiss"*. She remembers how her, Young D and DeJuan laughed about Young D's comment, *"Not having to worry about a guy from her past."*

He's been *all* of her first, as far as he's concerned. On 2nd thought, he may not take to this information, very well. But she's going to tell him. Whatever happens. They'll work it out from there. An innocent kiss is nothing compared to an outside child.

"He still doesn't have anything to worry about. But he may just worry, anyway. Only because Teddy junior's a pro. Derrick will *definitely* demand to be trained now. He's isn't gonna be comfortable with Teddy junior being around me. He's gonna think Teddy junior still likes me. He'll wanna confront him. The fact that Teddy junior is a pro, *will* bother Derrick. He'll flat out object to us going out of town on jobs, together."

I can make sure TJ doesn't send us out, as partners. So that my husband won't have that worry.

She smiles as she thinks of how quickly the tables turned. Even though her situation is a mole hill, compared to his *Mount Everest*. She has always prided herself on being squeaky clean when it comes to the opposite sex. She smiles again. Then she gets back to work.

She cast her eyes upon the lone file which she'd taken from the safe. She places it on the desk and goes back to the stacks of invoices.

I know there's something here that'll give me exactly what I need to see. I need to see my brother's ties to Kierra. Have they used any of my money to pay her bills? She looks like the gold digger type. What is her real stake, in this? No one believes Derrick fathered her daughter. Except for her and Kid. Kid has already proven he'd try to do or say anything that would make me leave Derrick. I've already seen the proof that he funded the hits on both of us. I just need to clear this matter of that five year old little girl. Then I can send his ass to meet Satan. His maker!

She couldn't have been more correct about Kid, being willing to try *anything*. The answers she needs are still so close. That if it could leap up and bite. She would've been bitten 12 times, already. What she needs to see, is in the lone file. Only she hasn't concentrated on the lone file yet.

****

Meanwhile, out on the tour with Young D and H-Town records, they're in Mobile Alabama.

"It's time to grub, my *brotherz!*" Gat Em yells.

They had just finished sound check. It's 630pm. They have dinner reservations at, *Two Dollar Bills' Kinfolks Catfish Restaurant* for 7:30pm. They've just enough time to get a shower and eat. Then they'll have to get ready for their show. They're going to perform at the *Mobile Civic Center* . Their show starts at 11pm.

They finish their pre-show meal. Then Young D goes to relax in his hotel suite. He's feeling horny and lonely. He has a couple of hours before show time. He calls Baby Girl to thank her for sending them to Two Dollar Bills. And to flirt a bit too.

"It was off the chain, baby," he says, "I'm as full as a tick, on a mangy ass pit bull." They laugh hard.

"You're country as hell too, Derrick," she says as she continues to laugh, "You sound like daddy Don, with those country sayings."

"And you love it." he says.

"True that," she says as she agrees with him.

He's in a great mood. He quickly admits that he's thinking about his pre-show. Which is why he's calling her. He wants to talk about it since he can't actually do it.

"I can't be mad at that," she says, "I'd love some pre-show, *myself.*"

"Give me the audio version," he says as he chuckles.

He'll settle for phone sex with her, at this point. She's game for it too. They both dig in.

They talk about some sexual things while he opens his suitcase. He pulls out and surveys the show gear she'd packed for tonight's show. He likes the ensemble she put together. He has always liked the way she styles him. He pours himself a Hennessey neat and smokes his show blunt while they trade sex talk.

"My nipples are hard, just hearing you pour up that Hennessey," she says.

"My dick is hard while I'm thinking about those hard ass nipples too, baby," he counters.

They both giggle. They really do miss each other, a lot. But they both still have work to get back too.

"Call the boys in so I can tell them goodnight," he says. She summons Cherry and Maggie to bring their sons into the office.

Lil Man comes tearing around the corner from their dayroom. Baby Girl has put Young D on the house intercom system so he can speak to all the staff too. His junior can hear him. Which has sent his energy into overdrive.

"My daddy talking to me?" Lil Man screams as he comes running into the office. He yells into the speakerphone, "Daddy you coming back now?!"

"I have to work, man," Young D says, "But mommy's gonna try and bring you to see me."

"And my brother too?" Lil Man asks.

"Oh, yes sir," Young D says, "I wanna see both of y'all and mommy too."

"Okay, daddy. I'm coming to your work, okay?" Lil Man continues, "But right now. I gotta go take the bath. I gotta get in the water. I gotta *big* water, daddy."

"Uh huh. Cherry letting you bathe in the Jacuzzi?" Young D asks as he chuckles.

"I getting in the cuzzi," Lil Man says as he giggles at himself for not being able to pronounce it. He tries again, "the *cuzzi*," he laughs again and so does his parents.

Maggie passes Don Prince to Baby Girl. She tells him his daddy is on the phone.

"Say hey, daddy!" she tells him.

"Hey la-di-dah," he mimics her, "da-da-da-da."

They all laugh. The boys have to say goodnight so they can take their baths. After saying I love you, they hang up. Young D relaxes in his suite. Baby Girl gets back to her files.

Out in Houston, Kierra has gone in to work, early. She needs to talk to her bosses. She wants to know where Kid is and why she hasn't heard from him over the Thanksgiving holiday.

"We haven't heard from him either," 1 boss says.

As far as Kid's partners are concerned. They don't reveal anything about Kid being the private partner. Kierra doesn't either because Kid had told her to keep it a secret. He has her thinking it's because the other bosses will want more money, if they know he's the money partner. When the truth is, his partners know he's the silent partner and they're going to keep him silent because that is what Kid stipulated to them.

"I wonder if everything is alright," Kierra asks, "Can y'all call his family and check on him? I can't get him on his cell phone."

"If it was something drastic," boss 1 says, "Somebody would contact us."

"For what reason?" Kierra asks, trying to see if they'll slip up and admit that Kid is a partner.

The boss says, "Because he's a damn good friend of mine. His folks would let us know if he was ill or something like that."

"Well, I hope that's not the case," Kierra says.

"Why do you care, *anyway*?" boss 2 asks, "I thought you had it bad for *MC Young D*. Your rapper fantasy."

The 2 bosses laugh. Kierra blushes openly.

Boss 1 adds, "She does man. Look at her blushing."

"I'm not blushing.   just agree with you. That motherfucker *is* fine as hell. *Shit*. Who wouldn't want that?"

"You're after the money," Boss 1 says, "You're a God damn ready teller, when it comes to a niggaz money, up in here. I know you're *extra* hell, outside."

They all laugh.

255

"Speaking of money," she says, "I'm starting early, tonight. I need to clean up these damn tips. Christmas is right around the corner."

"What happen to your cake daddy?" Boss 2 says.

She doesn't know if he's aware that she was getting money from Young D. But she does know, for certain that Kid had never told them about her daughter being for Young D. He'd just told them that she had it bad for him. She leaves them to discuss her, after she's gone to the dressing room to change her clothes. She thinks to herself as she changes into her stripper gear.

Kid better come through for me, for the holidays. He done fucked up my shit with D. Me and Danica haven't gotten no parts of money since his wife found out. And I haven't had no more of my dick either! Something has got to give and soon. I know what I can do? I'm putting his ass on child support. He ain't gonna want this shit in the media. So he'll be trying to keep me quiet again. Yeah boy! I'll be getting that dick again, in no time.

She laughs as she heads for the stage.

****

In Harrisburg, James Lawson has a new letter from his pen pal. In the letter, there's a mild hint and more hints, that he'll get a lot more information as it becomes available. What Baby Girl is doing is stringing him along. In the letter today, she lets him in some of her own background. In the letter, part of it reads;

"That bowlegged woman that was staying in her house. Her folks left her wealthy. Not rich but wealthy. That's the kind of money most black folks don't know shit about. Generations of money. Old money. She bought Deloris property. PLUS bought Deloris a

brand new house. She set her up with a middle to high range, 5 figure salary at one of their many companies. I'm not sure which company she's working out of, yet. But I got my people on it. I'll know, in a little while. I do know that the bowlegged woman owns companies in Harrisburg too. They got shipping companies on the docks. Morales Enterprises is on damn near every container at our Harrisburg port and that's the company the bowlegged bitch owns. Everything from shipping to freight trains. Deloris could be at either company. When I first heard she was working for that woman and I knew that the woman was also from the label that the twins signed too. I automatically thought that Deloris had gone south. Now I see that she may not be. She wouldn't have had to go south. Not just to work for that company. You understand? She may still be in the Harrisburg area, pal. But with a new job, new car and a new house. I figure that was all done to throw you off of her scent. You know? If I was you. I would check out the docks. And for sure, keep an eye on her brother."

After reading the letter, James jumps into his F-150 pickup and heads to the Harrisburg docks.

He isn't allowed entrance without a badge or a pass. So he stakes it out, for about an hour. He's looking at the lay of the land. Trying to figure out which building housed the clerical jobs. He automatically assumes Deloris would be doing clerical work. But he doesn't know what kind of car she'd be driving now. So at 11pm, when there's a shift change. He peers into each and every vehicle as it comes and goes from the shipyard. But all he see are males.

"I'll have to get back here early," he says to himself. "When the day shift people come. I'll go asked what time do the business offices open."

He gets out of his pickup and approaches the security booth

again. This time, he's going to asks a legitimate question.

He says, "Hi. Can you tell me what time the business offices open? I wanted to check on an application that I have in."

"The business office opens at nine a-m," the guard says, "But all applications are done at the employment office. Our personnel director goes to the employment office and looks through them. She does the interviews there, on site. They don't do any of that here."

James asks, "Who is the personnel director? So I'll know who to ask for when I get there?"

"Her name is Mildred Greenwald," the guard says, "She'll be there Monday morning, for sure. She always goes in on Monday, to update and interview for the register. We keep a waiting list of folks trying to get hired on here. President George Bush ain't leaving us much to eat with, bro. Everybody without a job is trying to get one. And everyone with one job. Are trying to supplement that one."

"Alright, I'll go see her on Monday," James says as he walks away.

He's disappointed that the personnel director isn't Deloris. But he's still going to show up on Monday and ask Mildred Greenwald about a new hire name Deloris Flowers.

"I'll be down there, bright and early Monday morning," he says to himself. "That bitch thank she can leave me. I told her she'll never be able to hide for long. I'll find her. And when I do. I'm gonna cut her Goddamn heart out."

****

Back at the manor, it's a crispy cool night. The boys are sound asleep by now. Young D's show should be just kicking off.

258

Meanwhile, Baby Girl is still in the office, cooped up and working. She can now understand why her daddy spent long hours in this office, every day. When she wanted him to go shooting with her or riding horses or playing a game of basketball. Often times he would tell her that he was doing daddy's work. *Daddy's work* is very time consuming. But it's necessary, in order to find what you need. Especially when a member has gone rogue. Perhaps daddy Don was always watching Gus and countering his moves. Even back then. There certainly aren't any traces of his screw ups before the Don died. So that's all she can figure. Her daddy Don had kept his business files on the up and up. Even though, through Gus' computer, he may have thought he was casting a bad rep for *The Organization.*

All of that started about 6 years ago. Shortly after The Don had died. She's going to get to the bottom of it, if it's the last thing she does. She hasn't found any payments to Kierra, in all of the invoices she's viewed.

She calls TJ, Teddy Jr and Alfred. They hadn't seen any payments to Kierra Ramsey either. She hangs up and searches her brain.

"It's here and I know it is," she says aloud, as *this time* she pulls the lone file which she'd laid on the desk. She pulls it in front of her. It's the 1 which she'd gotten out of the safe with the invoices. Still she hasn't opened it.

I need to know why would Kid want me and Derrick dead? What happened? What did we do to him?

She thinks to herself while she thumbs through, invoice after invoice. She's finding very little new information. She already knows Kid is the buyer. Now she wants to know why.

Why does he hate Derrick so much? Enough to want us dead?

259

She thinks it over in her mind, to see if she can come up with any other clue. Anything Young D may have done to warrant this anger from Kid.

Surely it ain't behind that tramp ass bitch! It can't be. Is it the closeness we have? Is it because Derrick became my protector?

Young D did come into her life at a time when Kid was a hero to her. Kid was the 1 she looked up too. The brother who always gave her money or whatever else she wanted. He was her protector, in the wards. Young D changed all of that, very quickly after he came into the mix. He became the 1 who spoiled her and he was her man, as well. Kid would use the fact that she was *"young and innocent and he wanted her to stay that way"* as his reason for not wanting them to be together, back then. That was his main reason. *Then*. But her and Young D are married with 2 children now. They're both very successful and very much in love with each other. Surely that can't still be the……..!

I wonder why this file was in the safe and not filed with the rest of them? Got to be some juice here. What the fuck am I waiting on to search this one?

She opens it and pulls out it's contents. The 1st thing she spots are medical forms. She examines them closely.

This better not be something about my parents!

As she examines them closer. She notices what kind of medical forms they are.

"These are from paternity test. Two of them. Two different doctors."

She looks for the names that are printed on the 2 documents. She sees 4 names on each 1 of them. One test was administered by a Dr. Fallows. The other by a Dr. Rawls. She reads the names aloud, "Derrick Blake. Bradley Walker. Kierra Ramsey. Danica Ramsey."

The same 4 names are on both test. Why are there 2 test for the same people? And why was Kid tested? He's sleeping with that tramp bitch?! That can't be why he hates Derrick.

According to the dates. The first paternity test on Young D and Kid was the 1 done by a Dr. Kenneth Fallows. She reads those results, first. Her heads begins to pound. She can feel her emotions boiling up and forming *Mount St. Helens*!

"Oh my GOD! Oh my GOD! Oh Derrick! Oh GOD!" she yells, for that is all the words she can form, just now.
When she can speak, the only words that form are,
"They set Derrick up. Muthafuck Gus and Kid!"
She sees their names as the ones who hired the 2nd doctor. Dr. Rawls. She can't even believe what she has in her hands. What she's just found is monumental.

First, she looks over the 2 test again. She starts with Young D's portion of Dr. Fallows test. *The accurate test.* The 1 done and completed, 2 weeks before the fake doctor was hired and paid off. On the unblemished test, it has 99.9% that Young D is NOT a match for Kierra Ramsey and Danica Ramsey. She looks at Kid's portion of the unblemished test. It is 99.9% positive for Kierra Ramsey and Danica Ramsey. Kid is the father of Kierra's daughter. Not Young D!
"Son of a Bitch!" she screams to the top of her voice.
But these are screams of mixed emotions. She's happy for her husband, herself and their entire 12 year relationship. But she's angry as hell at her stepbrother Kid. She reads more of the file. The more she reads. The more she learns that this conspiracy is against her! The file has more in it. The more she

digs into it. The more she uncovers of the plot that is very descriptive. She sees the plan which was laid out for Young D. From the time him and Kierra met until his *"future"* demise. It was all staged and written out, like a movie script. She looks back at the copy of the fake test by Dr. Richard Rawls. This is the 1 Young D received. This is the 1 he'd told her about. The only 1 he'd gotten. She digs deeper into the stack of papers which she had pulled from the file. Finally she sees something which explains why she had to be killed. It's the explanation of what Emilio Pantango had touched on, when they were on the phone.

This was never about Derrick. It was about me, all the time. Derrick was collateral damage. This is what I've been looking for. The answer to my question, why?

She pulls out a long letter that was handwritten on a legal pad. It's written in Gus' handwriting. There is no doubt about it. She knows his writing, from the many packages she had. She reads the letter aloud. She cringes while trying to maintain her emotions.

<u>*B&G business plan*</u>
    <u>*The Morales empire*</u> *is more than capable of funding B&G Landscaping's interest in <u>the project</u>. Though Donnie Morales wasn't willing to fund us. We're going to convince his successor to do so. We'll need to have his heir, on our side, to secure the funds. And we will get her. Either willingly or by force.*
    In the event, the heir to Donnie Morales doesn't cooperate with the project. Then we'll need to remove her from the equation. She's the best at taking marks down. So to have her killed, will prove difficult. We need to try selling her on the

project, first. But we don't need her spouse as a beneficiary of hers. For she will be terminated. At a later date, for sure. Even if she does agree to stay on. We don't need another partner in B&G. Once the project has been completed and we have her trust. Then we can terminate her and gain her shares. Thus, we don't need her spouse around to inherit her fortune. B&G Landscaping needs to inherit her shares. We need control of the entire project and her fortune, as well. To remain as viable candidates for future developments. Her beneficiary will need to be terminated. He's high profile. This will cause a problem again. Her husband needs to be terminated, first. Then B, of B&G, will gain her complete trust. For he will take on the position as her comforter and confidante again. During this time that he's gaining her trust. He will learn the total assets of the Empire, including all gate codes, business codes, passwords, account numbers, safety deposit boxes, accounts receivable, payable and the net worth of the entire estate. With this knowledge, B&G Landscaping will soon have control of Morales Empire and the ability to fund many more projects. Not only in Orleans Parish but outside areas, as well. Not to exclude international. Step 1 is underway.

The dismantling of her spouses credibility. This is only the first step. Showing that he has fathered an outside child. The heir prides their relationship on the fact that she will be the only mother of his children. But she will learn of the outside child. Hopefully, their union will be severed. Thus relieving him of any hold on the heirs assets. But they have offspring now. B&G will need to secure guardianship of them from other empire employees: [Butler, head chef and head nanny] or terminate them as well.

She trembles. She can't read anymore. She sees all she needs to see and she's thoroughly disgusted.

263

Now I know why this file and this paperwork was hidden in his private safe. This was Gus and Kid's attempt at taking over my daddy's entire life's work. Everything my daddy, The Don had inherited. Everything his family had built. Everything that he past on to me, for my family, my offspring, my babies. They were willing to squander it, me, my husband, our children and their Godparents. They were ready to kill me and everyone whom I love and who loves me. And for what? GREED!

She reads every single document in the file. She now knows this plan was started, right after The Don had died. She sees a closed document which speaks on her mother.

Oh God. Please don't dare let me see anything that shows me that they had anything to do with the deaths of either of my parents. Please God. Because my emotions will get the best of me. I know it. And I will kill Kid out of rage and go to prison.

She looks at the file from end to end, for the 4th time. She finds no such information in the file which would indicate there was any foul play in the deaths of Big Dog, Don or Wanda. She calms down on that bit. With her emotions now intact again, she hashes her a plan of her own. 1 which will afford her the opportunity to clear the Morales name, keep her fortune and get rid of Bradley "Kid" Walker, once and for all.

"Because this motherfucker is so rogue that he has already plotted on killing my children. So Kid wants to control my mind, my life and my fortune. That is Derrick Jr and Don Prince's jobs, Kid. Now what does Kierra know of this whole plot? Because I don't see her name in my handwritten death certificate file letter."

Kierra's name was nowhere in the legal pad letter. So she really wants to know how much of this plan she has knowledge

264

of. She retrieves Kierra's phone numbers from the file. Then she puts the file back together neatly and locks it in The Don's office safe.

She calls the Commissioner and asks him to arrange a meeting between her and Kid, tonight. She thinks of a fabricated story to tell him.

She says, "I found some files from my fathers estate which Brian aka Kid and Gus, had altered. Some are missing. I need to know what they've done with them and I need to know immediately. It concerns campaign contributions too. I can't allow misappropriations. This will not wait until Monday."

The commissioner says, "It's done. Give me an hour. Then go to the parish jail."

He's thinking about saving his own ass. She knew he would. The Don definitely taught her how to play the game. She calls Charles and tells him what's going down.

She says, "I need you to drive me to see Kid, in one hour."

He tells her, he'll be out front and ready in 30 minutes. She locks the office and goes to freshen up.

While in the master suite, she calls DeJuan. The show starts in 15 minutes so she knows Young D will be in show mode, by now. DeJuan recognizes her number on his caller ID and answers his phone.

"Hello?"

"How's security?" she asks.

DeJuan says, "Not a blemish. Everything's been straight, out here, Baby Girl. *Everything.* How are things at the manor?"

"Couldn't be better. Tell Derrick I'll see him, day after tomorrow. I'm going back to Houston, first. For some loose ends. Tell him to call me, after the show."

"Automatic," DeJuan says and they hang up.

She makes a round trip reservation for her only, to go to

Houston tomorrow. She won't be going to their Estate. So she isn't taking their sons with her. Bruce and Jordan will fly to Houston, first thing in the morning. They have school on Monday. Her flight for her face to face with Kierra, leaves at noon.

After her flight is confirmed. She continues setting her plan for Kierra and Kid, in motion.

CHAPTER THIRTY TWO
ALWAYS OR NEVER AGAIN

Annie and Angela had gone to Kierra's and picked up Danica for the weekend, when they returned from New Orleans, earlier today. Annie figures this would be the best time to go and get her. Since Young D and the crew are all, still on Tour and won't be around the property. With Baby Girl, Bruce, Jordan and the kids still in New Orleans, Annie decides to let Danica come to the main house to visit and spend the weekend. Danica has never spent a night at Young D's estate. She has only visited twice. Kierra was more than happy to send her with them to stay. It gives her more time to do nothing, just as she's doing right now. She had laid down to take a nap after Annie, Angela and Danica left. It's hours later and she's just waking up. She decides she needs to call Annie to check on Danica. Just to seem as if she's responsible. She makes the call to Angela's mobile phone and gets a less than glorious greeting.

"Hello?" Angela says in an irritated tone, as she flips open her cell phone.

"Hey Angela. It's Kierra"

"I know. What is it now?" Angela asks, intentionally trying to sound bothered.

"I wanted to check on Danica before I leave for work," Kierra says.
Angela tells her that her little girl is doing fine. They're watching DVD's and munching out in the home theater room. They hang up.

Kierra is at her apartment with her roommate Trina. She noticed Angela's non-interest in talking with her and how she rushed her off of the phone. She talks about it with Trina.

"Well hell, girlfriend. I just wanted to know if D even knows that Danica is was over there," Kierra says to Trina.

"But Angela was rushing me off of the damn phone. She was rude as *fuck*."

"I'll bet you he don't know she's over there," Trina says, "He doesn't ever seem that concerned about her. Not to me, he don't."

Kierra ignores Trina and continues to get dressed for The Anatomy. Trina notices how Kierra ignored her comment about Young D's lack of interest in Danica. She changes the subject.

"Is Kid coming down, this weekend?" Trina asks.

"I haven't heard from him, in three days," Kierra says, "I don't even fucking know if he's coming. If he's already here or what the fuck he's doing."

Trina can feel that Kierra isn't as fond of Kid, as she had once been. Not since finding out that Kid was just using her to get Young D busted by his wife, has Kierra's reaction to mentions of Kid been pleasant. Kid does want Kierra as his side piece, though. But that's mainly for his own selfish reasons. He wants to use her to set up men and get their assets. He has plans of using her for everything from infidelity and extortion. To drug robberies. In the meantime, he plans to keep her in *Gucci* and *Prada*. Because he feels that she's mentally superficial. So he figures if he keeps her in designer names. She'll be willing to do whatever he ask her to do, to keep getting them. She'll benefit from her extortions of other men. But he stands to make *way* more than he'll ever give to her.

Today, Trina stays in her roommates ear about Kid. Her feelings about his intentions have changed drastically, since their trip to San Francisco. Since that botched trip, Trina's feelings have been that once Kid is done using Kierra. He'll have *her* killed. Even Kierra had started to believe the same.

Today is just one of those days when Trina feels like voicing it.

"If he'll hurt his own little sister, by trying to kill her husband," Trina says, "You should know that nigga don't give a fuck about taking you out the game too."

Kierra agrees as she says, "I've been feeling the same thing, home girl. My new feeling is, that nigga don't give a damn about nobody but his damn self. Now let's be out."

Already late for work, they head off for *The Anatomy*.

****

Baby Girl and Charles arrive at Orleans Parish correctional facility, at nearly midnight. They're escorted to the tier which houses Kid and seated in the visitors section. Within in minutes, Kid is escorted to the window directly in front of them. He picks up the phone. She does the same.

"Hey, Lil Lovely," he says with a smile.

A fake smile is how she sees it. And knowing what she knows about him now. That's the only kind it can ever be, as far as she's concerned. She will never feel love for Kid again. But she can fake it for now, to get to the greater good. But she does have to straighten him out on 1 thing. The name he is to call her.

"Don't call me Lovely, Kid," she says, "Only Derrick is allowed to call me by my government name. That was taught to me by my daddy Don. You and everyone else, are to call me, Baby Girl. Cool?"

"Cool," Kid concedes easily. Then he speaks again.

"Hey, Baby Girl," he says, still smiling.

"Kid. How long are you gonna be in here?" she asks.

"I got a hearing, Monday morning," he begins, "The thing is. I'm not even charged, right now. It's some bullshit, Lil

269

sis. Don't worry yourself about me. I'll be okay until Monday. But I'm gonna need for you to make these motherfuckahs get a move on, by then, though."
You must be kidding? Who's worried? Me? I'm not worried about your dirty ass. I just want to know when you're getting out so I can murk, yo bitch ass!

"I promise I won't worry," she tells him. "I just wanted to know how long you're gonna be locked up."
It takes everything she has inside of her to fake with a happy expression on her face. She makes small talk, initially. Telling him about Thanksgiving and how much fun his kids had at her manor. She made sure to look directly into his eyes, as she puts the emphasis on, *Her Manor*. He shifts from side to side on his metal stool and she can tell that he's nervous about talking to her. Even though, he's trying to appear unaffected by her sudden visit.
Why do I make you nervous, Kid?

She wants to go into a little more detail. So she asks Charles to have the guard on duty, move them to a room where they can talk without the use of the jail phones.
Charles goes to the guard and on his cell phone, he calls the commissioner. Then the commissioner talks with the senior officer on duty. The face to face visit is granted within minutes. They're moved to the contact visiting room, immediately. Baby Girl and Kid can continue their conversation, in complete privacy.
"Wow," Kid says, "You got a lil pull in here, ha?"
Kid asks as he sits down at the table in the contact visitors room. She doesn't answer him. She's ready to get down to what it is, she actually came to say.

First and foremost, she isn't going to let him know that she's located the *lone* file. Not at all. She's only going to give him enough information so that he knows she's on to him. But without alerting him that she knows the depths of him and Gus' scheme to take what's rightfully hers.

She starts off by talking about the bouncer from the Anatomy, whom she'd killed at Arnold Air Force Base.

"I asked to come in here. Because I didn't wanna put you at risk, by talking on those phones," she says.

"Put me at risk, how?" he asks, further playing out his innocent stance.

"You go to Anatomy a lot, don't you?" she asks as she watches his movements and reactions.

"Yes indeed," he says, "Usually every time I'm in Houston. Why?"

"I heard some bouncer got killed from there," she says, "But he was out of town when he got popped. Did you do that?"

"Nah. I didn't," he says.

"His name was Damien? Damien Glover. He worked at the Anatomy, for four years," she says, "You never heard of him nor saw him?"

"I may have. I don't know the bouncers. Not like I know the dancers. You know," he says as he grins, "I'm a man, lil sis. I'm more concerned with knowing the bitches who strip in there. Or bitches, period," he chuckles.
Oh you are quite full of yourself, aren't you?

He's laughing. She's not. She's still watching his reaction to her questions. Charles moves out of earshot, in hopes that Kid will open up a little more.

"It just seems strange to me that you don't know him,

271

Kid," she says, "You use to tell me that you kept up with everything and everybody, around you."

"I do, to a certain extent," he says, "But if I ain't doing business with them. Then I'm not gonna remember them."

"So you and Damien never had any type of business together? Is that what you're saying?"

"That's what I'm saying," he answers.

"I know you know Kierra. She works there, right?" she says "She knew him and you know her, right?"

"That means nothing," he says quickly.

Neither do you! Not to me!

She has to shake his ass up, just a little bit. She leans in, so he can hear her whispers.

"Cut to the chase, Kid," she says, "That's what you use to tell me. Right? Skip the dumb shit? Isn't that what you use to tell me?"

"Yes. A phrase to live by, Lovely," he says.

"Only my daddy and my husband sound good calling me that," she says, "And my daddy's dead. Both of them."

"I've always called you that too," he tries.

"Yes you have," she says, "But I just told you, not to call me that. Plus you never sounded right saying it."

"Oh well. Okay," he says as he shrugs his shoulders.

She can tell he's putting a lot of effort into acting unconcerned about her last comment. Which is why he repeated her birth name again. Though she'd told him at the start of their talk, not to call her by her government name. She must cover more.

"So let's cut to the chase. I know you hired Damien to kill Derrick," she says suddenly.

Out of habit, he looks at her. Then quickly he looks away. Then back at her again.

"You're guessing that," he tries, "You've got the wrong dude, sis. D is my brother-in-law."

He stutters over that response but she can tell that he was preoccupied with something else that she'd said before the last accusation. She guesses he's preoccupied with her mentioning Kierra.

Does he think I've talked to Kierra?

He's wondering. Not only if Baby Girl has talked to her. But also, if she knows about the switch him and Gus pulled with the paternity test. And if Kierra told her about his ownership of The Anatomy. But still he doesn't crack. He doesn't give up anything.

He's so use to fucking over people that this shit hasn't even rattled him.

She goes in for the sustenance. The real meat of what she wants him to know, tonight.

"Derrick is my husband and you're like a brother to me. You are my brother's, brother," she says, "It really disappoints me to know that you care so little about me."

"I don't know where you're coming from, with this," he tries, "I would never hurt you."

"It's not the hurting that I'm worried about," she says, "It's the killing, that's got me bothered."

"Baby Girl, you've got it wrong," he persist.

"You don't sound any better saying Baby Girl. It must be fake," she says, "It sounds forced."

He decides not to comment, this time. She tells him she doesn't believe him and he'll need to prove it to her.

She says, "Kid. I love Derrick and he loves me. He may fuck off with a groupie, every now and then. But he's coming home to

273

Me. Every night. He takes care of us, like a man is suppose too. As my brother, you should love that. But you hate Derrick. So you want to set him up with a stripper bitch like Kierra. Why?"

"I didn't set him up with anybody," he says, "He was grown, then. Just like he's grown now. He wasn't good enough for you, then. And he's not good enough for you now. I've always told you that."

"Yes, you have," she says. Then she asks him, "So who is good enough, Kid? You?"

"You're my sister, Baby Girl," he says, "Of course, not me. But someone who has what you have-"

"He does. He's got a son name Derrick Jr and a son named Donovan Prince. He has seven homes in four states. He owns an Empire and businesses, all over this country and international too. That's just to name a few things that he has, just like me."

"I'm not talking about what he got through you."

"He didn't get it through me," she says, "He's built his own, with daddy's help. Just like you. And you're a hypocrite."

"How am I a hypocrite?" he asks.

"The same way that I got mine and he got his. Is the same way that you got yours," she says, "Daddy helped you come up on everything that you have today, Kid. He did the same thing for Derrick, Terry, Craig, William, Marcus and Greg, as he did for you and Roger junior. He helped each one of you get in touch with the right music industry people. And that's how all of you got the Unity contracts, in the first place."

"I never said he didn't help us get set up," he says, "I knew he helped Soldier, Baby Boy and all of them, get set up too. When they left our label. He helped them to get their own thing jumped off. Yeah. I know that."

"And you hold a grudge because of that?" she asks quickly.

"No. I don't hold a grudge," he says.

"Is the grudge because I own just as much of your company, as you do?" she asks.

"Nah, baby girl."

This is the first time she had even considered this as a reason Kid would want to take over Don's efforts. Because Don had helped the guys who left Kid's label, still become successful without Kid and Six Nine. If that were a reason. She thinks that would only be a minor piece to the puzzle. She's thinking that Kid could want to get control of all of her stocks so that he can have ownership of her and all of the brothers plus Young D too. Like he did before they discovered that he was a selfish asshole and split from his label. Or could it be that he wants her out of their cookie jar? But she knows it's more than that. No matter how many pieces to the puzzle she discovers. They don't over shadow what she concludes is his main reason. Kid and Gus' ultimate reason for the nearly decade old, *whole plot*, was simply greed.

"And you know I own a percentage of each of their labels too," she says, before taunting him with, "Don't you?"

"Yes I know that," he says, "I know you own shares in my label. Just like you own shares in Geezy and Young G too. And their labels just started in the last four years. That was after the Don died."

"I have shares in their labels because they asked me to take shares and give them guidance," she says, "Or should I say. They wanted the benefit of the insight they could receive from my staff and employees. I have the same benefits at Derrick's label. And he got his own distribution deal. He didn't go to Unity. But I own a third of you and Six Nine's label."

"I know he went to Atlantis, *instead*," he says, "I know he worked that out without The Don. But I'm sure you had a lot to do with the whole connection."

He avoids discussing the fact that she owns just as much of his label as *he* does.

She says, "You're wrong again. Derrick and his manager JB, pulled that deal with Atlantis together. Without me or my staff. He can make moves with his label without one word from me. Which is something you can't do. I have to sign off on everything your label does."

And that's why you want my shares and holdings. You asshole.

"Okay. I know he got that deal *alone*," he says, "That didn't come until after Don had died already. So why are you bringing it up?"

"That's not the proof that daddy didn't help him get it," she says, "Soldier and Craig's labels came after he died too. So neither is that proof that daddy wasn't apart of theirs. My *word* is. And I'm so sick of you running down my husband's name like he's some gold digger. That's what *your* bitch is. The one you're sending after *my* man."

"I'm not sending anybody," he lies.

"You keep referring to Derrick as a deadbeat who's after my money," she says, "These are the facts. The income from Derrick's businesses are what pays all our overhead. Including the bills at the manor. Even though daddy left specific funds for the up keep of the manor. My husband pays for all of it. Including the staff's salaries because he wants daddy Don's money left for our sons, as well as the rest of the assets. And for the staff's children too. He did this out of his loyalty and respect to my daddy and to show his appreciation for what he *did* do for him. Because he loves and respects my

276

parents and me. Now. Where is your loyalty to my daddy? I mean. Can't you see that this meeting is about more than just Derrick? Can you, Kid?"

Kid still denies setting up the hits on Young D. Again, Baby Girl tells him how much she loves her husband and how much he loves her.

"I need for you to tell me exactly what the whole situation with you and Gus is about. And will you stop trying to mark my husband? That's all I need to hear from you."

He starts, "I don't know what it's about, Baby Girl. Because I don't know what the hell you're talking about-"

"I got the five hundred gee's out of Gus's safe," she says, "The three hundred fifty thousand from you, for me to kill my own husband in San Francisco. You must've known that one wasn't going to happen. Because you put down an additional one hundred and fifty thousand toward our demise. I got it all. It's all mine. I'm the only pro to get work from *The Morales Organization.* Oh yes. And the extra one fifty? That was for those four packages Gus had done before he met his maker. The ones you paid him to arrange with all the clues open to get me caught up. One of those tainted packages is the reason you're in here, as we speak."

She smiles coyly. Instantly, Kid becomes nervous and it shows. He knows that secret file was in Gus's safe, along with that money she has just mentioned. He knows the file held the secrets of what their ultimate goal was. And it also held the information that'll prove he was setting up her husband with Kierra. He wonders if she'd found it. But still, he plays ignorant to her accusations.

"What five hundred gee's?" he asks.

"Quit playing stupid. I know about the hit on me from fourth of July. Mark Genolli? That was from you too?"

She plays as if she doesn't know it was him who hired Mark. She watches him stumble over phases as he changes and shifts on the bench, to find the next words. She continues talking before he can say anything. She wants him to think she hasn't seen the secret file.

"Alfred, TJ, Teddy junior and Charles was in Gus' house, with me. They got all the files and the other stuff, out of his house and his safe. They moved it all to the main house and they're going over it, piece by piece. I got the money, though. Because it's mine. When you kill a pro who has an order to kill you. That when you collect. Mark had a mark for me. But I bust his ass and his second rate professional bodyguard too. You should've known you was fucking with the best, Kid. I'm the best to ever do this, is what my daddy Don and big Dog told me."

"You've got me confused with someone else, Baby Girl," he still tries.

"No more hits on Derrick, Kid," she says calmly. "Now the next thing I'll do is I'm going to go to Houston and talk to your bitch. If she doesn't come clean with me. I'm gonna slit her fucking throat, collect her blood in a bottle and make you drink it. Now. It's time for me get back to the manor and see what the men have found out. For your sake. Your name had better not be in it. And as for now. I'll just say you may see me forever or never again. It all depends on what that file holds."

Charles knows this is her time to leave. He can see her emotions coming into play.

"Baby Girl. It's time," Charles says.

She stands and turns to leave. Kid is still seated. The look on his face, shows that he knows his game will end soon. He's pondering all that has taken place in their meeting. Baby Girl turns back to him, bends down to his ear and whispers,

"It's either now or never. Will you leave my family alone? Yes or no?"

"I never have bothered you or Young D and I never will. Now come on and get me the fuck out of here, sis," he tries.

You're safer in this motherfucker,. You bastard!

She walks out without even looking back at him. On her way out of the tier, she has an order for the guards.

"Do not let him use the phone before he gets released," she tells them. "He's angry with his girl and he's going to upset her, if he has the opportunity to call."

"The Commissioner will call you and put his stamp on it," Charles clarifies, "He'll be calling, within the hour. I don't want my family harassed by this man."

The correctional officer says, "Yes sir. We'll take care of it."

The lead guard adds Kid to the no-call list immediately. Baby Girl is satisfied that he cannot call Kierra before she'll see her, tomorrow. She only needs to learn what, if anything, Kierra knew about this greedy plot that Kid and Gus were executing. According to the file, Kierra only seems to be a pawn in Kid and Gus' game. But Baby Girl has to be absolutely sure. Kierra's apartment is where Kid stays, whenever he's in Houston without his wife and kids. Baby Girl wants to know did she or did she not know that Young D wasn't the *real* father of her daughter.

For her sake, her involvement better be minimal or I'm cancelling her ass for good measure. I'd have to do her, after today but that's no big deal. That bitch has been fucking my husband. My man! That's cause enough for me to take her tramp ass out. I only hope she can shed some light on why, she was chosen. Plus I wanna know does she know her child is not

279

Derrick's. Because if she does know it. Then she's using him just like Kid was.

    While Baby Girl and Charles head back to the manor. She's going over all of the things she discussed with Kid, as she reflects on how he tried to deny his intentions and involvement. But she has his ass right where she needs him. Her senior staff is going to make arrangements for Kid to stay in jail until she's done with his package. His day to be marked is approaching rapidly. She already has that taste in her mouth. When she does kill him. She'll be correcting a few things. 1, she will be cleansing her family tree, saving herself, her husband and her fortune. While at the same time. She'll be getting some revenge for her fellow victims of Katrina, who was about to *forever* lose any claim to their land and the city they love and was displaced from.

    "Charles I feel a certain type of relief, *this* early morning," she says, as they ride back to the manor. "I feel as if a weight has been lifted off of my shoulders."

    "Misses Baby Girl you *should* feel pretty good," Charles says, "You have uncovered a gold mine. Alfred, Addie Mae, Cherry and I have been bidding our time. Just waiting on the day that Gus did something irreversible. We knew you would get him and put him in his proper place."

    "Did y'all know what him and Kid were up too?"

    "We always knew Gus was a rogue," he admits. "Donnie knew that too. He only kept him here for a closer view. He knew if he fired him. He would go somewhere else and really become a problem. We feel like he left him here, so you could expose and dispose of him."

    "He told me Gus couldn't be trusted. I could never understand why he kept him here," she says, "I thought maybe

280

he had a gambling problem or something like that. And couldn't be trusted with money."

"No. Gus was his *own* problem," Charles says, "Don had us all set up, *real* nice. I mean from the original Don Morales, two generations before your daddy. Each one of his senior staff have legitimate businesses which are all protected under the Don's umbrella. We all have something to pass on to our *children's* children. Gus had the same. But his greed caused him to lose it all. *Twice*."

"How did he lose it?" she asks as they pull in through the manor gates and her phone begins to ring.

"You've got an important call to attend too," Charles says, "We can go over that, at another time."
She smiles as she listens to her ring tone.

I've been really trying, baby. Trying to hold back this feeling, for so long. And if you feel…, like I feel baby. Come on. Oh! Come on. Woo! Let's get it on. Aaahhh baby!… Let's get it on!

It's Young D's ring tone. He's done with his Mobile show. Baby Girl answers as she gets out of the limousine and heads inside her mansion.

"Hey, baby. How was the show?" she asks.
He says, ""It was alright. But I need you to be here, for the show to be great."
They laugh. He always says that. He tells her, he's going to grab a quick shower. Then he wants her to call him back when she gets in the bed.
"I'm not hitting the clubs, tonight," he says, "I wanna phone fuck you."
They laugh again.

"You know I'm always down for some Derrick sex.

281

Anyway I can get it," she says as she agrees to call him back, a little later.

They hang up. She goes into her son's rooms and kiss them both goodnight, before she heads to her master suite.

She takes a shower. As soon as she's under her covers, she calls Young D back.

Young D answers with a funny line. He chuckles and says, "This is the Derrick Blake's Lovely Girl bus station. Where you can hop on my seat and I'll ride you, for cheap."

"Oh *God*, Derrick," Baby Girl giggles, "You've got a million of those things. Don't you?"

"Yes."

She says, "Because you only have one dick. And it belongs to me."

"Come on and get your property, baby girl," he says, sounding almost demanding.

"I wish I could be there, right now and tuck you in."

"So do I," he says, "I would try to break this bone off in that pussy, right about now. If I could get my hands on you. We wouldn't stop until the cops come knocking."

"They would have to break down the door," she says, "Because we would be knocking boots, harder than they could beat on *any* door."

They chuckle.

"I need to feel your pussy, Lovely," he reiterates.

"That pussy you're talking about, is *your* pussy, Derrick," she says.

"I wanna fuck, Lovely," he says.

"Lovely wants to fuck you too," she says as they both laugh again.

"This shit is unreal," he says, "I'm thinking about all the changes we've been through, in just *this* year."

"We've got a few more changes to get through," she says, "But they're good changes."

"What's happening?" he asks, "You got something? Please tell me you got something, good."

"Oh I do, Derrick," she says, "But I'll have to tell you in person. It's just that good. You're gonna want to fuck me, instantly. So I can't tell you until I see you. I'm bringing it to you personally. On Monday. I have a few more loose ends to tie up, first. But it's looking really good."

In a demanding tone, he says, "Then let me know what time you're getting here."

"I'm making our reservations, right now," she says.

She has her laptop in bed with her, making airline reservation for her and their 2 sons, to Birmingham, Alabama for the next day.

"We'll fly out tomorrow morning at ten minutes to nine," she tells him, "We'll arrive in Birmingham at one, in the afternoon. Will the tour bus be there, by then?"

"Oh for sure and I'll make sure we do," he says, "We're leaving out before ten, tomorrow morning. I'll get DeJuan to get a rental car, when we get there. We'll be there and waiting when y'all land."

"Something else to look forward too," she says.

They get back to the phone sex. He's satisfied he'll see his family, in 36 hours. He can relax his mind now and talk about what new sex positions he wants to try with her when she arrives. They talk for an hour before he demands she get some sleep. She tells him the same.

"Kiss my sons, for me," he says.

"I did already," she says, "They're sleeping peacefully.

"Then I can too," he says, "I love you, Lovely girl."

"I love you too, Derrick," she says.

They exchange a few kisses by phone. Then they hang up. She falls asleep, almost immediately.

****

Charles calls Annie, first thing Sunday morning. He reminds her that he's putting Bruce and Jordan on a flight home. She confirms that Corleone will pick them up at the airport, in Houston. She also tells him, she had picked up Danica when she returned and allowed her to spend the weekend with them. He informs Annie that Baby Girl isn't coming back today.

"She has a mountain of work to finish up, today," he tells Annie, "Then I have to take her and the boys to the airport. The same time, tomorrow morning. They're going to Birmingham to meet Young D."

"He'll be happy," Annie says, "I haven't told them about me picking up Danica."

"I want mention it either," Charles says.

"Oh okay. But you can tell Baby Girl, Charles," Annie says, "I want her to know that she's been here."

"Okay. I'll tell her when I get back," Charles says and they hang up.

As he drives to the airport with Bruce and Jordan, Charles is thinking about the conversation Baby Girl had with Kid. Then he thinks about the conversation he had with Baby Girl, on the way back for Orleans parish jail. He can't wait to get the senior staff together so they can tell her what made Gus a rogue, decades ago. He then thinks about his conversation with Annie.

Well she did the responsible and human thing. She went to get the little girl for a visit. Annie always said that wasn't her grandchild. Just as all of us, on the staff said. But still she's doing her duty as the only grandmother the little girl knows. I just can't wait until Baby Girl uncovers the obvious dirt behind that paternity.

Charles arrives back at the Manor, from his 1st airport trip today. But he has another one to make. The next airport trip is for Baby Girl. He drives Baby Girl to the airport to catch her flight. She's going to Houston.

Charles and Baby Girl head into the airport and make their way to her flight gate. Charles makes sure to let Baby Girl know about his talk with Annie and make certain she knows, he didn't disclose this trip to her mother-in-law.

Baby Girl says, "I know you wouldn't do that, sir. So, mama Annie has the little girl at that house?"

"Yes. She said she was going to keep her today. While Young D was on the road," Charles tells her.

"Oh. Okay. That's fine," Baby Girl says, "Sir Charles. I'm not going home when I get to Houston. I'm going to Kierra's place. I found something in the files that I have to know the answers too. Before I can even think about a package for her."

"So you're not planning to kill her, today?" he asks.

"No sir. I just wanna know if she knew that Derrick wasn't her daughter's father," she says.

"You found proof, didn't you?"

"I sure did, Charles," she says, "All of y'all was right. That's not Derrick's baby. Kid is actually the father. Gus helped him to fake a test and fool Derrick."

"I want you to make plans to be at the manor, when you tell Young D the entire story," Charles says, "So we can help both of you understand why Gus was labeled a rogue. And

285

why you was the person the Don wanted to terminate his ass."

"It's a date," she says with a smile, "And please let mama Annie know that I don't have a problem with Danica visiting the house. After all, she *is still* my niece. But I want Derrick to be the first one I tell about the real paternity."

Charles says, "We'll have to introduce that little girl to Joyce Wesley. Let her know that's her *true* grandmother."

She says, "Yes. And it's because of the news you guys helped me to uncover. Today may very well be the last time Danica sees mama Annie, as her granddaughter. I think that little girl would be better off without either of her biological parents. They're both losers. I feel sorry for her and I don't even know her. Really I do."

"But you're not killing her mother, today. Correct?" Charles asks again, "I'm just trying to be clear on that."

"Nor her father," Baby Girl says, "Not today, I'm not. But I'm not ruling it out. The father is going to die. The jury is still out on the mother, at this point. I'm going to see her today. Then I'll make that determination."

"Have a safe flight, Misses Baby Girl," he says as she heads through her flight gate and down the gang blank to the tarmac.

****

James Lawson received another letter from his pen pal yesterday. He's giddy with excitement because his pen pal finally reveals where Deloris is living, for certain. The pen pal tells him that she lives in the southern united states. The letter tells James what Deloris' exact job description is.

The letter reads:

She works for a shipping company, down in Houston Texas. She

286

is the personal assistant to the CEO of the company. I don't know that persons name. I live in Houston, myself now. Because my leads brought me here. I have a personal interest in seeing Deloris get what she deserves. She lives in Houston. So make plans to travel here soon. She has met a man and she meets him downtown. When I write to you next. I will have her job address, her home address and her hotel rendezvous schedule. Then, if you can find a way to get here and catch her while she's out. She's all yours. But she lives on the same property as that Hip Hop artist and his wife. That artist that signed her twins and took them off with him. Which ultimately caused Deloris to leave you and follow them. You might want to get their asses too. But 1 step at a time. I'll let you know where the hotel is and when she'll be going back there. Because going to her house is impossible. They live a gated community with armed guards, all around the properties. I don't want you getting arrested in Houston because I already know she has ruined your life and got you on papers, in Harrisburg, as it is. We'll get her. Me or you, one.

James Lawson is beside himself with anticipation, excitement and anxiousness. He now has a destination city to which he can use his free airline ticket to travel too.

"I told you I would find you, wherever you ran off too, bitch," he says to himself as he glares at his free airline ticket and the letters he'd received.

He says, "I'll never let you leave me and live!"

****

Kid insisted on using the phone, all night but his request were denied. He resumes his request again today. But all of his request are denied by order of the commissioner,

287

again. The commissioner had sent the order to deny him phone privileges until he's released. The commissioner called Charles as he was returning from his second trip from the airport after dropping Baby Girl off for her flight, to make him aware.

The commissioner says, "He tried everything, man. But we're holding him down."

"We'll be sure an show our appreciation, like always," Charles tells him.

When commissioner and Charles phone call ends, Charles sends a text to Baby Girl's cell phone to pass that info on to her.

Baby Girl has only packed her day bag, for Houston. She didn't bring a hit bag along. She's hoping she won't need it. She left with all of Kierra's phone numbers. She'd called DeJuan before her flight and gotten Kierra's address. She tries swearing him to secrecy and promises she'll tell him what transpires, as soon as she can. She hangs up without saying goodbye because the flight attendants are standing over her, demanding she turn her cell phone off, so they can depart. She does and they depart, on time.

But what Baby Girl didn't know was that Young D was walking into the room as DeJuan was giving her the information on Kierra. Young D heard DeJuan say Kierra's name and then give Baby Girl, Kierra's address. When DeJuan hangs up the phone and turns around. He's staring Young D, right in the face. Young D has a look of betrayal on his face. He wants to know what's going on, immediately. Keeping his voice calm, is easy for Young D. However, his line of questioning is straight and to the point.

"Why are you giving my wife the address to *that* bitch's apartment?" he asks, "What the fuck is going on?"

DeJuan doesn't answer. He tries to divert the question.

"She didn't believe she lived in the Houston area, bro," DeJuan tries.

"Come on, Juan," Young D says, "I've been your boy since third grade, man. Lying was never something you could get by me with. What's the deal? Is she going to kill her? Yes or no?"

"No."

"Why did she need it?" Young D asks.

"She needs to talk to her."

"You could've given her the phone number," he says, "If all she wanted to do was talk."

Young D is dialing Baby Girl's cell phone but he isn't getting an answer. He doesn't know Baby Girl is in flight. He wasn't told that she was going to Houston today. He dials her number again and this time, he leaves a voice mail and marks it urgent.

"Lovely. This is your husband. I need to talk to you, right now. Please don't do anything that will get you caught up. If you do her. The police are going to look at every lead. Her little girl will lead to me and then you. Baby, please don't do this one. Call me!"

He hangs up and looks at DeJuan, in anger.

Then he says, "I can't believe you gave her that Goddamn address. She's going to get caught up, on this one! I need to call mama."

"Don't call your mama, man," DeJuan says, "She don't know Baby Girl is coming in either."

"More reason to tell her," Young D says, "I can't afford to not say something. I cannot live without that woman."

"She's not gonna kill her, bro," DeJuan says, "She was in a damn good mood. She said she has some good news and some very important information that she wants to confront Kierra with. And it couldn't wait until tomorrow."

"Is Kid in Houston?"

"I don't know," DeJuan says, "She's going there to talk to Kierra. But she told me something else about your mama's house."

"What?"

"Danica is over there," DeJuan tells him, "She's staying for the weekend."

"That explains why mama hasn't called me," he says, "And that could also be why Lovely thinks this is the best time to smoke her."

DeJuan gives him a doubtful look.

"Nah. You'd better be right, brother," Young D says, "Because if anything happens to my wife. It's gonna be the end of our friendship. And you know I'm not lying."

"I know and I accept that," DeJuan says, "That's a bet. Now calm down and wait for Baby Girl to call back. Alright?"

"Alright. Cool," he says, "But I'm calling mama about her little weekend company."

He calls Annie's house.

****

Baby Girl's flight arrives in Houston, in the early afternoon. As soon her plane starts it's taxi to the terminal, she powers up her cell phone. She's thinking.

Should I go get my back up gun?

No! Annie and Angela are there. Plus Jordan and Bruce are back home now too. They'll know I'm in town and so will the police. Because I flew here. Damn!

God please don't let this bitch piss me off.

By the time they reach the gate, she has 10 missed calls in her log and an urgent voice mail. She gets off the plane and into the terminal before checking her call log.

It's Derrick. He's called me 10 times, back to back. Oh God! Something's wrong! I have an urgent voice mail. Let me listen and find out what the urgency is about.

She listens to his voice mail as she heads toward the rental car agency.

"*Lovely. This is your husband. I need to talk to you, right now. Please don't do anything that will get you caught up. If you do her. The police are going to look at every lead. Her little girl will lead to me and then you. Baby, please don't do this one. Call me!*"

She smiles and concludes that he'd overhead DeJuan's end of their call.

"DeJuan's going to stay in training opts until he learns how to shake Derrick," she says aloud, just before reaching the rental agents counter.

Derrick don't worry about the police being led to you. That's the good news I'm bringing tomorrow. Then I'll have to stop you from killing her.

Or maybe I won't.

She rents a car and begins her drive from Hobby airport. She forgets about swinging by the house for her tools. She calls her husband, who answers on the first ring.

"Hello," he says, anticipation in his voice.

"Hi Derrick. What's so urgent?" she asks as she smiles.

"Lovely, baby. What are you gonna do?" Young D asks. "Please tell me you're not on a hit. You haven't done anything, have you?"

"No, Derrick. I've just arrived and rented a car," she

291

says, "I'm not going to hurt anyone. Don't worry."

"You can forget that," he says, "I worry every time you're out of my sight. It's a natural instinct now. I can't control it."

She says, "I'm just gonna talk to her, Derrick. I'm not going for any drama. Hang on, while I connect her on three way. Then you can *hear* how calm I am. Okay?"

"Uh huh," he says, still not even wanting her to be near Kierra.

She holds his call and dials Kierra. Then she clicks him back over, so he can listen.

She's driving straight to the 5th ward and straight to Kierra's apartment. She's less than 10 minutes away. After 4 rings, Kierra answers. She's still groggy from her late night at work.

"Hello."

"May I speak with Kierra Ramsey, please?" Baby Girl asks, recognizing Kierra's voice.

"Who is this?" Kierra asks.

"This is Derrick Blake's wife. Lovely Blake."

Kierra is stunned. Baby Girl can hear her fumble with the phone. She smiles to herself.

Be afraid, bitch. Be very afraid.

CHAPTER THIRTY THREE
THE UNRAVELING

"This is Kierra. Can I help you?"

"It's, *may* I help you?" Baby Girl corrects her.

She chooses the intimidation play on the phone, just to get Kierra back on her heels for when she arrives. Kierra is none the wiser. Baby Girl gets on to the point of the call, while Young D listens on 3-way,

"But whether you can help me or not. Is what I'm here to find out. I need a few minutes of your time, Kierra," Baby Girl says. "I have some questions for you and a few suggestions too. Are you open for it?"

"What questions?" Kierra asks.

She says, "Face to Face, Kierra. I'm not going into this, on the phone."

Baby Girl pulls up to the apartment complex, gets out with her laptop and the file. She goes up to the door of Kierra's apartment. Kierra is still on the line. She thinks this is a set up.

"So now I'm suppose to meet you somewhere, so you can jump me *again*?" she asks. "I ain't stupid."

"You don't have to meet me anywhere. I'm at your door, Kierra. This is where I wanna talk to you at. Right here, at your apartment. This is serious business and it's about your daughter. Now do you want to hear what I have to say or not?"

Kierra looks out the peephole of her apartment door. She can see Baby Girl standing at her door.

"Is that *all* you wanna do is talk?" she asks.

"Just talk. That's all."

"Okay. Here I come," Kierra says and they hang up.

Kierra drops her cell phone on her coffee table. It takes her a few minutes before she comes to the door. Because she's telling Trina what's going on. Baby Girl tells Young D, she needs to hang up and she will call him and DeJuan back, as soon as she's done here. He doesn't want to hang up. But she insists. She doesn't want him to hear what she tells Kierra. She wants to tell him in person and see his reaction, firsthand. He finally hangs up, just as Kierra is opening the door.

"Hey. Come on in," Kierra says.

Baby Girl enters the apartment. Her nose catches a very familiar scent, right away, as her eyes survey the room. Trina is there too. Kierra has asks her to join them so she will feel comfortable having Baby Girl here. Trina's sitting on the couch. There's a picture of Danica on the coffee table. It seems out of place. Like it had *just* been placed there. Kierra offers her a seat, directly in front of the picture.

Yeah she just put it here for me to see. Lol It's my niece, bitch. Not my man's baby. You and your home girl look scared as fuck. Lol

Baby Girl greets both females and lets Trina know that she is welcome to stay too.

"I have no problem with talking, while both of you are here," Baby Girl says as both females smile, nervously.

Baby Girl sits down, opens her laptop and gets right down to the business of her visit.

"I know you were seeing my husband," Baby Girl says, "And I emphasize, *were*. He broke it off with you, after May thirtieth. I know you've been knowing him, for over seven years. I know you had a daughter in two thousand two, which is suppose to be his. Am I right, so far?"

With a stunned expression, Kierra says, "Yeah."

Baby Girl says, "Okay. We'll start there, first. Do you have a copy of the paternity test?"

"Yes," Kierra says.

Baby Girl asks, "May I see it? Can you get it for me, please?"
Kierra says, "Sure."
She heads to her *important* papers drawer. She retrieves the copy of the paternity test, she has. Then she returns to the living room. She hands her copy to Baby Girl. Immediately, Baby Girl see that this is the test done by Dr. Richard Rawls. *The false test.* She smiles as she glares at the phony document she's holding in her hands.
If this is her only form of knowledge about the paternity. Then she's in the clear, as far as the setting up of Derrick. Just as long as she didn't know that this doctor faked these results. But that's what I need to know. Did she know this shit was fake?

"Is this all that you have?" Baby Girl asks.

"Yeah. That's what the doctor gave us?" Kierra says, feeling braver now. "And as you see. It shows that D is the father."

"And they didn't even have to go to *The Maury Povich show* to get that truth," Trina adds as the 2 females snicker.
Baby Girl stays calm. She knows she'll have the last laugh.

"Is this doctor's office here or in New Orleans?"
Baby Girl asks Kierra this question because she wants to know if she knows the doctor, *personally.* If he's local. Then that's a possibility. But Kid has spent a lot of time in Houston in the past decade and so did Gus. This could be, *all* their doings. Baby Girl is going to get to the bottom of who perpetrated this fraud. She waits for Kierra to answer.
Kierra says, "He's got a office here and in New Orleans."

"Why did you end up going to him?" Baby Girl asks.
Kierra stops to think. She doesn't want to implement Kid. But she may not have a choice. She doesn't want to look like a liar, either.

Baby Girl presses, "Tell me the truth. Please. It's important that I know *who* hired *this* doctor."

"A friend of mine, told me about him," Kierra tries, "The first doctor wasn't able to do it. Or he never got the results back to us. So a friend of mine, told us about this doctor. We went to him and he did the test, right away."

Baby Girl asks, "Did you set up the appointment? Who told Derrick about the doctor and did you and him go, at the same time? Or did y'all go on separate visits? It's important that I know how you ended up using doctor Rawls. But I would like to know if you and my husband went together too."

No. That has nothing to do with anything else. I just want to know that for myself.

Baby Girl's eyes are smiling as she looks from Kierra to Trina. Before Kierra answers, Baby Girl asks Trina,

"Did you tell her about this doctor."

She's trying to break the ice with Trina, to make sure she feels included. At the same time, she's hoping they'll stop trying to cover for Kid. She can see that they're about to unravel.

"No. I didn't even know Kierra, then," Trina says, "I met her when Danica was six months old."

Baby Girl turns her attention back to Kierra.

She asks, "So how did this appointment and test happen?"

"My friend set it all up and told Young D where to go and take the test," Kierra says.

"This friend. This is someone whom Derrick knows pretty well, isn't it?" Baby Girl asks.

She's digging in now.

Kierra says, "Yes."

She knows she has to come clean about Kid and she's willing too now. Baby Girl is surprises to see how willing she is to unload this burden. Although at this point, Kierra doesn't know that her test results are as phony as a ten thousand dollar bill. But there is something Baby Girl hadn't realized, upon showing up here. She hadn't realized that the woman she has paid a surprised visit, is a woman *scorned*. And it's only going to get much worse.

Unbeknownst to Baby Girl, Kierra is tired of holding secrets for Kid with no reciprocity. He had promised her, he would deliver Young D to her. As *her* man. He'd also claimed then, that him and Young D were like brothers. Only for Kierra to learn later, that not only are Young D and Kid not like brothers. But they barely speak to each other. And more important, she had discovered that Young D was married to Kid's sister. For the short time Baby Girl has been here, Kierra can see that she has the upper hand in this whole circle. She can see the confidence Baby Girl exudes. It's becoming more and more clear to Kierra that the only thing Kid runs, is his club, his imagination and his mouth. She decides to tell Baby Girl everything she knows, while Trina listens and adlibs.

Kierra offers, "Kid told me about the doctor. Miss Annie had found the first doctor and told me to go to him. That's when Kid found out about the test that was being done. So he put pressure on that other doctor to hurry up. Kid said he got angry or something like that. And he said that doctor refused to do the service and gave him the money back. Kid took the money back to Young D and everything. Then Kid found *this* doctor. He set up the appointments and he told Young D where to go and when to go."

Baby Girl is satisfied with Kierra's admission. But she had no idea that Kierra knew this next part. Which she's about to reveal to her.

"Kid wants Young D out of your life. He wants you to find out about Danica so you will leave him. That's why he told you. He knows I want Young D and he said he was helping me to get him," Kierra admits.

She wrings her hands together, as if to be drying water from them. She continues as she looks down at her hands,

"But I found out *that* was a lie. Kid was lying. He was just using me. The same way he used Young D and anybody else, who's dumb enough to believe him."

Baby Girl lets her speak, freely. She wants to hear everything Kierra knows about the whole situation. And even what she knows about her.

Kierra starts by telling her, how she had come to meet Kid.

"He came down here in Ninety eight, to *Club Exposé*. That was the first club I worked in. That's where I met Kid and we started dating. Then I found out he had a woman. *He said* he had a baby mama. That was after The Anatomy opened, a year later. Which was in early, Ninety nine. The same year I met Young D. But that was later, like spring break time, when I met him. He had come back to Houston, to visit. He came to the Anatomy with DeJuan. Well, they came with Kid, so I thought they were all boys."

Baby Girl knows she's being truthful, so far. The time frames match up perfectly.

Kierra continues, "I liked Young D, from the first time I laid eyes on him. He was gorgeous and he still is. So who wouldn't? But he told me about you, from the beginning. He said he thought you was seeing someone else, in college. Because you stayed busy. *Too* busy for him."

Baby Girl sighs. She knows that was when she turned pro. Her and Young D have had this discussion, many times already.

298

"Go on," she tells Kierra.

"Well, we started messing around but it was later. Like, a couple of months later."

"When was the first time?" Baby Girl asks, "The first time that y'all were sexual."

"April of Ninety Nine," Kierra says, "But we did it once. And he didn't keep in touch with me, after that. That's when I told Kid, we had slept together but Young D vamped out. Kid took over, from there. *Kind of*. He would call Young D and give him messages from me. For like, the next three weeks. Young D would tell him, to tell me that he was gonna come by the club or by my place. He finally came to visit me, one more time. By then, that was the end of the year. He said he had moved back home to Houston. But a month after that, when your father died. He moved back to New Orleans for a few months, to be with you."

Baby Girl reminisces on the year 2000. It was a rocky one, for her whole family. Suddenly, losing the Don in January, threw her mother into a depression and her, as well. Young D was there for them. But her and him weren't the best of friends, at that time. She *knew* he'd been unfaithful with a girl, from her high school and he thought for sure, that she had a relationship going on, at LSU and wasn't admitting it. Further, *Baby Boy* and *Soldier* had beef with Kid, during that time. They had gotten into a huge family fight. A fight were all of them had brought out guns and everything else. Each 1 of them was shot, that same summer. Baby Boy and Soldier was against Kid. Young G and Geezy was still with Kid's label. But they wasn't taking sides. They were just still on the 3rd Ward label. No business was being done with them, because of the infighting. Baby Girl's entire family was in turmoil, is what that time felt like. Soon after, Soldier was shot by 1 of Kid's boys. That's

299

when Young G or William, decided to leave the label. Young G had always seen Soldier as his big brother. Same as Baby Girl had and still does. When Soldier left, Young G left with him. Young G left the label and moved to Atlanta. Geezy stayed with 3rd Ward while Baby Boy moved on to Houston and worked with DeJuan. Young D went on the road with Soldier, for awhile. That's how he met his current manager, JB. This was all in the year 2000. Baby Girl went back to LSU, for her senior year. Young D was on the road with Soldier. Baby Boy and DeJuan had joined them, on the road. Young D still kept in touch with Baby Girl and he visited her too. But they wasn't able to get the real closeness they'd once had. But neither were willing to leave the other. They still loved each other. But liking each other was the main problem, back then. Baby Girl don't even care to reminisce on that era anymore. She tells Kierra to continue. She does.

"The day your father had passed away and D went back to New Orleans for the funeral. Kid was *here*. He always stayed with me, when he was in Houston. He still does. But he was going back for the funeral and that's the day when I found out he didn't want D with you, at all. After D left for New Orleans. Kid told me he wanted that nigga out of your life, for good. He always said your father didn't like D with you because he fucked around, a lot. But I didn't believe that part because he really didn't. Well, he didn't with me. Not like that," Kierra says.

She continues, "As time went on. Me and Kid kept seeing each other. I didn't see D again, as far as sleeping with him. Until two thousand and two. It was after New Year's. I was seeing Kid heavily, by then. Young D came to the club. I saw him and went after him. I wanted him more than I've ever wanted Kid. But the feeling wasn't mutual. I admit that. But we hooked up, *that* night. The next month, I missed my period and I was pregnant with Danica."

Baby Girl asks, "You and Kid was dating heavily and he was living with you, while in Houston?"

"Yeah."

"He never told you, he was married?" Baby Girl asks.

"No."

Baby Girl asks, "So were you there to actually *see* Kid get tested?"

"Nah. I wasn't there with either of them," she says, "I just took my baby and we went."

"That was the week *after* we met," Trina adds, "Danica was six months old, when they did the test."

"She only did one test and you only did one test?" Baby Girl asks.

"Yes," Kierra says.

"Kid didn't get tested or he fouled it up, intentionally," Baby Girl finally says.

Kierra tries to counter with,

"He did get tested but we knew it wasn't him because he's sterile."

"*What*?" Baby Girl asks in a yell, while holding in a gut busting laugh.

"He showed me the bills from his surgery," Kierra tells her.

"What surgery? What kind of surgery?"

Kierra tells her, she had seen lab test and results, showing Kid had a vasectomy when he was a young teen. Baby Girl has to laugh. Now she knows for certain, that Kierra is in the dark about who had actually fathered her daughter.

"Kid is a liar," Baby Girl says, "And I *almost* feel sorry for you. I do feel sorry for this little girl, though."

She picks up Danica's picture. Next, she pulls out the real paternity test from the file she'd brought with her. She hands it to Kierra and says, "Look at these."

Baby Girl shows Kierra and Trina the *real* paternity test. The one by Dr. Fallows.

"Do you see the date of this test?" Baby Girl asks Kierra. "It's dated, March two thousand three. All the way down. Danica was born, September of Oh Two, so that would be six months. The ones by doctor Rawls have two different years, on them. October, two thousand three and December, two thousand and four. This one here by Fallows, is the real test and the correct results. Derrick is not Danica's father. Kid is. Oh and yes. Look at these."

She shows them the pictures of Kid's children. Then she says, "Kid has *five* children, when you include Danica. He's been fathering kids since he was a teen. There's *no way* he's sterile. He lied to you about all of it. He's married and has two kids with his wife. That's the oldest two. He has three more, outside of his marriage, when you include Danica. He's been married since after his first daughter Breanne, was born. Danica has four siblings. Two brothers and two sisters, that I know of. This is Bradley Walker Jr or Little Kid and he's twelve. Then this is Breanne and she's ten. These are the two by his high school sweetheart. Whom he married before Breanne was born. He's been married, almost eleven years. This is his daughter Catina. She just turned six. The baby boy Brandon, is four. They are from two other women. One of them lives in New Orleans and the other one, lives in Atlanta. He has custody of all four of his kids. They live with him and his wife, in New Orleans. My guess is, he will do the same with Danica. Because no matter what he has you believing. Kid doesn't want to pay anyone, *anything*. He got custody of number three and four because he did not want to pay child support to either lady."

"Oh my God," Trina says as she looks at the pictures. "Danica looks just like them. Breanne and Danica could pass for twins."

Kierra looks at the pictures too. She's dumbfounded. Her expression says emphatically that she had no clue that Young D was being falsely accused.

Kierra says, "I'm so sorry. Oh my *God*! I have to tell Young D. I am *so* sorry. Please believe, I didn't know this."

Baby Girl says, "Oh I do. I believe you didn't. But Kid *did*. He set it up. All of it. He wants Derrick out of my life, alright. But not to be with you. He wants him dead."

"I *knew* it," Trina says, "He wanted him to get killed, in San Francisco. Ain't that right?"

"Oh yes. He sure did," Baby Girl says, "*And* I think he was setting the two of you up to be killed, as well."

Kierra is very heated, by now. She realizes that Kid has used her, entirely. The whole time. It has become vividly clear that she was a pawn in Kid's chess game, for whatever he stood to gain. She wants to save face here and show Baby Girl that she cares for Young D and wasn't trying to use him. Nor set him up. She really wants to be with him. *Next*. She reveals another fact that she knows. About the subject of Kid wanting Young D dead. Before she can begin, Baby Girly has a few questions for her.

She asks, "Before you tell me that. I wanna know was you involved with Kid finding out that Derrick came to Lafayette to meet me there?"

"Yes. I didn't know where he went. But when I went by the house-."

"You went to my house?" Baby Girl asks.

"I was outside the door. But the guys would never let me come inside. I had gotten this fresh old man to bring me in the main gate," Kierra goes on, as Baby Girl holds direct eye contact with her. "The labelmates told me, Young D was gone to meet his wife."

"What did you want with him?" Baby Girl asks.

"To spend time," Kierra admits.

Baby Girl says, "But you already had."

This shocks Kierra *and* Trina. Neither of them were aware that Baby Girl knew about that last meeting. Baby Girl clarifies.

"He fucked with you, on the thirtieth of May. Do you know how I know?"

"How?"

"For one. He told me," Baby Girl says, "But it was much later. And two. I smelled your perfume. I remember how stinking it was. I knew I'd smelled it before. At our events? But DeJuan covered for you and said he had worn the shirt and had sex while wearing it. He didn't offer your name. But Derrick did. *Later*. He admitted it. Then he told me about Danica and told me, he had ended it, *that* day. He also said he was never attracted to you and that you was black mailing him, for sex. Or you would tell me about the little girl. I know I'm right, so far. So I want even asks. But Derrick admitted it. He had too. He loves me. And he wants to spend his life, with me. He knew he couldn't do that, if he was going to be living a lie. So go on with your accounts. Please."

Kierra is stunned speechless. She's intimidated by how confident and in control, Baby Girl is about the whole affair. Kierra gathers her composure and continues to tell Baby Girl what she knows about Kid's attempts on Young D's life.

Kierra says, "Well. First, I just thought he wanted me to break y'all up. He said he was doing it, for me. He always said he was

304

doing it because he knew I was in love with Young D-"

"I doubt that," Baby Girl says, "You're infatuated with whom you can't have. But go on."

"Well. I knew he wanted him dead. I found that out, before he took me to San Francisco," Kierra says.

"He took me too," Trina chimes in.

Baby Girl says, "I know. I saw both of you. I'll tell you later. Go on, Kierra. How did you find out that Kid wanted Derrick dead?"

"I over heard him on the phone, one morning. When he had spent the night here," Kierra says, "He thought I was still asleep but I was in that hallway, over there. Listening to him. I heard him on the phone with somebody. He bought a separate hotel room, in San Francisco. He flew out there and brought me and Trina along. He told me, I was suppose to be meeting Young D in that room, for a hook up. He was gonna make sure that you found out about us. He was gonna find a way to get you a key to that room. He told me, that me and Young D was suppose to be in the room fucking. And you was going to walk in and you was suppose to go off on him. Then I was suppose to tell you, why I was with him. That's when I was suppose to tell you about Danica. Then, Kid said you would leave Young D and I would have a chance to console him and get with him."

"Kid really doesn't have a clue about *whom* I am, as far as where it relates to my husband," Baby Girl says as she shakes her head. "And it's obvious, he has no clue about the type of man, Derrick is either. Derrick's not trying to leave me. Not for you or anyone else. If anything. He was thinking about me, in order to get off with you."

Kierra doesn't even *try* to argue that one. She thinks back to the few times she was able to convince Young D to fuck with her. He always seemed to be, miles away. She shrugs her shoulders in submission and continues, "But I knew he was lying about that part, after a while. Because Young D never acted like he wanted to be with me, after Danica was born. And there wasn't even any talk of it, before that. He was always worrying about, whom you was messing with."

"I wasn't messing with anybody," Baby Girl says, "I went to college before I was fifteen years old. It was a very different situation, for me. Then for most people at the college level. The other students was at least, three years older than me. There was never another man in my life. I've been with Derrick exclusively. Kid knows that. And he also knows that Derrick is with me because he loves me, *exclusively*. However, Derrick *is* a man. But love was never apart of his trice, with *any* other woman. I'm confident of that. But please. Go on with the rest of what Kid did. I am *so* over trying to explain my marriage to him."

"Well, when he spent the night, that night. He got up early the next morning and he was on the phone. He was telling somebody something totally different then what he'd been telling me, for years. I don't know who that was on the phone. But they must've said that Kid wasn't given you credit for having sense or something like that. Because Kid asks them, *'How am I underestimating Lovely?'* His voice was so impatient, until he was damn near growling at them. I thought it was like some kind of drug deal or something. I didn't want him to know I was listening because I already knew he was holding out on money he'd been promising me. I was eavesdropping. Trying to get a heads up. That's why I stayed hid. I had been feeling like he was up to something that he wasn't telling me about. And that's when I heard him say, as plain as daylight, *'I know she's sharp. But once she sees Young D fucking up. Her emotions will take over. She'll kill his ass and this bitch too.'*

That's when I knew he didn't give a damn about Young D or me. He was in my apartment. He was talking about me, when he said, '*This bitch.*' I went to get Trina up, so we could get out of here."

Trina adds, "And we left, saying we was going to eat. So she could get outta here and tell me what she had just heard."

"And y'all still went to Cali, with him?" Baby Girl asks.

"Yes. He was taking us shopping and we knew you was suppose to come," Kierra says, "So we tried to make it a getaway, for you and Young D."

"And she knew that, as long as she wasn't with Young D," Trina says, "Then there was no way, you was gonna catch him with her and be mad enough to wanna kill him."

"I was suppose to be *that* call girl or hooker," Kierra says, "Kid was suppose to have somebody to alert you that Young D was in a hotel with another woman. You was gonna go there and catch him. But once I found out he was trying to set him and me up, to get us killed. That's when me and Trina said we would turn it against him and make it a romantic meeting for y'all."

"How?" Baby Girl asks.

"She didn't go in the room and stay," Trina says, "She was suppose to be in the room, when he went in there. But she didn't stay in there. We waited in the lobby and we saw him come in and go upstairs. He was dressed up like he had a meeting or something. Then we saw you come in too. But we left and came back, in like twenty minutes and no one was in the room. Didn't either one of y'all stay up there."

"No, we sure didn't," Baby Girl says, as she thinks of a lie to throw them off of her profession.

She says, "I went to the wrong *damn* floor. He gave me the key to the wrong room. He must've been up to more than just

307

trying to kill you and Derrick. Because the room I went to, had Japanese people in it. But he *was* trying to have some gang member to go in that room. And kill Derrick and you. He lied to you *and* me. Kid had sent Derrick to that room and he had him thinking he was meeting some CEO of a major trading company, for a new business deal. He knew he would go for that. And that is the part that really pisses me off. He wanted to kill the only man that I've ever loved. And his reason is greed and greed only. Derrick has never done anything wrong to Kid. And Kid lied about my daddy, not liking him. My mother and father *loved* Derrick. They loved him so much, that he was written into the will *with* me. That's another thing that Kid doesn't know anything about. The terms of half of the shit they left me includes Derrick. And the only way for us to have it all, is to be together. Derrick don't even know that part either. He's with me because this is where he wants to be. Kid doesn't know that or maybe he would've tried something else." Kierra believes her but she has even more, she wants to confess.

"Kid is a liar and I see that, all to clearly now," Kierra says, "If I had been able to *just* talk to you, along time ago. This would never have gone, this far. He used me and now, every secret that I know of his. I wanna tell."

"By all means," Baby Girl says, "Vent, at your leisure," she chuckles and adds, "There are a few more pieces to this puzzle that I *really* need to solve."

"I'm willing to tell you, what I know," Kierra says, "If you can protect me from Kid."

"And me too," Trina says, "He'll kill us both, I think. I think he has the money and power to have people killed. We had a body guard that got killed in Tennessee. I think he had that done. Because they were always having private meetings, at the club. And this Sergeant who was working in New Orleans too. Sergeant Moore, his first name was Kevin. He was suppose to introduce us. We talked on the phone, a few times and I was suppose to go down there and meet him, in person. We was going to do it for Thanksgiving, as a matter of fact. But I didn't hear nothing from Sergeant Moore and Kid hasn't called Kierra either. He's just one big fat ass lie, after another one."

Baby Girl is in thought, right now. She's listening to Trina and Kierra talk. She lets them talk to each other while she's making mental notes.

Kid and Gus were both in the same ignorance, when it came to The Brotherhood *and* The Organization. *Neither of them understood, rage has no part in this killing game. Only the five A's matter. Accuracy, Acuteness, Ability and Absolute Anonymity. I can't wait to part his fucking fro.*

Trina and Kierra prepare to give up the next batch of Kids secrets while Baby Girl is in thought. But suddenly, her cell phone rings.

I've been really trying baby. Trying to hold back this feeling, for so long. And if you feel, like I feel baby. Come on. Oh! Come on. Woo, let's get it on. Aaahhh baby…. Let's get it on!

It's her *very* impatient husband's ring tone again. As *Marvin Gaye's*, *Let's Get It On*, oozes out of her Iphone, she begins to smile. Then she says,

"I need to take this, ladies. Hang on a second."

She answers her phone, "hello?"

"Hey, baby. Is everything okay?" Young D asks.

"Yes, Derrick," she says, "Everything is fine. I haven't

killed *anyone*. Kierra and Trina are both sitting here, waiting to finish telling me *just* how big of an asshole, my brother Kid is."

"Are you for real?" Young D asks.

"Seriously," she says, "The three of us are sitting here talking."

She turns to Kierra and Trina. She says, "Will y'all say hello. So Derrick will know I haven't killed y'all nor threatened too." She chuckles.

Trina smiles and yells, "Hello!"

"Hello, D," Kierra says as she smiles too.

Young D can tell from the sound of their voices, he had interrupted some serious girl talk. He isn't thrilled with the idea of Baby Girl talking to Kierra. But he's happy it's at a civil level. And that his wife is handling the matters with her, from now on. He has no idea he's off the *'he's the daddy'* hook, yet. Baby Girl will give him that news in Birmingham.

While Trina and Kierra discuss the next secret, they'll expose for Baby Girl. She finishes up her call with Young D.

She says, "See. I told you we was having girl chat. They are just about to finish up telling me about Kid and everything he has tried to do, to break us up since daddy died. Derrick this stuff is going to blow your mind."

Young D says, "Okay. Well get through, so you can leave there. Mama got the little girl. I guess you'll see her. Sooner or later."

"Derrick, say her name," Baby Girl tells him, with a smile, "Her name is Danica. Not little girl."

"Okay. I'll talk you before you go to bed, tonight," he says, "And don't miss that flight, in the morning. I've got it bad."

"I'll be there to fix it, baby," she says as they chuckle and then hang up.

Kierra and Trina are in awe at the playfulness and connection, Baby Girl and Young D have. Neither of them have ever seen this side of Young D and they never will. With her pleasure call done, Baby Girl gets back to the business of why she came here.

"So Kierra. It's safe to say that you had no idea that my husband was not the father of Danica," Baby Girl says as Kierra shakes her head in agreement.

"She didn't know," Trina says, "I didn't either. And we have both talked about why she didn't look like him."

"Oh y'all did?" Baby Girl asks.

"Yes."

"He did too," Baby Girl says, "So did his mother and DeJuan. Let me just cut to the chase. Everybody knew about Danica. Except me. Even my senior staff in New Orleans, all of my brothers, Derrick's family. Everybody. Except me and my sons. I knew something was wrong as soon as I found out about her. Because Annie had never had her at her house and she lives for her grandchildren. But as soon as I found out. I talked to her. She told me she didn't believe she was her grandchild. But her son is taking care of her and she wasn't going to leave her out of anything that she did for the other grandchildren. I agreed with her and I still do. Danica is related to my relatives. So she's *my* relative. She's my relative. Not my husband's. So Danica will become a legitimate part of our family. It isn't her fault that y'all adults screwed up and she's not going to suffer from it, either. I know she's visiting today. You can thank *me* for that. Even though I wasn't okay, knowing Derrick had kept this a secret. Still, it wasn't Danica's fault and she will be included, from now on. Are you okay with that?"

"I'm okay with it," Kierra says, "I always wanted her to be able to go over there. But he said no."

"Of course he was going to say no," Baby Girl tells her. "I didn't know about her. Nobody wanted me to know about her. Not even you. Because you was blackmailing my husband, for my goods."
Baby Girl is looking directly at her but Kierra looks away.
Figures! I know you didn't think I was going to leave that out. Hell to the nah!

"I'm over it now, Kierra," Baby Girl says, "I knew it was you. I knew it, years ago. I've smelled your funky ass perfume, on my husbands clothes, from time to time. I knew it was you because I could smell it on you. That t-shirt that Derrick wore on May thirtieth. Smelled like this apartment smells, right now. That could've been partly the reason he wasn't attracted to you. Because I was always talking about the smell of affairs, in my house. You really should change perfumes because I hate it now."
Neither Trina nor Kierra make eye contact after those comments. So Baby Girl lightens up, just a bit.
"I heard you was the one who called Corleone about the attempt on Derrick's life, in Gary."
        "I did. I overheard Kid talking on the phone again," Kierra says, "This time, we was on our way to the club when he was on the phone. But somebody killed that guy too. That's why we know Kid will have us killed. Everybody we know of him dealing with, comes up dead. He was a gang banger, from Cali. He had done time at the death house and when he got out. He came here to meet one of the strippers at The Anatomy. They had been pen pals or something. She met him while he was locked up. But that's how I knew about Gary and San Francisco."
Baby Girl asks, "You knew bout San Fran before we left?"

"Yeah."

"Why didn't you tell him about that one?"

"I tried too," Kierra says.

"When?"

"I went to Galveston and I was trying to get backstage to tell him," she says, "I hate to say this. But I had to fuck my way back there. I was willing to do that, just so I could tell him and hopefully save his life. I got backstage but he wouldn't allow me to come near him or his dressing room. I was waiting for DeJuan to come out, so I could tell him. But then, you showed up."

"Oh yes, I did and we know how that ended already," Baby Girl says with a chuckle, "You should've said something when I asked you, *who are you back here for*? And, *what do you want*? You didn't say anything. You just looked guilty of trying to fuck my husband. Plus, that was after the t-shirt and I smelt it on you, that night too."

"I should have but you was already getting ready to fight," Kierra says, "What would you have thought if I would've said something like that?"

"It would've stalled me on kicking your ass, Kierra," she says, "I care about my husband's *entire* existence. Not just his dick. I love all of him. *Alive!*"

Kierra says, "I wished I would've said something, years ago. But anyway. After that, I was banned from even coming to the cookouts."

"You still are," Baby Girl says, "But Danica can come. It's weird that you thought she was Derrick's child. Yet, you never brought her along when you came to the events."

"He didn't want me too," Kierra says, "He didn't want you to see her."

"I would've known she wasn't from Derrick," Baby

313

Girl tells her, "I saw Breanne and Catina in her, as soon as I looked at that picture. But things are going to be different. First off, Kid is going to refund every dime that my husband has given to you. With the exception of birthday monies. Because she can keep that. I give my nieces and nephews huge birthday money, as it is. One hundred dollars per birthday, is nothing. Any child support, rent, etcetera. *Will* be refunded. I'll take that out of Kid's share of the label."

"You can do that?" Kierra asks as Trina looks on in awe.

"I can do anything I want," Baby Girl says, "I own more of the company than him or Six Nine does. My daddy got them that deal. He helped all of them get what they have now. Derrick went the extra step and got his own distribution. But he ships through our trucking and shipping company and has his literature and logo's printed through our own company too."

"You must be rich?" Trina asks.

Baby Girl chuckles and says, "No. Derrick is rich. I'm wealthy. And together, we're filthy rich. That's his joke, not mine."

"So why did Kid want Young D dead. *Really*," Kierra asks, "because Trina thinks that he wants you. His own sister."

"No. That's not it," she says, "Though we're not blood. Six Nine is my blood brother. We have the same *real* father. What Kid is after, is my wealth. He's a greedy, son of bitch, who will stop at nothing to get his hands on my inheritance. My daddy Don Morales married my mother, when I was like two years old. He left me everything. So I'm a major contributor to a lot of shit and I own a lot of shit too."

"Did you help Kid buy The Anatomy?" Trina asks as Kierra looks at her.

"He didn't want me to tell no one about that," Kierra

314

says, "But I told you I'm coming clean today. I don't want any bad blood between us."

"Kierra, we will never be buddies," Baby Girl tells her, "I'll just go on and let you know that now. But as long as you stay away from Derrick. We want be fighting again. Tell me about this Anatomy thing. And no. I didn't help Kid buy it."

"He's the silent partner of the club," Kierra says, "He told me not to tell nobody. Because then, they would be hitting him up for cash."

"Do you really believe that?" Baby Girl asks, "Who needs money from Kid? Besides you?"

"He said folks at the club would be asking him for raises," Trina adds as she laughs.

"Kid is mixed up in some crooked shit," Baby Girl says, "He has been hiring people to kill me and my husband. And some of those people worked at that club."

"I saw you and Angela in there, one night," Kierra says.

"I was coming to see if he was there," Baby Girl says, "I had a feeling he owned that club. There was at least three folks, who worked with him, that tried to kill Derrick, me or both of us. Kid wouldn't get shit, if we died. Our sons would and the senior staff are their guardians. After that, mama Annie is. Kid has been mixed up in some murderous shit. That's why he's locked up, right now."

"*Who is*?" Kierra asks as Trina looks on.

"Kid is in jail, in New Orleans."

"*Damn*. I know I haven't heard from him," Kierra says, "I was wondering where he was. I even asked the other bosses and they played me off."

Baby Girl has done what she needed to do here. As she prepares to leave, she leaves 1 more jewel with the 2 females.

"I do believe he's being held in connection with a

315

murder," she says, "And I think it may have something to do with that guy that you mentioned earlier. That Sergeant."

"Sergeant Moore?" Trina asks.

"I heard it on the news, for two nights straight," Baby Girl says, "Sergeant Moore, from the New Orleans military processing station, was found dead in his apartment in New Orleans east. And Kid has been in jail since that shit hit the news."

"Oh my God!" Trina says, "I called his phone, one night and somebody answered it. I asked to speak to him and they said he wasn't available. It sounded like a white man. But then, he started asking me all sorts of questions so I hung up in his face."

"It was probably the police," Baby Girl says.

"He called her back too," Kierra says, "Then Houston police came out here. They asks us all kinds of stuff. But they didn't tell us that he was dead."

"After they found out that we had never met him, in person," Trina says, "And that we was at work, on these two days that they was looking into. Once they figured we didn't know anything about his whereabouts. They left us alone. But all last week, they was on our asses."

"Until we told them that Kid is the one who got us connected on the phone and he was going to introduce us," Kierra says.

Baby Girl smiles. Rather these females know it or not. They had done her a tremendous favor. By alerting the police that Kid knew Sergeant Moore. They've aided her in the *ultimate* package. The 1 she's wrapping up nicely and putting Kid's name on.

"Well, at least now I know why Kid was so chummy with you," Baby Girl says to Kierra. "I was wondering if he knew that you wanted my husband. Finding out that he was trying to make it happen, was disappointing. Kierra and Trina, I have to go, for now," she says, "Kid won't be coming to Houston, for awhile. He doesn't have a bond and he can't use the phone. That's by order of the commissioner. So he won't be moving, for a minute. I'm gonna see about getting your child support started. And so that y'all feel safe against whomever you think he may send. I just rented y'all a room at the Crowne Plaza hotel downtown. Go stay down there, for a few nights. Until you know the coast is clear. And if you break some shit. You will be responsible for it. You can't call me. But I will call and check on you two. Okay?"

"Alright. Thank you, so much," Kierra says, "You really are a good person."

"Yes. Thank you. I'm glad to have finally met you," Trina says, "You're way nicer than Kid is."

"That's because you've never pissed me off," she says as she laughs.

She packs up her laptop and slips her file back into the laptop bag. She heads for the door.

"I have a flight back to New Orleans, in a couple of hours," she says, "So I want get to see Danica, this time. But I'll see her when I can get back home. Is there anything you need me to tell Kid?"

"Yes. Tell him I want my child support," Kierra says as her and Trina burst out in laughter. Kierra adds, "And if you will. Please tell Young D that I'm *so* sorry and that I didn't know what Kid was doing."

"I'll see him tomorrow, around lunch time," Baby Girl says, "I'll be telling him *all* of this stuff. He still doesn't know that he isn't her father. That's something that I'll tell him, face to face. Me finding this paperwork. Saved him from getting high blood pressure," Lovely says as she giggles again.

Kierra and Trina walk her out to her rental car.

"Is this your car too?" Trina asks.

"No. It's a rental. I grabbed it at the airport, so I could zip by here and get back, on time. I'll call and check on y'all later. Try to get some rest and keep the things we discussed under wraps, for now. The less Kid knows about this meeting. The safer you are."

"We won't say shit, then," Kierra says.

"Oh and one more thing," Baby Girl says, "Always call Derrick, D and not Derrick. And never try calling him daddy again. That's only for me and our sons. Okay?"

"Cool. My bad," Kierra says, "That was during my salty days. I respect that he loves you and I'm never going that route again. I promise you."

"Good. Then I won't have to kill you," Baby Girl says as she grins.

She gets into her rented *Chevy Malibu* and starts it up. She waves goodbye to the 2 females as she whips out of the parking lot and heads back to Hobby airport. She flips out her Iphone and calls her husband, on the way.

"Hello, sexy," Young D says as she can hear him smiling.

"Hey sexy, yourself," she says as she giggles, "I'm on my way back to the airport. I thought I would ease your mind."

"That's why I love you, Lovely," he says, "You're always thinking about me. I've learned to think about you, all the time too. Hell. I can't help it."

They both chuckle before he asks, "So how did it go?"

"It went great, actually," she says, "She gave up the goods on Kid. Did you know he owns the anatomy club?"

"Nah. I didn't."

"He does," she says, "He never mentioned that. You remember how he was bugging me, last year about selling him my shares from the Third Ward label?"

"Yes. I do. He was claiming he needed the money, more than you did," Young D says.

"That's a given," Baby Girl says, "I don't need any money. But I'm not trying to give away any, either."

"You don't have too," he says, "He was trying to play on your sympathy."

"He doesn't have that option anymore," she says, "He can get out of my life and stay out."

"I understand how you feel," he says, "Baby, just have a safe trip to the IN OH. Then I need for you to get some rest, so you and my sons can come and see me, in the morning. Oh yeah. We got a last minute show in Montgomery, tonight."

"Get your paper, Derrick," she says, "You're in demand, like usual."

"We're gonna stay for the after party," he says, "We'll hit the road at two. So we'll be in Birmingham, two hours before y'all leave New Orleans."

"Sounds like a winner to me," she says, "Well, I'm back at Hobby. I need to return this rental so I can get to my gate. I've got an hour before my flight out."

"Okay, Lovely," he says, "I love you."

"I love the way you say that, Derrick," she says as she smiles. Then she says, "I love you too. I'll see you tomorrow. If you get bored. Call me tonight."

He says he will. They say goodbye and hang up. Baby Girl returns the Malibu. Then hurries to her gate where her flight departs on time.

319

At Kierra's apartment, her and Trina had packed enough clothes for the week and hurried downtown to the Crowne plaza hotel.

Kierra calls Annie and lets her know where they'll be. She ask her if she wants her to come and get Danica.

"No. You can't get in here anyway," Annie says, "I'll bring her to the hotel before seven. Just make sure you're there."

"Okay. I'll be here. And thanks, so much," Kierra says and they hang up.

Annie is puzzled by how giddy Kierra was on the phone. She wonders what's got her acting so docile, all of a sudden. Annie doesn't know that she was right about Danica, all along. Baby Girl told Kierra not to tell anyone until she has told Young D, first. And she won't do that until tomorrow afternoon.

****

Kid's wife tries to visit him, this evening. She is told he doesn't have visitation rights. She's confused as to why she can't see nor talk to her own husband, on the phone. Without giving her anymore information, she's escorted away from the Orleans parish jail and ordered not to return until she receives a call from Kid. She leaves the jail and heads straight to The Manor.

CHAPTER   THIRTY FOUR
THE NEW HIRE

Charles meets Baby Girl at her gate, in Louis Armstrong international airport. He escorts her to the limousine, seats her and they head to The Manor.

Charles says to her, "You have a guest there, waiting to asked you for a favor. It's Kid's wife, Marisa."

"Oh. Okay," Baby Girl says, "She must've tried to visit him and was told that she couldn't?"

"Exactly. She wants you to make it happen," he says.

She says, "Call the commissioner. Ask him for a visit tonight. Tell him, I'm gonna bring her with me. Are the kids with her?"

"No, she's alone," he says.

"Get the visit," she says, "I need him to know I have the power to rock his whole entire world, right now. Kierra and her roommate Trina gave him up, on the San Francisco fiasco. They even told Houston police that he was linked to the sergeant, I polished in the east."

"Sounds to me like somebody is saving you a lot of work on his package, Baby Girl," Charles says as he chuckles.

"Oh Charles. It's a beautiful day in Morales land," she says, chuckling too. She adds, "This is going to be one of the most well put together packages, *ever*. TJ may want to give those girls a bonus, for their part in it."

"Our bright futures, depend on how well you rid the family tree of that nonproductive branch," he says, "I need to feel confident that the senior staff's futures are going to be *very* bright."

"Invest in shade then, mister Charles," she says, "You might wanna start a line of sun visors too. Based on the new info I have. You're looking at a very *bright* future."

They both laugh as he makes his way down Morales highway

and turns into the manors property. They're still smiling.

Charles says, "I'll get the commissioner on the line, as soon as I get you safe inside the main house, misses Lovely.

"Thank you, mister Charles."

They pull on up in front of the main entrance and Charles parks the limousine. Baby Girl's cell phone rings, just as she's getting out of the limousine. She answers to Deloris, on the other end.

"Hi, Miss Deloris. Is everything okay?"

"Oh yes it *is,* Baby Girl," she says, "I wanted to ask you for a small favor."

"What is it," Baby Girl asks.

"I gave TJ my cell phone number, when I was there for Thanksgiving," she says, "I lost that phone today and have to wait for the replacement. I don't wanna miss his call tonight. Could you give him my home number. Please?"

"Why of course I can and I surely will," Baby Girl says with a grin. She adds, "Is love in the air or what?"

"He is *so* charming and sweet. I do like him, a lot," she says, "I haven't told the twins yet. But I want him to visit me, here in Houston."

"Well alright!" Baby Girl yells, "I'll pass that number on to him. As soon as I get inside, see my sons and get settled. I'll call him and give him the number. And I'll tell him to call you, right away."

Deloris thanks her and they hang up.

Lovely heads inside of the mansion. Cherry and Maggie are both in the foyer with her sons.

"They wanted to say hello, before they have their baths," Cherry says with a smile.

Baby Girl tells her that she's going to play with them while she meets with her guest.

"She's waiting in the parlor, ma'am," Maggie says, "We'll bring the boys in. I just have to change them into their parlor shoes and we'll be right in."
Maggie takes Lil Man and Don Prince to their wing to put on their house slippers.

Baby Girl goes on into the parlor. Marisa is seated in a leather wingback chair, which is close to the 1st fireplace. She's looking into the flames, as the fire crackles and pops. A fierce and warm fire heating the right side of the huge parlor, gives off a welcoming ambiance. Marisa seems as engulfed in her inner thoughts, as the logs are engulfed by the flames.

There are 3 fireplaces in the parlor which expands to 35 square feet, by itself. This was Wanda's peace and quiet room. Her escape from the hustle and bustle of the mansion. Her meeting room. The room where she entertained the wives of the Don's business associates. As well as the ladies from their church. The parlor was decorated to be warm, relaxing and inviting. It was important to The Don, that his wife was able to bond with the women who accompanied the men, he met with in his den. He knew women *likes* went along way with a man, when he was deciding on where and with whom, to spend his money. Wanda's country girl morals and genuine good nature, wowed each woman The Don left in her presence. Much like she had charmed him without even trying. Baby Girl has her mother's ways when it comes to her good nature and morals. And even her charm. But it's The Don's patience or lack there of. And no nonsense demeanor, that she exudes in her business practices. She's beholding to no one except her sons, her husband, his loved ones and her loyal staff. Anyone other than those, whom she chooses to love, are expendable. She doesn't sweat the small shit and she hasn't found time, to have time to waste. She knew the day would come, when she would hold the

future of the 1 who tried to set her death certificate date, ahead of schedule. But when she imagined ending the buyers life, as he knew it. She had no idea that he was a member of her family. Knowing that now, makes no difference. Other than, she'll most likely assume the responsibility of the financier of his offspring.
Just so long as that bastard has no breath left.

She walks into the parlor and speaks to Marisa.

"Hi sister-in-law. What brings you out, this evening?" Baby Girl asks.

"I wanted to know if you can help me out," Marisa says. Baby Girl can see that she's distressed. She's been crying, a lot and her eyes are still swollen and puffy.
Guess that's what happens when you marry a jackass and uphold him in his bullshit. He leaves you nothing to sponsor. While he has to get permission to wipe his own ass. I hold his fate. Only because he tried to change mine. There's only one God! Mine!

"What's the problem?" Baby Girl asks, as if she doesn't know, already.

"I need to see Bradley senior," she says, "He's in jail. He has been in there since before Thanksgiving. That's where he was, all this time. They're not allowing him to even have a phone call. And they won't even tell me, *why* he's in there. They won't let me visit him. I don't know what to know. I miss him, so much. And I'm really worried. Baby Girl can you have your people to help us out?"

Before Baby Girl can answer her, Maggie arrives with her sons. They tear into the parlor and head straight for their mother. She's seated on the wingback sofa, adjacent to the chair which holds Marisa.

324

"Hi mommy. I love you," Lil Man says as she pounces on her.

"Love you, mommy," Don Prince mimics his older brother, as he struggles to climb up on the sofa.
Baby Girl gives him a lift and pulls him to her. He finds a comfortable spot on her lab. Once her sons are seated and comfortable with knowing they have her until they slumber. She answers Marisa.

"Give me time to get my boys settled into bed. Then I'll see if I can get them to allow us to visit him. Okay?"

"Okay. Thank you, Baby Girl," Marisa says, "I know you love your brothers. I knew you would be willing to make sure that he gets justice."

"Oh you can be sure of that," Baby Girl says, "Wait here. I'll be back, after I've had time with my sons."

Baby Girl takes her sons to their wing. She goes to their playroom and lets them pull out their favorite toys.

"It's time to play with mommy," she says, "I missed you guys, *so* much. What do you wanna play with, first?"
Her sons are pulling out every toy in their storage. She takes her time and plays with her sons for an hour. While Marisa waits in the parlor. Then Charles comes to the playroom and tells her, the commissioner has set up a visit with Kid.

"Okay," she says.

"I've got the car, out front, already," he says.

"Let Marisa know we can visit him," she says, "And give me fifteen more minutes."

Charles heads to the parlor. He gives Marisa the news. She smiles through her tears, as she grabs her *Marc Jacob* bag and follows Charles to the car.

In the kids wing, Baby Girl helps Maggie and Cherry

put her sons to bed. They've enjoyed their hour or so, with her. They're ready to slumber. She takes out their clothes for their trip to meet Young D, on the road. Baby Girl goes up to her master suite and pulls out her things for tomorrow's trip, as well. Cherry and Maggie are going to pack for the 3 of them, while Baby Girl is visiting Kid, at the jail.

"Thanks, ladies," Baby Girl says to Cherry and Magee. She adds, "I'll be back, *shortly*."

Cherry smiles. She knows this isn't going to be a pleasure visit. Not for Baby Girl, it isn't. For her, this visit is a means to an end.

"Take care of your business, Baby Girl," Cherry says, after Maggie has gone to pack for the boys. She adds, "Everything will be ready for your trip to see mister Derrick."

Baby Girl smiles at Cherry and says, "On the family's honor. I will *definitely* handle business."

Another hour later, Baby Girl and Marisa are seated in the family visitation room with Kid. He's happy to see his wife but he's very antsy. He can see in Baby Girl's eyes that she's got something on him. Instead of catching up with Marisa, Kid has many questions for his half sister.

"How are you, today?" he asks.

"So much better than yesterday," Baby Girl says, "And apparently, better than you are. This here ain't the spot."

"I agree with you on that," Kid says, "I thought you would've had me out of here, by now."

"I don't have that kind of pull," Baby Girl says, just to tick him off.

"*Shit*. You got all the power, baby sis," he says, "You're not gonna be selfish with it, are you?"

Baby Girl knows he's trying to put her on the spot, in front of

Marisa. He wants Marisa to think she's just a wayward family member, who doesn't help out her kinfolks. She has a card to play that will send him running for the hills. And she's going to play it.

"I couldn't get in touch with anyone who would help me with you," is how she starts. "I flew all the way to Houston. I checked with some of your employees, from the strip club that you own."

"I don't own a club-"

"Oh please stop with the lies, Kid," she says, "You're in here for murder. Aren't you gonna tell your wife? She's worried *sick* over you. She's asking me to help you. But she doesn't know how non-supportive *you've* been with me and my marriage. Does she Kid? Tell Marisa how you've been moving on me and my husband. And that way, she won't be running to me, expecting me to bail out a Cain ass nigga, who tried to hurt me and my husband!"

Kid climbs back into his shell. He doesn't want to go there.

"What is she talking about, Brad?" Marisa asks.

"Tell her, Brad," Baby Girl insists, "Or you can tell her that I don't owe you shit. Have her call doctor Rawls and have him fix things up, the way you want them. Fix them up to your advantage."

She's on a roll. While Kid is acting as if he's going to pass out. Marisa is firing questions at him, like hot lead from a loaded gun. He can't answer her. Or rather, he *won't* answer her. Baby Girl wants to keep her package in tact, so she pulls up. Kid gets the point. He won't dare try to play her weak or put her on the spot again. He now sees that she can play hardball. Even with him. Still, after Marisa heard the bit about the strip club. She's now wanting clarity. Baby Girl doesn't even want to cast shade onto her package. She's going to eat Kid alive, in due time. She's said enough to back him all the way off of her. Now that the ball is in her court. She's going to play him like dominoes.

"Answer your wife about The Anatomy," she says, "Tell her about your a silent partnership with the strip club. Tell her about all the motherfuckers from that club, who have been dying, *up* out of there."

Kid now knows he can either tell his wife or Baby Girl will fill her in later. He doesn't want Marisa to go to Baby Girl about any of his business. Because he now knows, at this point, she's going to clean him out. He looks at Baby Girl with those eyes he use to use, when she was a kid. Those eyes that she use to respect. Now, she can see through them. She looks back at him with eyes that say, "I ain't got nothing for you, man."

He decides to fess up about the club.

"I own a club named, The Anatomy," he admits.

"You own a strip club?" Marisa asks with a rise in her voice. She goes on, saying, "Since when and why haven't you told me? And are you in here for murder? Who's murder, *Brad*? I need to know what's going on?"

"I own a strip club, in Houston," he says, "But I haven't killed anyone. Somebody set me up-"

"-Somebody set you up?" Baby Girl asks. She goes on, asking, "Was this the same person who you was helping to set *me* up?"

Marisa looks from Kid to Lovely and back to Kid. She can see it in his eyes. He's caught up. She can see in Baby Girl's eyes that she's fed up. Baby Girl has a look of disgust on her face and her posture says that she is fresh out of patience.

Kid says, "I don't know who's trying to set me up or who tried to set you up, baby sis. I just need to get in front of a judge, so I can go home to my family."

"Which family is that?" Baby Girl asks, totally throwing him for a loop.

"*Ha? What?*" Marisa asks, "What *other* family do you have?"

Kid is almost frozen speechless. He recovers quickly, realizing he has to make nice with his sister. Or she's going to sale him down the river, right here and right now.

"I don't have but one family, Marisa," he says, hoping Baby Girl won't reveal what she knows. He says, "I just didn't have Baby Girl's back, when a nigga tried to fuck over her and Young D. She's gonna hold that against me. She has a right too. I should've been there to get her back and I didn't."

"Do you have a family living somewhere else?" Marisa persists.

Kid holds his breath and closes his eyes. He expects Baby Girl to come in and blow his spot up. But she doesn't. He opens his eyes and sees that Baby Girl is holding Marisa's hand. They're both looking at him.

"Nah. I don't have another family," he says in a very low voice. Still with a low voice, he says, "And I have to start taking care of the family that I *do* have."

Baby Girl lets him make it with that. She's done what she came to do, for tonight. She leaves Marisa in the room with Kid, so they can have some conjugal time. She joins Charles, out front.

Charles asks, "So did you kill him and leave him breathing?"

"Yes and only because I had to," Baby Girl says, "We're in jail. I don't even like to visit here. So taking up residence is out of the question."

Her and Charles laugh while they wait for Marisa to finish up her private time with Kid. He's in the best place he can be, as far as Baby Girl is concerned. Behind prison bars with her in the drivers seat. And his team quickly becoming informants of hers. Her thoughts switch to Birmingham and her husband and how she's steadily gathering information and the reigns that will put him in the best possible mood. While at the same time, taking the pressure off of him about a secret he had harbored from years, *unnecessarily.*

After 30 minutes, the guards tell them Marisa will have to leave. Baby Girl goes back in with the guard to escort Marisa out of the visitation room.

After Marisa has been taken out of earshot and before Baby Girl leaves Kid, she has a message for him. She can't leave without making him aware of the correct file that she's seen. There's no way she's leaving without giving him a morsel to chew on, for later. She gets close enough to him to whisper. She's acting as if there is something she was suppose to tell him but she had simply forgotten it. Then, as if she has a sudden recollection, she leans into him and says,

"Before I go. There was something else I was suppose to tell you. Oh yeah. Your woman in Houston. *Kierra.* You know her, from your *other* family? Yes. Well she told me to tell you that she wants her fucking child support," Baby girl says that with a smile. Then she adds, "She also asked me to apologize to Derrick for falsely accusing him of being the father of your daughter Danica. Good ole doctor Rawls, right? It's amazing how a little money can make a professional, risk his license and life's work to try to fuck over a boss. Isn't it?"

She can hear *Disturbing The Peace* artist *Shareefa*'s song, *I Need A Boss* in her head, as she continues to smile. Kid can't even look at her, at this point. He already knows she has found irrefutable evidence that he was behind the extortion of Young D. Kid drops his head as the guards re-shackle him and escort him back to his cell.

330

"Bye Kid. See you next time," Baby Girl says in a chummy tone.

She *is* planning on seeing him again. In the parish jail. Before he's allowed to have a bond. The court appearance he's expecting tomorrow morning, isn't going to happen. Baby Girl has to go see her husband and spend time on the road for a few days. She wants Kid held until she can get back to Houston with Young D and start the clock on his ass.

Their visit being over now. Her and Charles escort Marisa to the car. Marissa is crying because she has to leave Kid behind. They allow her to cry, in peace. As they drive back to The Manor. Neither of them say anything to her. Baby Girl is only thinking of her 9am flight to Birmingham and making sweet love to her man and the father to only, *her sons*.

****

James Lawson is up late, writing the return letter to his pen pal. He's so anxious to know the inside scoop on Deloris, down in Houston, that he's sending his letter by *Express* mail.

"It's time for you to face me, woman," he says as he talks to himself. "I told you I would never live without you. And there is no way that I am gonna allow you to carry on that life you have. Without me. I'll be to see you, Dee Dee. As the gospel song says, *Soon and Very Soon*."

He's so full of himself tonight. Only because he knows he's only days away from knowing Deloris' location. He's planning to use his free ticket, during the Christmas season.

****

The show in Montgomery Alabama was so full of

energy, that H-Town records are leaving on a high, like never before. As they head to the after party, Young D whips out his blackberry to call his wife. Baby Girl answers on the 1st ring.

"Hello, baby," she says as she smiles big, "How did the show go, tonight?"

"The show was good. But you know that's not what I called for," he says, in an impatient voice. He says, "I know I told you we were gonna go to the after party. But that's not where my mind is, Lovely. It's on you."

"Perfect place for it to be," she says, "My mind is on you. And in about twelve hours. My lips will be on you too. I mean, all over you. I can't wait. But Derrick, you can't disappoint your fans. You have to go to your party."

"Lovely."

"Derrick. Go to your party," she says, "It'll help you pass the time until we get to you. I promise you. It's worth the wait."

It takes some convincing but Young D finally agrees to attend the party and allow his artist to unwind too. He talks to Baby Girl until they reach the club where the after party is being held.

"Alright, baby," he says, "We're here. I'm going on in. Only because you insist."

"Well okay. That's good," she says and they both laugh.

"I just miss you, baby," he says, "And I've been worried about all this shit with Kid and Kierra and all."

"I'll help you relax when I get there," she says, "I promise. Okay?"

"Okay, baby. I love you," he says.

"I love you too, Derrick," she says, "I always have and I always will."

"Me too," he says.

They say goodbye and hang up, just as Charles is pulling up, in front of The Manor. He walks Marisa to her car and makes sure she's able to drive home. He's sees after her until she's off the premises. Then he prepares a vehicle for the drive to the airport, the next day.

Baby Girl calls Teddy Jr. He's still up. He says he'll meet her in the parlor, in just a few minutes. He stays in the main house. Even though his father TJ stays in 1 of the Villa homes, just as he always did. Teddy Jr likes to stay closer to Baby Girl. Just in case she needs something, *anything*, in the middle of the night. Much like tonight.

"Meet me in the office, instead of the parlor," Baby Girl tells Teddy Jr and they hang up.

Within minutes, they're together in The Don's office, with the door closed. Teddy Jr has been wanting to talk to Baby Girl, alone, since he got here. He doesn't waste any time getting his point across.

"Baby Girl, you *stay* on the go, don't you?" he asks.

"Life in *The Organization* is a busy one," she says, "Are you ready for that?"

"I'm ready for anything, you're putting out," he says. There's an awkward silence before Baby Girl burst into laughter. Teddy Jr laughs too. Although, he isn't sure of why she's laughing. Still he laughs cautiously, along with her.

"Teddy junior, are you trying to make me feel shy again?" she asks, "Because I've grown up, a lot more since age nine."

"You use to be so shy and quiet, though," he says, "And you still have the prettiest smile I have ever seen. Misses Wanda named you *perfectly*."

She responds quickly, saying, "I was never *that* shy. Daddy

333

Don taught me to listen rather than to speak, a lot. I always took his advice too. Best advice I've had in my life. God blessed my mama to meet and bring him into our lives."

Teddy Jr is openly flirting with her and letting her know that he has the hots for her. That he's thought about her, a whole lot, over the years. She tries changing the subject again.

She asks, "You know miss Deloris likes big TJ, don't you?"

"You know Teddy junior likes you, don't you?" he asks, as he flashes her his bright and handsome smile.

She feels suddenly nervous, around him. Getting this kind of attention from him, isn't something she had anticipated. She had never thought of how she would react if she got attention from any man. Other than her husband, for that matter. Still, she hasn't made herself halt his flirtatious behavior yet. She feels guilty for liking the fact that he's still into her, after all of these years. But she knows it's not going to advance any farther than flirting. She just has to find a way to make sure he knows that, as well.

"I know you'll be twenty four, Tuesday after next," she says without making eye contact.

"My birthday is still December fourth. Yes," he says, "Can we go get a drink or something?"

"I don't think that's wise, Teddy," she says.

She can't avoid the timid-like smile that follows that statement. For God sakes, she has no idea what has come over her.

Why am I not putting him in his place? I'm not interested in Teddy junior, like that. Derrick will kill him and me too.

"Do you remember our first kiss? Because I sure do," he says, "I've thought about it, for years. Every time I think about New Orleans or this place. It's all about you."

"Okay, Teddy but I'm married," she says.

334

"Didn't stop you from still looking gorgeous to me," he says, "I see your wedding rings, Baby Girl. I remember the ring, I gave you too."

They both laugh at his comments. Baby Girl is laughing as a relief or as an out, from the rest of their conversation. She remembers when he gave her a ring pop and they said they were married. All of that happened before they even kissed.

"Teddy *this* set of rings are the truth, though," she says, "I absolutely adore Derrick. He's my soul mate."

"You would be saying that about me, if I'd lived closer to you," he says.

"We need to get to work, Ted," she says, "I have an early flight and I need to get some sleep."

"I can help you relax too. I don't only crack safes. I crack backs too," he says, still smiling.

"No thank you, Teddy," she says, "Now let me see what you have on the packages. Did TJ get to do anymore on Kid?"

"Okay. I see you're changing the subject, so okay," he says, "He got a good plan going on him, so far. He didn't know if you wanted an assistant or if you wanted to go solo."

"Derrick won't be okay with us traveling together, Teddy," she says, "Not if he knows what your feelings are."

"He doesn't have to know that I like you," he tries.

But she quickly shoots him down, saying, "I don't keep secrets from my husband. And I don't put him in uncomfortable situations."

"I'm a professional, Baby Girl," he says, "We should both be professional and just get the job done."

"You should've been thinking that way, when you first started this conversation," she says, as she looks at him with a raised brow. She adds, "Because now, I know how you feel. Which would make me dishonest and an enabler, if I didn't tell

335

my husband. Or if I go on trips with you. And if he knows how you feel. Then me going on trips alone with you, would cause unnecessary strain and stress in my home."

"So far he has dual assassins on his package," he says, before turning somber. He says, "I was really looking forward to my first gig with The Organization."

"I'll get with him about it, after the tour," she says, "Derrick will need to be there, if he's going with the Houston package that I suggested."

"Yes. That's the one with the alternative aid, in Houston," he says.

"The alternate is Kierra," she says, "She's going to get the ball rolling. He'll go running down there, as soon as he makes bail. But I'm keeping her hid until we can open the package. It'll be your birthday week before Derrick gets a break in his tour schedule. We're going to use Kierra as bait. And to do that. Derrick and I have to be there."

"Sounds like a winner," he says, "What about the abuser from PEE AY?"

"James Lawson? Oh I'm working him up, as we speak," she says, "I'm waiting on his return letter to the P.O. Box, in Houston."

"When are you gonna have him fly in?" he asks.

"I'm trying to make it coincide with the Kid package," she says, "While we're there with the alternate. So it will be next week too. We're going to splurge on a nice suite at the Crowne Plaza for Deloris and big TJ. Keeping TJ aware, of course. And let mister Lawson fly right on into Houston."

"And into his death date," he adds and they both laugh.

"That's going to be your first work with The Organization," she says, "Kid will be the second."

"Unless something pops up sooner, ha?" he asks.

"God willing."
They laugh again as she prepares to lock up the office. She tells him goodnight and he heads to his suite. Baby Girl goes to tuck her sons in and kiss them goodnight. Then she's off the bed, herself.

****

Baby Girl, Lil Man and Don P arrive in Birmingham at 1:20pm. Young D and DeJuan are there to pick them up. Young D hugs his sons. Then he holds Baby Girl in his arms, for more than a minute, while giving her a kiss which last just as long.

"I missed you, woman," he says as he finally releases her lips and smiles big.

"You'll get to show me *all* of that, real soon," she says, smiling just as big.
Young D nods in agreement, as they pile into the rental car and drive back to the Marriott.

After playing with his sons, for half an hour and tiring them out, Young D leaves DeJuan in charge of them. While he and Baby Girl lock up in his suite for some alone time.

As soon as they get inside the suite and get comfortable, Baby Girl gets right to the new findings.

"I have some good news for you, Derrick," she says, as soon as he locks the door. She adds, "Here's the reason I went to see Kierra."
He says, "It'd better be *damn* good. Especially, if you expect me to read paperwork before I wet that pussy."
His face holds a stone expression.

"I promised you, what I was bringing was gonna be worth the wait," she says, "Didn't I?"

337

"Yes you did," he says.

She says, "And you already know this pussy, which belongs to you, is worth waiting for. But this, right here, is what I call, the elimination of future high blood pressure and a heart attack. Check it out, Derrick and breathe freely."

She whips out the file and pulls the paperwork out. She lays the 2 sets of paternity test in front of him. Young D frowns as he strains his eyes to see what it is he's suppose to see, on the paperwork. Within seconds, he recognizes the test from Dr. Rawls.

"I saw this, already," he says in a disappointed tone. Then he says, "I got this, baby. *I* showed it to *you*."

"I know you did, Derrick," she says, "But that test is as fake as a three dollar bill. Gus and Kid set that up and Kid paid this doctor to do that fake test. *Twice*. Kid even tried to changed the dates on each of them, so it would read the date that you actually went. But the test lab kept the true dates of both of the test. Doctor Rawls tests were done in October, two thousand two and December, two thousand. You went in March of two thousand three. Look at this. You can see Doctor Fallows test. It has the exact date that you went in and gave your saliva. Kid's doctor, doctor Rawls, used Kid's saliva. But he put your name on it, as the donor. I want you to look at the real test. You can see on this *real* test with *your* sample that you are not the father of Danica."

Young D stares at the real test. He feels almost faint. He can't believe what he's seeing. And how obvious it is that he's been had. He has spent *years* praying for news, like this. He's also finding it hard to remain calm, after finding out that the little girl that *his mother* told him had none of the family features. Isn't his daughter, after all.

"That bitch set me up!" he yells.

"Not Kierra, Derrick." Baby Girl says, "She didn't know either. That's why I had to see her, face to face. She had the same test that you had. This trickery was done by Kid and Gus, all the way. They hired *and* paid this doctor Rawls, to set you up. Kid told Kierra that doctor Fallows refused to finish his test."

Young D adds, "Yea, I remember him telling me that shit too."

"It was a lie," she says, "All of it. And Kid owns The Anatomy Club. Kierra told me about that too. And now that she knows you're not the father. She asks me to tell you that she's sorry for accusing you. She was only going by the test and her longing to have you. Kid and Gus promised her that if she helped them to break us up. She would have you, for herself. But they was gonna make sure you and me wasn't together. Even if they had to kill us. Kierra overheard him on the phone. She alerted Corleone about the hit, in Gary. But I had the jump already. In Galveston, when I whooped her ass. She was not just coming to try to fuck you. She was gonna tell you about the San Francisco hit."

"San Francisco?" he asks, "That was a smooth set up. I fell for that shit, all the way."

"I'm just glad they was dumb enough to make me the pro, on that job," she says, "Because back then. I didn't have a clue of who was setting us up. Well, I had a clue. But I didn't wanna believe it. After we did away with Mark and Billy. I felt like it was an inside job. That would've been the only thing that would've made Mark Genolli think he could *possibly* get to me."

"Why would your own *family* wanna kill me?" he asks. He's still not getting it.

"The truth is, you was collateral to Gus and Kid, baby" she corrects him. She says, "My family didn't want you dead.

339

The two rogues did. The senior staff was on your side, all the way."

"They know about all of this?" he asks.

"Of course. They're my guardians," she says with a smile, "They helped with Gus."

"Whoa!"

"Yes indeed. The whole deal for you in San Francisco, was fake. As we all know, by now. But Kid was the buyer of all of the contracts on you and me. And him and Gus set this fake test up. That is when they began, what eventually graduated to putting contract hits on us."

"But why, Lovely?" he asks, "They hated us together, *that* much?!"

"It was never about you, me or our sons," she says, "It was all about my daddy's fortune. It gets *so* much worse. You wasn't ever the primary mark. *I* was."

She shows him the ledger with Gus' handwriting. It details what B&G Landscaping had planned for them and possibly the senior staff too. Young D takes the time to read the entire ledger. He becomes disgusted, instantly.

"That muthafuckin snake in the grass," he says, "How the fuck can two people, who are suppose to be protecting you from harm. Do shit like this? Oh *Goddamn*! I know we're killing that bitch ass muthafucka, Kid. That nigga is an asshole. You got plans for doing his ass in, by now. Don't you?"

"That cake is already being baked, *whoadie*," she says as she smiles slightly.

Young D won't even allow himself to smile. Not just yet. Though he's overjoyed with the news she has brought to him about Danica and Kierra. He's even more anxious about getting even with Kid. The part of the ledger where Kid and

340

Gus suggested taking custody of their sons, has set his emotions to an all new high.

"They was trying to fuck with my boys too," he says, "I'll kill that bitch, on sight. Baby Girl, it ain't no fuckin way that I ain't riding on *his* ass. You better be done cut me in. Not on the money either. Just the action."

"There won't be any money. Well, the senior staff might put out a bounty on him," she says with a smile. She says, "But you're already apart of his demise. Those are my boys too. It's already in the package and you will be riding on it."

"Good. This shits got me heated, Baby Girl," he says, "That bitch ass nigga was helping this bitch, *blackmail* me. But all the time, he was telling me the reason he didn't want me with you, was because I had cheated before. He was helping her extort me!"

"He sure was," she says, "And if you had told me sooner. They wouldn't have gotten this far."

"You're right, baby and I'm sorry," he says, "I don't have anymore secrets. I promise you. *Damn*! Kid and Gus was trying to take over your fortune! What *The Don* left for you. Why would The Don allow Gus to work for him and live there? Because I know he had to know he was foul."

"Oh, he did," she says, "But he wanted *me* to kill him. If it had happened before daddy died. Either of my fathers, for that matter, that would've cast shade on *The Organization*. With them gone and Teddy in a hospital, at the time Gus died. There was nothing to point to The Manor. I feel like Gus and Kid are the reason daddy trained me, in the first place. No one suspects me. I guess that's because I'm a female."

"You did Gus, didn't you?" he asks, "You never told me if you did."

She gives him a *why-even-bother-to-asks-me-that-question* look.

"Yea I figured that out, the day the call came in from the manor, about his punk ass," he says, "I could tell by your reaction. You wasn't stressing it, at all. Plus you wanted *me* to answer your phone. You never do that."

She smiles and says, "That's the way you learn the signs. Half of the happenings in this business are nonverbal. I've been training you on what to look for, without even trying too."

"He owns Anatomy. Is that where that Hiram dude, that we left under the overpass, came from?" he asks.

"Nah. He was actually from Cali, by way of the Texas state penitentiary," she says, "He had met one of the strippers online. They started seeing each other while he was doing time. Kid got his contact information from there, some how. I guess Kid was fucking that stripper too. Or maybe he was checking her calls or emails. I really don't know *how* he got connected to Hiram. But we know he did. And that guy out at Arnold's Air Force Base. He was a bouncer at the club."

"So when you left me on the road, was it because you was leaving me? Or *saving* me?" he asks, finally getting it.

"You know that answer, already baby," she says, "I needed to get the senior staff involved to eliminate the threat, completely. I popped a military guy, when I left. He was gonna hit you in Des Moines."

"I was stressed out, on that run," he says, "My head was so tight. That's why I cut my braids off."

"You look sexy as hell, either way," she says with a smile.

"So when do we kill Kid," he asks impatiently.

"TJ is finishing the package, I started for him," she tells him. She says, "We're gonna use Kierra and Trina. Like he did. But this time, it's going to be, to smoke him out."

"*When?*"

She says, "We'll do that part, next week. While we're in Houston for three days. Then we'll kill him, before the New Year. Or shortly after. We have to get the fix, *all* the way on, before we snuff him."

"Who is *we*?" he asks, "Just you and me?"

"You, me, DeJuan and Teddy junior," she says.

"What's up with him anyway. This Teddy junior?"

"He's the new hire," she says, "Daddy Don intended for him to be in The Brotherhood. His daddy and my *real father*, was his main pro's for years."

"Yea, but I don't like how he stares at you," he says, "He's hot for you. Ain't he, baby? Tell me the truth. He wants you. Don't he?"

She's quiet for a minute. But coming clean is her only option. Especially after the come on, Teddy Jr pulled last night in The Don's office.

She says, "Derrick. I need to tell you something else."

"I'm listening," he say as his brows knit together.

"When we was little," she says, "Me and him kissed."

"What? *How* little? It was before me, right?" he asks.

"Yes it was before you, Derrick. I was barely nine."

"So I wasn't the first boy you kissed?" he asks, looking dejected.

"Yes you are. That kiss between me and Teddy wasn't a kiss, like ours," she says, "It was the kind of kiss, Lil Man gives to people outside of the family."

"Teeth clinched. Lips folded together and nose turned up?" he ask.

"Exactly. And fingers crossed," she says, "But he was hoping for more. I would be lying-"

"More what? Did he come on to you since he came back or not?" he asks, "Don't bullshit me."

343

"Yes. Yes he did."

"Get him out of the mansion, baby," he says, "You will *not* be at the manor without me. That'll drive me crazy."

"He knows he has to move to the villa," she says, "He also knows that I'm here, telling you about it today. Teddy knows there's no chance that we'll hook up. We have to work together and we have to-"

"I'm not gonna be okay with y'all going off together," he says, "Even before I knew about this. I wasn't comfortable with him being alone with you."

"I know that. But Derrick, you're going to have trust me. Just like you always have. Because I'm gonna get angry, if you stop trusting me, based on the actions of someone else."
Young D is quiet. She can tell he's conflicted about what he wants to say next. Every ounce of him wants to confront Teddy Jr and kick his ass. He looks at her.

"Do you promise me that there's nothing there?" he asks, his eyes welling up with tears.
She pulls his face to hers and kisses him hard. Then she pulls his head to hers and hugs him tight. He starts to kiss on her neck and she lets him.

"I promise you, Derrick," she says, "There is no other man in this world for me. But you. You will be the only man that I'll ever be intimate with. I can't change that innocent kiss. But I do control what I do *now*. And whatever I do *now*, is with you."

"You don't feel like you owe me one? I mean, because of the Kierra thing?" he asks, as he facial expression tells her, he's worried and worried, a lot.
She can see in his tear filled eyes, that he feels like he deserves to be cheated on.

"No. I don't feel like I need to sin against God or my

344

marriage. What I owe you, is a good fucking. Every single time I see you, Derrick," she says, "That's all I owe you. I'm not going against my upbringing, to settle some whore score. I love you unconditionally. And I need the same from you."

"You got it, Lovely," he says as he pulls her face to his. He whispers, "It's time for me to feel your body. Maybe my hands can say what my mouth can't."

He pulls her to him and puts his tongue in her mouth. This sends chills down her body. He's breathing so hard. His whole body is shaking. She can feel that he's emotional.

"I love you so much, for just loving me," he whispers as he sucks on her earlobe. He whispers, "Thank you for saving my life, once again."

All she can do is moan. Just the way he's handling her, right now, tells her that this is going to be a very intense lovemaking session.

He goes from her ear to her neck and straight to her breast. Sucking and licking on her, wildly. As if he's starved for sex. She would bet her bottom dollar that he's starving. She could eat too.

"I wanna taste you," he whispers as he heads south.

"I want some sixty nine, Derrick," she whispers back. She adds, "I wanna taste you too."

He obliges as he flips her up on top of him and they both dive in.

From the onset, Young D is ravished. He gets up close and personal with her clitoris. While she takes his hard dick into her mouth. She rolls her tongue around it, before sucking it in and to the back of her throat. He moans as his entire body jerks. She moans. She's pleased at the pleasure she's giving him. He braces her thighs apart with his forearms. While his tongue licks her swiftly. Her orgasm comes strong and rapid.

She's out of control, within seconds. She tries to hold onto his penis. But she's forced to let it go when she feels him pulling away from her. He's trying to turn his body around. Soon, he flips her onto her back, pulls her thighs apart and lays between them. His long and lean penis stands up stiff against his washboard abdomen. He wants a kiss, as he dives in to fetch her tongue. She makes finding it, very easy as she shoves it into his mouth. He pulls her hips toward him and enters her in a rush.

"Ah shit. I missed my pussy, baby," he whispers, which causes her to shutter as if she caught a chill.

"I missed you too, baby," she moans as she tries to adjust her rear end on the bed.

She struggles to accommodate his huge penis which has her pussy *fully* stuffed.

She says, "Oh God! You feel like a steel pipe, baby."

"I told you I had it bad, out here," he whispers, "Can you feel how much I've been thinking about this?"

"Yes. *God* yes."

He begins to grind slowly, As if, as *Bernie Mac* would say, he's stirring coffee. With every stroke, she's getting more wet as she holds him close to her breast. His kisses are very intense. He's making eye contact with her at every body shift. Behind every moan, he digs into her deeper. Seeking the pleasure indicator that he's use too. Her screaming and calling his name, is all he wants to hear. Her yelps as he fucks her harder, don't do anything to stop his deep and deeper penetrations. He's going for that pocket inside of her, that makes her, *"wet my dick"* as he always says. He isn't far from it. She can feel her loins tighten. Her insides tingle with excitement. Anticipation. She can feel her toes start to straighten and then curl. Her eyes seem to close automatically, as defined lines appear on her forehead. Her body jolts initially. Then it stiffens to board hard, as her juices flow southward. She's in ecstasy. Again!

As she screams his name, her nails dig into his back. Her hips go to automatic pilot. Her whispers with her eyes now barely open, mixed with random inaudible admissions. Find him staring directly at her face. His own face, wet with tears. Young D is emotional about this lovemaking session. He's relieved to not have fathered a child, other than with her. But now, he has the pressure of another young man, a professional killer, who is pursuing the woman he loves. His mind has taken him from mild jealousy. To insecurity with a touch of anger. To now, the fear that she may find Teddy Jr, the least bit interesting. He can't allow that to happen. As he greases her loins thoroughly and she unwinds in orgasmic bliss. He goes into a state of desperation.

"I love you, Lovely. I need you, baby girl," he whispers in her ear, as she spirals in and throughout her lasting orgasm.

"I love you too," she manages, "Oh Derrick! It's so good!"
She's fucking him, like this is her last opportunity to make it good to him. Finally, she opens her eyes fully and looks upon his face. What she sees, takes her back for a few seconds. But she quickly gathers her composure. She reaches for his face and holds it in her hands.
"Are you okay, Derrick?"
He's crying as he grinds into her with a steady stroke which allows her second orgasm to continue to escape. She pulls him to her, as she explodes again. He's kissing her wildly. He has teardrops mixed with his sweat, dripping onto her skin. She's still trying to inquire about his status. But he's not trying to answer her. He just holds her tighter and loves her harder. He's on a mission to save his marriage. Even though, it isn't

even in trouble. As far as he's concerned, it is. And he's doing what his mind is telling him is needed. As *J. Holiday's* song, *Bed* plays on the hotel radio. Baby Girl is in sexual bliss. Young D has fully satisfied her. But he's still not done.

Suddenly he rips himself away from her arms, pulls himself from her and heads south. He wants her juices on the tip of his tongue. Again!

"Oh baby!" she screams, as he captures her already jolting clitoris.

"I want you to love it, baby," he moans as he lashes her with his tongue, "Mmmm. You're so sweet, Lovely."
Just like that, she's coming again. It's number 3 and she's near exhaustion. He appears to have a second wind. Something he does often, after she's at the point where she could roll over and slumber. He's not allowing her body a chance, at not moving. He rolls her over and enters her from behind. Pulling her up on her knees for full penetration, he works her over.

"Oh daddy!!! Oh!!!"
He's in the zone. Still, his face stained with tears, he starts to talk to her.

"I love you! I've never cared for *any other* woman, like this! In my life!" he yells as he fucks. He continues, "I really need you to believe me and know that I need you in my life! As my wife, Lovely!"
The tears come back heavier.

"I'm not going anywhere, Derrick," she whispers cautiously. She adds, "I love you. And I need you too. I always have. And I always will."
She holds onto her pillow. Digging her nails into it with every deep stroke from him. He's kissing the back of her neck and her shoulders. As his tears continue to drip. She needs him to know that he's in no danger of losing her.

"Let me get on top," she request.

After another minute or so, he allows her to climb on top of him. She takes him into her, instantly. Her over moist pussy enables his dick to slip right in and fill her up to capacity.

"Oh," she moans, as his *hard-as-an-iron-pipe* penis, invades every inch of pussy tunnel that she has.

He's breathing heavily as his tears continue to run down into his ears. She leans into him and kisses him with fervor. He feels vulnerable. She wants to assure him. She gives him the best ride, she has. He captures her hips in his strong hands and gives her, all of him.

He soon cums with the forces of Hurricane feeder bands. His pumping action causes her to flip over. He's back on top. He grinds as he cums and grunts and yells too. His orgasm is both heart felt and violent. He loves her and he has something to prove. He's sorry about Kierra. But he's ready to kill Teddy Jr.

His orgasm becomes smoother now. Allowing him to show her passion and compassion. He's kissing her, like her tongue is his life line and he's on his last breath. Slowly but surely, they both come to a rest stop, at sexual satisfaction. He holds her tight and she hold him back. They're crying together now.

He never wanted to hurt her. She's never going to hurt him. Somehow they get that point across, through their kisses and embrace. Still, with the tears flowing, they lay still and allow their breathing patterns to harmonize as they fall into a restful sleep.

=========END OF PART TWO=========
349

The end of; Still By My Lonely-The Organization-part two
The prequel; *All By My Lonely-The Organization-part one*

If you were charged more than $25(US dollars) and shipping & handling was not included, contact us immediately:
[Black Coffee's websites]
www.blackdollone.com or www.truesrelatepublishing.com
On Twitter: http://twitter.com/AuthorBlkCoffee
INSTAGRAM: AuthorBlkCoffee
Linked-In: Author Black Coffee
Facebook: Black Coffee
Facebook Groups:
Black Coffee's Crew Nation
The Organization
Page: True's Relate Publishing & Black Coffee's Books
All books available in print and eBooks
Amazon Kindle

Be sure to pick up the *Time Will Reveal Series*
Time To Learn-RELOADED-Time Will Reveal part 1
Time To Grow-RELOADED-Time Will Reveal part 2
Time To Love-RELOADED-Time Will Reveal part 3
Time to Know-RELOADED-Time Will Reveal part 4
Time To Feel-RELOADED-Time Will Reveal part 5
The Making of AJAY- "Every Man"-RELOADED
(Time Will Reveal- short stories)
#1 MORE THE 4 ADMIRERS-RELOADED
#2 MR. WRONG AND THE RATS-RELOADED
#3 THE CREW'S PRIORITY(TBA)
And more of the Time Will Reveal series to come!
Time To Show-RELOADED-Time Will Reveal part 6 [2015]
Ajay and Ebony 1-Time Will Reveal 7-Time To Give(TBA)
Ajay and Ebony 2-Time Will Reveal 8- Time To Live(TBA)
350

<u>Look for these future releases by Black Coffee [TBA]</u>
The Foe, The Friend-Poetry [print & audio](Winter 2015)
To Hell and Back [3 recovering addicts]
Set up to Fail
Katrina-The Catastrophe heard around the world
To Strong to fall Off
How the Internet challenged Privacy
Bigotry bleeds and breeds
The Jessie Lee Williams Jr story
9/11-The homegrown terror

Contact me online and let me know what you think!
-Black Coffee
"Stay Blessed and Vigilant"
#NoJusticeNoPeace
#ByAnyMeansNecessary

351